Be Bop A Lula

A Novel by Lou Duro

Cover Design by George Drakakis

ISPN:9781520616858

It was a time when The Crowd was a sacred sect meeting in a candy-store temple, and Hanging Out was a full-time obligation, with occasional time-outs for gang wars and bar fights; drive-ins and making out; hot rods and motorcycles. Eggcreams and cherry-cokes were the nectar of the Gods, and Coney Island hot dogs were tube steaks to teenage gourmets.

It was the 1950s...

and *coming of age*

will never be like this again!

This is a book of fiction based on fact. Only those who were there will be able to separate the two. Be Bop A Lula is dedicated to all of them...

THE CROWD

and to my wife, Sofia, who came of age in a different world, but shared mine through innumerable readings over all the years it took the manuscript, itself, to *come of age.*

PROLOGUE

ATHENS, 1987

"BO IS DEAD. STOP. SERVICES FRIDAY. STOP. PLEASE CALL. STOP. KATE."

The telegram, dated two weeks before, had been waiting for him on the bedside table when they wheeled him in from the operating room. Due to the anesthesia, it was several hours before he was able to read it. Even then, the words did not register in his drug-filled mind immediately. He had to re-read the wire several times before the impact of the message became clear.

"Oh, God, no," Eddie Casale groaned. He began crying. A nurse heard him, appeared at the door and went in search of a doctor who spoke some English.

"Leg much pain?" a grim-faced doctor asked with a trace of annoyance, after maneuvering his way through the crowded orthopedic ward and stopping at the foot of Casale's bed. At his heels were two harried looking nurses in soiled uniforms pushing a rattling medical cart.

Eddie looked at him through tear-filled eyes. He tried to speak, but choked on the words. He swallowed hard several times.

"N-o," he said, finally, shaking his head slowly and tapping a finger on his chest. "Heart much pain."

"*Ti?*" the doctor asked in Greek, confusion clouding his face. He turned to the nurses, shrugging his shoulders and raising his eyebrows. They mimicked the gesture. Then the doctor noticed the telegram still clutched tightly in Eddie's right hand. "*Katalaveno, katalaveno,*" he said, slowly nodding his head in understanding. He pointed to the yellow sheet of paper. "Problem from America, yes?"

"Very big prob –- " The rest of Casale's words were choked off by sobs, as the tears fell again.

The doctor patted the patient gently on his freshly cast-covered leg then turned to leave, signaling the nurses to follow with a snap of the fingers.

Eddie wiped his eyes with the edge of the bed sheet. He held the telegram in both hands and stared at it for a long time, as if trying to read more than was written. There was something else, he thought. Something he was missing. He was sure of it. But, it couldn't quite push its way through the lingering traces of anesthesia still clouding his mind. Suddenly, he crumbled the telegram, started to rip it, and then stopped. He unraveled the paper. The printed words were still clear: "BO IS DEAD." He folded the paper into a neat square, and pressed it smooth between his palms, then put it into the drawer of his bedside table.

"FUCK, NOOO," he half shouted and half moaned a moment later, startling the roomful of patients and visitors who had been trying not to pay attention to the foreigner in the corner bed. He reached into the drawer, grabbed the telegram, and savagely tore it into confetti-sized pieces. He let out a long sigh, the small scraps of paper falling from his hand and fluttering to the floor. He suddenly felt calmness, as if the act of destroying the telegram actually brought relief. At least the cold, hard printed words were now gone.

Eddie eased himself back onto the rock-hard pillow, trying to find the least uncomfortable spot. He closed his eyes, squeezing them tightly, in an attempt to fight off the frustration which was quickly enveloping him; frustration over the fact that he was confined to a hospital bed while his oldest friend, the guy who helped him survive on the streets of New York all those years ago, was laid in the ground 5,000 miles away.

When he opened his eyes a short time later, his wife, Maria, was sitting on the edge of the bed, smiling at him.

"I just spoke to the surgeon," she beamed, as Eddie blinked awake. "He said the operation went perfectly. Isn't that great?" She read it in his eyes first, and then noticed the quiver of his lower lip. Her smile faltered, then faded completely. She knew she was losing the battle for composure.

"Oh, God, sweetheart," she said, in a voice beginning to crack with emotion. "I know it must be terrible for you now, but you'll feel better soon. The doctor said . . ."

"Bo is dead," Eddie blurted out, and immediately tears tracked down his cheeks again.

"What . . . ? Who . . . ?" She looked confused, then her eyes widened in understanding. "Oh, my God, no!" She reached for his hand and squeezed gently. "I'm so sorry. What happened?"

"I - I don't know." He told her about the telegram, how it had taken two weeks to track him to the hospital, where he was undergoing a series of operations on his right leg. "You'll have to call his sister for me and explain why I wasn't there for the funeral. You know, find out what happened, and . . . and. . . . Oh, Maria, I can't fuckin' believe it. Bo was indestructible. He never even caught a cold. How can he be dead?" He started to cry again. She leaned over, put her arms around his shoulders and held him close, wet cheek against wet cheek. Neither spoke. The sounds of each other's sobbing were all the comforting they needed for the moment.

Maria Casale had never met Bob "Bo" Brody, her husband's childhood friend. She and Eddie met later in life, married quickly, and abandoned New York for Maria's homeland five years ago. Nevertheless, she saw him through her husband's eyes, heard him through his words, and witnessed their adventures through often-repeated detailed accounts of their teenaged exploits. And, over the years, she eventually began to share some of her husband's love for the friend she never met.

Maria heard the stories of how Bo and Eddie came through the 50s together, rocking and rolling every step of the way. Those were the years legends were born, legends so powerful the world knew them by just one name: Elvis, Marlon, Marilyn. And, in Eddie's world of New York City's Queens County, it was simply "Bo." He was the street-smart hero in the days when The Crowd was a sacred sect meeting in a candy-store temple, and "Hanging Out" was a full-time obligation, with occasional time-outs for gang wars and bar fights; drive-ins and making out; hot rods and motorcycles. Eggcreams and cherry-cokes were the nectar of the Gods. For Eddie and Bo, and the rest of their crowd, the 50s could have lasted forever, but they ended three years too soon. It was 1957, when draft notices and marriage licenses turned growing up into serious business.

At the hospital the next day, Maria told Eddie she called Bo's sister and found out he had died of a heart attack while out on his boat. "I explained why you couldn't be there, your accident and all," Maria said. "She said she was sorry about your leg, and to tell you to get well soon."

"I don't believe it," Eddie said. "A heart attack, for chrisake. He was only 50. After all the shit we went through. How'd it happen?"

"She said he took his boat out on Long Island Sound, you know, to watch the tall ships and all over the holiday weekend. Apparently, he just collapsed – "

"Holiday weekend?" Eddie interrupted. He leaned forward with a painful grunt and grabbed his wife's shoulder with his hand. "W-what d-day?"

"Kate said it was that Saturday, July 5th," she began, "when he – " She stopped short. Eddie felt a chill run up his spine, in spite of the pain. Speechless for the moment, they just stared at each other. Then they spoke in unison.

"That was the same day as . . . "

It hit Eddie like a Marciano right hook. Bo died in New York the same day Eddie was knocked unconscious and almost died in a motorcycle accident in Greece. He completely lost control. He broke up crying in great convulsive sobs in his wife's arms.

"Come on, Eddie," Maria said, putting her arms over he husband's troubled shoulders. "I know it's not easy, but you must try to put it out of your mind for now and concentrate on getting better yourself."

It was several long moments before he was able to calm himself. He swallowed hard three or four times. He reached over and ripped a piece of toilet paper from the roll on the nightstand, and blew his nose. Then, he looked at his wife and tried a wry smile. It almost worked. "You're right," he said weakly, and now a smile did start to take shape. "And, sometimes the best way to forget is to remember, right?"

"What do you mean?" she asked, with a tilt of her head.

The next day, Maria delivered a stack of yellow legal-sized pads and half a dozen black felt tips. And, for the next three weeks, while confined to his hospital bed, Eddie Casale forgot the pain of Bo's death by remembering the pleasure of their life, and that last crazy year together. It was 1957 – a year crammed with extra abandon, a new level of recklessness, as they realized their teenage games were about to be called on account of growing up.

It was one hell of a year!

ONE

ROCK AROUND THE CLOCK

It looked more like an alleyway behind a seedy lower East Side barroom rather than the backyard of a substantial brick-and-shingle home in one of New York's more fashionable suburban communities. There were 204 beer cans, seven fifths of Seagram's 7, four pints of Three Feathers, and an assortment of other bottles in various shapes and sizes that ranged from Thunderbird wine to Old Mister Boston Sloe Gin. Of course, they were all empty. Eddie Casale knew the count was right. All Sunday morning, as he tried to sleep off a record-book hangover, his father had meticulously gathered the evidence, which had been stuffed inside rose bushes, thrown behind hedges, and tossed in the reflecting pool of the life-sized blue and white statue of the Blessed Virgin Mary. Now, Mr. Casale handed his son an inventory list which would have made an accountant proud.

They were standing on the multi-colored slate patio just outside the back door. Mr. Casale, an experienced trial lawyer, was interrogating his son like a hostile witness. Eddie, still dressed in his old faded, too-small Roy Rogers bathrobe, hemmed and hawed, but avoided answering anything until his brain showed some signs of becoming functional. Meanwhile, at his father's command, he tried desperately to focus his blurred vision from the sheet of paper to the desecrated lawn and shrubbery, which had been immaculately groomed at this time yesterday.

Such devastation might be expected if it had been a lawn party. However, the actual soiree had been held in Eddie's basement, which had been converted into a finished party room complete with pinball machine and juke box, "where you can bring your friends over whenever you want." That was Mr. Casale's original plan in his continuing efforts to keep tabs on the ever-expanding life style of a teenage son "in these unpredictable times." After some of his son's recent stunts, though, he was sorry he didn't make it into a library. Eddie practically needed a court order now if he wanted to invite more than three people at any one time. Like last night, for instance.

Eddie had worked hard for two weeks before getting the go-ahead to produce his latest extravaganza. He had diligently applied the "Three Ps" of teenage-parent negotiations – pleading, promising and pouting – at every possible opportunity. He begged for them to understand his need for self expression, he pledged to abide by whatever rules were set forth, and he sulked continually, from time to time throwing in a mournful sigh. Also, he made an elaborate display of taking the garbage out every night without being told. Finally, they gave in, mostly just to be rid of him. Of course, they made the usual conditions and demands.

"Absolutely no *drinking, and* this *time I mean it!" Mr. Casale had said emphatically. "Even if I have to search everyone as they come in. And, I don't care if some of them are over eighteen."*

"Yeah, yeah," Eddie said, knowing that the six-packs and whiskey bottles would be passed from the cars through the small window in the utility room which opened onto the driveway.

"I want you and your friends to clean up the mess afterwards," Mrs. Casale had said. "This time I'm *not going to do it."*

"Yeah, yeah," Eddie said, knowing that his mother, who cleaned before the cleaning lady came on Fridays, would attack the basement with bucket, mop and Lysol at the crack of the following dawn.

Eddie scanned the back of the patio where all the cans and bottles were lined up. Dead soldiers, he thought. It was how his crowd referred to the empties. *Shit, this was a whole fucking army, another Fort Bragg, for Chrissake.* He had told his friends they had to get rid of the empties, to take some when they left the party and dump them. "What stupid fucks."

"*What* did you say? I didn't quite get that." Mr. Casale looked astonished. He leaned closer to his son, as if to hear his words better.

Eddie froze. He had no idea his thought had actually been spoken. He glanced at his father, then quickly averted his eyes again. His brain was still engulfed in a fog consisting of three parts alcohol, one part sleep. He took a couple of deep breaths, gulping in fresh springtime air. It helped a little.

"What putrid luck," Eddie finally managed meekly, but a little more distinctly than his last statement. He stole another quick glance at his father, whose face screwed to a grimace momentarily, then back to the perpetual scowl of the morning.

Eddie nervously finger-combed his long, sleep-tousled, dark brown hair. Although he was a good five inches taller than his dad, he was still intimidated. Mr. Casale's practiced courtroom presence always made him appear to loom much larger than his actual height of five-foot-eight – a fact Eddie always had problems coming to grips with. Dressed in one of his many navy blue suits, with starched white shirt and wide solid maroon tie, Mr. Casale stood with arms folded across his chest, right foot tapping incessantly. He looked like Perry Mason waiting impatiently for an answer to the question, "Where were you on the night of . . ."

Eddie shifted his feet, searched the ground, then scanned the sky, and eventually made a visual inspection of the rain gutters along the roof of the house. He looked anyplace except at his father. He just didn't feel strong enough to return that stare, and certainly didn't trust himself to say anything yet.

"How in the world can 30 teenagers drink so much alcohol?"

Eddie's mind was still a bit fuzzy, but clearing rapidly. Enough, he quickly thanked God, to stop him from blurting out: "Because we were thirsty." This was definitely not the time for flippancy, the usually flippant Eddie reasoned. Instead, he decided to handle this situation as he usually handled almost all confrontations with his father. He would lie. If he put on his dumb and innocent act, Eddie reasoned, at least his father might believe half the story. It was the innocent part that Eddie always had the most trouble portraying.

"Dad! Do ya mean to stand there an' tell me that my friends, my very *good* friends, who promised me not to drink after I *told* them my father didn't allow it, went back on their word?" Eddie finally glanced at his father, then wished he hadn't. He continued anyway. "I jus' can't believe it! They musta snuck it in when I wasn't lookin', an' drank it while I was dancin'. An', wow, Kate an' I didn't stop doin' the Lindy all night."

Eddie started humming, shaking his hips and waving his arms. The lariat belt of his robe came loose. Mr. Casale stepped back, astonished, and nearly fell off the patio. The startled movement gave Eddie the false hope of possible victory in the verbal sparring match with his dad. He moved forward, adding an off-key vocal accompaniment to his impromptu dancing."One, two, three o'clock, four o'clock, rock." He spun around. *"Five, six, seven o'clock, eight o'clock rock. We're gonna rock around the clock . . ."* Mr. Casale stepped in quickly, reached up, grabbed his son tightly by the shoulders and held him still.

"I *know* how dumb you are without you proving it," Mr. Casale said, stepping back and shaking his head in disgust. "But don't try to play *innocent* with me." Eddie decided to change gears. He would try the "out of sight, out of mind" routine. In this case, he figured, if he got rid of the evidence, the crime may be forgotten much sooner.

"Look, Dad," Eddie said, donning a sincere expression. "I'll get the trash cans, clean up this mess, and put the cans out front for the garbage men to pick up. OK?" He turned to go, but stopped abruptly when his father suddenly grabbed his arm.

"Don't touch a thing!" Mr. Casale gasped with a touch of alarm. "Do you think I want the whole neighborhood to see all these cans and bottles in front of *our* house? They'll think we're just a bunch of alcoholics, for God's sake." He glanced over the redwood fence surreptitiously. He regained his composure and resumed his normal father-berating-son tone, with even added emphasis. "And, that's the *last* party for you, young man. You seem to forget the fact that you're still *only* sixteen."

Eddie cringed at the words. He hated when his father said that to him. Not about the party. Shit, he thought, that's nothing. But that "only sixteen" crap really pissed him off, and his father knew it. Eddie couldn't help showing his irritation, although he tried to mask it with a fake smile. Mr. Casale countered with a sadistic smile, and Eddie braced himself for what he knew was coming next.

"You may think you're grown up because you're tall, but it takes more than size to make a man. You must remember you still have the mind of a child."

Eddie knew his father was trying to get him to dig himself deeper, of course, but couldn't help himself. He hated to be called a "child" almost as much as he hated to be called "chicken." Maybe more. He didn't speak, fearful that the only words out of his mouth would be, "Fuck you and the horse you rode in on." But Mr. Casale played the waiting game expertly. Eddie shifted again, then once more. His father remained imperturbable, his irritating cloak of superiority draped in front of his son like a red cape at a bull.

The back door swung open and Eddie's mother popped her head out of the house. "Hurry up you two," she called. "The twelve o'clock Mass starts in twenty minutes and you still have to get ready, Edward. You don't want to be late." Then she was gone, the door banging shut behind her, like a judge's gavel signaling an end to any further discussion.

The spell of the confrontation broken, Eddie felt the tension lift from his shoulders. He let out a deep breath, regained his composure, and smiled inwardly, happy to have avoided falling into his father's trap. Well, Eddie thought, if he wants a child, I'll give him a child. He snapped his "little-boy-innocent" expression into place. "Ya don't want me to be late for Mass, now do ya, Daddy? *Mommy* wouldn't like that."

Mr. Casale stared at Eddie for several moments. He started to say something, stopped, glanced at the back door, then around the yard. He gave his son one last hard look, shook his head in disgust, and walked into the house without another word. As the door closed behind him, Eddie started to give his father the finger – his courageous way of getting in the last word, when all else failed. As his right hand was about waist high, with only the middle finger extended, Mr. Casale's face suddenly appeared behind the little glass window pane set in the wooden door. Eddie realized too late that he had been baited, after all. Panic stricken, he decided to continue with the movement, bringing his arm up and using "the finger" to pick his nose. He looked back at the door. His father's face was beaming back at him through the little window.

That night, under the cover of darkness, Mr. Casale skulked through the neighborhood distributing empty beer cans and liquor bottles in each of the garbage cans which had been set out in front of the houses along their street for early Monday morning collection. He placed two neatly packed brown paper bags in each can. Eddie watched through the Venetian blinds, laughing silently, as his father, dressed in dark trousers and windbreaker like a cat burglar, tiptoed from one garbage can to the next, his arms laden with paper bags. Whenever he spotted someone, either walking or in a car, he straightened up and took normal strides, pretending to be returning home with a load of groceries.

It was Sunday night, almost eight o'clock, so Eddie knew his father would be back in the house soon. Not even "The Great Whiskey Bottle Rebel" would miss *Ed Sullivan.* He went back into the living room where his mother and sister were watching a religious program on television. His mother watched every Catholic show on TV, including some Protestant ones she thought were Catholic. Eddie plopped down in his father's easy chair, the only place in the room to sit without fear of sliding to the floor on thick clear vinyl seat covers. There were two priests glaring at Eddie from the TV screen, discussing why eating meat on Fridays was a sin. He immediately thought of the White Castle hamburgers he ate last Friday night and was overcome with guilt. He reached for the copy of *Collier's* with the photo layout of Marilyn Monroe in *Bus Stop*, and buried his head in the magazine, waiting for his father to come in and take possession of his chair and the television.

When it came to TV, the old man was easily satisfied, Eddie thought. Just don't fuck with his weekend nights. It was *Perry Como* on Saturdays and *Ed Sullivan* on Sundays. At one time, it was Tuesdays, too, but that was when *Milton Berle* was still on the air. However, Eddie remembered with a trace of glee that was a conflict his father never won.

At 8 p.m. on Tuesdays, Mr. Casale would tune into NBC to watch "The *Milton Berle Show*." Mrs. Casale would immediately switch the station to watch Bishop Fulton J. Sheen's *Life Is Worth Living* show," which came on at the same time. Thus, the weekly "Berle and The Bishop" dispute would ensue at the Casale household. It wasn't that Mr. Casale was not a good Catholic. It was just that his idea of "good" was to sit in the back of the church for an hour on Sunday mornings and put five dollars in the collection basket; not to watch a priest – even a bishop – pontificate while Berle was bantering.

Mrs. Casale had different ideas about devotion. She tried to attend Mass every morning, and receive communion, too. She made every novena the church offered, and, at least once a week, said the Stations of the Cross, kneeling before each of the fourteen icons with rosary beads in hand. She had made a three-day "Retreat of Atonement" once, at the Sisters of Mercy Convent in upstate Peekskill, but when she returned home the house was in such a shambles she prayed that God would understand that her *true* penance in life was to clean, cook and care for her family.

All week, Eddie's father, mother and sister watched television together in harmony. They laughed at *I Love Lucy* and *Jack Benny.* They shouted answers at *What's My Line* and *The $64,000 Question.* They marveled at the feats of *Lassie* and *Flicka*. They thrilled to the daring of *Wyatt Earp* and *Marshall Dillon*. They were enthralled by the drama of *Playhouse 90* and *Kraft Television Theater*. It all went well, except for Tuesday nights, and *Uncle Miltie*.

It usually went something like this:

"Let's watch Milton Berle tonight." Mr. Casale would venture hopefully, turning to channel four.

"We're watching Bishop Sheen." Mrs. Casale would insist, twisting the dial back to channel nine.

"Milton Berle."

"Bishop Sheen."

"Uncle Miltie!"

"The Bishop!"

At about this point, Mrs. Casale would whip out her rosary and begin to recite "Hail Marys," punctuating each prayer with a loud sigh. To Mrs. Casale, it was a sin not to watch a priest on television. Failure to watch a Bishop was practically grounds for excommunication. And, if you didn't tune into the Bishop because you chose to watch some silly man in a woman's dress prance around in high heel shoes, you may even turn to stone.

Well, God and Eddie's mother proved a little too much, even for the formidable Mr. Casale. Many Tuesday nights, Eddie's father was banished to the basement to watch a miniature *Uncle Miltie* on the old Dumont TV set with the seven-inch screen, while his mother and sister, together with what seemed to be a strange apparition in an easy chair, solemnly viewed an all-knowing Bishop Fulton J. Sheen on the new large-screen Magnavox.

Eddie shoved his head further into the magazine. He was always overcome with this strange feeling when he thought about his family's confrontation over Berle and The Bishop. Sure, it was funny, ha-ha; but it was also funny, strange. Not only was his father a loser on that one, but "Mr. Television," as Milton Berle was known due his once overehelming popularity, didn't fare too well, either. He was off the air completely now. Was the cleric's job done? His mission accomplished? Was the comedian, like his father, a victim of the combined forces of God, Bishop and Mother?

Mr. Casale, lawyer by day and trash distributor by night, returned from his rounds, washed up and joined his family. He expected to relax in his chair, which was always left empty for him, or vacated as soon as he entered the room. Eddie, still smarting over the patio incident, remained seated, and continued to hide his face behind the magazine, staring at a full-page photo of Marilyn Monroe in tights. He could feel his father standing in front of him, hands on his hips, waiting. The TV priests were still going at it, now dealing with the evils of cigarette smoking. They made mention of Humphrey Bogart's death last month from throat cancer. Eddie tried not to think about the pack of Luckies in the pocket of his jeans.

"Get the hell – er, heck, out of my chair." Eddie dropped the magazine to one side, in an animated act of surprise at his father's presence.

"Oh, sorry, Dad. Didn't know ya were here," he said calmly, pushing himself up slowly from the soft cushion. He glanced at his mother to see if she had overheard his father's "curse" word. She was hurriedly making the sign of the cross. Eddie knew his mother would nag her husband for hours about his "sinful" language, especially "in front of the children."

"Wipe that smirk off your face," Mr. Casale ordered, lowering himself into his chair. "And . . ." Eddie froze. Oh, no, he thought. ". . . forget about television for tonight." Wham! Eddie felt the shock of his father's words just as he was about to take up his usual viewing position sprawled on the deep-pile carpet. He turned, but before he could register a complaint, Mr. Casale continued. "Did you finish your homework? And how about studying? Tomorrow's a school day, you know. And, your finals are coming up soon, don't forget."

His father was hitting him with everything but the marble-based ash tray next to his chair. There was only one thing to do – whine.

"Aw, gee, Dad, come on, willya, huh? I did most of it. Really. Just got a little left. No big deal. I'll finish it right after Sullivan, awright? He's gonna have the

Everly Brothers on. Ya know, *Wake Up Little Susie* and *Bye-bye Love."*

Now it was Mr. Casale's turn to smirk. "Stop your whining and just forget Ed Sullivan. And say 'bye-bye' to your 'little Susan.' Go to your room and finish it *now*," he commanded. "Your sister *never* had to be told to finish her homework when she was in school. Right, Anna?"

"Yes, Daddy. And, on weekends I *always* did it on Friday afternoons, as soon as I came home from school, so the lessons were still fresh in my mind." Thanks, Sis, Eddie thought, I can always depend on ya never to miss a cue to fuck me over. What should I expect from someone whose favorite singer is Pat Boone?

"Do as your father says. . ." Mrs. Casale chimed in, as she walked over to the TV set, after the priests had ended their show with a blessing, to perform her duty as channel changer. *He knows what's best.* Eddie mouthed the words without speaking them.

". . . he knows what's best," his mother concluded on her way back to the couch.

With a contented sigh, and a nod at his wife in appreciation for her usual support, Mr. Casale settled deeper into the soft cushions of his chair, just as the dancers began the opening number for Sullivan's *Toast of The Town* show.

Eddie decided to give it one more shot, but this time he'd try to be a little clever, more creative. "Come on, Dad. After all, ya know what Sinatra says. Horse an' carriage? Love an' marriage? Well, it's the same with Sunday an' Sullivan. They just naturally go together. Huh? Ya know, a Sunday without Sullivan is like, well, like a Sunday without church. So, whadaya say, Dad? Huh?"

Eddie was proud of his little impromptu routine. At first, he was sure he had impressed his father, too, with the way he started smiling. The first hint that he had made a serious blunder came when he realized his father's smile was cold, without the slightest trace of amusement.

"Yes, I know it's like Sunday without church," Mr. Casale said very slowly, precisely, and a little too loudly. "But, that shouldn't be a problem for *you*, now should it?" He paused for effect, smile frozen into shape, and Eddie had his first inkling of what was coming next. He felt, rather than actually saw, his mother's head turn in their direction. "Since you *didn't* go to church this morning," his father continued, "you shouldn't mind missing Sullivan, either. Right, *Mr. Wisenheimer*? Maybe you should tell your friend, Mr. Sinatra, *that*."

Eddie heard the vinyl crinkle and crack on the sofa and he knew his mother was on the move. "No, no. Ya don't know – er, I mean. . ." he floundered in a weak voice. Then, with more conviction, "I swear to God I was in church this mornin'." He was starting to get his confidence back, but his voice was still a few octaves too high. He knew he was on safe ground with this one, though. "May God strike me *dead* if I wasn't in that church this mornin'," he added with emphasis.

"Oh, sure you were, sure you were." Mr. Casale conceded that point, but he was almost gloating now. "Sure you were," he continued, "for all of thirty seconds. You went in the front door, and right out the side door. You forgot to stay for Mass. Don't try playing semantics with me, young man. I'm way out of your league."

Oh, shit, Eddie thought, feeling something which he knew must be a second cousin to shell shock. *The old man's goin' for the jugular this time. He's been hip that I cut out of Mass a lot, but he's never said anything in front of the old lady before.*

Mrs. Casale was on her feet and heading for him. There was fire in her eyes.

"You mean you missed Mass this morning?" she asked incredulously, a trace of hysteria in her voice.

One of Mrs. Casale's main functions on Sunday mornings – in addition to attending nine o'clock Mass and starting the sauce for the ravioli or lasagna dinner – was to get Eddie up and out the door, regardless of the shape he was in from the night before, for twelve o'clock services at St. Joseph's, just two blocks away. In fact, the convenience of the church was a major factor in choosing this particular home in Queens County when the matriarch decided ten years ago to move her young family from Corona, the over-crowded Italian neighborhood. After much house – and church – hunting, Mrs. Casale had found the right combination on 210th Street in Bayside, a community of one-family homes with spacious grounds. However, for Eddie it had always been a thorn in his side. His mother was able to stand in front of their house and watch him until he actually passed through the front doors of the church. A number of times he had been caught, as a result of his mother's dedicated vigilance, sneaking out five minutes later. He was always sent scurrying back with a shout that carried the two-block distance with such resonance it must have been, Eddie deduced, amplified with the wrath of God. It was only about a year ago, due to increased attendance, that the church began utilizing its side doors. This allowed Eddie an unobserved escape route to Dick's Candy Store where he would commiserate with friends over eggcreams until it was time to return home. Of course, his father had figured it out right away, even caught him at Dick's a few times, but had never said anything in front of his mother – until now.

"I'm *talking* to you," Mrs. Casale yelled at her son, while roughly shaking his right arm with both her hands. "Did you miss Mass this morning? Yes or no." At a stocky five-foot-six, with brown eyes that turned black when she became angry, Mrs. Casale was big for a daughter of Sicilian immigrants, and she possessed the temperament that went with her heritage. Eddie, almost a foot taller than his mother, felt intimidated.

"Well, see Mom, it's not exactly like - "

"And, don't *lie*!" she cut him off. "That's the worst sin of all, and God will punish you even more."

That did it! Eddie broke free of his mother's grasp, and dashed for the stairs, taking the steps two at a time. He needed time – for his Mom to cool down and for him to come up with a good story. "You're right, Dad," he called through the slats of the banister, "I'd better finish that homework right now."

Before closing the door to the relative safety of his bedroom, Eddie heard his mother ask his father, "Are you *sure* he wasn't at Mass this morning?" while, in the background, Ed Sullivan began telling his audience about the "reeeealy big shooow" they were about to see.

Eddie stripped down to his Jockey shorts, dumped his clothes in a heap by his dresser, and climbed into bed with his world history reader and ratty, dog-eared Composition notebook. The notebook was filled mostly with scribbles, doodles and ballpoint hearts with various sets of initials, the most prominent of which being, "P.R." Penny Randazzo was Eddie's steady girl. But, he also liked other girls. And he loved dancing with Kate Brody, those great tits pressing . . . Eddie felt his cock stiffen. He grabbed his history book, opened it to the assigned chapter fourteen, and glanced at the page headed: "European Industrialization of 1870." It was no use; his cock continued to grow and stiffen. "Fuck this shit," he said out loud, slamming the book shut and dropping it to the floor, "at least I tried." He gave his cock, which was now rock-hard, a squeeze and felt that familiar shiver of pleasure pulsate through his body.

This fuckin' thing has a mind of its own, Eddie marveled, as he often did, when he got hard-ons for no apparent reason. Then he reasoned, *It* knew what I was gonna do even before *I* knew it! He chuckled out loud. Well, that's not too difficult, he rationalized in his own mind, since I do it practically every night anyway.

He slipped out of bed and adjusted his cock in his shorts, using the gesture as an excuse to give himself another satisfying squeeze, this time intensifying the pleasure by adding a slight tug. He opened the bottom drawer of his dresser, and reached under the neatly folded "Joe College" wide-striped polo shirts he never wore. This was his "safe" drawer. It contained shirts he received for Christmas or birthday presents which he wouldn't be caught dead in. Next to the polo shirts, of course, were the oxfords with button-down collars. Since he never wore these shirts, his mother didn't have to wash, iron and replace them.

Eddie had three magazines to choose from at the moment: *Sun*, *Playboy* and *Nugget*. *Sun* was a slick black and white publication of indefinite age filled with photos of totally naked men and women playing volley ball or sitting around a swimming pool at some nudist colony. Most of the girls were kind of flabby, but some had nice big tits. They just weren't too sexy, though. Eddie considered this more of a prestige book than anything else. He placed it neatly back under the shirts. The *Playboy* was fairly new. He had copped it from the United Cigar Store by the subway stop at Main Street, Flushing, during a busy rush hour last December, along with a couple of Baby Ruths. It had a great centerfold of a redhead named *Kelley* with enormous, jutting tits and huge nipples which almost jumped out of the page. I had her last night, Eddie thought. He put it back with the other and closed the drawer. The two-year-old worn and dog-eared *Nugget* was his favorite. The girls were more dirty looking than the ones in *Playboy*, although their tits usually weren't as big. And, Eddie liked the way the photographs in *Nugget* were taken, too, in settings and situations which he could easily project himself into and be right there with the girls. Before returning to bed with *Nugget*, Eddie grabbed the jar of Dixie Peach Hair Pomade, which he seldom used for his hair, and slid the chair behind the door. The chair was probably unnecessary, even though he was forbidden to lock his door. His mother or father have never entered his room without knocking, as agreed, since he became a teenager three years ago. However, whenever he was about to masturbate, he had horrible flashbacks to the time when he was eight, before he really knew what jerking off was all about.

At that time, little Eddie just enjoyed sleeping on his stomach, especially when his thing got hard and rubbed against the smoothness of the mattress covering. It didn't take him long to figure out that it felt even better when he moved his hips until his whole body shuddered and thrilled. The problem was that it sometimes made him wet his bed, when, without warning, his thing would squirt, leaving a little telltale spot on the sheet. And, he always went to the bathroom before going to bed, too. As the weeks went by, the wetting occurred more and more. Eddie was ashamed. He was smart enough to realize he must be doing something wrong if it made him a bed-wetter, something he never did before, even when he was much younger. This was something he could never speak about. If his friends found out they would laugh and call him names. He often vowed never to do it again, a promise he kept until he went to bed the following night. And, then it was "just this one more time."

Eddie was into his third month of "one more times" when, one night, he had been attacking his mattress with such voracity that his parents, downstairs watching television, thought he was having a seizure. Panic stricken, they ran to his room and threw open the door, ready for almost any emergency – but not what confronted them. Their son, startled, turned instinctively toward the interruption, covers thrown back. His engorged penis, sheet-burned to a bright red, flounced and flapped in front of him, uncontrollably emitting little spurts of an almost clear secretion. Momentarily stunned, Mr. and Mrs. Casale just stood in the doorway, eyes wide, simply staring, strangely reminding Eddie for an instant of the farmer and his wife in that painting he remembered from the art book at the school library. As the scene registered, their faces reddened in a combination of anger and embarrassment.

"What a bad *boy!" Mrs. Casale cried.*

"You should be ashamed!*" Mr. Casale yelled.*

"I'm s-s-sorry," Eddie wept, as he watched his thing soften, shrivel up and practically disappear. He looked up through tear-filled eyes. His parents were still staring at it, too. Overcome with a shame he didn't quite understand, he belatedly reached down and pulled the sheet up around his head, covering his nakedness and his humiliation. He sobbed loudly, expecting further wrath from his parents. He became confused when their anger was suddenly directed toward each other.

"I told *you!" his mother snapped.*

"Me? Me? His father retorted. "You're the one with all the pamphlets from the Church explaining what to say, for Chrissake."

"It's your duty, you're the father. And, don't use blasphemy in this *house!"*

"I'm just saying, maybe it's the Church's responsibility. I mean, they know how to handle these *things."*

"I can't believe it. You're a lawyer. *You make your living* talking *to people."*

"But they're strangers. And, we don't talk about this *kind of thing."*

"Dear God in Heaven," his mother began to wail, "Please forgive him for he knows not what he does." Eddie wasn't sure if she was praying for him or his

father, but he was relieved to hear them both heading back down the stairs. He fell asleep wondering what really happened.

The next day his mother had dragged him to old Father Norman, pastor of Blessed Savior Roman Catholic Church, and headmaster of the church's elementary school, where Eddie attended second grade. After a brief, whispered conversation, his mother left him in the pastor's office, which always smelled of old whiskey fumes and cigar smoke. The ancient priest, who had seemed to be having trouble keeping his eyes open, leaned back in his chair. Also present was the huge and sinister Sister Thomas, the school's principal. It had been a joke among the students that she played left tackle for the Sisters of Mercy football team while at the Convent. And they beat Notre Dame!

After being nudged by Sister Thomas' beefy hand, Father Norman had begun by clearing his throat. It didn't work. When he spoke his voice was still phlegmy.

"Well, my son, in a few months you will receive your first Communion and you will learn that what you have done is a terrible sin — a mortal sin — for which you must confess to God and beg His forgiveness." As he spoke, Father Norman's voice had seemed to clear and take on force, his hands raised toward heaven for emphasis.

Eddie became frightened, then cowered when the priest suddenly shot a finger at him, and raised his voice even more. "You must control yourself from these evil thoughts and actions, or suffer the damnation of everlasting hell." By this time Father Norman was half out of his chair, his tired face suddenly charged with excitement. Then, as if the exertion had been too much for him, he sighed and fell back in his seat. "Of course," he continued, almost mumbling, "it feels good when you're doing it. . ." He glanced at Sister Thomas. She shot him a menacing frown. ". . . Ahem, but you always feel deeply saddened right afterward. That's God's way of telling you how unhappy you have made Him." Eddie had never felt sad afterwards, except when his parents caught him, but he kept his mouth shut. "And, don't be fooled, either," the priest concluded, "It is just as great *of a sin to do it like you did as if you had used your hand. Er, Sister?"*

Sister Thomas stepped forward, her six-foot frame towering over Eddie. She promised a "hell right here on earth" by using her ruler to beat his hand raw if he ever used it to "touch yourself where you shouldn't."

Eddie had tears in his eyes by the time they finished. Before letting him go he was made to vow, repeating after Father Norman, "never to be impure with myself in any manner." That night Eddie discovered, thanks to the information supplied by Father Norman and Sister Thomas, that by using his hand to rub his thing he could achieve the same results without all the noise of bed banging.

Now, with chair securely in place, Eddie slipped back into bed, pulled down his shorts to below the knees, and cleared his mind of Father Norman, Sister Thomas, and the persistent rumors of early blindness. The magazine flipped open, almost automatically, to his favorite girl, Ginger. There she was, as always, waiting for him; blonde, pig-tailed, standing in front of the haystack, tits with erect nipples protruding from an open red and black plaid flannel shirt, the zipper on her short-short cut-off jeans pulled halfway down. She looked out at him with searching blue eyes, long golden legs slightly parted, left hand on a jutting hip, the tip of her right index finger stuck in the corner of her mouth, between pouting red lips.

Eddie propped Ginger against the pillow. He was already breathing heavy when he dipped the middle and index fingers of his right hand into the Dixie Peach. He moaned as he touched the ointment to the head of his already throbbing cock. He hardly had time to jump on the blonde and throw her back onto the haystack before he was stifling groans with his left hand and cumming into his right.

Shit, that was fast, Eddie thought a few moments later, his mind clearing and his breathing returning to normal. He reached over to the night table for a wad of Kleenex to wipe himself off, then tossed Ginger onto the floor, propped the pillow back behind his head, and went into his usual post-masturbation contemplations.

I guess I'm really getting good at this, it hardly takes me any time at all, now. Well, as they say, practice makes perfect, right? But I wonder if it's the same with a real girl. It's hard to think of it bein' much better, but I guess it is. Otherwise, why fuckin' bother, huh? Well, shit, I have to find out for myself soon. I mean, most of my friends have gotten laid already. Prob'bly a lot of it is bullshit, though. Yeah, sure. Except maybe for Bo. And Dancer, for sure. Well, I better find out before I get any older, for Chrissake.

Before nodding off to sleep, Eddie recited his usual nighttime prayer: "Dear God, please let me get laid, just once, and I will never jerk off again. *This* time I mean it."

TWO

SCHOOL DAYS

Up in the morning and out to school
The teacher is teaching the golden rule

"Sure, Chuck Berry can sing about it," Eddie muttered, as he opened one eye and glanced at his GE clock-radio. "If I had his money I'd be singin' about it, too. But personally I think school sucks. 'Specially on Mondays." Seven forty-five. Eddie closed his eye and rolled over. *It should be coming any minute, now,* he thought.

Ring, ring goes the bell . . .

Chuck Berry's soulful tune was interrupted by Mrs. Casale shouting up from the bottom of the stairs. "Turn that noise down and get out of bed. Your sister's finished with the bathroom."

Eddie moaned. His mother was right on schedule. He threw the covers down and contemplated the hard-on pressing against his Jockey shorts. Should he jerk off again or take a piss? He knew what he felt like doing, but was worried about his eyesight. He ran to the bathroom with his hands in front of his crotch. As his bladder emptied, his cock softened, a phenomenon they never explained in Eddie's biology class.

Stepping from the shower, he slipped into his bathrobe and toweled his hair. Using the end of the towel, he circled a clearing in the steamed mirror and inspected his face for traces of a beard. Nothing. The Gillette Blue Blade he had stashed behind the Bromo Seltzer bottle would have to wait a little longer.

He did, however, discover an early-warning sign of an up-coming zit – that little spot of redness that hurt like hell when you touched it – and the son-of-a-bitch had chosen a prominent place on Eddie's face to fester. He found his sister's Clearasil and smeared some over the area, ending up with a bright pink glob on his right cheek, like a neon sign advertising Zit City. He washed it off and left it alone, knowing from experience that no matter what he did the fucking pimple would break through his skin anytime it felt like it, probably about an hour before his next date.

Eddie selected his toothbrush from among the four displayed in the rack above the sink, squeezed on some Pepsodent, and brushed with his usual back-and-forth motion. Then he squeezed huge dabs of Brylcreem into each hand and rubbed them vigorously into his hair. He used the wide-toothed end of the comb to carefully sculpture his hair, pushing the sides smooth and slick until they met, evenly, at the center of the back of his head. He took his mother's make-up mirror, held it behind his head, and checked the reflection in the large bathroom mirror. A perfect duck's ass. He took great pride in his hair, which he knew was one of his strong points with the girls. As a finishing touch, he used the tip of the comb to flip a few strands of hair down over his forehead into a Bill Haley spit curl.

"Hurry up or you'll be late for school. You spend more time in that bathroom than your sister," Mrs. Casale yelled from the bottom of the stairs. "God only knows what you do in there all that time."

Eddie hated when his mother said things like that. It always made him wonder if God *really* knew what he did in the bathroom sometimes. Anyway, Eddie knew the time now. It was his mother's eight fifteen warning. Her next one, at exactly eight thirty, would be: "Get down here this instant, or I'll come up there with the spoon. I'm not writing anymore late notes for you."

"The Spoon" was the long-handled wooden spoon which Mrs. Casale used deftly, whether to create sauces or inflict pain on various parts of Eddie's body. Because of this, Eddie considered his Mom to be the best talking alarm clock in the world. He heard that GE and some other companies were developing clocks that could speak, but he figured if they ever invented one that told you the time, then threatened you with pain if you didn't get up, they'd *really* make a fortune.

Eddie grabbed his clothes from the hanger on the back of the bathroom door. Bayside High School had a strict dress code. For boys, it was neatly pressed slacks, a clean shirt with a button front, and shoes – no boots or sneakers. However, that was for the rest of the kids. Eddie's crowd had a special deal, worked out with Dr. Martell, the principal, "for the sake of peace and harmony in the classroom." He pulled on his dungarees, and buckled the wide, metal-studded garrison belt off to the side, with the big buckle resting on his left hip. He held his red T-shirt up to the light from the bathroom window. It passed the eye test. He smelled the shirt's armpits. It passed the nose test. He rubbed an extra dose of Mennen deodorant under his arms, and slipped the T-shirt over his head, stretching the neck opening extra wide so he wouldn't mess up his hair.

Eddie studied the results in the mirror. Damn, if he didn't look pretty fuckin' good, he thought. Almost like Elvis himself. All he needed now was *The Smile*. He tried to curl his lip the way Elvis Presley did, but his face became contorted, causing Eddie to appear slightly retarded. He needed more practice. When Eddie smiled his lips shot straight out, then curved slightly upward at the corners. A normal, everyday asshole smile, Eddie thought. That damned Presley. How does he do it? Eddie used his thumb and forefinger to twist the corner of his upper lip into a curl, but when he took his hand away, his lip straightened. The only thing that remained was a bright red mark from where he bruised his skin by pinching it. "Fuck ya, Elvis," Eddie snarled in-to the mirror.

"Get down here this instant, or I'll come up there with the spoon. I'm not writing anymore late notes for you." Mrs. Casale gave her eight thirty alarm. Eddie rubbed a little after shave talc on his bruise, gave the sides of his hair a final pat, and rushed out of the bathroom and down the stairs.

"Sit, and have your breakfast. You have time if you eat fast," Eddie's mother said, as she set a plate of scrambled eggs, four strips of bacon and two slices of buttered toast on the kitchen table, next to a water tumbler full of fresh-squeezed orange juice. No crisis is too great to cause a person not to eat: Mrs. Casale's Rule Number One.

"Thanks, Mom, but I'm not hungry. This is all I want." Eddie grabbed the orange juice and gulped it down while still standing.

"What do you mean, not hungry. You got to eat." Eddie knew his mother's next line, and mouthed the words as she said them. "Besides, it's a sin to waste food. There are children starving to death in China."

"Then wrap up the bacon an' eggs an' send 'em to the Chinks," Eddie called over his shoulder as he grabbed his black leather jacket and notebook, and headed quickly for the door, knowing that his mother was on her way to the drawer where she kept quite a large selection of wooden spoons.

Eddie stepped out into a beautiful April morning. It was still quite cool, but with a sunshine full of promises of the warmness to come. He hooked his jacket on his thumb, and carried it over his left shoulder, upset that he took it with him, but not daring to put it back in the house.

"Shit, now I gotta carry it around all fuckin' day," he muttered to himself, kicking at a small stone in the driveway with his heavy black boot. The stone skittered along and bounced off the right front fender of Mr. Casale's two-month old Buick Roadmaster, taking a decent sized paint chip with it when it left. Eddie froze in his tracks, his eyes darting to his father's upstairs bedroom window. It was closed tight, thank God. He let his breath out slowly, and continued walking. What a way to start the day, he thought. I've been out of the house for less than a minute, and I feel like shit already. What next?

When he reached the end of his driveway, however, his spirits lifted, and a smile spread across his face. There was Bo Brody, who lived across the street, wheeling his Triumph motorcycle out of the garage. Eddie always smiled when he saw Bo. Everyone did. Bo had that sort of effect on people. It felt good just being in his presence.

"Hi, man," Eddie said, walking across the street to greet his friend. "How's the bike runnin'?"

"Great, man," Bo said, speaking softly as always. "That re-built carb is givin' me jus' the right mixture now." He checked his watch. "Gotta get to the job. I'm runnin' late this mornin'."

Bo was nineteen, just under six feet tall, with reddish-brown hair, and a complexion that authenticated his Irish-German heritage. He had massive shoulders and chest, and arms like tree trunks. He didn't need to lift weights to be strong, but he lifted weights, anyway.

Although Eddie and Bo lived across the street from each other for many years, they had never been friends, and hardly had spoken more than a greeting until about a year ago. After all, Bo and his friends were three years older than "that little kid." But, by the time Eddie was fifteen, "that little kid" was six-foot-four, one hundred eighty five pounds, and looking every bit of eighteen or nineteen himself. Finally, he was accepted by the older crowd. Now when they went to bars, he was hardly ever asked for proof, and it made Eddie happy when some of the older guys were proofed, and he wasn't. The thing that made Eddie the happiest, however, was the fact that he and Bo became the best of friends.

"So, didya dig the party Saturday night?

"Yeah. It was a gas," Bo said, buttoning up his Levi jacket. "Cept I didn't know whether to take Barbara or Judy home, so I just ended up takin' my bike out for a run." He pulled the collar of his jacket up, and looked at Eddie. "Say, yer ol' man didn't get bent outa shape 'cause of all that shit we drank, did he?"

"No way, man," Eddie replied, averting his eyes. "He's pretty cool 'bout those things. Besides, I know how to handle him."

Bo caught the eye movement, and flashed a knowing smile.

"Well, I guess he was a little pissed," Eddie said reluctantly. "But, at me, not you guys," he added quickly. "He still thinks I'm a baby."

"You are a fuckin' baby, whadaya expect?" Bo teased, slipping on his aviator sun glasses. "By the way, how's my alma mater? You keepin' those asshole teachers in line?"

"Yer spirit still haunts the hallways," Eddie said with a feeling of pride. "I make sure of that."

Just then, the front door of Bo's house opened and Kate Brody, Bo's fifteen-year-old sister stepped onto the top of the stoop. Kate was hot. She looked hot, acted hot, and, if you danced with her, you didn't try it without an asbestos suit. Just seeing her now forced Eddie to relive the physical and mental torture of Saturday night.

Someone played a slow-dance record like Earth Angel *or* Sincerely, *and Kate asked Eddie to dance* The Fish, *because her boyfriend, Hank, was either 'not drunk enough' or 'too drunk' to dance. The trouble was that as soon as Eddie pressed Kate's great body against his own and began to move, he'd get a huge erection. And, with a pair of baggy, powder blue pegged pants, there was nothing to hide it or hold it down. It pressed against Kate's belly, and Kate would press back harder, breathing in his ear. For a guy who would get a hard-on in Algebra class just looking at the back of Gloria's ponytail, this was hell. It took every trick in the book not to erupt. Eddie closed his eyes and went through the line-up of the 1955 world champion Brooklyn Dodgers.*

The dance ended and Kate immediately walked to her chair against the wall on the girl's side of the room, leaving Eddie in the center of the floor with Old Glory at full staff. The girls quickly gathered around Kate, whispering, looking at Eddie and giggling. The guys had been a little more obvious.

"Hey, what'd ya drop a beer bottle down yer pants?" Cootie, who was loud even when sober – and he wasn't sober – yelled out across the room.

Of course, after that outburst even those who may have been otherwise occupied – like making out – were now directing their attention to the dance floor.

"Lookit, everybody. Omar The Tent maker has a new construction site." That was Kenny Fletcher, who unglued his lips from Joan Ford's for the first time that night – at Eddie's expense.

Now, the whole room was pointing and laughing, and Eddie felt ridiculous. The only effect was that the humiliation made the rise in his pants subside. He walked to the table and picked up a bottle of Thunderbird, downing four large gulps without a glass. He began to feel better. He vowed he would never do The Fish *with Kate Brody again. That was until someone played Johnny Ace's* Pledging My Love *and Kate touched his arm, looked up with those big brown eyes, and said, "Let's dance." Eddie just looked down at those big tits in the tight white sweater, and said, "Ya bet."*

What it came down to, Eddie figured, was that three minutes of pressing a hard-on against Kate's stomach was worth all the mental torture of the giggling and wisecracking. It was even worth the physical torture which would come later that night – a devastating case of blue-balls.

Now Eddie's eyes were on Kate's breasts again, this time those two glorious globes were doing wonders for a green Angora sweater. He tried, unsuccessfully, not to stare at her bouncing boobs as she skipped down her front steps. He sneaked a glance at Bo to see if he was witnessing the ogling of his sister, but Eddie couldn't see Bo's eyes behind the dark glasses, which he was adjusting with thumb and forefinger.

Eddie hoped Kate wouldn't make any cracks about the party, especially in front of her brother. He held his breath. He was relieved as she passed, simply calling out a cheerful "good morning." About twenty feet up the street, she stopped, turned, and with a perfectly innocent smile and an over-animated voice, said: "Oh *Eeeddiee,* that was a *divine* party. And, I just *adore* the way you dance." She turned abruptly, her flare skirt flaring to the knees, and continued on her way to Bayside High School.

Eddie didn't answer. He felt himself begin to blush. He looked at Bo to see if his friend caught the meaning of the remark. After all, Bo never mentioned how he felt about guys getting hard-ons with his sister, and Eddie wasn't about to bring the subject up. At the moment, however, Bo seemed more intent on starting his bike. On the third kick the engine caught. He revved the throttle a few times, then toed the bike into first gear. He looked up.

"Remember," he said to Eddie, "I'm always three years older and *one* step ahead of ya."

"Yeah, I *know.* Catch ya later," Eddie said, now anxious to be on his way.

Bo nodded, rolled a few feet, then braked sharply. "Hey, man!" he called. Eddie stiffened, then turned slowly. Bo was looking back over his shoulder at him. For a few seconds they just stared at each other. Slowly, that easy smile broke over Bo's face. "Keep a cool tool, fool," he said. "I'm wise to that rise in your Levi's." Then, with a roar of the engine, he was gone.

Bayside High was only four blocks from Eddie's house, allowing ample time to make the final eight fifty-five bell. Not that he *ever* made the final bell. When he reached the park adjacent to the school, Eddie spotted some of his friends, as usual, already lounging on the grass waiting for him.

Dan Manning was sitting with his arms folded around propped up knees. In his hands was a dog-eared paperback copy of *The Amboy Dukes,* a novel about teenage street gangs from Brooklyn. The book had made the rounds of all the guys, and Manning got it last because he was the slowest reader. He sat there staring wide-eyed at a page, strands of his straight red hair falling over his high forehead, a look of wonderment on his face, while his lips formed each word carefully. Once in a while he'd yell, "Wow," or "Holy Shit," or ask in bewilderment something like, "What is c-a-t-a-s-t-r-o-p-h-e?" ("That's you reading a fuckin' book," Johnny Logan had replied.) Dan had the book for three weeks, reading it incessantly – in school, the park, the candy store, just about everywhere. He was now up to page fifty seven. All the guys were getting to the point of hating to be near him. They tried everything to get him to stop reading that damned book, including telling him how it ended. All he had said was, "Wow! I can't wait to get to *that* part."

Dan, though, did have something pretty impressive going for him, which was why his friends risked the possibility of a nervous breakdown by continuing to let him hang out. Being left back several times throughout his academic career, he was now eighteen, in possession of a legal driver's license, and was the only one of the "school" crowd to drive a car. It was a huge 1940 black Packard sedan, right out of a George Raft movie, which was used to transport up to twelve kids at a time, or stage mock "rubouts" on street corners by blasting unsuspecting pedestrians with bullet-like squirts from water machine guns.

Joe Ross was lying on his back, his arms folded behind his head. His eyes were covered by very dark Ray Charles-type sun glasses. Joe had his red nylon jacket off and propped behind his head, careful not to mess his dark blond hair. A pack of cigarettes was rolled into the sleeve of his white T-shirt, the dark red Lucky Strikes emblem showing through. Ross stood five-foot-seven, and didn't weigh more than one hundred and twenty pounds. He wasn't much in a fight, but he was always ready to use his mouth. Eddie didn't know if he was sleeping or not.

"What the hell took ya so long?" Ross asked, remaining perfectly still, only his lips moving. "Did ya still have a hard-on from Saturday night, an' had to take care of business before school?"

"Fuck ya, Ross," Eddie responded. "At least when I get a hard-on people notice. Ya need a magnifyin' glass an' tweezers jus' to jerk off."

"People notice, awright," Ross shot back. "They notice Kate an' the rest of the bitches makin' an asshole out of ya, an' laughin' their asses off. An' I bet your pillow noticed, too, when ya humped the shit out of it that night."

"Oh, yeah? Oh, yeah?" Eddie was trying to think of a good comeback. "I saw *yer* pillow goin' out with Cootie because it can't get satisfied at home."

"Bullshit," Ross said, sitting up. "I *loaned* my pillow to Cootie that night because he needed a date. Whadaya jealous?"

The rank-out session was suddenly interrupted by someone shouting: "Look out behind ya! He's got a push-button. He's gonna cut ya!"

Ross sprang to his feet, heavy engineer boots gouging two heel marks in the young spring grass. Eddie turned, dropped in a crouch, arms up in defense. They looked around. The only one near them was Manning.

"I told ya to watch out for that bastard," he continued shouting to page fifty seven of the book, a look of deep concern on his face.

"Jesus H. Christ!" Ross snarled. "That fuckin' does it! I can't take this shit no more. I'm leavin' an' I ain't comin' back 'til this idiot finishes that fuckin' book. Which may be never. Ya comin'? Or ya stayin' with him? Yer choice." Ross started walking away, tossing his windbreaker over his shoulder.

"What choice?" Eddie answered, matter-of-factly. "He got the fuckin' car, asshole."

Ross stopped dead in his tracks after only several feet. He turned slowly. "Some friend ya are," he said, more calmly now. "But ya do put up a hell of an argument."

"Think of it this way, ol' buddy," Eddie said, walking over and putting an arm around his friend's shoulder. "He can't read when he drives."

"That fuckin' idiot can't read when he *reads*," Ross said, slipping on his jacket.

Laughing, Eddie walked over to Manning and kicked his boot.

"Hey, man," Manning said in surprise, looking up from the book for the first time. "When'd ya get here?"

"Jus' a little while ago," Eddie said, "but I didn't want to interrupt yer readin'."

"Yeah. This is a great book, awright," Manning said with enthusiasm. "These Dukes are some real tough sons-a-bitches, huh?"

"Yeah, sure," Eddie agreed, as he heard Ross moan behind him. "But put the book away 'til you get to class, willya? We're gonna split now."

"Hey, wait up ya guys," Johnny Logan called. He was trotting across the grass towards the group just as the eight fifty-five bell rang. With the arrival of Logan, a tall sixteen-year-old with long, brown hair, the high school contingent of The Bayside Crowd was complete. Of the twenty or so guys who hung out at Dick's Candy Store, these were the only four still in school.

Ross unraveled the Luckies from his sleeve and passed the pack around, followed by his Zippo lighter. All four lit up. They strolled casually toward the school, just jiving, punching each other on the arms, and taking deep drags on the smokes. It just wasn't cool to be on time for home room. They liked to swagger in a few minutes after nine and piss off the teacher by disrupting the class – just late enough to make a grand entrance, but not so late that they would be sent to the dean's office for a late pass, three of which would necessitate a note from a parent. They had it down to a science.

Students were forbidden to use the huge, ornate main entrance to Bayside High School. That sacred archway was reserved for teachers, VIP's, and, AOA's (Assorted Other Assholes). The only time pupils were allowed to ascend the wide stone steps into the hallowed halls of high school officialdom was when they were bringing their parents in for a requested conference with the dean or principal. Otherwise, they were required to use the two metal doors on the street level of the three-story building, using the clearly marked "up" or "down" staircases to maneuver to classrooms.

As the four boys, with Eddie in the lead, pushed open the twelve-foot door and entered the school's main lobby, their heavy black boots scuffing the highly-polished marble floor, they found George St. Claire, Dean of Boys, waiting for them. He stood there with a smug look on his pinched face, his bony arms folded across his narrow chest, while tapping his right foot in anticipation. Like always, he wore a snap-on bowtie with an elastic band around the collar, and a baggy blue serge suit two sizes too big for his five-foot-three frame. The one interesting thing about St. Claire was the fact that so little hair – just a wisp around the ears – could produce a record amount of dandruff on his shoulders. His main job, it seemed, was the harassment of Eddie and his friends. He was always following them during change of class, peeking into classrooms, watching, or spying from around corners of the building – his detention pad at the ready.

In return, he suffered anguish and frustration. Dr. H. Bruce Martell, the principal, realizing it had become almost an obsession with his dean, paid little or no attention to St. Claire when he harped on so many minor infractions, like running in hallways or sitting in class with legs crossed. When St. Claire reported these, and even some of the more serious offenses, or if the boys had not shown up for detention, Martell would simply say, "Fine, George, fine. I'll handle it from here." After the dean would leave his office, the principal would shake his head and look up St. Claire's retirement date, hoping the man would be able to hang in and make it. It was Martell's policy, which he impressed upon his staff, not to get involved with these boys for anything short of a capital crime. His dean just didn't seem to get the message.

The boys approached St. Claire, who stood in the center of the lobby like a sentry on duty. He unfolded his arms, reached into a jacket pocket, whipped out several slips of paper and thrust them forward.

"Three hours of detention each for using an unauthorized entrance," he said gleefully. "I was watching you cross the street. I *knew* you were heading this way." When he spoke, he had a habit of pushing himself up on his toes, in an attempt to appear larger. He was still unable, however, to delude anyone from noting that he was perhaps the tiniest person in the school, with the exception of several freshmen girls.

The boys all grabbed their slips at the same time. Logan pulled out the dean's bowtie, stuffed his paper behind it, and snapped the tie back, crushing the paper. Ross blew his nose in his slip, then tossed it over his shoulder. Manning made an ass-wiping motion with his, then held it under St. Claire's nose with thumb and forefinger like soiled toilet paper. Eddie folded his paper into an airplane and sent it soaring, with several loops, twenty feet down the hallway, receiving plaudits from his pals for his latest aeronautical design.

The boys left St. Claire stunned, motionless, like a statue with an outstretched hand, and headed for home room, dragging their boots along the waxed floor. However, they felt they owed their dean some parting remarks.

"If ya put a ski lift on yer shoulders ya'd make a fortune with all that snow," Ross advised.

"The next time ya buy a suit try the little boys' department at Barney's," Eddie added. "Ya might find one that fits ya."

"Now you've done it! Now you've done it!" St. Claire shouted after them when he finally regained his composure. "We'll see what Dr. Martell has to say about *this* little episode," he called over his shoulder while rushing off to the principal's office.

Ross, Logan and Eddie bopped into home room 308. Manning was assigned to a different class – not special, just different. Not that it really mattered anymore. They were all in their junior year. Next year they would graduate. They weren't supposed to know it, but it was all arranged, as long as they didn't do anything serious enough to be expelled. The word from the top was to move those troublemakers along and out as fast as possible.

"Hey, teach! How's it hangin'?" Logan called loudly across the room, as they entered the class with all the flair of Bill Haley and The Comets taking the stage at the Brooklyn Paramount. Morton Greenbaum, the teacher, looked up from the book he was reading. He saw who it was, shook his head in dismay, and chose not to get into a confrontation. He buried his head back behind the book.

Logan plopped down at a desk in the last row, and propped his long legs on the desk across the aisle. The boy sitting there wisely moved to another one. Ross sat on the other side of Logan, behind a girl with a long, black ponytail, which he began to fondle. The girl whispered something to her friend and they both looked back and giggled. Eddie helped himself to a folding chair from the supply closet and set it up in the aisle next to Penny Randazzo's desk. Despite being Eddie's steady girl, it always seemed Penny was pissed off at him about something or other. Today appeared to be no exception. Her hands were folded primly on the desk and she was staring straight ahead. She didn't greet him. Penny wore her light brown hair in waves down to her shoulders. Her eyes were dark brown, her lips full. Her parents didn't allow her to wear makeup, but she didn't need any. Today she was wearing her pink sweater with her name embroidered in blue over the curve of her left breast.

"Hi, Penny," Eddie said with a smile as he sat down. "What's the name of the *other* one?" It was his standard greeting whenever she wore that sweater, and it always produced a giggle. Today, nothing. "Hey, what's a matter, baby?" He touched her arm gently. Her body stiffened, she continued staring ahead.

Wow! Super pissed today. Eddie figured it had to do with the party and what happened every time he had danced with Kate – and only sometimes when he danced with her.

"Hey, look, honey, that stuff at the party don't mean nothin'," Eddie explained. "Kate's just a good friend. Comeon, she goes steady with Hank. She ain't as pretty as you, anyway." He decided not to add, *but her tits are bigger.*

Penny turned and looked sharply at Eddie. Her eyes were ringed with red.

"Ah, comeon, baby, don't cry over somethin' as dumb as that," Eddie said, putting his hands on her shoulders and trying to pull her close.

She shrugged them off and pulled away. "It has nothing to do with Kate, you animal, and don't ever put those filthy hands on me again."

She was talking loud enough now to disturb Greenbaum's reading. He looked up from his book, annoyed.

"Whadaya talkin' about?" Eddie asked, now totally bewildered.

Greenbaum was about to say something, but the bell rang for change of class. Penny picked up her books, stood, and turned to leave. Eddie grabbed her arm. Roughly, she pulled it away.

"I told you never to touch me again," she ordered loudly. Then, lowering her voice, she said, "If you can put those hands - and everything else – all over that dirty slut Helen Roberts, I never want them to touch *me*." She blinked several times and tears filled her eyes again.

"What the hell are ya talkin' about," Eddie asked again. Now he was almost pleading, even more confused with the mention of Helen Roberts.

"Willy Shaw is telling the entire school about you and that pig *doing it* in the boy's bathroom last week," Penny blurted out, her voice cracking. Then she turned and stormed out of the room. Her friends Lori and Tricia were waiting by the door, and all three gave him a final dirty look, turned up their noses and walked off.

Holy shit, Eddie thought. *What the hell's goin' on?* He had to think. Helen Roberts was the school pump. *The Slut*. She would put out for anyone, anytime, anyplace. None of the girls would associate with her, and guys would only meet her someplace private – like the boy's bathroom, the abandoned freight car near the railroad station, or the back seat of a car at night. All the guys had fucked her, or at least had hand jobs or blow jobs.

Well, almost all. Eddie had come close last week, but just couldn't go through with it.

Eddie was with Logan and Ross, cutting study class, out in the park smoking Luckies, when they spotted Al Lupia and several other seniors crossing the street with Helen Roberts in tow. Al, one of The Bayside Crowd's few "outside" friends in school, waved them to follow, then signaled by making a circle with the thumb and forefinger of one hand and inserting the middle finger of the other. They continued to the park's equipment shack, broke the padlock with a rock and went inside.

"Comeon," Logan said. "I fucked her twice already. She ain't half bad."

"Yeah," Ross added. "Just tie a two-by-four on yer ass so ya don't fall in."

"Yeah," Eddie lied. "Might as well fuck her again, right? Nothin' else around." Eddie couldn't believe it. He was finally going to get his first piece of ass. Even if it was Helen Roberts.

By the time they reached the equipment shack there were fourteen guys crowded into the small room. Al Lupia called out, "I'm first." Someone else followed with the usual shout of, "Sloppy seconds."

From the sweat-stained wrestling mat where Helen Roberts was laying with her skirt pulled up and her panties pushed down, she said, in all seriousness. "Sloppy seconds? You're about the sloppy one thousandth."

Eddie looked around. All the guys were laughing and jockeying for position on line, his own friends included. Lupia lowered himself on Helen, her thick legs, bobby socks still on her feet, raised in the air. Are they crazy, or is it me? Eddie thought. He shook his head. He didn't know. He was sure of one thing, though. When he does do it for the first time, it has to be better than this. He backed out the door and no one noticed him leaving.

Now Willy Shaw was spreading rumors about Eddie and Helen Roberts. True or not, it didn't matter, though. Shaw had no right to be talking about Eddie, and Shaw knew it. That was an insult Eddie couldn't ignore. Eddie had to go after Shaw, and that would mean a war with the Bayside Bombers, a tough, mostly Irish street gang from Bayside West, a poorer section of the neighborhood, an area which included the high school. Eddie had it figured out in an instant. He would kick Willy Shaw's ass. Then his older brother, Dutch Shaw, and Jack Callahan, leader of the Bombers, along with the rest of the gang, would jump Eddie in the park. Most of the Bombers didn't work, so they could wait for Eddie during the day, while most of Eddie's friends had jobs and weren't around in the afternoons. It was a perfect set up, Eddie thought, but one he had to walk into or be labeled a punk.

Johnny Logan and Joe Ross were at Eddie's side leaving the classroom, wondering what the hell had happened. He explained what Penny had told him.

"That mothafucka," Ross said. "He knows damn well ya don't talk about shit like that."

"Fuckin' A," Logan added.

"I didn't do it anyway," Eddie protested. "Shit, I'm prob'bly the only guy in fuckin' school that never touched that pig, for Chrissake."

"Doesn't matter, right?" Ross asked. "Who the fuck would believe it? She tells people herself that she's fucked or sucked every boy in the school."

"Right!"

"Yeah, right."

"So, it's a good bet the Bombers put him up to it," Ross continued. "They prob'bly want an excuse to stomp yer ass. They know what Penny is like. They figure, spread some shit 'bout ya an' The Slut, let it be known it comes from Willy, an' ya *gotta* make a move."

"Fuckin' A," Logan said again. "They know ya can wipe the floor with Willy, an' when ya do, the

Bombers will be all over ya. I bet they've been wantin' yer ass ever since ya left the Blessed Sacrament dance last month with one of their chicks. What was her name, Beth or Tess, or somethin'?"

"Yeah, Beth," Eddie said, remembering, with a fond smile, the girl with long red hair he took to the park that night. "An' she gave me some good tit, too. Real nice pair on her." Of course, when he found out she lived in Bayside West, Bomber turf, he knew he would probably never see her again.

"Man, I hope they were worth it, but personally *I* ain't never seen tits on an Irish girl worth takin' a beatin' for," Logan said, bringing Eddie back to the present crisis.

"Yeah, well, I don't plan to start now, either," Eddie said. "Look, I know the script, but I gotta play it out, ya know? I'll take care of our friend Willy durin' gym class. Ya guys just play chickie in case any teachers come aroun', or if his friends try to jump in. Whatever happens after that, fuck it. I'll deal with it when the time comes."

There were about a dozen guys already in the locker room changing into their orange and blue gym suits when Eddie and his friends came in for the eleven thirty class. Eddie stopped just inside the door and scanned the room. He spotted Willy Shaw dressed in the school-colored orange and blue T-shirt and shorts over in the far corner talking to one of his friends, a small pimply-faced punk called Alfie.

"Hey, there's the WOP bastard, now," Shaw called out loudly when he spotted Eddie. "Whadaya know? We was jus' talkin' 'bout the dago, an' in he slides."

Eddie stared hard at Willy, while the other kids in the locker room, knowing trouble was coming, finished dressing on the move, rushing out the door to the gym. Eddie walked directly at Shaw, pacing himself carefully, without saying a word. Logan kept five steps behind, watching his back. Ross stayed by the door, propped it open a crack, and kept an eye peeled for teachers, or any other intruders.

"It seems ya been talkin' about me quite a bit lately, huh?" Eddie said, his voice low, menacing. He was standing directly in front of the other boy now, in close, ready for action, his eyes watching Shaw's eyes for the first hint of attack. In his peripheral vision he caught Alfie backing away from the action, hands in the air as if being robbed at gun point, letting it be known that he was not going to be involved.

"That's right," Shaw said, getting up slowly from the bench, circling to his left. He was flashing a crack-toothed smile, but his words came out hard and cold. "You and that cocksucker Helen Roberts are a hot fuckin' item, huh?" He kept circling, his smile widening. "Ya know, asshole, when ya kiss her yer tastin' every cock in school, 'specially mine." He was taunting, trying to get Eddie to blow his cool, make a mistake. Eddie waited, maintaining eye contact, while Shaw kept circling and taunting. "Now I hear ya gonna have a real ginzo weddin'. Ya know, plenty of spaghetti and *grease*-balls."

Shaw was about three inches shorter than Eddie, and a good thirty pounds lighter, but very solid. And, he was fast, very fast. He ran every day in the gym, and beat everyone, even some members of the track and field team, which he always refused to join to the frustration of the coach.

"It's yer move, ya dumb Mick mothafucka." Now, it was Eddie's turn to taunt, and he did it in the same low, menacing voice. "Ya did all the talkin'. Maybe that's all ya know how to do, is talk."

Shaw kept circling, but now he leaned slightly forward in a crouch, arms swinging. Eddie shifted his weight to the balls of his feet, turning with him, but remaining in the same spot. He continued to wait, trying to control his excitement with his breathing, forcing himself to be patient. He knew Shaw would eventually make the first move.

Otherwise, once Eddie grabbed Shaw, it would all be over. Eddie held eye contact, knowing that was where Shaw would telegraph his intentions a spilt second before any physical movement.

There it was! A rapid double blink and Shaw was on the move, leaping in the air, his muscular leg shooting forward with a kick aimed directly at Eddie's balls. Almost at the same instant, though, Eddie was moving, too, twisting to his right. The kick caught his left hip bone, and he was glad Shaw was wearing his gym shoes and not his engineer boots. He felt pain, anyway, from the sheer power of the blow, but not enough to stop him from grabbing Shaw's leg as he side-stepped. He pulled it straight up, and flipped him back, slamming him hard onto the tile floor. Shaw's head cracked loudly when it hit, dazing him, and Eddie was on him in an instant, a knee pressed against his chest, fists exploding in his face. Blood spurted from Shaw's nose, ran down his chin and was absorbed into his T-shirt.

"Chickie! Chickie! Here comes Johnson." Ross shouted a warning from the door. Eddie jumped to his feet, and was backing away, just as Ned Johnson, the gym teacher, burst into the locker room from the gym. The entire fight lasted no more than forty seconds.

"What's going on in here?" Johnson demanded, looking at Shaw, as the boy picked himself up from the floor and grabbed a towel to hold to his bleeding face.

"Nuttin'," Shaw mumbled. "I jus' fell an' hit my head on the bench. That's all. It's nuttin'."

Johnson glared at Eddie, then back at Shaw. "You, Shaw, get your rump up to the nurse's office," the teacher ordered. "And, the rest of you bums get out of here. Now! I don't even want you in gym class today. Personally, I don't care if you hoodlums kill each other. But do it on someone else's time, not mine. In *my* class, if anyone wants to fight they can always try me." He looked at each of the boys in turn. They all turned away. No one ever fucked with Johnson. He was a gym teacher who took his job seriously. In top physical shape, he had big, muscular arms, and a tight, hard body. He was the only teacher in school that never received any back talk.

As Shaw bent over to pull on his pants, he leaned close to Eddie. "This ain't over yet, scumbag," he whispered through puffed lips. "We'll finish it after school tomorrow in the park. Jus' you an' me."

"I'll be there, punk," Eddie replied. "Jus' make sure ya don't chicken out."

"Move! Get going! Get out of here!" Johnson shouted, shoving the boys towards the door. "I have work to do, students to train. Something you bums don't know anything about. Now, scram!"

Eddie, Logan and Ross ran up the "down" staircase, and out the side door. They lit up Luckies. Eddie's hands were still shaking from the excitement of the fight, his knuckles slightly bruised.

"Well, whadawe gonna do 'bout tomorrow?" Ross asked, unable to hide the nervousness in his voice. "Ya know that Jack Callahan an' the rest of those lowlifes will be waitin' for us."

"I know, I know. But it's me they want, not ya guys. I'll just go an' see what happens, get it over with, ya know?" Eddie was trying to sound braver than he actually felt. It wasn't working.

"Shit, man, I bet there'll be at least twenty or more of 'em," Ross said. "An', except for us three – well, four countin' Manning – the rest of our crowd will be workin'."

"Hey, thanks for that glowin' report," Eddie said. "I never realized just how fuckin' bleak our situation was until now. Thanks a lot, ya fuckin' asshole."

"Oh, shit, man, I was only – "

"I know," Eddie said. "I know. Maybe we're makin' too much out of it anyway. Maybe the Bombers won't show, and it'll just be me and Shaw, one-on-one."

"Yeah. An' maybe the rabbi's a catholic," Logan said. "Either way, ya know *I'll* back ya up.

"Yeah, sure," Ross said, biting the nail of his left pinky. "We'll be with ya."

Eddie knew he could count on Johnny Logan, regardless of the odds, but Joe Ross was a different story. He couldn't fight his way out of a wet paper bag, and would probably find ten excuses not to try. Eddie figured Ross would drop a brick on his foot tonight so he couldn't walk to school tomorrow. What the hell, Eddie knew it didn't matter anyway. The guys he *needed* to have there were Bo and Ox and Dancer. Yeah, and Al Chavello who used to hang with the Fordham Road Baldies, and Mike Mancuso who once ran with the Corona Dukes. And Buffalo and Cootie and Handsome Hank Coleman and the rest of The Bayside Crowd. But they would all be working. It would be just him and his school friends in the park at 3 p.m. tomorrow, and if the Bombers jumped them, they would get their asses stomped, no two ways about it.

THREE

RIP IT UP

Eddie wiped his dish with the last piece of crusty Italian bread, and sat back from the table, stuffed. Earlier, he had been considering coming up with an excuse to skip dinner so he could get down to Dick's early to commiserate with his friends over his pending predicament. Then he spotted the pot simmering on the stove, and remembered it was Monday, the night of his favorite dinner.

Now, after two helpings of macaroni in a thick tomato sauce made with chunks of pork and veal, he felt pretty good. There must be something about all that crap in movies about a favorite "last meal" for those guys on death row, he thought, patting his full belly. Then he froze. *What am I thinking?* He felt depression push past contentment to resume its previous place of occupation. Frowning, he pushed his chair back and excused himself from the table.

"Wait! Where are you going so fast?" Mrs. Casale asked.

"Out," Eddie replied, grabbing his leather jacket and heading for the door.

"And, what are you going to do?" she persisted.

"Nothin'," her son said, his hand turning the door knob.

"I never heard of anyone going out so often just to do nothing," Mr. Casale said, still sitting at the table over a second cup of coffee.

"Oh, you know him," Eddie's sister said, as she stacked dirty dishes in the sink. "He can't miss a night of visiting with those friends of his at that candy store."

Eddie didn't answer. He was in no mood for their bullshit. He just had to get out of the house.

"Don't come home late, young man. . ." his mother called after him, as usual. He pulled the door closed quickly, almost slamming it, so he wouldn't be subjected to her final nightly proclamation: ". . . you have to get up for school tomorrow."

He turned the corner and walked along Bell Boulevard, heading towards Dick's Candy Store. Nervous, he felt himself rushing, walking much too fast. He was anxious to get there, but he tried to walk slowly. He expected most of the crowd to be there, as usual, and he had to play it cool. Although he was worried about the next day, he couldn't let it show. Several feet from the door of the candy store, he heard the juke box blasting the voice of Carl Perkins:

You can do anything
But lay off my blue suede shoes.

Eddie pulled up the collar of his jacket, ran his fingers through his hair and, after checking his reflection in the storefront window, walked into the "Headquarters" of The Bayside Crowd.

Dick's was similar to many other candy stores or soda fountains in New York neighborhoods. On the right were floor displays, shelves and revolving racks with everything from thirty-nine-cent toys, to paperback books, magazines and comics, to a full compliment of school supplies. On the left, where the cash register was, were two glass display cases featuring a wide array of candy like Good 'n' Plenty, Baby Ruth, Three Musketeers, and Chuckles, plus penny items like jawbreakers, jelly beans, sour balls and strands of black, brown and red licorice. The bubble gums – Bazooka with its color comic strip, and Topps with its five baseball cards – were on top of the counter next to the register. Along the left wall was a long counter and soda fountain, with stools, and, on the right were vinyl booths with Formica-top tables. The constantly-playing juke box was against the back wall.

It was still early, so the crowd in Dick's was light. Kate Brody was sitting in a booth with Diane Roth and Barbara Saunders. They were sipping cherry-Cokes and leaning close to each other in private conversation. Johnny Logan was sitting on a stool next to Handsome Hank Coleman, while Steve Kolinski, better known as Cootie, was studying the selections on the juke box, the tip of his tongue protruding from the corner of his mouth as a sign of his concentration, trying to decide what six songs to play for his quarter. It was a major undertaking, one which could consume a good portion of the next half hour.

"Play C-24!" Eddie called out. He walked over to Hank and slid onto the stool next to him. He could tell by the way he was greeted that they all had heard about the fight that afternoon, and about the impending trouble, too. He figured Logan must have spread the word. Hank proved him right.

"Johnny told us what happened today." The nineteen-year-old gave the younger boy an approving smile, nodding his head. "Yeah, sounds like ya really messed up that asshole, huh?"

"Oh, he's nothin' but a piece a shit," Eddie replied. "I can stomp his Irish ass every day, an' twice on Sundays."

Cootie finally pressed the last of his buttons on the juke box. He came over and sat next to Eddie, as Fats Domino began singing about how much he hated *Blue Monday*. Just then, Dan Manning came rushing into the store, and pushed himself between Cootie and Eddie.

"I heard what happened in the locker room," Manning said, excitedly. "Damn, I'm sorry I missed it."

"Well, you may get your chance tomorrow if those punk Bombers show up," Cootie said with concern in his voice. "I wish to hell I didn't have to work so I could be there."

"That makes two of us," Hank added.

The door swung open and big Paul "Ox" Zarora strode in, followed by Larry "Buffalo" Baker and Kenny Fletcher.

"What's happenin', guys?" Ox's voice boomed across the room. His voice, big and powerful, suited his almost six foot, barrel-chested frame.

As the new arrivals were being filled in on the action, Chuck Hoffman, Al Chavello and Mike Mancuso entered, and were immediately brought up to date, too. During the next half hour, Dancer Bob Larkin and Leo "The Shadow" Silverman came in, along with Big Judy Bender and Joan Ford, and the store was buzzing with so much excitement it was difficult to hear The Five Keys singing *Close Your Eyes.*

What *could* be heard, though, was the sound everyone, in their own way, was waiting for. The distinctive roar of the Triumph motorcycle as Bo Brody wheeled to the curb directly in front of the door. With a final rev of the engine, he turned the bike off and, seconds later, strode easily into the store, removing his aviator glasses as he walked. The noise subsided noticeably. His presence alone seemed to produce a calming effect, and almost everyone called out to greet him. Several of the guys nearly tripped over themselves as they rushed to be the first to provide Bo with the "hot" news of the day.

Eddie remained seated, drinking a vanilla eggcream, while trying to act cool and indifferent – like James Dean in *Rebel Without A Cause.* He hoped he was pulling it off.

At least three guys surrounded Bo, but it was Ross who was doing most of the talking now, his hands darting as he emphasized certain points. Bo looked from face to face, nodding occasionally. Then, with a final nod and a "thumb-up" signal, he slid away from the little group and walked over to Eddie, taking the stool Cootie had vacated.

"Sounds like ya got a problem," Bo said his voice soft.

"Aw, shit, man. I dunno know why everyone's makin' such a fuss," Eddie said. "I can take care of myself, ya know? Fuck those punks."

Bo looked at Eddie hard for an instant, then flashed one of his knowing smiles. "Sure ya can, buddy, sure ya can," he said, placing a big hand on his friend's shoulder, and squeezing lightly. "But, remember. I'm always three years older and *one* step ahead of ya. An' it's about time we gave those Bombers an explosion of their own. They've been bullyin' their way aroun' this town too long, anyway."

Bo slid off the stool, strode over to the juke box, and in the middle of Bill Doggett's *Honky Tonk,* pulled the machine from the wall and unplugged it. As the music slowed to a stop, all eyes turned towards Bo. No one spoke. Some stood. Others turned in their seats to face Bo.

"Tomorrow is a local holiday," Bo began, his voice carrying clearly throughout the room, a hint of a smile on his face. "It's 'Bayside Day'. That means nobody has to go to work. An' we can all meet in the park at the high school at three o'clock to celebrate."

For several seconds there was silence, then pandemonium broke out as the meaning of his words sank in. Everyone began yelling and clapping and stomping their feet.

Ox Zarora stepped forward and draped a huge arm around Bo's massive shoulders. They made a formidable pair. "Are ya with us?" he shouted, making sure he was the first to endorse Bo's action. He made a fist with his other hand and, raising it in the air, shouted again, even louder, "Are ya *with* us?" Everyone shouted back their support with such enthusiasm that the Coke glasses on the counter shook as if a minor quake had hit the region.

Dick, the owner of the store, looked like he was about to have a coronary. He kept running back and forth behind the counter yelling "Don't break anything! Don't break anything!"

"Don't worry, Dick. The only things we'll break are the heads of the Bombers," Buffalo Baker yelled, pounding his fist on a Formica table for emphasis, and sending a Coke glass crashing to the floor. With all the noise, Dick didn't hear it, and Kenny Fletcher quickly pushed the pieces under the table with his foot.

Eddie hadn't moved. He had remained on his stool, watching and listening to all the excitement filling the store. He now felt a lot more confident about the following day, and so damned proud to have friends like these guys. Yeah, these were his pals, all right, but they wouldn't be backing him up tomorrow if it weren't for Bo. He looked over to where Bo was still standing by the juke box, surrounded by Ox, Chuck Hoffman and Al Chavello. Bo caught his eye and winked, nodding once, and Eddie had to turn away. He felt his eyes get watery.

Someone plugged the juke box back in and rock 'n' roll blended with the many conversations, which now had returned to a near-normal pitch.

"Yeah, man! That's *exactly* what we're gonna do," Dancer Bob Larkin said as he cha-cha-chaed over to Eddie, flipping his thumb over his shoulder toward the juke box. Bob Larkin got his nickname because he never walked. He *did* The Walk, of course, as he did The Stroll, and all the other dances, and that was the only way he moved. He slid onto a stool, and began playing the counter as if it were a keyboard, while singing along with Little Richard:

I'm gonna rip it up
I'm gonna rock it up.

Joe Ross didn't show up for school the next day. Eddie, Logan and Manning, as they waited in the park for final bell, joked about what excuse he'd come up with this time. They suspected he kept a special emergency kit, complete with Ace bandages, adhesive tape and an array of Johnson & Johnson products, as well as props like crutches and a sling for his arm. If a fight broke out suddenly, like on the street or in a bar, he would just happen to be making an emergency call at a telephone booth or ducking into a store for a much-needed *whatever*. The guys didn't mind, they even laughed about it, because they knew he had no *heart*. And, even if he did, he had nothing to back it up with, anyway.

Eddie and Johnny Logan were in pretty good spirits when they reached home room. They were talkative, and full of nervous energy. It was obvious by the stares and whispers of the other kids in the class that the news of the fight had spread throughout the school. Eddie didn't approach Penny Randazzo, as he usually did, but sat in the last row next to Logan. Penny looked upset. She kept glancing over her shoulder at Eddie, who was trying hard to ignore her. When the bell rang, Penny ran over and stopped Eddie by the door.

"I heard about the fight yesterday in the locker room," she said softly, her voice cracking slightly. "A-a-and that maybe there's going to be another one today?

"Hey, whadaya expect after that shit ya laid on me," Eddie said. With satisfaction, he heard her gasp. "Ya don't think I'd let that creep Shaw spread lies about me, do ya?"

"You mean it's *really* not true about you and Helen?" she asked, blinking several times to clear her large brown eyes. She stood on her toes to bring her face closer, since, at five-foot-four, Penny was a foot shorter than Eddie.

"Of course not," he said softly, looking down, maintaining deep eye contact. He took her hand gently in both of his hands, and pulled her close, kissing her briefly in turn on the forehead, the nose and the lips. "Ya know yer the only girl for me, baby."

It worked!

"Oh, God, I'm so sorry," she blurted out, tears now rolling freely down her cheeks. "I should have known better. The whole thing's my fault. Can you ever forgive me?"

"Hey, cool it, baby. It's OK," Eddie said soothingly. He squeezed her hand gently. "That asshole won't be givin' us any more trouble after today. I promise. Now get to yer next class an' I'll catch ya later, beautiful."

"Please be careful, and don't get hurt," she said, sniffling into a crumpled Kleenex which she pulled from inside the sleeve of her green sweater. She leaned forward and tip-toed a quick kiss to the lips. Then she turned, and rushed down the hall where her friends were waiting. She turned one last time, and flashed a smile over her shoulder. Eddie tried to wink, that cool eye movement that Bo did with confidence, but, like always, he felt both eyes close at the same time, and knew he looked silly. Luckily, Penny had already turned back and continued to walk away. He stood alone for some time watching her. The way her long brown hair flowed over her shoulders, the sway of her body when she walked, the curves of her legs as her full skirt bounced to the knee. He felt a sudden urge to run after her; to hold her close and tell her how much he really cared – even loved – her. But the moment vanished when his friend grabbed his arm.

"Hey, whadaya deaf or somethin'?" Logan said. "I've been callin' ya, but ya just stand there with this dumb expression on yer face."

"Oh, sorry, man. I was just thinkin' about the fight," Eddie lied. "Let's split."

After a few steps, Logan turned to Eddie. "Bullshit, ya were thinkin' 'bout the fight," he said with a smile.

"Personally, I think I just saved ya from somethin' a hell of a lot more dangerous than the fuckin' Bombers."

"Fuck ya," Eddie said, and punched his friend's upper arm playfully.

The day seemed to fly by. Eddie and Logan attended all of their classes – except gym, even though they had heard earlier that Willy Shaw wasn't in school. They didn't pull any of their usual pranks, or do anything to disrupt the classes. The teachers seemed dumbstruck, and kept glancing at the two boys in disbelief, unable to comprehend the sudden change in behavior. Of course, all the kids understood and, from time to time, came forward with "good lucks" and "kick their asses'." Many of them had been victims of the Bombers at one time or another, and would love to see the gang members get back what they've been handing out.

The last class for Eddie and Logan was study hall, which was in the auditorium, together with about two hundred other kids from several other classes as well. They always cut this class and left school early. Today, however, they decided to attend.

Ben Wilson, one of the four study hall teachers, walked up and down the long rows of seats with his roll book open, taking attendance by calling out the names of students assigned to specific seats, according to the cards originally filled out by the students. When he reached the two boys, he stopped, checked his book, looked at them again, and re-checked his book.

"Are you two supposed to be in this class?" Wilson asked.

"Of course," Eddie said. "It's on our schedule."

"Well, I know your names. God knows, we *all* know your names." He turned the pages of his roll book, glancing up and down each page. "But there are no cards for you."

"We filled out those cards on our first day." Logan said. "Ya musta lost 'em."

"Yes, I'm sure you did," Wilson said sarcastically. "Then why haven't I seen you in this class before? Never mind, never mind. I really don't care. Just sit there quietly and don't bother anyone." The teacher continued along his way, calling names, shaking his head.

Actually, the boys had filled out class seating cards for study hall on the first day of school. That was when another teacher, Glenda Hanley, was assigned to the class. She had passed out the cards, and Logan had written the name of "Emanuel Labour." Eddie had signed his, "Dick Hertz."

On the second day of class, Miss Hanley had taken attendance according to the seating arrangements. When she called "Emanuel Labour," Logan had yelled back "He's out working." Of course, everyone had chuckled over that one. The flustered Miss Hanley had blushed, but went on.

"Dick Hertz!" she had called out next. No one answered. "Dick Hertz!" she had said even louder. Still no answer. "Who's Dick Hertz?" she had asked quite loudly, obviously annoyed.

"Mine does," Eddie had yelled across the room, grabbing the crotch of his jeans.

The kids roared with laughter, and Miss Hanley had dropped the roll book and ran from the study hall in tears. She had been re-assigned the next day as a home economics teacher.

The final bell rang. Dan Manning was waiting in the hallway as Eddie and Logan left the auditorium. "Well, here we go," he said, as he fell in step beside his friends.

They ran down the up staircase, and out the side door. Willy Shaw and his friend, Alfie White, were waiting on the sidewalk across the street, by the entrance to the park. Willy's brother, Dutch, along with Jack Callahan, Don Gilmartin, Tippy O'Connor and about fifteen other members of the Bombers were standing inside the park on the grass. Eddie felt the hairs on the back of his neck rise. His eyes scanned the rest of the park. It was empty. He glanced behind the equipment shack, the bathrooms. Nothing. He searched up and down the broad street in front of the school. His heart sank. There was no sign of Bo and the other guys who vowed to back him up. *Was it all talk?* No, at least not with Bo, anyway. But, where the hell was he? Maybe they couldn't get out of work. Maybe . . .

"Hey, shithead," Shaw taunted. "Ya gonna stand there all day with yer finga up yer ass, or we gonna get it on? Let's go in the park an' I'll kick yer fuckin' ass up one side an' down the otha."

"Ya couldn't kick an ol' lady's ass." Eddie said, looking him straight in the eyes. "That's why you brought along big brother an' the rest of his punk friends."

"Hey, man," Shaw said, feigning indignation. "They're jus' here to make sure it's a fair fight, and to stop yer friends from jumpin' in when I'm stompin' yer head into the ground."

"Fair fight?" Eddie replied with a humorless laugh. "Ya guys never fought fair in yer lives. But, what the hell. Let's go to it."

Eddie, flanked by his two friends, started across the street. "Where the hell are they?" Manning said, unable to keep his voice from trembling. Eddie watched as the Bombers slowly began to spread out into an arc, some smiling coldly, some sneering, clenched fists pounding into open palms. Manning's step faltered, as he dropped back several paces. Eddie thought he would lose him, but he didn't turn to look. A moment later Manning was back by his side, mumbling an apology.

The familiar roar of the engines came just as the three boys stepped into the park. They stopped, and looked down the street. Three motorcycles, riding abreast, led a motorcade of four cars. Bo, on his Triumph, was in the middle, flanked by Ox riding his maroon Indian Chief, and Cootie straddling his big yellow Harley 74. Following in tight formation was Hank Coleman in his customized black '56 Ford, Buffalo Baker in his green '56 Olds 88, Kenny Fletcher in his '50 Ford convertible, and Al Chavello in his red and white '55 Chevy. Eddie let out a big sigh of relief, and looked at his two friends. They both had big shit-eating grins on their faces. He figured he must have the same stupid expression, but who cared? Willy and Alfie joined the rest of the Bombers in the park, who were now gathered in a tight group talking among themselves. *They certainly didn't look as cocky, or happy, as they did a minute ago,* Eddie thought.

The bikes and cars pulled to the curb directly in front of the park entrance. Car doors swung open and guys started piling out. Practically the whole crowd was there, fourteen new arrivals in all.

"I hope ya didn't start without us," Bo said, smiling, as he slid off his bike.

"What?" Eddie said in mock surprise. "And deprive my friends of havin' some fun? Never happen."

Bo carefully removed his aviator sun glasses and hung them on the handlebar of his bike. He looked into the park at the bombers. Jack Callahan was standing at the head of his gang, hands on his hips, staring back. At thirty yards their eyes met and locked. Bo was still smiling, but now it was a hard, mirthless grin, with tight lips drawn back. "Let's go," he said, without taking his eyes off Callahan, and The Bayside Crowd moved forward, spreading out as they walked. Callahan gave his gang the word, and they began spreading out, too. "I'll take Gilmartin if he makes a move," Ox informed his friends. No one argued. Next to Callahan, Gilmartin was considered to be the best fighter on the

Bombers. Some even say he could kick Callahan's ass.

Bo stopped about three feet in front of Callahan, their eyes still locked. Eddie walked up to Shaw, standing to Callahan's right, and stared him down. Shaw's nose was swollen, his lips puffed, and there was an ugly bruise over his right eye, souvenirs of his earlier encounter with Eddie. He broke eye contact almost immediately, and glanced over at Callahan for support. But the gang leader was busy evil-eyeing Bo.

Bo's eyes hardened. His lips tightened even more. He spoke softly, but the meaning of his words was deafening.

"This is between these two," he said, with a slight flick of his head in the direction of Eddie and Willy Shaw. "Ya wanna keep it that way, or you lookin' for an all-out rumble?"

"Hey, we're jus' here to watch yer friend get stomped," Callahan replied, not breaking eye contact. His voice was cold, hard. He was about the same height as Bo, but more lean, lanky. He had the strong, tough body of an Irish brawler, and the face to go with it – it looked like Patton's army had marched over it. He pushed his scarred face closer to Bo's. "Jus' make sure you or yer punk friends don't jump in when he cries for help. Ya dig?"

Bo didn't reply to the warning verbally, but his jaw muscles tightened.

Shaw stepped back and took off his red nylon jacket. Eddie had already tossed his leather jacket on the grass. The Bombers and The Bayside Crowd each formed a half circle, facing each other. Eddie and Willy stepped in the center, and immediately started circling. Eddie watched his opponent's eyes, even though he knew Shaw's first move would be a leaping kick, just like in the locker room. *I was ready for it then, and I'll be ready for it now,* Eddie thought. He always remembered what the champ, Rocky

Marciano, said about the eyes signaling the attack. There it was again, the two quick blinks. This is too fuckin' easy, Eddie thought, almost smiling as he began to move.

Shaw jumped high in the air, his right leg coming straight out towards Eddie's mid-section. Eddie dodged to his right, but, suddenly, he stumbled. His foot caught on a big clod of crabgrass. It was enough to throw him off balance, leaving him totally exposed for Willy's heavy black boot which exploded in his gut. Eddie thought he would heave up his lunch. He doubled over, holding his stomach. Willy, moving fast, jumped in with another kick. This one connected with Eddie's side, and sent him sprawling to the ground in pain.

The Bombers were cheering, and shouting. "Finish him!" "Kill him!" "Stomp his face!" Eddie's friends were mostly silent now, some only groaning as the kicks landed. "Take yer time," Bo said, almost to himself. "Get yer shit together." "Get up, Eddie, get up," Johnny Logan pleaded.

Eddie hit the ground hard. Instantly Willy was over him, this time with a boot aimed at his head. Eddie threw his arms over his head to protect his face, and Willy's foot landed almost harmlessly on his thick bicep. That gave him the few seconds he needed to regain some composure, and, before Willy could throw another kick, Eddie rolled away and sprang to his feet, ignoring his nausea and the pain in his side. Willy must have thought Eddie was hurt more than he actually was, because he made the mistake of charging right at the much larger boy. Eddie planted his feet firmly on the ground, feinted left, then threw a hard right hand punch. Willy ran smack into it. Everyone heard the unmistakable sound of bones breaking as his nose flattened against his face. Suddenly, Willy's face was covered with blood, and he swayed like a Saturday night drunk trying to find his way home. Dazed, Willy was an easy target for Eddie's knee, which slammed hard between his legs. He went down in a heap with a terrible cry of pain. Eddie stood above him for several seconds to see if he'd get up. He debated whether or not to give him a final kick to the head, like some of his friends were suggesting with shouts, but he couldn't see any reason for it. Willy just rolled around moaning, doubled up in pain. He won the fight. As far as he was concerned, it was over.

Suddenly, Eddie felt a tremendous blow to his back. It was like a bomb had exploded in his kidney. He fell to his knees and glanced over his shoulder through eyes which were already beginning to water. Jack Callahan stood over him. His leg was drawn back, ready to kick him square in the face, and there was nothing he could do about it. He was stunned, unable to defend himself.

Poised on one leg, Callahan grimaced in pain, and his body flew forward, slamming hard into the ground next to Eddie. Bo, who was now standing above both of them, had slammed a huge forearm to the back of Callahan's head.

"I told ya to stay out of it, punk," Bo said in his quiet, menacing monotone. "Now, it's me an' you."

Eddie managed to get to his feet and join the rest of his friends. They had now formed a half-circle around Bo and Callahan, facing off the rest of the Bombers on the other side. Ox and Gilmartin were staring at each other, but neither one made the first move. This was Bo's and Callahan's show now. Shaw, still moaning, tried to get up, but was unable to stand on his own. Alfie threw an arm around him, and helped his friend over to where the action was taking place.

Callahan rolled over, propped himself up on his elbows, and shook his head in an attempt to clear it. Bo moved slowly, carefully, first to the left, then to the right. He leaned forward slightly, his muscled arms dangling loosely at his sides, like Gorgeous George in a wrestling match with The Golden Superman. He was waiting for Callahan to get to his feet, not wanting the Bombers to claim their leader was attacked from behind.

Color crept back into Callahan's face. His eyes focused on Bo, then turned into dark slits. He snarled. With the quickness of a prizefighter, he sprang to his feet and immediately assumed the classic stance of a boxer, bobbing and weaving. A couple of years ago, Callahan had been considered a pretty good light-heavyweight in the Junior Golden Gloves, until he had been disqualified because of fouls. Bo, on the other hand, was twenty pounds heavier, and kept in condition by lifting weights.

Callahan danced around Bo, feinting left and right, darting in, throwing quick left jabs, then backing away. He was fast, his punches almost a blur. Some connected, but Bo didn't seem to be bothered. He just flicked his head back as each blow landed, reducing the possibility of damage considerably. However, a welt did form at the corner of his right eye. He still kept coming forward, though, arms swinging at his sides, waiting for just the right moment. It came as Callahan was pulling back a double jab. With a quickness that defied his bulk, Bo leapt forward. Callahan sensed it coming and swung a powerful right. The punch caught Bo's left cheek hard, and ripped a gash in the skin. But by this time, Bo had his massive arms around Callahan.

With quick motions, as if it were a clean and jerk weight-lifting competition, he picked him up over his head and slammed him into the ground. Before Callahan could catch his breath, Bo reached down with his left hand, grabbed a handful of shirt and yanked him up. At the same time Callahan was coming up, Bo's big right fist was swinging down. Pieces of broken teeth flew in all directions as Callahan's mouth started to pump blood. In a daze, he tried to scramble away on his hands and feet. He made it as far as the wooden park bench, and dragged himself onto it for support. Bo was on him again. He pushed his face down on the bench, grabbed his two ears, and began smashing his face against the rock-hard wood, as if trying to squeeze Callahan's head through the narrow openings between the wooden slats. There was blood everywhere.

Angered at watching their leader take a beating, The Bombers became restless, and started inching forward. Don Gilmartin broke from the rest of the gang, making a move at Bo. Ox Zarora jumped out, blocking his way with his massive arms spread wide, egging Gilmartin on with pursed lips, taunting, "Let's go pussy, fuck wit' *me*." The rest of The Bombers kept moving forward. The Bayside Crowd kept pace, moving and watching carefully. Dutch Shaw pointed at Eddie and snarled, "Yer mine, mothafucka." Eddie beckoned him with a wave of his hand, saying, "Comeon, scumbag. It's a family special today. Ya get the same as yer brother. No extra charge."

The only thing that prevented an all-out rumble was the sound of the siren in the distance.

"Let's get outa here!" Cootie yelled. "The cops are comin'."

Everyone began running. There were shouts of "We'll meet again" and "This ain't over yet." Gilmartin and O'Connor carried the semi-conscious Callahan to a parked car, while Alfie helped a limping Willy Shaw. The Bayside Crowd ran to the cars and motorcycles. Eddie jumped on the back of Bo's Triumph. Within seconds, the air was filled with the smell of burning rubber, as tires peeled on pavement and everyone raced off. By the time the police car from the one eleven Precinct had rolled to a stop by the park's entrance, cars and motorcycles were safely speeding away in all directions, through the park, across the grass and over walk-ways.

FOUR

SEE YOU LATER, ALLIGATOR

Eddie had a fist full of Bo's Levi jacket with one hand, and a death-grip on the back-bar of the Triumph's "buddy" seat with the other. The bike's rear wheel spit up dirt, grass and stones as it roared through the park, bouncing and skidding. Eddie fought to stay on. Bo hit a paved walk-way, picked up speed on the smoothness, and raced to the opposite end of the park.

He swung a hard right behind the playground area, using his right leg as a pivot, and maneuvered through a small cluster of trees, finally breaking out of the park with an airborne leap over a small rise which dropped onto 32nd Avenue. Eddie's grip tightened even more as the rear wheel fish-tailed several times before treads caught pavement, and the bike roared off in the direction of Fort Totten and the relative safety of the Cross Island Parkway.

Bo and Eddie cruised around without speaking. Whenever there was trouble, the guys stayed away from their usual hangouts for a while, just in case the cops decided to harass the crowd, or bring someone in. Bo swung onto the Cross Island at the Fort Totten entrance. He held the bike at a steady fifty in the light mid-afternoon traffic. He took the Cross Island to the Belt Parkway, headed west on the Belt to the Van Wyck Expressway, rode the Van Wyck south, returning to the northbound Cross Island, and back to the Fort Totten exit. It took them just twenty minutes to complete the fifteen mile loop, and Bo decided the timing was still not right to hit the candy store. He took the side streets to his house.

Bo rolled the bike into his backyard, out of sight, and nodded to Eddie an invitation to come inside. The boys entered the back door, stepping into the kitchen. Bo's mother and sister were sitting at the kitchen table. Mrs. Brody was leaning forward, wringing her hands, her face full of anguish. Kate Brody, who had been doing the talking, stopped in mid-sentence. They both looked up at the door as the boys came in the room.

"Oh my Lord!" Mrs. Brody screamed, rising from her chair, her hand to her mouth. She stared at her son. "What did they do to you? I'm calling an ambulance." She ran to the wall phone by the sink.

Bo and Eddie looked at each other in puzzlement. It was then that Eddie first noticed his friend's T-shirt. The front was splattered with blood – big, huge blotches soaked into the white material. The sight of it was shocking. Eddie stared, Bo looked down. Then the realization sank in that the blood was Callahan's, not Bo's. Of course, Mrs. Brody had no way of knowing that. She was already dialing the operator.

Bo sprang to action, crossing the room in four giant strides. He gently removed the receiver from his mother's hand, and hung it back up. There were tears brimming in Mrs. Brody's eyes as she looked up at her much-taller son. Her gray-brown hair was pulled tight in a bun on the top of her head, and Bo pressed his cheek against it as he put an arm around his mother's shoulders and led her back to her chair at the table. He assured her that he was not hurt, that it was someone else's blood on his shirt. Some guy started a fight, and he had to protect himself. Didn't he? However, she would not calm down until she inspected her son thoroughly. She rolled up his shirt, looked at his chest, felt his ribs. She examined the two-inch gash on his cheek, to make sure it didn't require stitches. She immediately washed the wound, swabbed on iodine, and covered it with a large Band-Aid. Satisfied that her son had suffered no major damage, Mrs. Brody's concern was quickly replaced with anger. She stood up in order to look down at her son who was sitting next to her.

"One of these days you and your friends are going to get into serious trouble, with all this fight business, mark my words," Mrs. Brody said, raising her voice, and shaking a finger in Bo's face. "Or, worse yet, you might get hurt badly or, God forbid, even killed. Or kill someone else. Anything can happen."

"Aw, Mom, don't worry," Bo said, standing, putting an arm around his mother again, and patting her shoulder. "He wasn't hurt that bad, nothin' to worry about. It's all over an' forgotten about."

She shrugged her son's arm off her shoulders, and stuck a wagging finger back in his face.

"Don't try to soft talk me, you big galoot," she said sternly, her face flushing with anger. "You were supposed to be at work, weren't you? How did you end up fighting at the high school like a wild animal? Explain that? Did that terrible bully start a fight at your job, then drag you *all* the way to the park? Is that what happened? Well, your sister's version is slightly different than yours. And, a lot more believable." She glared at her son, eyes ablaze, then turned to Eddie.

"And you! I know you were fighting, too. Don't think I won't tell your mother, young man."

Bo and Eddie were silent. They stood with their heads down, looking at the floor, from time to time glancing at Kate sitting across the table. She was blushing. Eddie shot her a dirty look, but Bo just shook his head slightly, and winked.

Bo apologized to his mom. Eddie nodded and mumbled in agreement. They both promised it wouldn't happen again, then headed up to Bo's room.

"Yes, that's what you always say," Mrs. Brody shouted after them. "But I'm warning you, if you don't stop this fighting you - "

The rest of her warning was cut off as Bo closed the door to his room, being careful not to slam it. The two friends looked at each other and smiled. Then each boy wagged his finger in the face of the other. That did it. All the tension of the day broke loose, and they started laughing. They tried not to look at each other, for each time they did, they laughed harder. It was useless. Soon, they were rolling on the bed, gasping, laughing uncontrollably, holding their stomachs in pain, while begging each other to stop.

The boys left for the candy store before six o'clock. Bo didn't want to be around when his old man got home from work. He told Eddie he'd treat him to a sack of hamburgers at White Castle, and Eddie called his mom to tell her he was "eating out" with Bo.

Buddy Holly's *That'll Be The Day* was playing on the juke box when Bo and Eddie walked into Dick's, but the music was all but drowned out by the level of excitement that filled the already-crowded store. Almost thirty guys and girls, just about everyone in The Bayside Crowd, were at the counter, in the booths, or standing around in small clusters. Dick was running around like a one-arm chicken-plucker pouring Cokes and mixing milk, syrup and seltzer for eggcreams. He didn't know why he was so busy at such an early hour, but he didn't care. There was almost a hint of a smile on his usually dour face as he rang up sales.

The crowd cheered as Bo and Eddie walked in, many jumping up to greet them like conquering heroes with back slaps and hand shakes. A few of the guys asked him if the cut was bad.

"Naw, just a fuckin' scratch," he replied. "I didn't even feel it."

Which was true. When Bo fought, he didn't seem to feel pain at all, which was one reason he was so dangerous. Last year, during a bar fight in Gaffney's in Port Washington, Bo went after a big Scandinavian-looking clam digger who had pinched Judy's ass. The big blond-headed guy, with arms thicker than his thighs from operating the clam rake all day, picked up a bar stool like it was a match stick and smashed it over Bo's head. Bo just blinked and kept going.

By the time Bo was finished with him, the clam digger looked as if he could have been served on a half shell. An hour later Bo was at Nassau Medical Center getting fourteen stitches in his head.

Eddie watched his friend with admiration, gritting his teeth every time he moved, thinking, Bo may not feel the pain, he thought, but I sure as hell do. Now that the excitement had worn off, Eddie felt the sharp pain where Callahan had kicked him. However, because it wasn't anything visible, no one asked him about it. Even if they did, he would never admit it, anyway. It just wouldn't be cool.

As the crowd began to settle down, Joe Ross came forward, the top of his head wrapped in a gauze bandage. Eddie had to suppress a laugh. *He must have bought a new one,* he thought. The bandage Joe wore after the last fight he missed was frayed around the edges.

"Hey, fellas," Ross said in a weak-sounding voice. "I'm sorry I missed the action, but I fell down the steps on my way to school and banged my head pretty hard on the concrete."

There were some chuckles from the crowd, which Ross ignored, but Bo and Eddie managed to keep smiles from their faces.

"Were ya hurt bad?" Bo asked.

"Howaya feelin' now?" Eddie asked.

"Well, still a little woozy, ya know," Ross said, swaying slightly for emphasis. "But the doctor said I should be awright in a few days."

"Oh, ya went to the doctor?" Eddie asked, trying even harder not to laugh. The effort caused a lightning rod of pain to shoot out from his kidney. He winced. Joe thought it was in sympathy for his own pain.

"Oh, it don't hurt *too* much," Ross said quickly. "I tried to tell my mom I was awright, 'cause I really wanted to be at school. For the fight, ya know. But, she *made* me go see the doctor an' have my head x-rayed." Wow, Eddie thought, he was playing the role to the hilt this time. He's out-Brandoing Brando.

"That's a shame," Bo said. "Ya better sit down an' take it easy. Ya don't look too good."

"Yeah," Ross said weakly, as he grasped the back of the booth to steady himself, then slid into the seat, moaning slightly as he moved.

Kenny Fletcher, who was standing next to the juke box, whistled sharply, pressing his lips back with two fingers. When everyone turned his way, he winked and hit the machine's reject button. Bonnie Lou suddenly stopped singing about *Daddy-O* and, several moments later, the store was filled with the sound of Fats Domino singing *Ain't That A Shame.*

The crowd, turning to their friend with the bandaged head, roared with laughter. Ross, still playing his game, didn't seem perturbed. He just held his head in his hands and moaned more loudly. Soon, most of the kids in the store were singing along, *"Ain't – that – a – shame. . . "*

Dancer grabbed Big Judy, who looked ready to pop right out of her tight black toreador pants and white peasant blouse, and started doing the Lindy. Dick frowned, but decided to continue to ring up sales instead of going over to stop the dancing. Most of the guys formed a circle around the couple, hand clapping, and ogling Judy, who was twisting and shaking and bumping and grinding, her long black ponytail whirling like that of a bucking bronco.

Kate grabbed Hank Coleman's arm and dragged him back to the booth. Diane Roth did the same with Kenny Fletcher. Both Barbara Saunders and Joan Ford vied for Bo's attention. Brenda Manzi fed a quarter into the juke box and picked six slow songs.

Things quieted down a little with Elvis Presley singing *Loving You,* but the jovial mood prevailed as spirits remained high from the day's activities. Cootie volunteered to keep watch by the door in case The Bombers tried a sneak attack, although no one thought that they would, certainly not without their leader.

Eddie sat on the front stool at the counter. He spun slowly around, surveying the room. I'm a lucky guy, he thought. These are my friends, real good people. He had a warm feeling, but, at the same time, he felt a little lonely. He watched so many of his friends sitting and talking with their girls. Even Bo had his head down and seemed to be talking trash to Barbara. Eddie wished Penny could be with him tonight, on such an important occasion. He really missed her. Her parents didn't let her out on school nights. Damn them, anyway, he thought, that's so old fashioned.

"A penny for your thoughts." The soft, familiar voice came from behind. It was Penny's favorite line.

Eddie swung around on his stool, a big grin on his face, his hand held out, palm up. "What are ya doing here? It's a school night."

"I'm not here, silly," Penny said, her grin matching his. She dropped a penny in his palm. "I'm at Lori's house doing homework and studying."

"That's right," Lori said, stepping up with Tricia. "And right now I'm studying 'the anatomy of man'." She had spotted Leo Silverman and was smiling at him.

"You're awful," Penny said, laughing.

"She certainly is," Tricia said, eyeing Mike Mancuso, but it was your idea to sneak out so you could see your 'hero'." The two girls giggled as they walked off in the direction of Leo and Mike. Penny blushed.

"Didya really say that?" Eddie asked.

"Hey, I'm not answering," Penny said. "I paid *you* for your thoughts, remember?"

"Yeah, I remember." Eddie, still sitting on the stool, took Penny's hand in his, and pulled her close. She moved between his legs, half sitting on his left thigh. "I was thinkin' about ya," he said, looking into her eyes.

"Really? And what were you thinking?" She moved her tight little ass slightly on his thigh, and her leg brushed briefly against his crotch. He started to get hard. She lifted her lovely face up close to his, the tip of her darting tongue wetting her full, slightly parted lips. He couldn't resist. He lowered his head. Suddenly they were alone in the crowded store, as lips met and tongues caressed. Eddie tightened his legs, drawing her closer. Her breath caught when she felt his hardness. She pulled away, taking a half step back.

"Look, Eddie, I think – "

"Wait, Penny," Eddie interrupted, "there's somethin' I wanna – "

"Hey, ya guys! The fuzz is comin'!" Cootie's resonant voice reverberated throughout the store.

Dick's fell silent, except for The Moonglows singing *Sincerely.* Suddenly, the door swung open and a size fifty six blue uniform filled the entrance. "Porky," the huge beat cop for Bell Boulevard, pushed his way into Dick's, followed by a slim negro officer, whose crisp, new, gray uniform signified his status as a recently-graduated rookie.

Officer George Reynolds - "Porky" to The Bayside Crowd – moved his five-foot-eleven, 300-pound frame through the store with all the grace of a bull in a china shop. He glared from face to face as he moved, nightstick swinging menacingly. He was thought to be one of the meanest cops in New York, and was known to especially hate teenagers. He relished any opportunity to break the balls of the crowd at Dick's, both literally and figuratively, since he liberally used his nightstick to punctuate his commands.

Of course, the guys gave him plenty of motives, too. They often called him Porky to his face, and asked him if he bought his uniforms at Barney's Fat Boy's Shop, then darted out of the way of the swinging nightstick. In fact, they'd called him Porky for so long that the insulting nickname was used by many other people, even some of the younger cops at the station house. But, what had pissed off Officer Reynolds more than anything else was when he had found out it had been The Bayside Crowd, and not "a concerned citizen," who had drafted the anonymous letter to his captain. It requested that Officer Reynolds be transferred from walking the Bell Boulevard beat because his tremendous weight left huge cracks in the sidewalk, posing a threat to the safety of pedestrians. It had made Porky especially mad because someone at the precinct thought it was funny enough to be posted on the bulletin board. They all had had a good laugh over that one.

No one was laughing now; all eyes were on Porky, wondering what he was up to. He walked over to the juke box, pulled the plug, then turned to face the crowd. His partner remained at the other end of the store, standing by the front booth.

"I heard you punks had some excitement today," Porky said with a smirk. "Had yourselves another fight, did you?" He looked around slowly.

There was a murmur of denials throughout the store, heads were shaking. The big cop paid no attention. He took a step forward, pounding his nightstick into the meaty palm of his right hand.

"The Captain asked me to bring one of you in for a little talk," he said, continuing to glance from face to face. "I told him it would be my pleasure."

Porky's eyes settled on Bo, who was sitting on the last stool at the counter. A thin smile cut across the cop's red beefy face.

"Well, well. What do we have here?" Porky said, walking over and standing directly in front of Bo.

"Mister Tough Guy, himself," Porky continued, taunting Bo. He was still slapping his stick in his palm. "What happened to your face, tough guy? Did some big bad man give Bo-Bo a boo-boo?" He snickered.

Bo didn't crack a smile. He didn't appreciate the cop's insulting remarks. "I cut myself shavin', *fatso*. What's it to ya?" Bo's words were cold, hard, and he said them staring into Porky's eyes.

Porky seemed shocked by Bo's aggressiveness, his eyes widening in surprise. He took a step backward, raising the nightstick. At the same time, Bo slid off the stool, arms poised, ready to defend himself.

At that moment, the colored cop shouted from across the room. "Hey, lookit here! Here's a guy that was in the fight, for sure."

Bo's and Porky's eyes remained locked for several seconds, neither wanting to be the first to break away. Finally, the cop turned to his partner. The rookie grabbed Joe Ross by the back of his turned-up collar and dragged him out of the booth.

"Look at this fresh bandage on his head," he said, dragging a protesting Ross across the room. "Someone must have belted him pretty hard, huh?"

Porky looked at Ross, then back at Bo. "Next time *you* may be the one with a broken head. And, I'll be the one to do it. Not the Bombers. Understand, tough guy?" Before Bo could reply, Porky turned away and strode across the store, roughly grabbing one of Ross' arms. The black cop had a firm grip on the other. "Good work, Officer Jones," Porky told his partner. "Let's get him out of here." To Ross he said, "Let's take a walk to the station house, punk.

We'd like you to answer some questions about this afternoon."

"B-b-but I was home all day. I swear to God. I was home all day. Jus' ask my mother, she'll tell ya. Jus' ask her." Ross' pleas were falling on deaf ears as the two officers half carried and half dragged him through the store and out the door.

Everyone was silent for several moments, staring at the door. Ox Zarora finally broke the silence.

"I keep tellin' that crazy son-of-a-bitch to stay outa fights or he'll get into trouble."

The tension broke and almost everyone started laughing at once. The crowd wasn't worried about their friend. They knew his mother. She was a big, tough widow, who weighed-in at about two hundred pounds. She protected her only son like a mountain lion with its cub. She'd be down to the precinct like a ball of fire, raising all kinds of righteous indignation. After all, he was the only one *not* at the fight. Cootie plugged in the juke box and some of the kids started singing along with Fats Domino's *I'm Walking*. The key phrase for the night became, "Good work, Officer Jones," which soon developed into a game – a sort of verbal tag – with the guys shouting the words into each other's ear.

Eddie, smiling, looked around for Penny, thinking they could go down to the park for some heavy making out. He remembered her backing away when Porky made his entrance, then Eddie's attention became centered on the actions of the cops. He looked over by the magazine rack, then checked all the booths. He didn't see her. He didn't see Lori or Tricia, either.

"If you're looking for Penny, she's gone," Brenda said, coming up and standing very close to Eddie. She gave him a seductive smile.

"Whadaya mean, gone?" Eddie asked.

"I mean gone, like splitsville, you dig?" Brenda said, moving even closer. She was wearing tight jeans and an even tighter black turtleneck. It was no secret that the fifteen-year-old brunette liked Eddie a lot.

"After the cops came, she slipped out the door," Brenda explained. "She said she wasn't supposed to be here. She was worried they'd take names and call parents, and she'd really be in trouble. You know?"

"Yeah, I know," Eddie said dejectedly. His plans for a hot night with Penny suddenly gone cold.

"Hey, comeon," Brenda purred, taking his arm. The movement caused Eddie's arm to brush across her full breasts. "You can drown your sorrows with a cherry-Coke. My treat."

Eddie hesitated, then, reluctantly, pulled his arm away. "Er, no thanks, Brenda. Some other time. I gotta talk to Bo." Eddie, not trusting himself, broke free and headed off before he could change his mind. That's all I need now, he thought, is for Penny to hear I was having a Coke with Brenda. Yeah, sure. As he walked away, however, he risked a glance back over his shoulder. Brenda, her long jean-clad legs slightly parted, was still smiling after him. His steps faltered, as well as his thoughts. *Hmmm. Well, she's not that cute, but she sure has a good body. Maybe –*

"GOOD WORK, OFFICER JONES," Cootie boomed into Eddie's ear, before scooting off, laughing and shouting.

The harsh interruption brought Eddie back to his senses. He turned away and continued his trek across the store, thinking again of the missed make-out session with Penny. "Yeah, *really* great work, Officer Jones!" Eddie said to no one in particular. "Thanks a lot."

Bayside High School was buzzing with excitement the next day. When not in class, kids were standing around in clusters talking about the fight. Eddie received many greetings of "Good going, man" and "It's about time he got his ass kicked." Apparently,

Eddie was getting the credit for Callahan's beating, too, and he just accepted the accolades with a cool nod of the head. Hell, he thought, no sense going into detailed explanations all day. Besides, it's great for my rep. Word spread that Callahan had been taken to Queens General Hospital and had been treated for deep head gashes and cracked facial bones, but had been released the same day.

Willy Shaw stayed out of school for a week. When he returned, he still had a bandage over his re-shaped nose. He and his friend Alfie avoided Eddie and his buddies, and everything remained quiet. Even the rest of The Bombers stayed away from the park across from the school. The one thing Eddie was pretty sure of was that they wouldn't make a move until Callahan was back in action. Meanwhile, there was trouble of another sort.

Somehow, Helen Roberts saw the fight from a different perspective. Eddie had become her knight in shining armor, defending her honor against all odds.

"Oh, I'm so proud of you, the way you beat up those boys for saying nasty things about me," Helen said, throwing her arms around Eddie and planting a sloppy kiss on his lips, before he could duck out of the way. They were in the hallway during change of class. Eddie looked around and it seemed as if half the student body was in the hall at the same time. They all stopped in their tracks and stared. Holy shit, Eddie thought, by lunch time the other half of the school will have heard about this crap.

"What the hell are ya talkin' about?" Eddie said loudly, as he pushed her gently, but firmly, away. "That fight had absolutely nothin' to do with ya."

"Oh, don't be so shy," Helen said, undaunted. "I know that you really care for me. And I feel the same about you. Always did. I like Italian boys, anyway. Does this mean we're going steady? Because – "

"Goin' steady!" Eddie interrupted her rambling. "What the hell are ya talkin' about?" he repeated. Now he was almost shouting. "Goin' steady? Are ya fuckin' crazy or somethin'? Get away from me ya stupid bitch." Eddie turned and walked away as fast as possible, trying to avoid the stares and smiles of the kids in the hall.

"I'll wait for you after school, honey, and we can go for a Coke," Helen shouted after him, as he ducked around a corner, where Johnny Logan was waiting.

By lunch time the story was even worse than Eddie had expected. Some of the girls he usually spoke to, or hung with in class, had started to avoid him. Luckily, he hadn't run into Penny yet. He spotted Dan Manning coming out of the school building. Good. He wanted to hear what Manning had heard.

"Congratulations," Manning said in greeting, after running across the street and into the park. He extended his right hand to Eddie.

"Fuck ya," Eddie grumbled, smacking it away.

Manning and Logan broke up laughing. Eddie cursed them both.

When Manning caught his breath, he related the latest version of the story which was going around the school. Helen was now showing everyone a ring, and telling them that Eddie, her "steady boy friend," gave it to her. Manning and Logan looked at each other and burst out laughing. Eddie gave them the finger.

"She's fuckin' crazy," Eddie muttered, shaking his head in disbelief. "A regular nut job ready for the funny farm."

"Here comes more trouble," Logan said, flicking his head at an approaching Elaine Blake.

Plain Elaine, as Eddie and his friends called her, was never seen outside of school – and the guys considered themselves lucky on that account. She was tall and skinny, and wore old baggy dresses that looked like they had been borrowed from her grandmother. She had straight brown hair and wore black horn-rimmed glasses. Plain Elaine, of course, was a straight-A student. And her only school friend was another straight-A student, Penny Randazzo. Plain Elaine's mission in life, besides making the dean's list, was to get her friend away from the evils of The Bayside Crowd, people she hated.

Plain Elaine was smiling as she walked up to the guys. That was a dead give-away that they were in for trouble. She stopped about three feet from Eddie. In her hand was a white envelope.

"Here!" she snapped, her smile gone now, replaced by a look of revulsion. "Penny told me to give this to you, you animal."

Before Eddie could reach for it, she dropped the envelope. It fluttered to the ground at his feet. She turned and quickly walked away.

"Whadaya afraid of?" he said angrily. "Think you might catch something?"

"I wouldn't doubt it," she said over her shoulder, as she kept walking.

Eddie snatched the envelope from the ground and ripped it open. He unfolded the piece of note paper which was inside, and immediately recognized Penny's small, neat handwriting. It was so familiar because of all those cute little love notes she wrote him. However, there was nothing cute about this note.

It was short and simple. "Eddie: You are a disgusting ('disgusting' underlined three times) pig. Don't ever (same underlining) try to see or call me again. Penny." There was something else in the envelope, which he shook out. It was the thin gold ankle bracelet he gave her when they started going steady, and she had worn ever since. The inscription read, "Penny, you leave me cents-less, love Eddie," followed by the date. He just stood there for several moments, dumbfounded, the note in one hand, the bracelet in the other, staring back and forth.

Logan put his arm around Eddie's shoulder and, in a consoling voice, said, "Hey, don't take it so hard, buddy. You can always have the inscription changed from Penny to Helen. It's the same amount of letters."

Manning piped in with, "An' have a matchin' one made with a chain an' lock so she can't spread her legs for the rest of the guys in school."

His friends' hooting and laughing brought Eddie out of his stupor. He shoved the note and bracelet in his pocket. He was really pissed off. He had to take it out on someone.

"Who the fuck do ya think ya guys are, Martin and Lewis?" Eddie shouted, reaching out to grab his friends. They ducked out of reach, and began running through the park, still laughing. Eddie was hot on their heels, shouting, "We'll see how funny it is when I get my hands on ya."

Penny stuck to her guns. She wouldn't talk to Eddie or reply to his notes. Helen Roberts kept following him around, like a lost puppy, waiting in hallways and outside of school. Eddie would tell her, "Get fuckin' lost." Helen would answer, "Stop playing hard to get." He would say, "I have the crabs." She would reply, "Oh, that's ok, I've had them several times myself."

Then, one night, cool as a cucumber, she walked into a crowded Dick's. *Lawdy, Miss Clawdy* by Lloyd Price was blasting from the juke box.

"Hi, Eddie, darling," she called out, walking up to him and planting a big wet kiss on his cheek, before he had time to react.

"Yuck!" he yelled in shock, wiping his cheek with the back of his hand, as the crowd roared with laughter. Cootie, caught in the middle of taking a drink, coughed up Coke through his nose. The snickers and wisecracks began immediately.

That's it, Eddie thought, no more Mr. Nice Guy. He jumped off the stool, grabbed her arm and roughly rushed her towards the door. His friends followed his actions with hoots and hollers, and a series of shouts, which included, "Look at the love birds, they want to be alone," "He's in a big hurry to get to the park, ain't he?" and "Do ya think they're gonna elope?"

Outside, he pushed Helen into the deserted doorway of the "Spot-Less Dry Cleaners" next to the candy store and put his hands around her neck. Eddie squeezed, but not too hard.

"Listen to me carefully, *bitch*," he said through clenched teeth, "if you ever, *ever* come near me again I'm gonna break yer fuckin' neck. Now, do ya *understand* what I'm sayin'?"

She looked at him wide-eyed for several moments, more from shocked disbelief than fear. Then she blinked rapidly, and her eyes filled with tears. She began sobbing quietly. Eddie felt a pang of guilt, and thought for a moment he may have been a little too rough on her. He removed his hands from her neck. There were already traces of a red welt.

"D-d-does t-t-this mean we're not going steady anymore?"

That did it! His guilt vanished, and his anger jumped several notches higher. He grabbed her by the shoulders and began shaking as he spoke in a menacing tone. "I dunno what the fuck yer talkin' about, ya dipshit. But I'm gonna spell it out in real simple language so even a stupid cunt like you could understand. Number one: don't ever talk to me again. Number two: don't ever come near me again. In fact, if we're walkin' down the same block, cross the fuckin' street. Because if ya *ever* come close enough to me so that I can reach ya, I'm gonna rip yer ugly cocksuckin' head off." With that, he gave her a final shake and shoved her away. He pushed a little too hard, and her shoe hit a crack in the sidewalk. She fell backwards, hitting the pavement heavy.

Oh shit, Eddie thought, I hope she's not hurt. The last thing I need now is an assault charge. He had to stop himself from helping her up.

Luckily Helen landed on her well-padded ass. She sat there a moment looking up at Eddie. Eddie stared back down, trying to keep his face hard, threatening. Finally, she picked herself up, brushed off the seat of her tight red pedal pushers, and took a few deep breaths to regain her composure. She wiped her eyes with the sleeve of her yellow sweater, and took a step closer to Eddie. Her face was only inches away. He felt her spittle when she spoke, and he cringed when he thought of all the cocks she had sucked.

"Nobody can treat me that way," Helen Roberts said with a trace of dignity. She held her head high. "I wouldn't go steady with you now if you were the last man on earth." She spun on her heels, the end of her dirty blonde ponytail whipping Eddie in the face, and strode down Bell Boulevard. Eddie just stood there, dumbfounded. Holy shit, he thought, what a fuckin' whacko. When she reached the corner, she turned back and shouted, "And, I'll return your ring in the morning."

"WHAT FUCKIN' RING!?" Eddie screamed at the top of his lungs. But, Helen had turned the corner and was out of sight.

For Eddie and his friends at school, who were looking forward to summer vacation, the days just seemed to drag by. April slipped into May, and May seemed to go on forever. Then it was Memorial Day and, after enduring the annual family barbecues, the boys jumped into June, knowing they were now "short-timers."

Everything remained quiet at school as most of the kids were thinking of the summer ahead, making plans and prepping for final exams. Eddie stopped trying to get back with Penny, finally realizing it was hopeless. It was inevitable that they should occasionally bump into each other in school, and when they did Penny managed a cordial, but cool greeting, before hurrying away. Helen Roberts, on the other hand, completely ignored him, looking the other way when their paths crossed in the halls of learning, which was fine with Eddie. She did, however, return "his" ring – a piece of cheap metal with an ugly blue stone – which Eddie had never seen before. He tossed it out of an open window. The story she told everyone was that she broke off with Eddie, and returned his ring, because "I didn't want to be tied down dating just one boy."

The first week of June brought with it New York's first heat wave of the year, with temperatures up into the nineties. That gave the boys an early case of the summertime blues. As a cure, most days they decided to play hooky. They would meet in the park in the morning, then hop into Dan Manning's old Packard and take off. Sometimes they would just go down the street to the jetty at Fort Totten, on Long Island Sound, and sit shirtless in the sun all day, smoking Luckies and bullshitting. Occasionally, they would drive to Brighton Beach in Brooklyn and hit on the Jewish women with big tits bulging out of too-tight bathing suits. They would go to the boardwalk at Rockaway where the Irish nannies walked with baby strollers, or Jones Beach on Long Island where young housewives in new fashionable bikini bathing suits lounged on the sand.

One morning, Eddie was sitting on the huge hood of the Packard, as Manning and Ross leaned against the front fender. They were waiting for Logan.

"Shit. It's gonna be another great fuckin' day," Eddie said, lying back across the hood, his hands folded behind his head, and eyes closed to the bright morning sun.

Suddenly, he heard the car doors slam and the engine start. He quickly sat up to jump off the car, but was too late. The Packard leapt forward in first gear, and Eddie had to grab the big metal hood ornament for support.

"Stop the fuckin' car, you assholes," he shouted over his shoulder, while holding on with both hands.

Manning and Ross were hysterical. Manning shifted to second, picked up more speed, then swung a right turn onto 210th Street. Eddie's body flew from one side to the other, his legs dangling over the fender. He felt the hood ornament give slightly from the weight of his body as he tried to right himself. He was scared shitless he would fall off, but then he had something else to worry about. He could see they were heading right towards his house, just as his father was leaving for work, backing the big black Buick out of the driveway.

Mr. Casale didn't see the Packard coming until the last minute, it was going so fast. He jammed on his brakes, and leaned out the window, ready to shout at the other driver to slow down on residential streets. His mouth just hung open as he watched the big car speed by with his son hanging from the hood, a feeble smile on his face.

Eddie knew he would have to deal with that later. For now, he thought, I have to stay on this car so these maniacs don't kill me. It wasn't easy. Manning raced up one street and down another, making sharp lefts and rights; hitting brake, gas, brake, gas. Eddie rocked, rolled and slid around the enormous hood. His hand-grip held. Somehow the hood emblem didn't break, and Eddie offered a silent prayer for the superior Packard craftsmanship. Finally, Manning grew tired of the game and returned to the park, where Logan was now waiting.

The car rolled to a stop. Eddie jumped off, anxious to get his hands on his two friends, but they remained in the car with the windows rolled up and the doors locked. Eddie pounded on the roof in frustration, but Manning and Ross just pointed at him and laughed until there were tears in their eyes.

"Hey, you make a good lookin' hood ornament," Logan said, laughing, as he walked over to the car.

Eddie glared at him. Then, realizing just how funny the whole scene must have been, he started laughing, too. Manning and Ross opened their doors, and soon all four boys were breaking up with laughter, holding on to each other for support. When they finally calmed down and caught their breath, they climbed into the car. Ross turned on the radio just as Herb Oscar Anderson was introducing the number one song in the country, and all the way to the jetty the boys tapped out the beat with their fingers on the dashboard and sang along with Shirley and Lee:

When you hold my hand
Say that I'm your man
When you thrill me so
I feel good

That evening, just after five, Eddie took out a couple of school books and note pads, and spread them over the kitchen table. A few minutes later, Mr. Casale, coming home from the office, walked in the back door, spotted Eddie and stopped in his tracks. He started to say something, but his son spoke first.

"Oh, hi Dad. Ya home already?" His tone was full of mock surprise, and he made an elaborate display of looking at his watch. "Oh my God! It's after five already. I was so involved in studying for my exams I lost all track of time."

"Don't use God's name like that," Mrs. Casale warned, as she entered the kitchen. She pecked her husband on the cheek, checked the chicken in the oven, and lit the gas under the pot of peas. "And," she added, "how can you lose track of time after only five minutes?"

Eddie froze. He glanced at his father. There was an evil smile coming to his face. Eddie's mind began racing, trying to come up with an answer, some response to his mother's remark which, because of her timing, undermined his whole set-up. Then, she provided him with a way out, too.

"Well, no matter, but finish your studying in your room," Mrs. Casale said, taking plates out of the cupboard. "I have to set the table now for dinner." Without a moment's hesitation, Eddie scooped up his books and scurried out of the kitchen.

All through dinner Eddie waited for his father to ask what he was doing on the hood of a speeding car instead of being in class. He really sweated it out, because, although he employed all of his creative powers, he was unable to come up with anything that came close to making any sense at all.

However, Mr. Casale never mentioned it. Occasionally, he looked up from his plate, and frowned, while nodding knowingly at his son, then continued eating. His son sweated a little more with each look. After eating, Eddie excused himself immediately with, "Well, back to my room to hit the books again," and rushed up the stairs. He stayed in his room all night and missed going to Dick's, but figured it was worth it not to confront his dad.

Final examinations were held towards the end of June, and Eddie and his friends went to school and took the tests. They answered the questions they could, leaving the others blank. They knew they would get at least a passing grade of sixty-five on all their papers. No teacher wanted them back again next year. Pass them along the system to the next grade, then let that teacher put up with their antics for a while. That seemed to be the new education system.

On the final day of school, Eddie picked up his report card, and scanned the column of scores. He smiled with satisfaction when he came to "English." It was marked with an eighty-four. English was the only subject he cared about. Mort Mayer, his teacher, told him he could get scores in the high nineties if he would just open a book. Mr. Mayer said he could be a good writer some day, or a journalist, if he would try a little harder. Eddie liked to write. The only things he worked on at all in school were his compositions, and he always received a "B." Mr. Mayer often said he would have gotten an "A" if the spelling wasn't so bad. But Eddie didn't have time to look something up in the dictionary, like his sister, Anna, told him to do every time he asked her how to spell a word. Eddie was satisfied, anyway. He knew his final grade of eighty-four was based on his four compositions over the term period.

"Hey, whadaya smilin' at?" Joe Ross said coming up behind Eddie. "Didn't ya expect to pass everything?"

"Yeah," Johnny Logan said, walking up next to Ross. "All sixty-fives. Makes it easy to figure my average."

"That's right," Ross said.

"Yeah, that's right," Eddie added, folding his report card and shoving it in the back pocket of his Levis. Shit, he thought, if they knew I got an eighty-four in English they would really rank me out.

No one cut classes on that last day. It was tradition to be around for the final bell on the final day of school. At two-forty five it rang, and bedlam broke out in the halls of Bayside High School. The kids went wild, racing through the corridors, throwing books at each other, tearing papers into confetti and tossing it in the air. All through the school, friends said their goodbyes for the summer with shouts of, "See you later, alligator," while others responded with, "After a while, crocodile."

Eddie, Logan, Ross and Manning walked out of the school, across the street and into the park. They lit up Luckies, sat on the grass and watched all the kids leaving school, laughing, happy as hell that there were no more classes, looking ahead to a summer of fun. That old children's rhyme they used to chant on the last day of grade school popped into Eddie's head:

No more classes, no more books
No more teachers' dirty looks

Fuckin' A, Eddie thought, in other words, no more bullshit. He looked over at his friends, and smiled. They were obviously deep in their own thoughts. He wondered if all three of them would come back as seniors next year. Hell, he wondered if he would be back. Next month he would turn seventeen, old enough to quit school if he wanted. The idea was weighing heavy on his mind lately. He thought about getting a job, having a paycheck in his pocket, buying a bike, fixing up a car, all those cool things. Of course, he would have to leave home if he did, he couldn't face his old man. Eddie shuddered. He didn't want to think about things like that now, he felt too damn good. It was the first day of summer vacation, and September was a light year away.

"Hey, ya assholes," he said, getting to his feet, and brushing grass and dirt from his Levis. "Whadawe sittin' here for? It's time to celebrate, 'an do some heavy drinkin'. Comeon. The first round of nickel Cokes are on me."

"Big fuckin' spender," Ross said, jumping up.

"Yeah, a regular Rockefeller," Logan added.

Four abreast, the friends walked across the park, on their way to Dick's Candy Store – and, hopefully, a summer of good times.

FIVE

BLACK DENIM TROUSERS

Marlon Brando, straddling a sleek Triumph motorcycle with a racing trophy tied to its handlebars, twisted the throttle and roared down a California two-lane blacktop followed by a gang of about 40 other cyclists. His black leather jacket was zippered up to the neck. He tugged on the visor of his motorcycle cap, adjusted his aviator-style sunglasses with thumb and forefinger, and leaned into a turn as he approached a crossroads. His gang, all with "Black Rebels Motorcycle Club" displayed on the back of their jackets, followed.

"This is the part I love best," Eddie Casale said, leaning forward in his seat.

"Ya say that about *every* fuckin' part," Buffalo Larry said with a snort of laughter.

"That's because they're *all* good," Cootie joined in, without taking his eyes from the screen. The tip of his tongue protruded from the right corner of his mouth as a sign of his deep concentration.

"Why don't ya all just shut up an' watch the flick, then?" Bo said. The statement may have been a question, but everyone who knew Bo understood it as an order.

Six friends from The Bayside Crowd were sitting in the balcony of the Beacon Theater on Broadway in Manhattan, a movie house which showed re-runs of classic films. The boys made the trip in from

Queens after spotting an ad in the Daily News for a special showing of *The Wild One.* They did this often, sometimes traveling as far as Jersey City across the river or the Loew's White Plains up in Westchester County to see their favorite movie. This was Eddie's tenth time. He took great pride in being able to mouth the words along with the characters on the screen, or act out the parts later at Dick's. Like when the chick says to Brando, "What are you rebelling against, Johnny?" and Brando says, "Whadaya got?"

On the screen, Johnny and his gang roared into a small town, forcing cars off the road and bringing people out of stores and houses. They rode their cycles around the town square, revving the powerful engines. Little kids waved and jumped up and down, while pretty teenage girls clapped, faces flushed with excitement. In the theater there were applause, whistles, hoots and hollers, and shouts of "Go, man, go."

The Wild One had been released in 1954 and since then, it had been shown continuously in one theater or another, and had remained as popular as ever. The movie had been responsible for the latest fashion crazes – the multi-zippered black leather jacket and the thick-bottomed, front-belted engineer boots. It had also caused a big boom in motorcycles sales - especially the English-made cycles which most of "The Rebels" rode.

The Bayside Crowd was no exception. But first, you had to get a driver's license, then the money for the bike. Finally, and most importantly, you had to find a place to keep the bike when your parents threatened to burn anything with two wheels and an engine which didn't mow the lawn.

Although Eddie was still a year away from meeting the first two requirements, he was already working on the third, with firm commitments from three of his friends to keep his bike safe when he got it. Meanwhile, Eddie, like the rest of his friends, was prematurely into the role. He already had his black leather jacket and engineer boots. And, when the time came, he would get *his* Triumph, too. For now, he was content to ride on the back of Bo's.

The fact that both Bo and Brando rode Triumphs was no coincidence, Eddie often thought, and someday I'll ride a Triumph, too. Bo handled that machine like a Cordon Bleu chef handled a carving knife, slicing through traffic and around curves with a sureness which could only be born from a confidence in the machine he rode, and, of course, his own ability. Straddling the buddy seat behind Bo, Eddie was able to experience the same confidence, both in the rider and the powerful engine between his legs.

As for the rest of the crowd, well, there was a whole compilation of cycles. A few opted for foreign bikes, as in the movie. Dancer rode a white BMW – nicknamed "The Ghost." Buffalo chose a silver-gray Norton 500 and Mike Mancuso had a red BSA Road Rocket. Cootie, the first in the crowd to ride a bike, kept to his original big yellow Harley Davidson 74, while Ox Zarora rode around on a 1947 showroom-shape Indian Chief, a restored police motorcycle with the original maroon paint and a hand-shift lever like a car. Hank Coleman motored a customized black and chrome Harley – almost a two-wheel version of his custom Ford Fairlane. Kenny Fletcher was the most creative, however. He bought a trunk-load of parts at a couple of junk yard auctions, dumped them in his garage, and six weeks later he rode out on his own *no-name* motorcycle.

Eddie nudged Cootie with his elbow, and nodded towards the screen. "Here he comes," he whispered. "The asshole's gonna fuck with Brando."

"Yeah, yeah. But don't tell me", Cootie said, annoyed, as if he didn't know what was going to happen. He inched forward even further on the edge of his seat.

Eddie stared wide-eyed at the screen, as Lee Marvin rode into town leading another gang of bikers, this one called "The Outlaws." *First, he'll steal Brando's trophy and put it on his own handlebars, then when Brando takes it back Marvin will taunt Brando, then the fight . . .* Eddie tried very hard not to let his mind race ahead of the film, but it was difficult since he knew it so well. What the hell, it was great to see it again anyway.

"The shame of it all. Oh, the shame of it all."

"Gimme a beer, and a *sidecar* for my friend."

"Write my mother and tell her I'm in jail, and send me a case of beer."

The guys shouted their favorite lines from the movie, as they left the theater, got on the bikes and headed down Broadway to Grant's, the huge 24-hour restaurant on Times Square which featured 10-cent beers, 15-cent hamburgers and 25-cent shots of whiskey (40 cents for a double). Whenever they were in Manhattan, they always stopped at Grant's, a Mecca for every bum, low-life and thrill-seeker in the city. It was always good for a few laughs before heading back to Queens. Sometimes they walked a few doors up from Grant's on 42nd Street to Hubert's Flea Circus and paid the 30-cent admission to check out Wanda, the woman with three tits, in the freak show in the basement. But sometimes even a three-titted woman, a no-arm man with hands growing out of his shoulders, and a bunch of costumed insects jumping through hoops and pulling miniature chariots were no competition for the *free* freak show at Grant's.

"Lookit those two," Mike said from where the guys were standing at the counter. He pointed with a half-eaten hamburger, grease running down his fingers, to two effeminate-looking men sitting close together holding hands in a booth midway across the room. One was stirring the other's coffee.

"There's something very *queer* going on in here," Larry said very loudly. Half the customers in the crowded restaurant turned, startled. The guys laughed.

Dancer took a white paper napkin from the dispenser, unfolded it and draped it over his left arm, waiter-style. He waltzed over to the booth, and, standing as close as possible to the astonished faces of the two occupants, he reached down with his right hand and grabbed his crotch. "Would you care for more *cream* in your coffee?" he said in a stage voice, squeezing his balls while he spoke. The guys at the counter were spitting out half chewed food and coughing up beer through their noses as they broke up with laughter. The hand-holders looked as if they were about to cry. While most of the other customers suddenly directed their concentration to the food or drink in front of them – proving they were old hands at ignoring other people's problems – a few nudged each other's attention to the drama suddenly unfolding before them. After all, this was the main reason some of them came to Grant's in the first place.

Willie Ray, the uniformed security guard usually stationed by the front door of Grant's, looked over. He started shuffling towards the guys. Willie's age was indeterminable, he could have been anywhere from late thirties to early sixties. His extremely black face was very smooth, which gave him a young appearance, but his body was that of an old man. He was very thin, with an almost sunken look, which was accented by his stooped shoulders, and made him seem shorter than his five-feet-eleven. His navy blue uniform looked several sizes too big, like a hand-me-down from an older brother. Willie was employed primarily to throw drunks out, keep old derelicts from coming in, and stop fags from sucking each other off in the men's room. He could look pretty tough if you were old, drunk or a homo, and he did that part of his job well. He had a problem, however, with anyone under the age of 65 who was relatively sober, and didn't swish when he walked.

And, when they were big tough-looking kids riding motorcycles, well they didn't pay him enough for that kind of shit.

"Comeon, gimme a break, willya," Willie began to whine when he was still several feet away from Dancer. He had a pained expression on his face. "Youse guys is gonna git me fired, an' - "

"An' I got a wif' an' four keeds ta feed," Eddie said, mimicking the guard, Amos and Andy style.

"Sheet, muthafucka, I ain't lyin' eitha," Dancer joined in, to the laughter of his friends.

"An' I ca't buy no mor' chick'n necks wid dem welfare checks," Larry said, fixing Willie with a cold, challenging stare. "An' youse know mah litt'l nigger babies loves dose chick'n necks. Ya-sah, dey sho' do."

The laughter continued, but suddenly there was more tension than humor in its sound. Willie looked around from face to face, finally settling on Bo's, knowing from past experience that these guys usually followed his lead. Besides, Bo was the only one who wasn't laughing. Willie was good at his job. He had to be, to hold on to it for six years. He knew when to act tough, and when to play the fool.

"Sheeeet," he began, flashing his wide-eyed, keyboard smile at Bo, "youse guys talk *nigger* betta den eyes do, an' dat is a fa't. Eyes do ho'ope ya doan wan' mah job, mon."

Bo gave Willie a hard look, squinting slightly, as he always did when studying a situation. Then his face softened and a smile appeared. He draped an arm loosely around Willie's round shoulders. "My man, nobody can talk *nigger* better than you, an' *dat's* a fa't," Bo said. Then, heading for the door, he called over his shoulder, "Let's get the hell outa here before Willie starts tap dancin' for us."

The guys, hooping and hollering, followed Bo out the door onto 42nd Street, where the motorcycles were illegally parked. Cootie was still munching on a hot dog and Buffalo smuggled out a half-full glass of beer under his shirt. It was still early, just past ten, but a surprise rain shower had cooled the otherwise muggy June night and momentarily cleared the street of most of the Times Square riffraff. The rain was just stopping, and prostitutes, fags and bums materialized from darkened doorways like zombies to resume their nightly parade along the world's most famous street.

Most of them, however, wisely kept their distance from the rowdy black-jacketed boys emerging from Grants. Dancer scooted back into the store, and re-emerged with fistfuls of paper napkins which he distributed to the rest of the guys to wipe the water off their seats. One by one they kicked their bikes to life, until the chorus of roaring engines dominated all other sounds on Times Square. Bo, with Eddie on the back, tapped the shift into first gear with the tip of his boot and began to release the clutch lever with his left hand when he noticed Ox Zarora still kicking his big Indian cycle. He eased the lever back to neutral, and hit the kill switch, turning off the engine. The other guys followed suit, until the only sound other than passing traffic was Ox's grunts as he worked up a sweat kicking against the high compression of the big Indian engine. Nothing happened.

"Fuck!" Ox shouted, climbing off the bike, stepping back and staring at the machine, hands on his hips. "Fuckfuckfuck!"

"That's pretty good," Buffalo Larry said, sliding off his Norton and walking over. "Is that what it says to do in the Indian Owner's Manual when it don't start? Try it *now* and see if it works after all those 'fucks'."

Ox ignored the hoots from the guys, reached under his seat for his tool kit, squatted down and started unscrewing one of the two spark plugs. "It's probably just wet," he said, more to himself than anyone else.

"Hey, buddy, ya need some help?"

Ox turned to the sound of the voice, and was rocked back on his heels by the sight and smell of a decrepit derelict who was squatting down next to him. In spite of the warm weather, the bum was wearing at least three layers of filthy clothing that emitted an odor strong enough to bring tears to your eyes. In fact, the only thing that smelled worse than his body was his breath.

"Get the fuck away from me," Ox managed, almost gagging.

"Aw, comeon buddy, I use' to be a priddy good wrench jockey. Lemme help." The bum smiled, flashing a matched set of two teeth in an otherwise empty mouth. Both teeth were broken and black.

"Yeah, let him help," the guys joined in, laughingly. "Give the poor slob a break, willya?"

A mischievous grin appeared on Ox's face. "Ok, I'll give him a break," he said over his shoulder. He turned to the bum. "Stand right over here, take this screw driver and put it in there, and hold on to this wire and let me know if I'm getting any spark when I kick the engine."

The bum, standing in a puddle of water in the gutter where Ox directed him, nodded eagerly, and did as instructed. "Ok, I'm ready," he said. Ox looked back at his friends, who were all trying to contain their laughter. He climbed on his bike and kicked the starter lever. The spark of electricity jumped from the powerful engine and through the bum, sending him a foot in the air, then flat on his back. The laughter that followed didn't last long, as the crowd realized the bum wasn't moving. They inched forward, looking at each other, unsure of their next move. They looked up. People were watching them from the window of Grants.

Bo was the first to speak. "Eddie, get to a phone and call - " He stopped in mid-sentence.

The bum's eyes fluttered open, much wider and clearer than just a few moments before. They searched out Ox, still sitting on his bike, frozen. The bum raised himself to a sitting position, and smiled his toothless smile.

"Yep," he said, as if nothing out of the ordinary had happened. "Yer gittin' spark in that cyl'na, now let's try the udda one."

The guys broke up with laughter, hanging on each other for support. It took another ten minutes before they calmed down, eventually sending the bum into Grants with 40 cents for a double shot, so Ox could finish drying off his spark plugs.

As the cycles roared down 42nd Street and turned onto 3rd Avenue, heading uptown towards the Queensborough Bridge at 59th Street, Eddie, sitting on the back of Bo's Triumph, started singing the cycle song recorded by The Cheers. By the time they started across the bridge, they were all singing to the background sound of throbbing engines:

He wore black denim trousers
And motorcycle boots
And a black leather jacket
With a eagle on its back
He had a hopped-up cycle
That took off like a gun
That fool was the terror
Of highway one-oh-one.

Although The Bayside Crowd had become much more mobile with the addition of several more bikes and cars, all the guys still hung out at Dick's Candy Store. After all, they had to maintain Bell Boulevard as their "turf." However, a couple of nights a week – usually Wednesdays and Fridays – they would hop on the cycles or pile into cars and head about ten miles out on Long Island to the Hide Out, a sprawling, seedy bar on Hillside Avenue, just over the Nassau County line, where they weren't too careful in checking draft cards. They seemed to have one rule: if you're past puberty you can drink. The place was a Mecca for guys from all the tough neighborhoods. They came from Bensonhurst and Bay Ridge in Brooklyn; Corona and Astoria in Queens, and Fordham Road in The Bronx. Three things you could count on at the Hide Out were cold pitchers of beer for a dollar, live country music, and a good knock-down, drag-out barroom brawl.

It was Friday night, the eve of a three-day July 4th holiday weekend, and by eight o'clock the curb in front of Dick's was lined with motorcycles. Inside the candy store, *Searchin'* by The Coasters blasted from the juke box, as most of the crowd lounged around in various groups sipping Cokes or eggcreams, and discussing everything from Brigitte Bardot to Nikita Khrushchev. Eddie, Dancer and Kenny Fletcher were over by the juke box harmonizing with The Coasters. Cootie was sitting alone at one of the booths, pages of the Daily News spread across the table, some ringed with wetness from his glass. His eyes were glued to the only page he ever read, the movie page.

"Shit!" Cootie exclaimed, as his eyes followed his finger down the page, his lips moving as he read. "Damn! *The Wild One* ain't playing nowhere in town this weekend." Cootie had become the official WOF, or the Wild One Finder. It was his job to check the newspapers to see if and where the movie was playing.

"Why don't you get a copy of LA Times?" Hank Coleman wisecracked. "Maybe it's playing out there."

"Naw, that's too fuckin' far," Cootie replied, in all seriousness, as he continued to study the page in front of him, the tip of his tongue protruding from the corner of his mouth.

A few of the guys snorted with laughter. Cootie looked up, suddenly realizing he was the butt of a joke again. "Fuck ya guys," he snarled, as he crumpled the page into a ball and threw it at Coleman. In doing so, he knocked over the glass of chocolate eggcream in front of him, splashing it all over his white shirt.

Now, everyone in the store was laughing, as all attention focused on Cootie, who sat there, totally pissed off, staring down at the sticky brown stain on the front of his shirt. Even the juke box trio wandered over, ignoring *Whispering Bells* by The Del-Vikings.

"Hey!" Chuck Hoffman called out. "Did anybody see a monkey with diarrhea runnin' aroun' here? I think it just shit on Cootie."

More laughter, as Cootie boomed even louder, "FUCK YA GUYS!"

"Someday," Leo Silverman told Cootie, "Bartlett's Book of Famous Quotations will accredit that line to you. Perhaps the most profound line by *any* Pollack." Silverman, who was the only guy in the crowd to attend college, would be starting his second year at Queens County Community College in September.

Some of the guys laughed even harder, and Cootie got hotter. "Fuck *ya,* Shadow, you *kike* bastard. And, fuck Bartlett, too, whoever the fuck he is."

Eddie, sitting next to Bo at the counter, looked over at Cootie's shirt, and laughed with the rest of the crowd. Then, the sight triggered the memory of the last time Cootie ruined his shirt, and Eddie laughed so hard that Bo had to catch him to keep him falling off the stool.

When Eddie, Bo and Cootie had arrived at Kiddie City, they made a beeline for the snack bar, found a table, threw their jackets on the chairs, and went over to the counter. Bo had been wearing a black Mister "V" shirt, and Eddie had on a white Fruit of the Loom T-shirt. Cootie, as usual, was wearing one of his numerous long sleeve white dress shirts, freshly washed and starched by his mother.

They got their franks and Cokes, stopped at the condiment counter, and walked back to the table. Bo and Eddie were already eating by the time Cootie joined them. His hot dog was piled about three inches high with mustard, relish, catsup, chopped raw onions, fried onions, chili beans and sauerkraut. He looked at his friends eating their franks with just a little dab of mustard, and laughed.

"Ya guys are crazy," he had snorted, holding his top-heavy hot dog with two hands, being careful with its balance. "All this stuff is free. It's like getting' a whole meal for the price of a frank. Ya jus' have to know how to take advantage of these things."

Trying not to spill anything, he lifted the frank slowly, then tilted it towards his mouth. The hot dog began to slide out of the roll, carrying with it its entire payload, like an over-loaded dump truck about to empty its cargo. It missed his mouth, bounced off his chin, landed on his starched collar first, then slid down the front of his white shirt. In its wake was left a huge stain of yellow, brown and red, with flecks of green, while strands of sauerkraut dangled from the opening of his shirt, slices of onion hung from his breast pocket and a nasty-looking clump of chili clung to his sleeve. Cootie just stood there, holding an empty roll, looking down at the colorful mess, and yelled, "SHIT!"

Bo and Eddie had their mouth full at that moment. They began laughing and choking at the same time. Chewed up bits of meat and bread burst from their lips like blasts from a double-barreled shotgun. They laughed so hard they fell off the chairs, their legs knocking over the table, sending large paper cups of Coke splashing to the floor. Each time they tried to stop, they looked at Cootie, who just stood there with a shocked expression, and broke up again. Finally, they caught their breaths, and managed to stop laughing by not looking at Cootie, or each other. They sat back in their seats.

That's when Cootie had said, "Fuck ya guys! They gave me a broken roll," and they were on the floor again.

The manager came running over in an attempt to quiet things down. By this time, though, Bo and Eddie were crawling towards the door, trying to get outside before their stomachs burst.

Cootie complained to the manager about getting a broken roll, and said he would send them a bill for his shirt if he didn't get another frank.

"I'll give you two," the manager had said, "if you keep those two lunatics out of here."

Bo and Eddie waited outside with tears in their eyes, and pains in their bellies, but their laughter had finally subsided into an occasional chuckle.

That is, until Cootie came out with a hot dog in each hand and an ugly streak down his shirt, and boasted, "Fuck ya guys! I beat 'em for an extra frank.

They immediately fell to the ground again, clutching their stomachs.

It was a little after nine when Bo suggested taking a ride out to the Hide Out, "to see what's goin' on."

"That's a capital idea," Ox Zarora said, raising his hand, forefinger in the air. "I second the motion."

Picking up on Zarora's lead, Kenny Fletcher stood up and said, "All in favor, say 'aye'."

All the guys shouted their approval, and immediately the usual plans were in the works as to who was taking cars or bikes, and who was riding with whom.

"Hey, what about the girls?" Barbara said. "Are we coming, too?"

"Naw, yer jus' breathing hard," Kenny wisecracked. There were chuckles from the guys, as they headed for the door.

"Don't waste your time," Judy Bender said to her friend. "They never take us anyplace."

That wasn't true, of course. The guys took the girls places. Sometimes they would go to the park to make out. And other times they would take them to drive-in movies to make out. But, to the Hide Out, never.

Things usually got pretty rough at the Hide Out, and they didn't want to worry about protecting the girls when a fight broke out. Besides, there was always a chance of picking up a girl out there, one that might put out right away. With the Bayside girls you had to go steady just to touch a tit. And that was only on the outside of the bra. (What are you doing back there? Hey! Get your fingers off that clip. Don't you dare unhook my bra. What are you, a sex maniac, or something?). And, most of the time, if the guy was eventually successful, he'd discover that the damn thing was padded, and for the past two months he was getting a boner from caressing foam rubber.

The Hide Out was already in full swing when the eight bikes and one car carrying the sixteen Bayside boys swung off Hillside Avenue and into the gravel parking area next to the bar. There were about thirty cars jammed in the lot, and twenty bikes lined parallel along the front of the building.

The guys parked and headed for the door. Eddie, Johnny Logan and Joe Ross were the only members of the crowd who were under eighteen, the legal drinking age, but they had fake draft cards. In fact, Eddie's card showed he was twenty-one, so he could use it in states where the drinking age was even higher. However, the only guy that didn't look eighteen was Ross, and he was proofed almost every time.

As usual, Blackie, the bouncer, was at the door. He stepped in front of The Bayside Crowd and spread his arms to block their way. However, he was careful not to touch anyone.

"Sorry, fellas," he said apologetically. "I got orders not to let you in no more. Not after what happened last time." He was supposed to be a dominating force, but when he spoke his words lacked conviction. Perhaps, it was due to the fact that traces of what *happened* last time – a cut cheek and a left eye that matched his name – were still visible on his face. Bo, up in front of the crowd, shot Blackie a cold stare, his lips pulled back in a tight smile. "An', who's gonna keep us out? *You?"*

The bouncer lowered his arms and dropped back a step. "Hey, fellas, it's not me. I jus' work here. Charlie's the owner, right? He tol' me not to let you in. I'm just followin' orders." His words tripped over each other, as if he couldn't get them out fast enough.

"Hey, Cootie," Bo called out, not taking his eyes off Blackie. "These guys say we can't come in an' have a beer. Whadaya have to say about that?'

Cootie made his way through the tight group at the door, and pushed his face about two inches in front of Blackie's. "Fuck ya guys!"

The boys burst out laughing. Blackie backed up another three steps. He turned to Charlie for support. His boss, who was behind the bar pouring beers, had an eye on the activity at the door. Blackie just stood there, arms slightly out from his sides, palms forward, as if to say, "What do I do now, boss?"

Charlie stopped what he was doing, and came rushing out from behind the bar. He was about fifty years old, with a totally bald head, a pot belly, and a perpetually worried expression. The expression came with the territory. Not that anyone ever took a swing at Charlie when he tried to break up fights. It was an unwritten rule that he would not get hurt. However, that rule didn't apply to his property, and that's what worried Charlie. Broken windows, mirrors, glasses, tables and chairs cost money.

"Aw, come on, you guys," Charlie pleaded, as he came up beside his bouncer. "Please go someplace else. I can't afford no more fights in here. Besides the damage, I have my license to worry about."

Bo put his big arm around the owner's shoulder, and said with a pleasant smile, "That's yer problem, Charlie, ya *worry* too much. Besides, ya know us. We don't start fights. We jus' finish 'em."

"Who knows from starting or finishing," the owner frowned. "I just know you're in them."

"Look, Charlie," Bo continued in his charming manner. "We just came here to have a few beers and listen to some music. Not to fight. Ok?"

"You promise no fights?" Charlie asked doubtfully.

"Of course we do," Bo reassured him. "Right, ya guys?" he called over his shoulder.

Buffalo Baker stepped forward with a very solemn look on his face. He raised his right hand, and said, "I swear on my Harley Davidson." He rode a Norton.

"Awright, awright," Charlie relented. "But this is the last time. Any more trouble and you're out for good. And I mean it!" He turned to his bouncer. "Ok, Blackie, let them in. But keep an eye on them," he added, before walking off. "Any sign of trouble and I want you to throw them out."

Blackie stared after his boss incredulously, as if he had been asked to go ten rounds with Floyd Patterson, until he was poked in the shoulder By Ox Zarora.

"Ya better keep the good eye on us," Ox said, pushing past the bouncer with the rest of the guys. "The other one looks like shit."

The Hide Out was a huge rectangular barn-like room, with a large oval-shaped bar in the middle. Most of the area surrounding the bar was cluttered with tables, chairs, and booths, all of them in some state of disrepair. The small dance floor was situated off the far end of the bar. In the middle of the oval, behind the shelves of bottles and glasses, was a raised platform which served as a stage for Johnny Lake, the guitar-banging, country-western singer who had been the Hide Out's only entertainment for the past two years. No one ever got tired of him, because no one ever really listened to him, except when they were drunk. Then they forgot him by the next day. Johnny Lake possessed just the right talent to play the Hide Out. He was loud. In fact, the joke among the crowd was that the only thing louder than Johnny Lake's singing were the blightly-colored cowboy shirts he wore.

As The Bayside Crowd walked along the front of the bar to take up their usual positions at the far end, Lake was pounding his guitar and shouting a bad rendition of Johnny Cash's *I Walk The Line.* He was wearing an electric blue satin shirt with long white fringes. When he spotted the new arrivals, he stopped singing, and with a big smile, said into the microphone, "The Bayside boys are here. Howdy, pardners. Your first round of beer is on me." Lake always bought the first round of beers for the guys from Bayside. They guessed he considered it something of an insurance policy.

"Forget the fuckin' beers," Cootie's voice boomed throughout the bar, without the aid of any microphone. "Jus' send over some ear plugs for yer singin' and sun glasses for yer shirt." There was a roar of laughter, as the smile froze on the now red-faced singer. He immediately went back to his song:

Because you're mine
I walk the line

Although there were still some empty tables, the bar was fairly crowded and most of the counter space was taken. Four guys, with glasses of beer in front of them, were occupying the crowd's favorite spot in the corner. Ox pulled out a white handkerchief, and draped it over his left arm like a waiter. He pushed his way between the guys, grabbed two of their glasses in each of his huge hands, and said, "Thank you for waiting, gentlemen. We now have a table for you. Walk this way, please." And, doing his best Groucho Marx shuffle, he walked over to the nearest table and plopped the four glasses down, causing half the beer to splash out.

"What the hell – " one of the guys began, turning, a snarl on his face. He suddenly stopped when he saw the crowd around him. "Come on," he said to his friends, wisely. "Let's sit at the fuckin' table. It's too crowded at the bar anyways."

Eddie and his friends ordered a pitcher of beer each – a dollar for the beer and a two-dollar deposit. It was an insurance premium to keep the glass pitchers safe during bar fights. At the end of the night, the deposit was returned if the pitcher was still in one piece. It worked, too. There were nights when the Hide Out was totally trashed by a fight, and, standing miraculously unscathed amidst the rumble, were 30 or 40 beer pitchers.

About six beers later, Johnny Lake was sounding much better, and his shirt was less offensive. More people drifted in and, by eleven o'clock every table, as well as the bar, was full. The small dance floor was jammed with swaying bodies.

Eddie was sitting at the bar, along with Bo, Cootie, Buffalo, Ox and Hank. Their stools were swung around, and they were leaning back against the bar, elbows propped on the bar top, surveying the action in the room. Some of their friends were standing nearby, while others were scattered throughout the bar scouting for single girls.

"Check out the fuckin' body on that bitch." It was Hank, and he was staring at the dance floor as if in a trance.

The rest of the guys at the bar followed his gaze to a pretty young blonde, only about five feet tall, with tits so big they could have made up fifty percent of her body weight. She was doing the Lindy with a tall, lanky guy with long sideburns. She was wearing skin-tight black Lee denim jeans and an equally-tight white turtleneck sweater. Her enormous tits and big, well-rounded ass were accentuated even more by a wide red elastic cinch belt pulled tight around her narrow waist. The girl's long ponytail, which fell to the mid-back, whirled around her writhing body as if it was whipping her into the state of ecstasy she seemed to be experiencing.

"Wow!"

"Holy shit!"

"I'd like to bite on those and pray for lockjaw."

"She can sit on my face anytime."

They all made comments as they watched her body wiggle, bounce and buck. When the music stopped, she and Sideburns embraced and walked hand-in-hand back to their large table, where several of their friends were sitting.

"We need a cold one after that," Bo said, turning back to the bar. He pounded his big fist on the counter, and shouted, "Innkeeper! A flagon of grog for me merry men."

Harry, one of the six regular bartenders, had been told, as they all had been, to keep an attentive eye on the boys from Bayside. He appeared immediately with fresh pitchers of cold beer, picking up soggy one dollar bills from the messy bar. The guys were at their *drinking-from-the-pitcher* stage.

"A toast," Eddie said, raising his pitcher. "Here's to little girls with big tits."

"I'll drink to that," Buffalo said, grabbing his pitcher.

"Ya'll drink to anything," Eddie quipped. "As long as someone else is payin'."

"Through the teeth an' over the gums, look out stomach here it comes," Cootie recited, then took a large gulp. He forgot he was drinking from a pitcher, and too much beer flowed out. It spilled over his face and down the front of his white shirt.

"Shit, man, it's supposed to hit yer stomach from the *inside,* not the *outside.*" Chuck Hoffman said.

"Hey, man, ya should drink that stuff, not wear it," Ox joined in.

"Fuck ya guys!" Cootie responded, wiping the front of his shirt with his sleeve.

Eddie chuckled, and took another swig. "Hey, Hank, whadaya on the wagon?" he asked, noticing that his friend's pitcher remained untouched on the bar. He turned and saw nothing but an empty stool. "Where the fuck . . . ?

Handsome Hank Coleman was leaning over a table with his arm around the pretty little blonde girl they had been watching on the dance floor only moments before. Hank's face was very close to hers, his lips near her ear. She had a shocked, wide-eyed expression.

Sideburns jumped up, knocking over his chair. He grabbed Hank by the hair, and yanked his head away from the girl, shouting, "You pervert!" With his other hand, he punched Hank in the face, and sent him reeling backwards into another table, which crashed to the floor under his weight. The five guys sitting at that table didn't appreciate having their drinks spilled. They looked around with fire in their eyes.

Without taking his eyes off the action, Eddie hit Bo in the side with his elbow and yelled, "Hank's in trouble!" He jumped off the stool and raced across the floor. The rest of the guys were only several steps behind.

Sideburns was pummeling Hank with both fists. Hank, unable to get to his feet, pulled his arms over his head in an attempt to protect his handsome face from the blows.

Eddie arrived on a full run, and without stopping, drew his right leg back and threw a perfect Green-Bay-Packer kick into the guy's chest. If it had been a football, it would have gone into the end zone. He heard the sound of ribs cracking as his boot made contact. Sideburns lifted two feet in the air, bounced off the wall, and landed at the feet of the five guys who had their drinks knocked over.

"That's the motherfucka," one of them shouted, then they all pounced on him.

In an instant, Sideburns' friends were all over Eddie. In another instant, they were off, flying across the room in various directions, as Eddie's friends were all involved now, punching, kicking and tossing guys around like rag dolls. Some guys were thrown into other tables, which pissed off the people at those tables. They joined the melee. Within seconds practically everyone in the bar was swinging it out, most of them not having any idea what caused the fight – and not caring.

A skinny kid with long brown hair ran up to Eddie and swung a wild, round-house right. He seemed drunk. He missed by a mile. Then he just stood there, swaying slightly, leaving himself wide open. Eddie stepped in with a hard, straight right hand to the jaw. The skinny kid's eyes turned white, his pupils rolling into his head. He didn't fall, however, and Eddie tried to shove him out of the way. Unfortunately, he still didn't go down, but wobbled a few feet and stumbled into Bo's back.

Bo reached over his shoulder, grabbed the guy's head with both hands, and flipped him over his back. The kid flew through the air and landed on top of the bar with such force that he bounced off, and smashed into the shelves of liquor behind the counter. Unconscious, he slid to the floor amid broken glass and a mixture of booze from at least a dozen bottles.

"Break it up! Where the hell is Blackie?" Charlie kept yelling, running around the bar. "That's it! I'm calling the cops!" he finally screamed. He ran into the telephone booth against the wall by the front door.

Ox Zarora and Chuck Hoffman, who had been fighting side by side, both spotted Charlie at the same time. They looked at each other, nodded, then dashed for the phone booth. As Charlie was dialing "O" for operator, the two big, powerful boys stood on each side of the booth, lifted it several inches in the air, and pulled it out from the wall, the wires snapping as it moved. Very carefully, in order to keep Charlie from being hurt, they swung the booth forward and placed it door-side down on the floor. Charlie, yelling and kicking, was unable to escape from his Ma Bell tomb.

Almost as fast as it started, the fight was over. There were half a dozen prone bodies on the floor along with broken furniture and glass. The Bayside Crowd formed a tight group and backed towards the door. Outside, they turned and ran for their bikes and cars. Suddenly, Bo held up his hand.

"Wait a minute!" he said, as everyone stopped. "Where's Hank?" He hadn't come out with The Bayside Crowd.

"I'm going back in," Bo said, getting off his Triumph. "He must still be inside." The rest of the crowd groaned, but they were ready to back him up.

Suddenly, they heard the roar of a Harley engine, and Hank rode out from behind the building. They were stunned. On the back of his big Harley was the sexy little blonde in the tight white sweater. She had her arms wrapped around him tightly, those enormous tits rubbing against his back, and her fingers played with the buttons on his shirt. Her pretty face was flushed with excitement.

"Yippie!" she yelled. "Let's see what this big mothafucka can do."

"Ya heard the lady," Hank said, trying to smile between his bruised lips. "Whadaya gonna do? Wait all night for the cops to come?" He twisted the throttle, popped the clutch, and as she squeezed him even tighter, the bike's rear wheel spit up gravel, bounced onto the pavement and roared down the street.

There was a moment of shocked silence as the guys stared at Hank's Harley racing away with the girl's ponytail whirling in the wind. Then, they were laughing and cursing at the same time, mumbling under their breath. But Hank ended up with the girl. After all, he *was* Handsome Hank. Seconds later they were all on the move, heading for their usual after-hours stop at the White Castle on Bell Boulevard.

It was late Saturday morning of the holiday weekend, and it was already hot, and getting hotter by the hour, with the temperature hitting the high eighties. Most of the kids who normally slept late on Saturdays were out early, taking advantage of Dick's new Fedder's air conditioner. *Tweedle Dee* by LaVerne Baker was playing on the juke box.

"Did ya see the way Johnny Lake made a beeline for the girl's bathroom as soon as the fight started," Kenny Fletcher said.

"Yeah, but he couldn't get in," Mike Mancuso said. "Blackie was awready inside with the door locked,"

"You missed all the action again, didn't you?" Johnny Logan said to Joe Ross.

"I was doin' somethin', wasn't I?" Ross protested. "I got all the deposits back for the pitchers. Did ya think of *that*?"

"Well, I guess we'll have to stay away from the Hide Out for a while," Bo said.

"Jus' for a *short* while," Eddie amended. "Charlie will cool off, then ya can smooth talk him into lettin' us in again. Right?"

Bo nodded and smiled. He glanced over at Chuck Hoffman, who was sitting quietly, looking depressed.

"What's buggin' you?" he asked. "Ya haven't said a word all morning."

"It's my old man, again," Chuck said, staring into his Coke glass. "We had another argument this morning about me getting a bike. He said if I got one he'd throw me *and* the motorcycle out."

Mr. Hoffman was a tough old German. He started out as a drill press operator and now had his own manufacturing plant, which he ran with an iron hand and an iron will, as all his employees, which included his son, knew too well. "Hard work and strict rules," he was fond of saying. "That's what it took." However, he ran his family like he ran his business. Mr. Hoffman owned one of the larger homes in Bayside, situated on a one acre plot, half of which was an immaculately-kept lawn. Chuck was the one who kept it immaculate, although his father could well afford a gardener. "Hard work won't hurt you," he would tell his son. "But hanging around with those bums will." Mr. Hoffman didn't approve of his son's friends and did his best to keep him away from them by providing chores around the house when he finished his day's work at the plant.

"For Chrissake!" Chuck pounded on the counter. "I'm nearly twenty years old. I should be able to have a motorcycle if I want one."

Bo walked over and sat on a stool next to Chuck. "Hell, he's not gonna throw ya out," he said, trying to console his friend. "Look. Jus' go home one day an' tell him ya bought a bike an' see what he says. Ya know, see how he handles it."

Suddenly, Chuck's face brightened. "Hey, maybe you have something. But let's take it a step further."

"Whadaya mean?" Bo seemed puzzled.

"I'll ride up on a bike and tell him I just bought it," Chuck said. "If he actually *sees* a bike, and thinks I already own it, he may not take it so bad."

"Yeah. But where are ya gonna get the bike?"

"Yours"

"Mine?"

"Yeah. I'll borrow your bike."

"Like hell ya will."

"No, wait. I'll drive and you ride on the back. We'll go together and I'll tell him I just bought it from you. And you confirm it. Ok?"

"I don't think it's such a good - "

"Aw, comeon." Chuck was excited now. "What can he do?" If he throws a fit I can always tell him we were joking around, and it's really not mine."

"Yer father doesn't have a sense of humor," Bo reminded him.

"Shit, man, it was your idea in the first place," Chuck persisted. "And it just might work."

"It wasn't my idea to use *my* bike," Bo said.

"No, but that just makes the whole thing better. Can't you see? If he thinks it's over and done with he just might accept it. Damn, what's the worse that could happen, anyhow?"

"Well, when would ya wanna pull this big scheme of yer's," Bo said lamely.

"No time like the present. That's one of my father's sayings, too." Chuck grabbed Bo by the arm and led him to the door. Bo resisted at first, then said, "What the hell." He reached into his dungarees pocket for the key to his Triumph and handed it to Chuck.

"This I gotta see," Ox Zarora said, coming over to Eddie. "Let's follow 'em there."

"Ok, but we'll watch from the street," Eddie said. "Chuck's old man has a big German Shepherd meaner than he is, an' there's no way I'm goin' on his property."

Eddie jumped on the back of Ox's Indian and they followed Bo and Chuck to the big Hoffman house, in the affluent section of Bayside known as The Gables.

Chuck rode the Triumph up the long, circular driveway in front of his spacious home. He stopped by the side lawn, not far from where his father was relaxing in a hammock. Chuck revved up the engine of the Triumph.

"Hey, Dad," he called, as the two boys climbed off the bike. "Look what I jus' bought."

Mr. Hoffman raised himself on one elbow and looked across the lawn at his son wheeling a motorcycle towards him on the grass.

"Ain't it a beaut, Dad? I jus' bought it," he repeated, in case his father missed it the first time.

Bo, reluctantly, followed a few paces behind his friend.

Anger flared in the eyes of Mr. Hoffman, as his face flushed beet-red in sharp contrast to his full head of snow-white hair. In his haste to get to his feet, he pushed the hammock a little too hard and it swung out, causing him to tumble to the ground.

"I don't think this was such a good idea," Bo called after his friend. "Let's get outa here."

By this time, Mr. Hoffman was on his feet, glaring at his son. Although he was short, about five foot six, he had broad shoulders, and was very fit for a man of sixty. Chuck, for the first time since suggesting his plan, seemed doubtful.

"N-now calm down, Dad. Let's just talk about it. Ok?"

"Talk?" Mr. Hoffman shouted. "You vant to talk? Ok, start talking. Talk all you vant. I love to hear you talk." With that, he started trotting over to the tool shed at the rear of the property.

"I don't think he wants to talk," Bo offered.

Mr. Hoffman came out of the tool shed moments later with a double-sided wood axe big enough to have been used by Paul Bunyan.

"Vell, Charles, I'm vaiting, but I don't hear you saying nothing," he said menacingly. He crossed the lawn with long strides, heading directly for the Triumph. Chuck seemed to be struck dumb, as he stared at the shiny blade of the axe reflecting the rays of the morning sun.

"Holy shit!" Bo cried out. He pushed his stunned friend aside roughly, and jumped on his bike. He kicked the starter, but the engine didn't catch. He forgot to turn on the key. Mr. Hoffman was only ten feet away now as he lifted the axe off his shoulder.

Chuck, snapped out of his stupor by Bo's push, ran up to his father in an attempt to stop him. "Dad, I was only kidding. It's *not* my bike, really – it's Bo's bike. I was only kidding."

"It von't be anybody's bike by the time I'm finished with it," Mr. Hoffman boomed, shoving his son aside.

Bo turned the key and kicked again. The engine roared to life. He shifted to first gear and released the clutch just as Mr. Hoffman swung the axe. The back wheel spun on the slippery grass, which had been watered earlier that morning, but the bike didn't move. The blade caught the rear of the seat, just behind Bo's ass, leaving a ten-inch gash in the leather and foam rubber. Bo swore over his shoulder, then gave it more gas. The spinning wheel finally ripped up enough wet grass to hit dry dirt. It caught and the bike leapt forward, just as the axe was about to fall again. The tire spit up grass and dirt everywhere, as the bike fishtailed across the once-immaculate lawn, leaving a single ugly dirt track in its wake.

The excitement attracted the attention of Mr. Hoffman's huge dog, who came running from behind the house to join his master in chasing the motorcycle. Bo hit the pavement, twisted the throttle even more, and sped out of The Gables, winding through gears like a Daytona racer.

Ox and Eddie were laughing so hard they had tears in their eyes. "That's like a scene from the Keystone Kops," Eddie managed, before breaking up again. They were still sitting on the big Indian motorcycle, parked by the curb in front of the yard, which allowed them an unobstructed view of the action. Suddenly, Eddie saw the German Shepherd's ears perk up, as he turned their way. Even at thirty yards, there was no mistaking that look. His mouth was pulled back exposing deadly teeth. The dog jumped, and was at full run in one motion, heading directly for the boys.

"Let's get the fuck outa here. Fast!" Eddie yelled in Ox's ear.

"Hey, whadaya yellin' – ?" As Ox turned, he saw the snarling dog, who had already covered half the distance between them. Ox quickly turned the key.

Eddie prayed that the Indian would start on the first kick for a change.

The German Shepherd took a giant leap covering the last two yards, and landed at the back of the bike. He went for Eddie's leg, but sank his teeth into the thick leather of his heavy engineer boot, which was hanging off the foot peg behind the exhaust pipe. At the same time, Ox kick-started the huge machine. It sprang to life with a deafening roar. As the dog was yanking and twisting Eddie's boot, his right ear was no more than an inch from the exhaust. It was like a shotgun blast to his head. The dog let go of the boot, jumped a foot in the air and began yelping like a scared puppy. As the boys raced away, the German Shepherd rolled on the ground, whining away, with his front paws over his ears.

It was a week before the crowd at Dick's saw Chuck again. He was busy re-sodding a good portion of his father's lawn, while the dog, with cotton stuffed in his ears, remained a recluse in his doghouse. Bo was most anxious to see Chuck, though. He was waiting with a bill of twenty dollars for a new seat.

By the time Bo, Ox and Eddie returned to Dick's a few more members of the crowd had arrived. Everyone wanted to know what happened.

Ox began the story, and the crowd started chuckling. Then Bo and Eddie got into it with more details, and before long all the humor of it came out and the entire crowd was laughing along.

It was only about twelve noon. The juke box was rocking with Little Richard's *Long Tall Sally.* The sun was blistering outside, but the Fedder's was doing its job indoors. Most of the crowd was content, doing their favorite thing – hanging out. The music was good and the Coke was cold. However, it was the guys with the motorcycles who always felt restless when the sun was shining.

"Let's take the bikes for a ride someplace," Mike Mancuso suggested.

"Yeah! We can take a run to Jones Beach an' check out the chicks in those bikinis," Dancer Bob Larkin said with a lecherous smile.

"Shit, no," Kenny Fletcher objected, looking at his girl, Joan Ford, out of the corner of his eye. "On a weekend like this it's jus' wall-to-wall people. An' the parkways will be jammed, too. Let's go someplace where we can open up the bikes.

"Yeah," Buffalo Larry Baker agreed. "Like Spinny Hill. Northern Boulevard will be empty today. We could have the hill to ourselves. That is," he added with a taunting smile, "unless ya guys are afraid to open it up out there."

Cootie was the first to spring for the bait. "Fuck ya guys! I can do the hill faster than any of ya."

"Bullshit," Buffalo responded, jumping off his stool to face Cootie. "That hog ya got may take my Norton on top end. But on cornerin'? No fuckin' way!"

"My fuckin' Road Rocket will blow ya both away," Mancuso piped in.

"Awright, awright!" Ox shouted, slamming his palm on the counter to get everyone's attention. "There's only one way to settle this. Let's ride to Spinny Hill now. Whadaya say, Bo?"

Bo looked around the room as everyone waited for his answer. "Well," he began with just a hint of a smile, "for me to race the hill with ya guys is like Mickey Mantle playin' in the Little League. But, if ya got the balls, let's go." He headed for the door and the rest of the crowd followed.

Eddie rode with Ox this time, as Bo was one of the racers. Seven bikes pulled out from in front of Dick's and headed down Bell Boulevard. They were followed by the rest of the crowd in three cars. The caravan swung a left, and headed east on Northern Boulevard, which would take them over the Nassau County line and into the hilly North shore of Long Island. Spinny Hill, in Manhasset, was a treacherous section of four-lane roadway. It ran for approximately half a mile, with almost a forty-five degree incline, and two tight, sharp "S" curves. The legal speed limit along this section was fifteen miles per hour. The guys were always trying to set new limits.

Traffic was extremely light. People were either out of town, or on the parkways heading for places like Jones Beach, Long Beach, Fire Island, Montauk and The Hamptons.

The group pulled to the side of the road at the top of the hill. "Perfect!" Ox exclaimed, as he surveyed the nearly deserted boulevard. Occasionally, a car maneuvered slowly up or down the hill, or entered the main road from a side street. "We practically got the road to ourselves. Ok, the race is between Bo, Cootie, Buffalo and Mike. Anybody else want in?" He looked around. There were no other takers.

Ox, the unofficial "official" of the race, took charge, putting people in position. There were two side streets in this section feeding into the main road, and a major intersection with a traffic light at the bottom of the hill. Ox stationed the guys at the various key locations, in order to keep the roadway clear, and to stop cars from using the downhill lanes at the same time as the racers.

"All set? Everybody know what to do?" he asked, looking around. Everyone nodded. "Ok, we'll be at bottom by the finish line, an' keep an eye on the traffic lights." He looked at the four racers. "Give us, let's say, five minutes to get in place, then hit it. An' remember. It's an honor-system race. The bikes make the run down the hill one at a time, an' ya tell us yer maximum speed. Ok, let's go."

Ox and Eddie started down the hill first. Dancer, with Johnny Logan on the back of his BMW, followed only a few yards behind. Although they weren't racing, both bikes picked up speed. Ox went into the first curve at almost forty miles per hour. The bike leaned sharply to the left, Eddie leaning with it. Immediately, they were out of the first curve and into the second, the bike now leaning even further to the right. There was a scraping noise. The bike bucked, and sparks flew from the footpeg hitting the pavement. Ox backed off on the throttle a bit, and the bike lifted just enough keep the metal clear of the ground. They hit the next set of curves, left and right again, and, when the big Indian straightened out, Ox down-shifted and braked at the same time, coming to a stop just before the intersection. Dancer and Logan on the BMW pulled up along side.

"Holy shit!" Eddie exclaimed. He swung his leg over the bike, in a hurry to feel solid ground under his feet again. He began breathing rapidly, suddenly realizing he had been holding his breath since going through the first curve. "That was better than the Cyclone at Coney Island," he said.

"Shit," Ox replied, with a wave of the hand. "That was nothin'. If I was ridin' solo I coulda really opened it up."

"You ain't lying," Mancuso agreed.

Yeah, right, Eddie thought, looking at his friends. You may be trying to play it cool, but your faces sure are flushed, too.

The boys took up their positions at the intersections. Because of the curves, the starting point at the top of the hill was not visible from the bottom, and the racers would not be seen until they went into the second curve. However, their engines would be heard long before that point, and the traffic, if any, would be stopped from crossing the intersection in ample time.

They heard the roar of the engine, and Eddie knew it was the Triumph even before he saw the bike. Moments later Bo burst into view, body bent low over the gas tank, his chin an inch above the handlebars. The Triumph was leaning at a 45-degree angle, leaving a wake of sparks as the footpeg dragged along the street. Bo banked sharply into the next curve, and seemed to pick up even more speed. Now the sparks flew from the other side of the bike as that footpeg made contact. Eddie checked the intersection, but there were no cars in sight. Bo pulled out of the last curve with a final twist of the throttle, and was still picking up speed as he raced past the intersection. He came to a stop about a hundred yards down the road, swung around and headed back. He was sporting a flushed face and a huge grin.

"I think I just established a new record for Spinny Hill," he beamed.

"Christ! How fast were ya goin'?" Ox asked.

"I hit fifty four in the final stretch," Bo said, with a hint of pride in his voice.

At that moment, they heard the roar of the next bike, and scrambled back to their positions. As Mancuso on his BSA Road Rocket sped into view, Eddie spotted a Chrysler Imperial approaching the intersection. He immediately jumped in front of the car, holding up his arm, palm out, like a traffic cop. The driver, a man of about fifty, rolled down the power window, and leaned out of his air-conditioned comfort with a snarl on his face. "Get the hell - " he began. The rest of his words were drowned out by the roar of the BSA as it raced past. Eddie stepped aside, and signaled for the driver to go with a wave of the arm. He muttered something about "crazy kids," then made a left and continued on his way. By this time, Mancuso made his U-turn and was rolling to a stop at the corner.

"I missed a gear," Mancuso said in disgust. "Shit, I only got it up to fifty. I know I can do better than that."

"Tough titty!" Ox responded. "Ya only get one shot at it. Ya know the rules."

"Yeah, but - "

"But, my ass!" Ox cut him off. "If ya can't shift that thing, maybe ya oughta get a bike with automatic transmission."

Before Mancuso could respond, the sound of the next bike could be heard coming down the hill. They quickly checked the intersection. It was clear.

Buffalo Larry was flat out on the tank of his Norton as he came into the final curve. The boys at the bottom of the hill watched as the bike leaned left, then right. Suddenly, there was a loud scraping noise and the bike shuddered and jolted upright. The footpeg momentarily dug into the pavement, throwing the bike off balance. The front wheel of the Norton began to wobble, and Buffalo fought to control the bike. The engine screamed as he down-shifted to cut speed, and they all knew that to brake at this time would cause the bike to go into a spin. Somehow, Buffalo kept the bike upright, and it finally slowed down enough for the wheel to stop wobbling.

The Bayside Crowd rushed over to Buffalo as he rolled to a stop at the intersection.

"Jesus! That was close!"

"Are ya awright?"

"I thought ya were gonna loose it for sure."

They were all speaking at once. Buffalo pushed his kick stand down, climbed off the bike, and took a bow.

"Jus' a little trick ridin', my friends," he said. "Nothin' to it."

As they were all carrying on, a Plymouth Fury approached the intersection. When the light turned green, the driver, a middle-aged woman, looked right, then left, then right and left, again, as if undecided as to which way to go. Finally, she turned right and headed slowly up the hill. She was in the opposite lanes so no one stopped her. Halfway up the hill, she stopped, and, as they watched in shock, she began to make a U-turn. A U-turn! On a hill – after a curve –across a double white line. At the same time, they heard the roar of the big Harley engine.

"Back up, ya bitch!"

"Get the fuck outa the road!"

They were all shouting at the same time. They started running towards her, yelling and waving their arms. The driver looked in the direction of the boys. Then she heard the engine and saw the motorcycle bearing down on her. She froze at the wheel and began screaming, with the Plymouth blocking most of the downhill lanes.

Cootie came out of the second curve with a roar, about to turn on a final burst of speed. He was almost on top of the car when he hit both the hand and foot brakes at the same time. He tried to lean the bike through the half lane which was not blocked. The rear wheel locked, and the bike slid sideways, slamming with tremendous force into the car's rear fender. Upon impact, Cootie was thrown from the bike. He landed with a sickening thud, and the sound of bones breaking, thirty yards away in front of Big Arthur's Bar-B-Q.

His friends were at his side within seconds. Cootie was lying on his back, his right leg at a grotesque angle behind him. He was bleeding from the ears, nose and mouth, as well as from a puncture wound in his side.

"Call the hospital!" Bo yelled, rushing over and kneeling beside his friend.

He checked his pulse. "He's still alive. Someone call the fuckin' hospital, now!" he ordered again. It was unnecessary. Buffalo was already on the pay phone inside the restaurant.

Eddie came over. He found it difficult to look at Cootie. Instead, he consoled his other friend.

"He'll be ok, Bo," he said, still standing. "I know he will."

Bo looked up at Eddie. "Yer damned right he will," he said with clenched teeth. Then he peeled off his T-shirt, folded it several times into a pad, and put it behind Cootie's head.

"Yer gonna make it, my man," he said to his unconscious friend, taking his hand. "Yer gonna - " His voice cracked. He was unable to continue. It was the first time in his life that Eddie saw tears roll down Bo's cheeks.

SIX

LET THE GOOD TIMES ROLL

"Fuck ya guys!" Cootie grumbled from his bed in room 305 of the orthopedic ward at the Manhasset Medical Center.

Three weeks after the accident, almost his entire body, from chest to toes, was still encased in plaster. Both legs were broken, the right one in three places. His left arm was fractured, as were three ribs. He suffered only a minor internal injury as a result of the puncture, which was caused by the jagged end of a broken shift lever ripping into his side. His cuts and lacerations were of little consequence; the worst requiring seventeen stitches in the back of his head, from when it made contact with Big Arthur's sidewalk. Luckily, there was only a minor concussion, and no brain damage.

"Of course there's no brain damage," Eddie quipped. "How can ya damage something which ain't there?"

"Fuck ya guys!" Cootie repeated as the laughing continued. He sucked up more beer from the can, slurping it through the curved plastic straw from his water glass.

Eddie, together with Johnny Logan, Joe Ross, Kenny Fletcher and Hank Coleman, were standing around the bed. The nurses had long since given up their attempt to enforce the two-visitors-at-a-time rule. In fact, they tried to avoid Cootie's room completely in order not to witness passing of contraband, like cans of Schaefer Beer or half pints of Three Feathers, to the patient. The younger nurses especially kept away from room 305, and it was the "forbidden zone" for candy stripers.

There were two other patients in the room. There used to be three, but the family of the third, a middle-aged businessman from Great Neck with his back in traction, demanded to have his room changed so he could get "some peace and quiet."

One of the beds was occupied by "Joe College," as The Bayside Crowd called him, recuperating from back surgery. He was a student from Hofstra University in Hempstead, who dislocated several vertebrae with a slide into second base during a school baseball game. He had three things going for him. He played baseball, drank beer, and had cute little co-eds coming to visit. The guys liked him. In the other bed was a very old man with both arms and both legs encased in plaster. He never said a word, just moaned occasionally, as he lay there, wired to traction, with his limbs pulled in the air like a dormant marionette. There were tubes extending from his nose, arms and crotch, and no one ever came to see him except a senior nurse, who, three times a day, changed the bottles at the end of each tube, and a bag attached to his side.

Handsome Hank used the "churchkey" from his key ring, opened another round of beers, and passed them around. He kept three for himself. He walked over to the next bed, and handed one to Joe College, and one to his pretty little redhead visitor.

In the next moment, Hank's arm was around the girl and they were tapping cans in a private toast, smiling into each other's eyes.

"What a guy!" Joe College called over to the rest of the crowd, obviously impressed, rather than annoyed, with Hank's conduct.

Actually, Joe College was impressed with everything the Bayside boys did, as he had never come in contact with a crowd like this before.

"Yeah, what a guy," they all said in concert, shaking their heads, as Hank now managed to draw the girl to the back of the room.

"Hey, don't get upset," Eddie offered to Joe College. "I mean, he's not *really* hitting on yer girl. That's jus' his way."

"Oh, no, no, I don't mind," Joe College said. "She's not my girl anyway. Hell, there's a couple a thousand like her at Hofstra. You know what they say, why buy the cow when the milk's free, anyway."

The boys watched in open mouth amazement as Hank smoothly maneuvered the coed to the empty bed, then rapidly drew the privacy curtain completely around.

"Oh God, he's so fuckin' bad," the guys said to each other. "Wow, he's so cool," Joe College said with obvious admiration. "He'd do great at Hofstra."

He'd do great any-fuckin'-where, Eddie thought, before continuing the story. "Well, anyway, then this car, the Plymouth Fury, stops, an' starts to make a fuckin' turn, right there in the . . ." It was the umpteenth rehash of "The Accident," and everyone listened as if hearing it for the first time.

Eddie had visited Cootie almost every night since he had been admitted, catching a ride with Bo or someone else heading out to the hospital. But, he also came to see his friend during every afternoon visiting session, when most of the other guys were at work. When Dan Manning was around, they made the ten-mile trip from Bayside to Manhasset in his Packard.

When he wasn't, Eddie took a chance and drove his uncle's 1947 gray Chrysler, with the fluid drive transmission. No one knew he had the Chrysler's spare key, and he risked taking the car out while his uncle was at work.

After another week in the hospital, Cootie was given a pair of crutches, ten minutes of instruction on how to use them, and his official release paper from the hospital. They were anxious to get rid of him, and his visitors, and return the ward to normal. His mother questioned the hospital's haste in releasing her son.

"Isn't it a bit early, after all he's been through," Mrs. Kolinski queried.

His surgeon made himself unavailable for any comments, leaving it up to the officials of the hospital. The administration office told Mrs. Kolinski that her son was "a big strong lad, who has responded well to the operations. He will convalesce just as well at home as in the hospital."

"In other words, yer givin' him the bum's rush," Bo said, his arm around the shoulder of the widowed Mrs. Kolinski. There was a murmur of denial. "Let's get him outta here an' back home. Yer'll take better care of him, anyway," Bo told Mrs. Kolinski, leading her out of the office. A moment later, Bo stuck his head back in. "If my friend has any problems," he said in his soft, but distinctive way, "I'll be back to *discuss* them with ya, personally."

Cootie was carried to the parking lot in a stretcher, where Manning's huge Packard was waiting to take him home. Mrs. Kolinski, at her son's urging, had refused the use of the hospital's ambulance.

Several nurses from the ward were standing by the glass doors watching the departure. They were smiling, making no secret of their pleasure in seeing this patient leave.

Eddie, who had packed up Cootie's belongings with Johnny Logan, and was bringing them down, spotted the nurses and became annoyed at their obvious attitude. He hit Logan with his elbow, waved his thumb towards the women in white, and mouthed the words, "Play along."

"Can ya believe it?" Eddie said loudly as they were alongside the nurses. "Rocky bein' admitted to the same room as Cootie? Ain't that something . . . two friends endin' up in the same room, one right after the other."

"No shit!" Logan said, picking up on the gag right away. "Cootie leaves, Rocky comes in. The same day, the same room. Whadda the odds on that?

"Let's go tell the crowd," Eddie said, in an excited voice. "We gotta come back tomorrow. Hey, maybe even bring Cootie."

The nurses, their smiles now gone, looked at each other wide-eyed. Then they rushed off, probably to check the admittance record for room 305. Eddie and Logan cracked up as they walked into the parking lot to help maneuver Cootie's prone body into the huge back seat of the Packard.

Three days after Cootie's release from the hospital, the telephone in the phone booth at Dick's rang. Eddie, standing closest to the booth, heard the ringing above Roy Orbison's *Ooby Dooby.* He ran for the phone.

"City Morgue," Eddie said, picking up the receiver. "Ya stab 'em, we slab 'em."

"Very funny, very funny." Eddie recognized Cootie's voice immediately, even without its usual raucous quality.

"Ya guys gotta get me outta here." There was desperation in his voice. "If my mother makes me eat another bowl of cabbage soup I'll throw up, I swear to God I will." Cabbage soup was the Polish equivalent to Jewish chicken soup.

Ten minutes later Eddie and Chuck Hoffman were helping Cootie into the backseat of Hoffman's 1954 blue Ford sedan, as Mrs. Kolinski watched in horror from the doorway of the house.

"Are you insane?" she yelled at her son for the third time. "You shouldn't be going out so soon."

"Yeah, yeah," Cootie called back. "Don't worry, I'll be careful." Then he cursed as he banged his head on the door handle.

"If you get hurt, again, Stanislaus, I'll kill you," Mrs. Kolinski shouted, using Cootie's Christian name and waving a fist in the air. Eddie and Chuck glanced at each other and smiled.

The Ford, of course, was much smaller than the Packard. Eddie was on one side pushing, while Chuck was around the other side pulling. Finally, with Cootie's cast-enclosed legs protruding from the back window, they were able to close the doors.

Driving back to Dick's, Eddie made an elaborate display of looking all around the car.

"Do ya see him?" he asked Chuck.

"No, I don't see him," Chuck said, holding back his laughter.

"How about you, Cootie?" Eddie asked. "Do ya see him?"

"See who?" Cootie asked. "Who the fuck ya talkin' about?"

"This guy *Stanislaus* yer old lady was talkin' to," Eddie said. "He must be a real asshole with a name like that."

They expected his usual response. Instead, Eddie was hit over the head with a crutch.

There was a loud round of applause when they entered the candy store. Cootie acknowledged the greeting with a big wave of his arm, which caused him to drop a crutch. A moment later, he fell forward, flat as a board. Several people rushed over to help him up.

"I'm ok, I'm ok," he said with a smile, as they propped him against the counter. "I just forgot for a second I couldn't walk without the crutches. Ain't that somethin'?" They all laughed.

"Christ," he continued, "I need some decent food for a change. Dick!" he called out in his most resonant voice. "Gimme two of yer greasiest burgers an' a black 'n' white malt."

Cootie laughed and everyone laughed with him. The spirits of the crowd seemed a bit higher now that Cootie was back and obviously in his old form again, at least mentally. He stood at the end of the counter accepting the "welcome backs" from his friends as he waited for his food.

Bo came from the front door of the store with a Paper Mate ball point pen, still in its package. "Put this on my check," he told Dick, holding up the twenty-nine-cent pen for him to see. He unwrapped it, and wrote on Cootie's cast, just above the area over his heart: "From my heart to yours, to help you heal with all the power generated through a true friendship."

Eddie took the pen from Bo, and wrote, "Down with all women drivers!"

Ox Zarora took the pen next, and, as the crowd lined up to sign Cootie's cast, the record on the juke box changed. Shirley and Lee started singing:

Come on, Baby, let the good times roll
Come on, Baby, let me thrill your soul

Cootie began wolfing down his burger, the grease running down his chin, then dripping onto the section of his white shirt which wasn't tucked into the top of the cast. It was the only article of clothing he was able to wear.

"Here, let me clean that off for ya," Eddie said, with a big stage-grin to his friends around the store. He grabbed a tall glass of ice water from the counter and poured its entire contents, cubes and all, down the front of Cootie's cast.

Cootie spit out a mouthful of burger and bun as he yelped from the shock of the cold water hitting his bare skin. A moment later, water dripped out of the opening in the cast at his crotch. The crowd pointed and laughed. Cootie moved forward to get hold of Eddie, but his friend easily stepped back, and Cootie started falling. Bo, still standing next to him, reached out and grabbed him by the back of the cast, and pulled him back.

"Shit, man, if you needed a bed pan, you should have asked," Leo Silverman remarked loudly.

"Hey, Cootie," Buffalo Baker joined in. "Why's that openin' so big? With yer dick ya only need a pinhole to piss outa."

"Fuck ya guys!" Cootie's voice boomed throughout the store, above the cries of laughter. Then he joined in, too. "It's great to be back," he said, looking around at his friends. "Hell, man, it's great to be alive!"

The crowd finally calmed down, returning to its normal level of stimulation. Diane Roth went over to feed the juke box, hitting the buttons like they were typewriter keys, her selections coming from memory. She walked back to her booth in tune with Frankie Lymon singing *Why Do Fools Fall In Love?*

A moment later, Kate Brody jumped up and moved to the middle of the store. "Hey everybody!" she shouted above the music. "Let me have your attention." She already had the guys', as soon as she moved. She was wearing tight dungaree shorts, rolled up as high as they could go, and a red T-shirt, at least a size too small. "I have a great idea. Let's have a party Saturday night. You know, like a welcome home party for Cootie."

The crowd voiced its agreement with hoots, hollers and applause. Any excuse for a party was a good one; this one, however, was excellent.

"Where should we have it?" Dancer called out, and immediately all eyes fell on Eddie.

"No, no, not me! No fuckin' way!" Eddie held his hands in front of his face, shielding himself from his friends' imploring eyes. "My old man would have a shit-fit if I even —"

"Aw, comeon," Kate said, walking over and taking his arm in hers, pressing it close to her body. "Let's talk about it." She led him over to a booth where Big Judy Bender, Barbara Saunders and Diane Roth were waiting, smiling up at him seductively.

"We can talk," Eddie said, with all the conviction he could muster, "But it won't do no good. I'm tellin' ya, there's no way I can have another party."

"Like leadin' a lamb to slaughter," Johnny Logan said.

"Ten to one he has the party," Joe Ross added.

"Ten to one?" Dancer was shocked at the odds. "I wouldn't take a hundred to one."

A few minutes later, Eddie was squeezed into one side of the booth between Kate and Judy, their naked thighs pressed against his, while, on the other side of the booth, Barbara and Diana smiled seductively, the tips of their tongues caressing their lips. It didn't take long. It was only seconds later that Eddie was trying desperately to figure out how in hell he would persuade his father to agree to the party which Eddie had just promised the girls would take place at his house in two nights. It was difficult for him to think. All the blood had rushed from his brain to his cock, now throbbing rock hard under the table.

"Good heavens! What are you doing out of bed so early?" Mrs. Casale asked. "You don't get up this early even when you have school."

"I decided now that I'm older I should be a little more responsible," Eddie said, walking into the kitchen. He stopped short, and winced, when he heard the sound of his own words. They sounded so unbelievable.

"That's nice," his mother said, nodding her head. His father just looked at him suspiciously, with squinting eyes.

Mr. and Mrs. Casale were sitting at the table having their usual morning coffee together, a relaxing time for Mr. Casale before he left for the office. That was why Eddie planned to ask the big question now. But first, a little more buttering up.

"Good mornin', Mom," Eddie continued with a big smile. He leaned over her side of the table and planted a big kiss on her cheek. "An', good mornin', Dad." He turned, leaning to the other side of the table, but brushed his father's elbow just as he was taking a sip from his cup. Coffee splashed on his tie. Fuck! Eddie thought. I'm off to a bad start.

"Damn!" Mr. Casale muttered, wiping his tie with a napkin.

"Don't swear!" Mrs. Casale exclaimed.

Mr. Casale glared at his son. The peace and tranquility of a moment ago was gone.

"I'm sorry, Dad. I'll get ya another tie." Eddie was upstairs and back in less than a minute with one of his father's many solid maroon ties. Since Mr. Casale was color blind, most of his ties were exactly the same so he wouldn't have trouble getting dressed in the morning. He took the tie from his son, held it against his navy blue suit, decided it matched, and started replacing the stained one. Eddie sat at the table. His mother had set a glass of orange juice at his place while he was gone.

"Dad, I was thinkin' - "

"No!"

"But, Dad, ya didn't even hear – "

"No! I told you last time, no more parties."

Holy shit! Eddie thought. How the hell does he do it? Is he a warlock or somethin'?

"Oh, pleeeease, Dad," Eddie pleaded." He immediately went to phase "one" of his two-pronged attack. "After all, I'm seventeen now, an' I didn't even have a party for my birthday, which was two weeks ago."

"I know when you were born. God only – "

Mrs. Casale cut her husband off with a sharp glance and a raised finger.

"Look, Dad," Eddie continued unperturbed, jumping right into phase "two" of his plan. "It's not for me, anyway. It's for Cootie, who just got out of the hospital, ya know. It'll make him feel so much better."

"Oh, that's such a nice idea," Mrs. Casale said. "That poor boy has been through an awful ordeal."

"You mean I can *have* the party, Mom?" Eddie asked hopefully.

"Well, your intentions are good. And, it's true, we didn't have a party for your birthday. But it's up to your father."

Mr. Casale looked at his wife incredulously. She smiled back pleasantly with an imperceptible nod. He then shot a look at his son. He started to say something, then stopped and sighed deeply, shaking his head.

"I have to go to the office," he said, frowning. "We'll talk about this party of yours when I get home."

This party of mine? Eddie thought. Did he say, this party of *mine*?

"Thanks, Dad," Eddie said, almost beaming, as his father headed for the door.

"I said, we'll *talk* about it!" he said sternly, then he was gone.

Eddie hung around the house in a state of sheer happiness. As a reward for his mother's support, he allowed her to prepare him a big breakfast, instead of the usual juice, milk and Thomas' English muffin.

That elated her morning considerably, too. As he waited for his pancakes and eggs, minus the bacon because it was Friday, he thought about the party. He was glad, now, that he hadn't asked to have one for his birthday. He had thought about it, but Bo had talked him out of it when he had mentioned it to his friend.

"Naw, don't bother, Eddie," Bo had said. They were sitting next to each other on stools at the counter in Dick's, listening to The Chords sing Sh-Boom. It was early evening, just a week after the accident.

"Ya know, with Cootie in the hospital, an' all, a party just wouldn't be the same. Let's wait til he comes out."

"Yeah, yer right," Eddie had agreed, nodding his head, although he couldn't help feeling a little disappointed. He took a drink from his Coke.

Bo swung around on the stool, and poked Eddie on the arm. "Besides," he said with a smile, "birthday parties are for kids. Yer a man, now, ain't ya?"

"Ya bet yer ass I am," Eddie said, still nodding, staring into his glass.

"Then we'll celebrate like men," Bo said. "We'll go out to dinner at Sal's. Jus' me an' you. My treat."

Eddie brightened immediately. I can dig that, he thought. Of course, Eddie had gone to Sal's many times before with Bo. His friend ate there every Friday night, and Eddie tagged along occasionally, whenever he could break away from his mother's meatless Friday night meals. This was different, however. It was the first time he was ever invited to a birthday dinner with his best friend. Eddie's birthday was Sunday, but Mrs. Casale had planned a big family dinner with relatives from Corona. The boys made their plans for Saturday night, and Bo said he would call for reservations.

Sal's Italian Restaurant was on Bell Boulevard, on the opposite end of the block from Dick's. Sal Bari, the owner, knew some of The Crowd well. That's why he greeted Bo and Eddie with a frown when they entered.

"Try-a controlla youself, an' keepa da voice-a down ta-night, capice?" he said, while showing them to their usual table in the furthest corner of the room. He would try to keep the nearest tables empty, just in case of another food fight or of an arm wrestling bout over the last piece of Italian bread.

As soon as they sat down, a waiter with a bored expression walked over. He began writing as he said, "The same." It was a statement rather than a question. They always ordered the same dishes.

"Noooo," Bo said, pondering the menu. "This week I'll try something different." The waiter stopped writing, looking a little surprised. He ripped the page off his pad and waited. "Let's see now. Lobster fra diavlo? No. Sirloin steak pizziolla? No. Hmmm. I

think I'll try the veal parmigiana." Same as he always ordered. Eddie laughed. The waiter didn't think it was so funny. He began writing again, pressing so hard he broke the pencil point. He took another one out of his breast pocket.

Eddie studied the menu for a full minute, while the waiter impatiently tapped his foot. Then he ordered his usual, too. "Chicken cacciatore," he said. "But easy on the 'caccias' and heavy on the 'tores'. Las' time ya gave me too much 'caccias' an' it gave me gas. Bo cracked up. The waiter walked away shaking his head.

The meal went along at a peaceful pace. Bo ordered a straw-wrapped bottle of Chianti wine, and they toasted Eddie's seventeenth birthday. They didn't even have to fight over the last piece of bread. Sal, like a warden watching convicts, kept a vigilant eye on the table, and quickly refilled the bread basket as soon as it went down to one slice.

"That was good," Eddie said, putting the last piece of mushroom and chicken in his mouth. "But I'm still a little hungry. I guess I'll have a hamburger when I get to Dick's"

"That's too bad," Bo said with a smile. "Yer all finished, an' I still have this big piece left." He jabbed his fork into a chunk of veal covered with melted mozzarella cheese, and pushed it around the plate, gathering up the remaining sauce. He held it tauntingly in front of Eddie's face.

"I always save the best til last," he teased, moving the fork slowly towards his open mouth.

"Hey, that's ok," Eddie said, taking on a somber expression. "In all seriousness, I jus' want to thank ya for this dinner. Ya made this a great birthday for me, my friend." He sniffed, as if fighting back tears. "There's jus' one thing I can wish for that can make it a little better, like perfect."

"What's that?" Bo asked, pausing, suddenly becoming serious, too.

"That last piece of fuckin' veal," Eddie yelled, snatching the chunk of meat from Bo's fork with his fingers and shoving it in his mouth.

Bo froze for a moment, stunned, staring at his empty fork poised in the air. That was all the time Eddie needed for a head start. He jumped up, knocking over his chair, and ran for the door. He looked over his shoulder. Bo was right behind him. And, behind Bo, standing by the now deserted table, was a shocked Sal, flanked by two waiters. In Sal's hands was a miniature birthday cake with a candle in the middle.

Later that night, after Bo apologized to Sal, and settled the bill, and after Eddie bought Bo a hamburger to make up for the veal he stole, the boys took a spin on the Triumph and ended up sitting on the jetty at Fort Totten.

"He took it pretty good?" Eddie asked, lighting up a Lucky with Bo's Zippo.

"Yeah, Sal's a good guy," Bo said. "An' the waiter was happy. I gave him a buck tip. The only thing was, they were disappointed they didn't get to sing 'Happy Birthday' to ya."

"I'm not," Eddie said. "I've heard them sing before."

The two boys laughed, then, for quite some time, there was silence as they each drifted off with their own thoughts. They took long drags from their cigarettes, watched the lights of the Bronx-Whitestone Bridge and listened to the sound of passing cars on the Cross Island Parkway. Occasionally, they could hear the scurrying of a water rat in the rocks. Eddie smiled to himself as he followed the movement of a used condom, riding the tide of the Long Island Sound. Coney Island white fish, he thought. Great name. Then his smile faded. He wondered if he would ever get a chance to use one. After all, he was seventeen now. He had carried a Trojan in his wallet for two years. How much longer would he have to wait before he could use it?

"It's over."

Eddie, his thoughts interrupted, turned to his friend. Bo was sitting on a flat rock, hunched forward, looking at the water.

"What?" Eddie said. "Did ya say somethin'?"

"It's over," Bo repeated, still staring at the water, as if transfixed by something in its dark depths.

"What's over?" Eddie asked.

"All this," Bo said, looking at his friend sadly, and spreading his arms. "I'm gonna be twenty in couple a months, for Chrissakes. I'm too old to be runnin' through restaurants, an' jus' hangin' an' shit. Besides, I'll be gettin' my draft notice soon. I'm thinkin' about enlistin' before it comes. Ya know, so I'll have a fuckin' choice, at least. Maybe learn something useful."

Eddie had been stunned. He didn't know what to say. He could see the depression in his friend's eyes, but, at the same time, there was determination in his words. He knew the older guys would get drafted some day, or get married, but he never gave it much thought. It was always in the future. For now, The Crowd would always be there for him.

"Look, it's not only me, ya know," Bo continued. "Most of the other guys are in the same boat. Sign up, get drafted or get hitched. Three choices. 'Cept for Cootie, of course, but that way is too fuckin' painful."

Eddie ignored Bo's attempt at humor. "B-but, what about me? What am I gonna do?" he asked.

Bo had reached out and put a hand on Eddie's shoulder. He squeezed gently. "Yer'll do the right thing, my man," he said softly, his words filled with emotion. "Ya always do."

Eddie wasn't too sure of that. He turned and looked at the water again. He didn't want Bo to see the tears brimming in his eyes. The right thing? What the fuck is that? he asked himself. I'm still a fuckin' teenager. What the hell will I do? Then he thought, fuck it! He blinked back his tears. Someday I may have to handle decisions like that, he thought, but, fuck it, I don't have to do it now. He looked over at Bo, who was back to staring at the water.

"WATCH OUT FOR THE RAT! he yelled, while pinching Bo sharply on the thigh.

Bo screamed like a schoolgirl at a Bella Lugosi movie. He jumped a foot in the air, stumbled over the jagged edge of an adjoining rock, and had to flounce his arms in the air like a tightrope walker to keep from tumbling into the Sound. By this time, Eddie was off and running, and howling with laughter. Bo caught up to him on the patchy grass next to the parkway, where they wrestled until Eddie cried "uncle."

"Remember," Bo had said, grabbing Eddie's hand and pulling him up from the grass. "I'll always be three years older and one *step ahead of ya."*

"That was delicious," Eddie said, wiping the last of the Vermont Maid maple syrup from his plate with a forkful of pancake and egg. "I'm stuffed. I think I'll take a walk down Bell to work this off." He headed for the door.

"Don't be late for dinner," Mrs. Casale called after her son.

"Dinner?" he said in mock surprise. "What's for lunch? I was thinkin' of comin' back early, an', ya know, just hangin' around here til Dad comes home."

"I'm sure you were," Mrs. Casale said, with a knowing smile. "If you want to come for lunch, fine, but you don't have to. This is the woman's day to clean and you'll just be in the way. Now, get out so I can clean up before she gets here. And, don't worry, I'm sure you'll be able to have your party."

Eddie stepped out into the August sunshine. His mother's words were better than the General Motors warranty for Cadillac. He knew her reasoning, too.

She wasn't stupid. If Eddie and his friends didn't have the party here, they would have it, just the same, "God knows where." Then, she would be up all night, worrying about his "drinking, fighting or whatever," until he made it home safely. At least, now, she could stay awake and do her worrying about his "drinking, fighting or whatever" with him in his own house.

Eddie felt great as he headed for Dick's. About a block from his house he started skipping like a kid, then broke into dance, doing his Gene Kelly *Singing-In-The-Rain* impersonation. When he leaped in the air to click his heels, he didn't make it nearly high enough. His feet were in an awkward position when he landed, and he nearly fell on his face. He looked around to see if anyone was watching. A little girl in a green pinafore walking with her mother was pointing at him and laughing. He walked the rest of the way.

Before getting to Dick's, Eddie stopped around the corner at Joe Ross' house, woke him up, and managed to get him to Dick's only with the promise of treating him to coffee and a toasted corn muffin.

The candy store was empty when they arrived. Dick was behind the counter grinding the grill clean with an abrasive stone. He looked up as the boys came in, checked his watch, then frowned. He couldn't believe they were starting so early today. He was still cleaning up from his usual breakfast crowd.

"Now you must vait," Dick said, "til I finish vid dis."

"No problem," Eddie said, as the boys stopped at the comic book rack in the front of the store. Ross chose a *Captain Marvel,* while Eddie grabbed the latest *Archie.* Before settling down to his reading, he went over to the juke box and dropped a quarter in the slot. Elvis Presley was singing *Hound Dog* by the time he got back to the table. Eddie opened up his comic book. He couldn't help wondering why Archie liked Veronica more than Betty. Veronica was always breaking his balls, while Betty kept playing up to him. The asshole had a better chance of getting laid with Betty. Besides, her tits were bigger, too. Eddie wished there was a "Betty" in his life.

Dan Manning showed up a little later and wanted to go to Jones Beach. Eddie declined, not wanting to take the chance of being late for dinner, but Ross ran home for his towel and bathing suit. His friends left, and Eddie took a *Sad Sack* comic from the rack.

Eddie was anxious for the girls to show up. He just had to tell a couple of them about the party, and that was it. The news would spread faster than if it was in the early edition of the Daily News. Every time the door opened, he glanced up, but it was always someone buying a pack of cigarettes or a package of Spearmint.

About an hour and three comic books later, Eddie shot a look towards the front of the store and did a double take, nearly knocking over his Coke glass. It was Diane Roth, Judy Bender and Kate Brody – and they weren't wearing any pants. Even Dick, usually immune to anything concerning The Crowd, nearly dropped the glass he was drying.

"Hi, there" the three smiling girls said in unison as they wiggled their way over to the table where a wide-eyed, slack-jawed Eddie was sitting.

"Put your eyes back in your head," Diane giggled.

"Pick your chin up off the table," Judy added.

"It's the latest style," Kate said, raising the bottom of her blue oxford shirt to reveal a pair of rolled-up denim shorts underneath. "We wear short-shorts with a long man's shirt on the outside so it looks like we don't have any pants on. Great, huh?" She slid in the booth next to Eddie, while the other girls sat across.

With all those naked thighs under the table in such close proximity to his, it took Eddie a while to collect his thoughts about the party.

The girls became ecstatic when he told them, even though he emphasized it wasn't a hundred percent certainty. But they had confidence in his persuasive abilities.

"By the way," Diane said," my cousin Ginny will be visiting from College Point. She goes to St. Agnes. You'll like her. She's from the Italian side of my family. Her last name's Marcessi, like my mother's maiden name."

"Yeah," Kate joined in. "We met her. She's perfect for you."

Eddie didn't notice the way the girls looked at each other and smiled. His mind was already conjuring up a "Ginny Marcessi from St. Agnes," and wondering if it was true what guys said about girls who went to Catholic high schools.

Eddie returned home shortly after five. As soon as he walked through the door he knew he would have a tough time getting through dinner. He was hit by the musty odor of simmering lentils, his mother's favorite meatless Friday night dinner. *Yuck. They smell as bad as they taste.* Usually, he begged his way out of the lentils meal, and was able to join Bo at Sal's, but tonight he was a man with a mission. He managed to get through the ordeal by washing down each mouthful of lentils with a large gulp of milk, and pausing occasionally for deep breaths. However, he was unable to keep from gagging several times, while his father, who always loved the savory little brown peas, seemed to be enjoying his dinner even more than usual.

After dinner, Eddie followed his father into the living room. Mr. Casale turned on the television and settled into his easy chair to watch the seven o'clock news. Eddie perched himself on the hassock directly in front of him.

"Look, Dad, about the party — "

"Ok, ok," Mr. Casale said, raising his hand like a traffic cop. "But here're the ground rules. Tell your friends they can bring beer, but no hard liquor."

He reached into his pocket, pulled out twenty dollars, and handed it to Eddie. "And buy some food, something to pick on, so at least you'll have something in your stomachs besides alcohol."

Just like that, Eddie thought. *Wham, bam, thank you, ma'am.* He couldn't believe it. No long speech. Nothing. He just sat there staring at the two tens in his hand. He figured he had to say something. "Well, gee, Dad, I – "

"Quiet!" Mr. Casale cut him off. "I want to hear this." He leaned forward in his chair, arms on his knees, and stared at the TV. Newscaster John Daly was announcing the indictment of a Soviet spy. *"Rudolf Abel is charged with three counts of divulging U.S. defense secrets from his Brooklyn apartment . . ."*

Eddie didn't have to be told twice. He pocketed the money and headed for the door, on his way to Dick's. He laughed to himself as he conjured up John Daly reporting, *"It has just been confirmed there will be a party in Bayside Saturday night."* Yeah, man.

SEVEN

OH WHAT A NIGHT

7 PM:
Kate Brody, Judy Bender, and Barbara Saunders arrived early to help Eddie get the basement ready for the party. Eddie still referred to the room as "the basement," although it became "the party room" to his parents when they finished it with a dropped ceiling, wood-paneled walls and a tile floor several years ago. Mrs. Casale wasn't too pleased with Eddie nailing several eight by ten glossies of people like Elvis Presley and Little Richard onto the expensive paneling. Likewise, Eddie wasn't happy about his mother's addition of an eleven by fourteen color portrait of The Virgin Mother with a Bleeding Heart.

Mrs. Casale had covered the ping-pong table with a white sheet and left stacks of paper cups and plates ready for use. Also, there were numerous trash bins and ash trays scattered around the room. The girls filled a dozen plates with potato chips, pretzels, popcorn and pork rinds, the only "food" Eddie bought. It cost him six dollars. He spent the rest of the money his father gave him on new records, fourteen of them, which he put into the 78 rpm Wurlitzer juke box. The old Wurlitzer, with the multi-colored bubbling lights, was a gift from his parents on Eddie's sixteenth birthday, as part of Mr. and Mrs. Casale's on-going crusade to keep their son at home.

When the girls finished with the snacks, they started going through Eddie's extensive record collection, which included some 45 rpms and several long-playing albums, looking for their current most-favorite songs – those with lyrics expressing their present feelings. Since the old juke box held only twenty-four records, the night's music would be supplemented with the new Motorola Hi-Fi, which was on a stand next to the Wurlitzer.

7:30 PM:

The juke box was fixed to play all the records automatically or by specific selections, with no money required.

Eddie pressed the buttons, selecting some of his favorite songs, while waiting for his friends to start drifting in.

8 PM:

The sound of Buddy Knox singing *Party Doll* greeted the first arrivals, which, as usual, were mostly the girls. Even those who had regular boyfriends always arrived at the parties by themselves, with guys usually trailing in later.

According to plan, Chuck Hoffman and Kenny Fletcher made an elaborate display of coming in the back door, which opened onto the entrance to the basement, with a case of beer each. That was for the benefit of Mr. Casale, who, with a clear view of the entranceway from his easy chair, kept a vigil on arrivals by peering over the top of the newspaper he was pretending to read.

"The rest of the beer, five more cases, is in the trunk of Buffalo's car," Hoffman said. "In a little while he'll pull in the driveway an' tap on the window. Then we'll pull 'em in."

As each guy arrived, a bottle of booze or wine was removed from under his shirt or inside his pants and placed on the table. Johnny Logan came in carrying two ten-pound bags of ice cubes. They were dumped over the beer cans in the utility sink in the small laundry room at the far end of the basement.

8:30 PM

The surprise of the evening was Mike Mancuso showing up with sexy Gloria Cooper on his arm, and the news that they just started going steady. Gloria was not one of the regulars, but everyone knew her, especially the guys. She was wearing his old high school ring on a gold chain around her neck. Mike even had a blue sport jacket on for the occasion. Gloria was poured into a tight white off-the-shoulder crepe dress, which clung to her every curve. The slit up the side, to mid-thigh, showed more leg than a Copacabana chorus girl. The guys just stared, while the girls tilted their heads together and shielded their mouths with their hands as they spoke. Mancuso was carrying a big brown paper bag with two packages of potato chips protruding from the top.

"Shit," Eddie said, "we got a lotta that stuff."

"Like hell ya do," Mancuso said with a smile. "We're celebratin' Italian style tonight." He took the chips and threw them on the table. Then he reached in the bag and pulled out a gallon of homemade *Guinea* red.

Eddie watched Gloria go over to the far corner of the room with Mike. She had a big round ass that rolled and swayed when she walked, like Marilyn Monroe in *Niagara.* The material of her dress was pulled so tight he could see the outline of her panties.

8:45 PM

Eddie heard his name called. He looked over to see Brenda Manzi smiling and waving at him as she came down the steps. He glanced back at Gloria. She was just lowering herself onto a bridge chair, swinging one leg over the other, the slit in her skirt exposing a shapely thigh. She shook her head, fluffing out her lustrous red hair, and leaned in close to whisper something in Mike's ear. Her big breasts, half-exposed from the top of the low-cut dress, brushed against his arm as she moved.

Eddie looked back at Brenda, who was walking up to him. At five-foot-seven, she was a big girl, running towards heavy. With a long face, spotted with adolescence pockmarks, she was just shy of pretty. But, what she lacked in facial features, she more than made up for in other areas. Brenda had long shapely legs and full breasts – what the guys called a *good body* – and was making the most of it tonight. She didn't have any slits in her tight navy blue skirt, but it was short enough – just above the knee – to show evidence of the shapely thigh above. Her powder blue blouse was unbuttoned daringly enough to expose signs of an exciting cleavage. Her normally dark brown eyes seemed even darker, perhaps due to the hint of makeup, and they were obviously set on Eddie.

Oh, what the hell, Eddie thought, Penny's history. Brenda may not be the cutest chick in the room, but she sure looks hot tonight. He walked up to greet her, returning her smile.

"Hi there," Brenda gushed, moving in very close. "This is for you." She thrust a flat package, which was obviously a record, into his hands. "A belated birthday gift." Eddie opened the envelope. It was *Happy, Happy Birthday Baby* by The Tune Weavers, one of the newest hit recordings.

"Hey, thanks a lot. I love this song."

"Yeah, me too," Brenda said. "And, it's fitting, too, you know? So's this." She leaned in even closer, her breasts pressing against his chest and, without warning, kissed him full on the lips. Eddie drew back at first, a little surprised at her boldness, then thought of her tits against his body. He moved in, putting an arm around Brenda's shoulders, and pressed close again, returning the kiss. They separated, Eddie a bit flushed – and flustered.

"Er, yeah, well, thanks again for the record an', er, the kiss, too," Eddie managed.

"You're welcome," Brenda purred. "But you have to promise to dance only with *me* when this song plays. Ok?" She gazed into his eyes, again rubbing up close to him. Eddie, caught up in the moment, just nodded his head and moved in for another kiss.

Suddenly, there was a commotion at the top of the stairs. Eddie pulled back and ran off to see what was happening. Brenda, standing in the middle of the room with her hands on her hips, stomped her foot in anger and disappointment.

"OUCH! TAKE IT EASY, YA FUCKIN' GUYS!" Cootie's deep, resonant voice bellowed down the steps. "I CAN'T FUCKIN' BEND, YA KNOW!" Then in a much softer, more respectful tone, he said, "Gee, I'm sorry, Mrs. Casale, I didn't see ya standin' there. I was just ova'come with pain an' didn't realize what I was sayin'.

Ox Zarora, holding Cootie by his cast-enclosed legs, came backing down the narrow cellar staircase, while Bo carried the guest of honor by the shoulders. Cootie, his face white with pain, was biting his knuckles to keep from cursing again, as his body banged and bumped from the wall on one side to the banister on the other.

"Over there," Bo said when they reached the basement. They carried Cootie to the other side of the room, and propped him against the wall between a small table and the juke box. He immediately reached inside the front of his cast and pulled out two flat-shaped pint bottles of Four Roses. He put one on the table, opened the other, and took a long swallow. As the whiskey went down his throat, color returned to his face. A third of the bottle was empty.

"*Awright!*" Cootie exclaimed, wiping his mouth with the sleeve of his freshly pressed white shirt. "I shoulda had that *before* comin' down those fuckin' steps."

9 PM:
Although no one was dancing yet, Dan Manning and Dancer Bob Larkin were finally getting things rolling by standing around the juke box and singing along with Chuck Berry's *Too Much Monkey Business.*

Same thing, every day
Gettin' up, goin' to school
No need of me complainin'
My objections overruled

All the parties usually started the same way. The girls sat on one side of the room talking; the guys stood around drinking. Mike and Gloria were the only exception, still sitting together in the corner. However, even Mike was spending more time with his lips wrapped around the mouth of the wine jug instead of around his girl's. Buffalo Larry Baker showed up, and the rest of the beer was lowered through the back window. Al Chavello came in with two more bags of ice cubes, and the second wash basin in the laundry room was filled, too. Hopefully, there would be enough cold beer until the end of the party.

Finally, Dancer got things hopping, as always. He grabbed Big Judy and started doing the Lindy to Carl Perkins' *Boppin' The Blues.*

Brenda kept trying to get Eddie's eye, but he purposely avoided looking her way. He was having second thoughts about getting involved with her. She seemed to kiss pretty good, he thought, and those boobs . . . but . . . well, hmmm, who knows. The night's young. He still had almost a third of a bottle of Thunderbird to finish, then – *well, we'll see.* Eddie put the quart bottle to his lips and took a long swallow of the cheap sweet yellowish wine. He remembered the silly rhyme they used to chant when he and his friends first started drinking the stuff:

What's the word? Thunderbird.

What's the price? Thirty twice.

Hey, for sixty cents a quart, how could you beat it? His thoughts were interrupted by a tap on the shoulder. He turned and saw Diane Roth standing there. "Hi," she said. "Sorry we're late, but we had to eat with the family first. You know, with my aunt and uncle coming over and all."

Eddie looked at her, puzzled.

"So what? That's ok," he said.

"Well," Diane said, "remember? I wanted you to meet my cousin, Ginny Marcessi."

"Oh, yeah, that's right. Great." He looked around. "Where is she?

"I'm right here." The voice came from behind Diane. Although she was just an average-sized teenager, Diane had somehow managed to block her cousin completely from view.

Ginny was that small, only four-foot-eleven, and just under ninety pounds. Everything was dark about her – her hair, her eyes, her complexion. She even had on dark clothes: a charcoal black pleated skirt, with a simple grey silk blouse buttoned to the neck. But, when she stepped around Diane, and smiled up at Eddie, the entire room seemed to brighten, and Eddie felt like he was hit by a lightning bolt from Zeus. Ginny had black curly hair, which fell down to her waist in wave upon wave, like ripples in the darkest sea. Her eyes were big, round, almost the size of saucers in a doll's tea set, and a deep dark green. But it was her smile that overshadowed everything else – a smile that struck Eddie dumb. He just couldn't stop staring at her. And Ginny stared right back. Much later, they would talk about love at first sight, but for now they were speechless. Almost everyone in the room, at least the more sober ones, was aware of what was happening – and they were enjoying the show. After all, he was over a foot taller than her. Brenda wasn't laughing, though. She wasn't even smiling.

Eddie realized he still held the bottle of wine. He reached behind him to place it on the table, without taking his eyes from Ginny. Bo, coming up next to his friend, signaled the rest of the room with a wink, then quickly pulled the table aside. Eddie released the bottle into thin air and it crashed to the floor. He still didn't turn away from Ginny. He was only half conscious of the laughter around him. The broken bottle, the comments of "Mutt and Jeff," the laughing. Nothing mattered except this doll-like creature in front of him.

Somehow, through the seemingly dense fog which had engulfed his brain and deadened his senses, Eddie recognized Elvis' voice coming from the juke box. He couldn't believe his good fortune. He was sure it was an omen.

"Do ya wanna dance?" he said, in the way of a greeting, looking deep into her eyes. He held out his arms, moving as if in a trance.

Ginny nodded, slid easily into his arms, and rested her head just below his chest. Together they moved slowly to the soft romantic sound of Elvis singing:

Love me tender, love me sweet
Never let me go
You have made my life complete
And I love you so

10 PM:

Eddie and Ginny danced through four consecutive records, all slow, romantic songs. By now, a few other guys, fueled with alcohol, made it to the dance floor with their girls.

When The Cadillacs started singing *Speedo,* Ginny and Eddie backed off from doing the Lindy. She said she wanted to sit with her cousin for a while, and talk to some of the other girls she had just met. She noticed the disappointment in his face as she started to move away. She quickly turned back, moving in close again. She stood on her tip-toes and kissed him briefly on the cheek.

"Don't worry," she said with a mischievous grin. "I won't forget about you while I'm gone." She started to turn away.

Eddie grabbed her by the arm and pulled her gently back, lowering his head to hers as she turned. He kissed her hard and long on the lips. "There's somethin' to remember me even more," he said as their lips parted.

Ginny looked surprised, then her smile returned. "You know, Eddie Casale," she said softly. "I really like you." She turned and headed over to where the other girls were sitting.

Eddie watched her go, marveling at the way she moved, a small package of curves and curls. "Hey!" he called after her loud enough to be heard above the sound of the music. She turned and looked at him. So did most of the other kids in the room. Eddie didn't care.

"Me, too, Ginny Marcessi," he said with a smile. "Me, too."

Eddie headed over to the table with the wine and whiskey, which was where most of the guys were still hanging out. They were waiting for him.

"Meeeee, tooooo," Leo Silverman said, drawing out the words for emphasis. "Now, ain't that just tooooo, tooooo, sweet."

"Kissy, kissy, kissy, kissy" Joe Ross chimed in, puckering his lips like a blowfish.

"She's the perfect size for ya," Johnny Logan added. "She don't even have ta get on her knees to give ya a blow job."

Instantly, Eddie's smile faded. His face reddened, tightened in anger. The guys, still laughing at Logan's wisecrack, were pretty drunk and didn't notice the change in their friend. But Bo stopped laughing and put his bottle on the table.

Suddenly, Eddie lunged at Logan. He grabbed him by the throat with his left hand and shoved him against the wall. "I'll kill ya, ya sonofabitch," he snarled, throwing a punch to his face with his right fist.

Eddie's swing was stopped midway by Bo's huge ham-like hand. Eddie tried to pull away, but Bo only tightened his grip on his friend's forearm.

"Cool down, cool down," Bo said in a low, calm voice. "He didn't mean nothin' by it. He just had too much to drink. We all did. Ya dig?"

Eddie looked at Bo, then back at Logan, who was still pressed against the wall with the hold on his throat. His face was turning white, as he gasped for breath. He tried to say something, but couldn't get the words out.

"Here, man, have a drink," Bo said, holding up a bottle of Thunderbird with one hand, while still gripping Eddie's arm with the other. He was smiling that easy smile of his. Eddie felt his anger subsiding. "Well, take the fuckin' bottle," Bo said. "I ain't gonna spoon-feed ya, ya know." Bo knew that Eddie had to let go of Logan's throat to take the bottle, since his other arm wasn't moving anywhere.

Eddie released Logan and grabbed the bottle. As he put it to his lips, Bo let go of his other arm. Eddie took a long swallow, then smiled at Bo. He gave him a diminutive nod. Bo winked.

The color returned to Logan's face as he rubbed his neck. "Christ, man, I didn't know ya felt that heavy about the chick," he said. "It was a bad joke. I'm sorry, ok? Ya don't have ta go fuckin' bananas."

"Hey, I over reacted, I guess," Eddie said. "I'm sorry, too. Here, buddy, have a drink." He passed the bottle to his friend. Soon, they were standing arm-in arm, singing along with Little Richard:

I got the heeby jeebies
And feel so sad
I got the heeby jeebies
Why you make me mad

11 PM:

Four couples were doing the Lindy to Joe Turner's *Shake, Rattle and roll,* but one person was dominating the floor – Gloria Cooper. Mancuso had finally consumed enough wine for Gloria to get him dancing.

He was holding his own, but Gloria was really ripping it up. With long legs swinging, and flaming hair swirling, she shimmied and shook, bopped and bounced, her movements pulling her dress even tighter, as if testing the manufacturer's warranty for stitching.

About halfway through the record, the other couples stopped dancing, formed a semi-circle, clapped hands in time with the beat, and joined everyone else in watching Gloria pulsate to the music. Mancuso, breathing heavy, finally got tired and gave up. With a wave of the hand, he muttered, "Go, baby, go," and returned to his half-finished jug of wine.

In addition to the clapping hands, the on-lookers started singing along with the record:

Shake, rattle and roll
Shake, rattle and roll
You don't do nothin'
To satisfy my soul

Her audience's enthusiasm goaded Gloria into a greater frenzy. It was like the music entered her body, absorbed through her pores, each beat causing her to writhe even more. Then she did something that some of the guys had seen only once before, at Minsky's Burlesque in Bayonne, New Jersey. With her eyes closed, and the tip of her tongue protruding from her moist red lips, Gloria put one hand behind her head, the other on the curve of her ass. She bent low, grinding her hips, and when she jutted her chest forward her tits nearly popped out of the top of her dress.

Cootie was watching along with all the other guys from his spot between the table and the juke box. He took a swig from his bottle, finishing off the last of his Four Roses, and missed the table when he went to put it down. It broke on the floor. Gloria did a final bump and grind, and the record ended.

"Lesh dance," Cootie slurred, reaching out for Gloria. He pushed himself off the wall, wavered momentarily, then tried to step forward, grabbing for her arm. With his arm outstretched, he looked like a tree with a solitary branch falling to the ground.

"Timber!" Eddie yelled, as he watched Cootie start to go over. He fell flat on his face with a loud crunch. There was a sudden silence in the room. Even the juke box happened to be momentarily still. Ox ran over, grabbed Cootie under the armpits and yanked him up. His eyes were closed, blood oozed from his nose. One eye opened, then the other. He wiped the blood off his nose with the sleeve of his white shirt, then looked around the room, trying to focus.

"I need anotha fuckin' drink!" he bellowed.

Everyone started talking and laughing at once, while *All Shook Up* by Elvis Presley came up on the juke box. Ox pushed Cootie back against the wall, this time propping him up with a long-handled broom, And Buffalo put a bottle of Seagram's 7 in his hand.

MIDNIGHT

The floor was full with couples slow-dancing as The Six Teens sang *A Casual Look.* Hank Coleman finally started dancing with his girlfriend, Kate. Even Bo was out there, moving awkwardly, trying desperately not to step on Barbara Saunders' feet. When it came to fighting, he was quick, sure and smooth. When dancing, he was clumsy, uncertain of how to move, out of step with the music. He figured it had something to do with the fact that he loved a good fight, but hated dancing. He did it just to please the girl, to get her to stop busting his balls. Like now. Between Barbara, and Big Judy, he had been asked to dance at least ten times since the party started. It was Barbara who finally wore him down. She had been after him for two years, so she had plenty of experience. She waited for him to have just the right amount of booze, and knew what records he liked. This one was one of his favorites, and she was whisper-singing the words in his ear:

A casual look a little wink
Can reveal just what you think
Don't be shy, don't even sigh
For you are my guy, you are my guy

Barbara carried a snapshot of Bo in her wallet. Bo was glancing back over his shoulder at the camera. She had pasted across the top the song title, *A Casual Look,* cut out from *Hit Parade Magazine.*

Eddie looked over Ginny's head at Bo and smiled. His friend looked so stiff. Maybe I can't out-fight him, but I sure can out-dance him, Eddie thought. He swung Ginny around, picked her up, twirled, then finished in a sweeping back-over dip, all in several smooth motions. She looked up at him and smiled. Eddie felt great. He had been dancing with Ginny all night. She was light as a feather, and followed his every move. She made him feel like Fred Astaire, she was his Ginger Rogers. Eddie never wanted to let her go. He was glad that it was that time of night when the juke box was set to play only slow-song records. "Are ya happy?" he asked softly, as they paused between records, still holding hands.

"I've never been happier," she murmured. She brought his hand up and pressed it against her smooth cheek. The whirring of the old Wurlitzer's mechanism could be heard selecting the next record and delivering it to the turntable. By the time the music started again, Eddie and Ginny were snuggled together, their arms around each other, his cheek resting on the top of her head. They stood in one spot, swaying gently to the sensual beat of *Happy, Happy Birthday Baby.* Suddenly, his arm was jerked roughly away from Ginny.

"Hey! This is *our* song. Remember?"

"What the – "

Annoyed, Eddie turned to face a wild-eyed Brenda.

"You bastard!" she snarled, her face contorted with anger. "You promised you'd only dance with me to this song." Brenda was swaying as she spoke, but not with the music. She was obviously drunk.

Eddie glanced at Ginny. She looked confused. He turned back to Brenda. "Look, I never promised ya anything," he explained. "Now, beat it. I'm dancin' with Ginny." He stepped in front of Brenda, shoving her aside with his hip, and took Ginny's hand.

"You lying bastard!" she spat, pulling Eddie back with one hand and shoving Ginny roughly with the other. "That's our song. I gave you the record!"

Now, Eddie was really pissed off. He glanced at Ginny again. She was getting angry, too. Her complexion had turned a shade darker. Her eyes were riveted on Brenda. Eddie went over to the juke box, turned it off, opened it, and pulled the record from its slot. He came back and handed it to Brenda. "I don't want it. I'm givin' it back. Now get the fuck away from me." He stepped in front of her again, giving her another hip-shove.

"You bastard! Brenda screamed, going wild. She swung the record and smashed it over his head. It shattered to pieces. She turned to Ginny. "And you, you little bitch, I'll smack the - " Brenda swung open handed.

Ginny moved fast. She grabbed Brenda's arm with two hands, one on the wrist, the other on the elbow, twisted around in a flash, and flipped the much larger girl over her hip. Brenda landed on her back with a loud thud, looked up in shock, then covered her eyes and cried like a baby.

Joan Ford and Big Judy came running over. "We'll take care of her," Joan said. "She just had too much to drink. She'll be ok in the morning, and sorry as hell." The girls helped their friend back to the chairs.

Diane came over to congratulate Ginny. "It's tough being half Irish and half Italian," Diane joked. "I don't know if I should be proud or embarrassed."

Kate told Eddie that she was really upset that he got hit with the record. He told her it didn't hurt at all. "I'm not talking about your head, stupid. I really like that song." She laughed and walked off.

Eddie laughed, too. He felt like hot shit. It was the first time that two girls had fought over him.

Conversations and laughter picked up where they left off, drinking resumed, and the music came back on. The party was back in full swing.

"Where the hell did ya learn *that*?" Eddie asked Ginny. It's judo, ain't it?"

"Yeah," Ginny said. "My dad showed me how to do it. He said I needed something to make up for my size. Now let's dance . . ." She grinned, and took his hand. ". . . before I flip you, too."

Eddie stopped. He became very serious. He looked into Ginny's eyes, holding her face with both hands. "Ya don't have to," he said softly. "I've *already* flipped for ya." He leaned down and kissed her. And, for the first time, their tongues touched.

1 AM

All the guys were at least a little high, some were down and out drunk, but they were grumbling that there was nothing left to drink. All the bottles – Seagram's, Four Roses, Three Feathers, Smirnoff's, Gilbey's, Thunderbird – were empty. The only alcohol remaining was five cans of Schaefer beer and the red wine which Mancuso was still drinking. Every few minutes he'd take a break from making out with Gloria, lift the big jug to his shoulder, and take a long swig, like a hillbilly drinking moonshine.

"Hey, something doesn't look kosher," Silverman said, as Eddie was replacing records in the juke box, adding more slow songs. "Watch this." He pointed towards the laundry room. A moment later a drunken Joe Ross emerged, wiping his mouth. He staggered over to Joan Ford. "He's been doing that every five minutes, and he's not drinking beer," Silverman said. "That sonofabitch must have a bottle stashed."

"Let's take a look," Eddie said. Shadow Silverman followed Eddie to the laundry room. It was a small cubicle with a double sink and a washer and dryer on the right, and a gas furnace on the left. There wasn't much room to move around, much less hide anything. It took the boys less than a minute to find what they were looking for.

"Here it is!" Eddie said, reaching into the front of the dryer and pulling out a bottle of Seagram's, about a quarter full. "In the most obvious fuckin' place, too."

"No one ever said he was smart, just sneaky." Shadow was angry. "Let's give him hell," he said, starting for the door.

"No, wait!" Eddie grabbed his friend by arm and pulled him back. "He's so fuckin' drunk it won't matter. We'll never get through to him by talkin'. Let's teach him a lesson he won't forget."

"You've got an evil grin, Eddie. Are you thinking what I think you're thinking?"

Eddie nodded, his grin widening. "Go get an empty bottle," he said.

Shadow ducked out of the room and returned a moment later. They took turns pissing into an empty Seagram's bottle. When they were finished, they held the two bottles up to the light. There was much more piss than there was whiskey.

"Sorry," Shadow said, "it was all that beer I drank. I *really* had to go. You think he'll know the difference?"

"No way," Eddie said. He poured a little whiskey into the piss bottle to give it the right smell, then replaced the "special blend" in Ross' hiding place. He started to leave. This time, he was stopped by Shadow.

"Where are you going with that bottle?" Shadow asked. "If you bring it out there, you'll have ten guys fighting over it, when it looks to me like there's only about two good swallows left."

Eddie looked at his friend. The two boys grinned at each other. "I do believe yer right," he said. "I'm glad to see they're teachin' ya something at Queens College." Eddie took the first hit, then Shadow drained the bottle.

In the main room, Eddie and Shadow positioned themselves against a wall a few feet from the laundry room to await Ross' next visit. Eddie was a little high, especially after that last long drink of whiskey, but not nearly as drunk as he usually got at parties. Because he had been dancing all night, his guzzling of Thunderbird was reduced considerably. Ginny came over and joined them.

"Where've you been?" she asked, slipping an arm around Eddie's waist. "I've missed you."

Eddie put his arm around her shoulder and pulled her against him. "Takin' care of business," he said. "Me an' Shadow have been workin' on a new formula for soberin' people up. If it works, we'll package it an' make a fortune."

Shadow laughed. "Yeah, and it's real cheap to produce, too." Eddie cracked up.

Ginny gave each of them a quizzical look. "What are you – ?"

"Hold on!" he said, spotting Ross weaving towards the laundry room. "Watch this first, then I'll explain."

Ross made it to the door, stopped, looked around surreptitiously, then slipped inside.

It was another few minutes before Ross emerged from the laundry room, white faced and red eyed.

There were tears rolling down his cheeks. The front of his yellow sport shirt and the lap of his brown slacks were soiled with vomit. He tried to walk normally, but after the first step he began retching again. He covered his mouth with his hand and made a beeline for the stairs and the back door.

Eddie and Shadow were cracking up as they watched their very sick friend run out. They shook hands, congratulating each other. Eddie explained to Ginny what they did, and why.

"Yuk! How could you?" she said, making a face. "That's disgusting." Then, with a trace of a smile coming to her lips, she added: "But he certainly had it coming."

1:30 AM

Eddie darkened the room by turning off most of the lights. He set the juke box for "automatic repeat" on everyone's favorite make-out record. For the rest of the night, Fats Domino would be providing romantic background music by singing:

I'm in the mood for love
Simply because you're near me
And baby when you're near me
I'm in the mood for love

All the regular-dating couples, plus those getting together just for the evening, settled down to do some serious making out. Kenny Fletcher and Joan Ford, Diane was with Al Chavello, Dancer and Big Judy got together, Shadow hit on a girl from Bay Terrace, and a new girl, Carol Michaels, cornered Chuck Hoffman. Even Barbara Saunders finally maneuvered Bo into a chair. Kate was on Hank Coleman's lap, but he was alternating between guzzling Schaefer beer and nodding out. Buffalo Baker, eyeing the passed out Brenda in a corner chair, plopped down on her lap, kissing and groping her dormant body.

Eddie led Ginny over to a chair in the opposite corner, and pulled her down onto his lap. She wrapped her arms around his neck and snuggled tight. The feel of her tight firm breasts against his chest excited him. They weren't big, but they weren't small, either. Eddie, who considered himself to be the world's number one "Tit Man," thought they were perfect for her size. However, he hoped to get his hands on them sometime soon for a much closer examination.

Ginny moved slightly to get more comfortable, her buttocks squirming deeper into his lap. Eddie felt his cock rise to the occasion. He leaned over and kissed her, pushing his tongue into her partially open mouth. She responded with a gentle touch of her own tongue. Eddie had one hand on the curve of her thigh, which he squeezed gently through her cotton skirt. The other hand found naked flesh, where the back of her silk blouse pulled out from the skirt. He was making circular motions with his thumb. His cock was now demanding attention, poking angrily into the left cheek of Ginny's ass. She shifted a bit, squirmed again. Her fingers danced down his back, over his spine, moved lower. She nibbled his lower lip. Eddie, breathing hard, moved his hand up her bare back, inching towards her bra strap.

Suddenly, the mood was broken by a shrill scream from across the room. Ginny pulled back. Eddie looked up, catching his breath. Gloria was on her feet. The front of her white dress was covered with an ugly purple stain. She was looking down at it, hands to her head, screaming. Mancuso, still sitting, was leaning forward, as regurgitated red wine spewed from his mouth.

"My beautiful new dress!" Gloria shouted. Tears rolled down her cheeks, streaking her makeup. "It's ruined! It's ruined!"

Kate and Judy rushed over and tried to calm Gloria down, and started to help her upstairs to the bathroom. Before she left, she ripped Mancuso's ring from around her neck and threw it at him.

"You disgusting pig!" she shouted, weaving slightly. "And to think I was going to do it with you tonight. I must have been crazy."

Eddie and Bo, who had come over to help their friend, looked at each other, then stared after Gloria. They watched the sensuous movements unique to a sexy woman in a tight dress climbing stairs. They looked down at Mancuso, who was swallowing hard, trying to get himself under control. "Asshole," they said in unison.

"I doan uner'shanit," Mancuso, tried to explain. "We were kishin' den my mout jush fillup."

"Don't worry about it," Eddie said. "Just take it easy for now. We'll getchya to yer car in a little while."

He went and found one of his mother's clean towels in the laundry room and threw it on the floor to cover up Mike's mess.

Kate came back down the steps. "Gloria needs a ride," she called out. "Can someone take her home?"

Five guys made a mad dash for the stairs, banging into each other, pushing and shoving. Even Hank Coleman, with a lewd grin, staggered over, but Kate threw a mean body block and sent him sprawling back into his chair. He immediately nodded off, again.

Eddie turned, and saw Ginny standing next to him, hands on her hips. She was feigning annoyance, but there was a trace of a smile on her face.

"Oh, no! No, not me!" Eddie said, holding up his hands in a show of innocence. "No way!"

"Well, I'm glad to hear that," Ginny said. "You're about the only one not running for the door."

"That's right," Eddie said in all seriousness. "I don't have a car."

"Oh you bum!" Ginny exclaimed, slapping him playfully on the arm. They both laughed.

Four of the boys returned from upstairs, grumbling that it wasn't fair because Chuck Hoffman was so big.

The tall, powerfully-built German, had scooped Gloria up in his arms and ran full speed to his car, making his getaway to the curses of the other guys, and the disappointment of Carol.

2 AM

The excitement had gotten everyone on their feet, and it seemed like a good time for the party to break up. Diane came over to collect her cousin, then waited by the steps to allow Eddie and Ginny some privacy for their good-night kisses. They exchanged phone numbers and reminded each other that they lived only a twenty-minute bus ride apart. Halfway up the stairs, Ginny turned back and threw Eddie a kiss with her hand. He caught it with pursed lips. She smiled, and left.

Eddie positioned himself by the bottom of the steps and reminded his friends to take empty bottles with them on the way out. "An' don't throw 'em in the *yard*," he kept repeating. "Take 'em with ya an' toss 'em down the block or somethin'."

Joan and Barbara gently slapped Brenda into consciousness. As they were helping her up the stairs, she turned, searched out Eddie with blurry eyes, and gave him the finger. Johnny Logan, not too sober himself, helped Mancuso to his car. However, Logan wasn't drunk enough to accept a ride home. He walked the ten blocks.

Buffalo Baker gave Kate a hand getting Hank up the stairs. Kate tried to get her boyfriend to spend the night on her couch but, as usual, he refused. He jumped into his customized Ford Fairlane, peeled rubber and roared down the street, nearly side-swiping several parked cars and a telephone pole.

Bo and Ox Zarora were the last to leave, telling Eddie it was another great party, even topping the last one. He smiled at his friends' approval.

Eddie took a quick look around the room. His smile vanished. *What a fuckin' mess,* he thought, shaking his head. *But what a fuckin' night! It's hard to imagine so much shit happening in such a short period of time, including falling in love. Wow!* He started for the steps, then froze. The juke box was still on. It had been changing selections again, and now a new song began playing. It was *Oh What A Night* by The Dells. It was freaky. *The fuckin' machine seems to have a mind of its own,* Eddie thought, feeling a chill go up his spine.

He went to turn it off. That's when he spotted Cootie, still propped against the wall, held tight by the broomstick. He was sound asleep.

"Hey, wait a minute," he shouted after Bo and Ox. "Ya forgot somethin'."

They came back down, saw Cootie, and cracked up laughing. Bo smacked him a few times to wake him up. "Fuck ya guys," Cootie mumbled, coming around. As they carried him out, he began singing what sounded like a Polish marching song at the top of his lungs. Eddie followed, shushing him all the way.

All the guys with cars had left. The only mode of transportation remaining was Ox's Indian motorcycle. They looked at each other and shrugged, picking up Cootie by each arm and lowering him on the back of the seat. The space between his cast-enclosed legs, however, was only wide enough for him to straddle the seat up to the knees. He had to be stuck on like an old clothespin.

Bo and Eddie watched Ox zigzag down the street, with Cootie, still singing at full volume, teetering dangerously from side to side.

"They'll make it," Bo said confidently. He turned and started across the street to his house. After a few steps, he stopped, looked back, and with an easy, knowing smile, said, "Somehow, with a little bit of luck, I think we'll all make it." He turned and left.

Before going in the house, Eddie stopped and

checked the backyard. Just as he thought. There were empty bottles scattered everywhere.

"Fuck it!" he said out loud. Tomorrow he'd face his father. For tonight, it was one hell of a party.

EIGHT

THE BIG BREAK

The first sign of serious trouble became apparent as soon as Eddie cracked open an eye Sunday morning, and peered at his clock radio. It was nine o'clock. Mrs. Casale had just woke him up to attend ten o'clock mass "with the family."

Shit, he thought, rubbing the sleepiness from his eyes. This is the first time she's done that in more than a year. Usually, she lets him sleep to the last minute, then gets him out on time for the last mass at noon. She must really be pissed off.

Wisely, he chose not to utter a word of complaint. Instead, he would play the role of "the good son" like David on *Ozzie and Harriet*. Perhaps, he reasoned, he could undo some of the damage of the night before. At least he didn't have his usual monster hangover – just a slight headache – and could function properly and think clearly. He would start by getting right up, dressing neatly in slacks and sport shirt, and rushing downstairs for church.

Unconsciously, he tweaked the hard-on under his Jockey shorts, and felt the familiar shiver of pleasure race through his body. It throbbed, demanding more attention.

"Oh, no," Eddie told it. "Not today. No way. I gotta be on time for mass. Yer not gonna win this time."

Resolutely, he swung his legs over the side of the bed. The movement caused his boner's sensitive head to rub against the cotton of his pants. His body quivered with pleasure again.

Oh, yeah? his cock seemed to be saying. *Feel*

that! Come on, Eddie, it won't take long. An' ya know how much better yer gonna feel, too.

Eddie's breath caught, and he moaned slightly. He started to lean back on the bed and reach for his cock. "No!" he shouted, suddenly jumping up. "This time I mean it."

As he stood, his hard-on poked its head out of the slit of his shorts. It seemed to be smiling up at him, tauntingly. He reached down to push it back in, before heading for the bathroom, determined to piss it into limpness. When his fingers touched the hot throbbing flesh, sparks flew.

Gotcha! his cock said with a sigh, as Eddie's fingers caressed it more firmly, squeezing gently, his forefinger finding and stroking the soft flesh-spot beneath its head.

"Oh God!" Eddie moaned, falling back on the bed, jerking his hand frantically.

When Eddie finally made it downstairs, after several warnings to "hurry up or else I'm coming up with the spoon" from his mother, he found his family waiting impatiently by the back door. It was nine forty-five.

"It's about time," Mrs. Casale said, starting for the door. "If we get there too late all the good seats up front will be taken."

So what, Eddie felt like saying. *Whadaya gonna miss? You've seen the same Mass a trillion times and it ain't changed yet.* Instead, he said, "I'm sorry. We'll be there in plenty of time if we hurry." He was walking on eggshells, careful not to mention anything connected with last night's party. He avoided his father's eyes completely.

"Well, I have no idea why it's so hard for you in the mornings," his mother said. "God only knows what takes you so long to get ready."

Eddie stopped short. He felt his face redden. *Could she . . . ?* He glanced at his mother. She was looking straight ahead. *Nah. No way could she know. Right?*

However, he suddenly realized he had something else to worry about. They were leaving by the back door, not the front. Another step or two would put him face-to-face with the backyard. *Oh, boy.*

Eddie stepped outside, holding his breath. It took several seconds for his eyes to adjust to the brightness of the morning sunshine. When he finally blinked his vision into focus, he surveyed a spotless lawn, not a bottle or beer can in sight. Holy shit! Eddie thought. The old man must have been up at the crack of dawn stuffing brown paper bags again. He let his breath out slowly, and shot a quick look at his father. Mr. Casale's face was impassive, just the slightest trace of a smile playing on his lips.

Eddie glanced at his mother and sister, Anna. They, too, sported the same strange look. He became nervous, and quickened his pace. He was suddenly in a hurry to reach the sanctuary of the church, and perhaps enlist God as an ally. He was sure he was going to need some help.

For the first time in months, Eddie walked through the front doors of St. Joseph's Roman Catholic Church and didn't exit immediately through the side doors. He genuflected while making the sign of the cross before slipping into a pew alongside his family. He immediately fell to his knees on the hardwood kneeler, ignoring the pain, and, with hands steepled in front of him, prayed.

"Oh my God, I am heartily sorry for having offended thee . . . " He started with the Act of Contrition, figuring that if he convinced God he was sorry for his sins he would be in a better bargaining position when he prayed for help in other things. However, he had forgotten most of the words after the opening line. He decided to try his luck with Mary. "Hail Mary, full of grace, the Lord is with thee, blessed art thou amongst woman . . . " Yeah! He remembered it all. Eddie said "Hail Marys" for his father not to be too mad. Then he prayed for his headache to go away. And, while he was at it, he slipped in a few prayers for a new Triumph motorcycle.

Back home, Eddie's faith in the power of prayer quickly faded. As soon as they walked in the door, Mr. Casale handed his son a sheet of yellow legal-size paper, then went into the living room to read the Sunday Journal-American.

Eddie stared at the sheet of paper. Printed across the top of the page in large letters were the words, PARTY INVOICE. Under that were two neat columns that read:

ITEM	***COST***
Backyard clean-up	*Mow lawn - 4 times*
Basement clean-up	*Take out garbage -2X*
Breaking of rules	*Grounded - 1 week*

Footnote: Since you will not be leaving the house, you will not need money. No allowance for one week.

PAYMENT BEGINS ON RECEIPT OF THIS INVOICE

Eddie stormed into the living room after his father. "Dad!" he almost shouted. "Is this some kind of joke, or what?"

Mr. Casale looked up from the newspaper, removed his reading glasses, and gave his son a piercing look. "Joke?" he asked. "Do you see me laughing?"

Oh, oh! It's whining time. "Aw, gee, Dad. Comeon. Huh? Please?"

"Very good," Mr. Casale said. "I can see you're learning to speak intelligibly in school."

"Comeon, Dad. Can't we at least talk about it?"

"Sure," his father said, laying the newspaper in his lap and folding his hands over it. Eddie began to see a ray of hope. It was quickly clouded out. "We can talk about it for as long as you like," Mr. Casale continued. "However, I must advise you that as a lawyer I receive forty dollars an hour for consultations. The cost will be added to your bill in the form of additional chores." He looked at his watch. "Ok, start talking."

Eddie's mouth hung open as he quickly assessed the situation. He decided to cut his losses before he got in any deeper.

"That's ok, forget about it," he said dejectedly, turning away, but not before noticing a satisfied smile breaking on his father's face just before Mr. Casale ducked behind the newspaper again.

The start of Eddie's one week house arrest was greeted with a text-book example of the infamous New York August weather. The hot and humid day was tailor-made for lounging on the beach, breezing along on the back of a motorcycle, or sitting in the balcony of an air-conditioned movie theater. It was a bitch, however, for mowing the lawn.

The Casales were just finishing their Sunday dinner of baked ziti with sausages. Eddie ripped apart a piece of Italian bread, forked the last sausage from the bowl, and stuck it between the two pieces of bread.

"That was great," he said. "I'm stuffed. I'll just take this for a snack for when I'm watchin' the ballgame. The Yankees are playin' the Red Sox."

"I don't think so," Mr. Casale said casually.

"Oh, yeah," Eddie insisted. "It's on the season schedule I got from Bayside Savings Bank."

"It may be on the Yankees' schedule, young man, but it's not on yours. You have an appointment with the lawn mower."

"Aw, gee whiz, Dad. In this hot sun?"

"It's the hot sun that makes the grass grow," Mr. Casale said. Then, with a slight lilt to his voice, he added, "along with a certain commodity that you seem to be full of. Now's a good time for the two of you to team up and fight back,"

Eddie, wide-eyed, gaped at his father. *Did he really say what I thought he said? Did he say I was full of shit?*

Eddie glanced at his mother, hoping that she caught the drift of his father's words, and would give her husband holy hell. She seemed oblivious, intent on clearing the dirty dishes from the table. However, his sister, Anna, picked up on their father's remark, and she had to use a napkin to suppress a giggle. Eddie, turning red with anger, glared at her.

"Oh, Momma," Anna began in a voice which was a little too animated, "is it ok if I don't help with the dishes today? It's so hot I'd like to pick up Marie and drive to the beach for a few hours.

"Of course, dear," Mrs. Casale replied.

"Thanks, Momma," Anna sang out. Then she looked around the room, saw no one was watching, and stuck her tongue out at her brother.

Eddie's short hairs bristled. He started for his sister, reaching out to grab her.

"Oh, Daddy!" she called out. Mr. Casale looked up. Eddie froze in mid-step, with an arm outstretched in the direction of his sister. "Would you please move your car so I can get mine out of the driveway?" she asked sweetly.

"Sure," Mr. Casale said. "Just let me know when you are ready to go." He looked at his son. "And what are you posing for?"

"Nuttin'," Eddie mumbled, relaxing a little. But he tensed up again when he heard Anna's taunting giggle.

"Well, get going, then," Mr. Casale ordered. The grass is getting higher by the minute."

Heading out the door, Eddie heard his mother caution her daughter to drive carefully, followed by the usual advice of "have fun and be good." That always cracked Eddie up. How the hell could you possibly do both? *Well,* Eddie reasoned, *if anybody could do it, my sister certainly could, the fuckin' square.*

Eddie stepped out of the back door and walked slam, bam into a wall of heat. The afternoon sun was so powerful he could see nothing but a white glare for several seconds. Gradually, the starkness faded into a sea of green which was the Casales' expansive backyard lawn. Eddie groaned. He had forgotten how big it actually was. He began sweating just looking at all that grass. *Christ,* he thought, *if ya put up goal posts ya could play a goddamn football game out there.*

The last time Eddie had mowed the lawn was in the summer of 1953, when he was thirteen. That was when he still had to do chores for his allowance. In July of that year, he had been invited to spend a few weeks at his cousin's beach house in Montauk Point. Eddie and his cousin, Jim, were about the same age, and good friends. It was a great summer, made even better by what had happened at home.

With Eddie gone, Mr. Casale had been faced with the prospect of mowing the lawn himself. He hadn't been looking forward to it.

Two neighborhood boys, armed with a lawn mower and hedge clipper, had passed by looking for work. Mr. Casale had hired them on the spot. They did such a good job, even gardening, pruning, and trimming, that he had kept them on a regular basis.

"Besides," he had told Eddie upon his return from Long Island, "I don't have to argue with them or listen to silly excuses. And, they really need the money. Their fathers can't afford to give them an allowance. That's the trouble with you. You don't realize how good you really have it. That's why you don't appreciate anything. When I was your age, I didn't have . . . "

And, for the next ten minutes Eddie had to listen to how hard his father had it, working all night making bread at the Silvercup Bakery in Long Island City to pay his way through college and law school.

Eddie had just sat there, thinking the lecture boring and repetitive, but nodding his head from time to time in an attempt to appear interested. One fact, however, had been made absolutely clear: he didn't have to mow the lawn anymore.

Eddie found the lawn mower in the back of the garage behind a couple of broken beach chairs and a set of snow tires. It was old and rusty. He wished he had one with a motor, like the fifteen-year-old kid his father had hired this year. The boy had invested in his own power mower, and serviced about seven or eight homes in the neighborhood. Mr. Casale had been impressed, calling the kid an "enterprising young man."

Well, fuck him and the power mower he rode in on, Eddie thought, as he pulled out the old clunker. It's kids like him who make it tough on guys like me.

By the time he dragged the mower onto the lawn, Eddie was already dripping with sweat. He tried pushing the mower, but the wheels and blades didn't turn. They were stuck tight with caked-on dried grass. He cursed the mower, and kicked it. Then, he cursed himself for kicking it. He was wearing open-toed sandals with no socks. His big toe began to throb. *Shit!*

Eddie got on his knees and tried to pull the dried grass from around the blades. He kept banging his knuckles. Now, both his hand and his foot were in pain, and he was getting angrier by the second.

Just then, Anna bounced out of the house, looking cool and jaunty. She was dressed for the seashore in a white and blue sun dress, and her long, black curly hair was pushed up under a floppy straw shade-hat, which was tied with a red ribbon under the chin. She was carrying a canvas beach bag, with a color picture of a sailor and the words "Ship Ahoy" in deep blue emblazoned on its side.

She smiled at him. He growled at her. She gaily pranced to her car, a new two-tone red and white Ford Crestline, humming loudly. He took a deep breath, and started counting to ten.

Eddie turned back to the grass-encrusted mower,

(one, two) forcing himself not to look at his sister.

"Wow, it's really a scorcher today," she sang out, getting into the car. He continued (three, four) cleaning the mower. She started the engine. "I can't wait to get to the beach and take a nice cool swim," she called through the open window. He yanked too hard at a clump of dried grass (five, six), and it suddenly broke free. His knuckles slammed into a blade (seven, eight), this time drawing blood. "Of course," she continued, "if *you* get too, toooo hot, you can always turn on the lawn sprinkler and run under it."

That did it! He jumped up. He put his left hand in the crook of his right arm, and, with clenched fist, raised it sharply from the elbow. It was a classic Italian gesture. "*Va fan culo*!" he snarled. "Fuck you!"

Anna's smile broadened. She was looking, not at Eddie, but, to the patio behind him. Eddie froze. Oh, no! he thought, as a wave of panic swept through him. *He had to move his car!* Eddie turned slowly. Sure enough. Mr. Casale was standing on the patio, hands on his hips, shooting daggers at him. With Anna's car idling, Eddie, his back to the house, hadn't heard his father come out.

She got me good this time, Eddie thought, as he watched his sister, still laughing, back out of the driveway after his father had moved his car. He immediately started formulating plans of retaliation. It was only those sinister thoughts which kept him going through the back-breaking drudgery of mowing the lawn.

Not counting getting the mower cleaned, it took Eddie over three hours to mow the lawn with only a couple of short breaks in between. And he couldn't even sneak a smoke. Mr. and Mrs. Casale had taken up positions on patio chairs under the shade of the huge umbrella with the cement base. His father, of course, knew he smoked, but Eddie could never do it in front of him. His mother just preferred to believe her son was a *Sen-Sen* addict, since he always seemed to be carrying those little packets of licorice-flavored breath fresheners.

After putting the mower away (without cleaning it) Eddie, his clothes soaked through with sweat and his hair matted to his head, plopped down on a patio chair. He couldn't remember ever being so exhausted.

"You look so hot," his mother said. "Why don't you turn on the sprinkler and run under it?"

Eddie snapped his head around to look at her. Was that a zinger? Eddie thought. Mrs. Casale, wearing sunglasses, was concentrating on her knitting. *Nah. It couldn't be . . . from my father, maybe, but not her.* He glanced quickly at his father.

Mr. Casale was leaning back in his chair, eyes closed to the sun. But, damn it, there was that faint smile playing on his lips again.

Eddie tried to relax, but he was too uncomfortable. He was wet, clammy, and his body had begun to ache. He had to go through this three more times? Shit!

"Dad?"

"What is it?"

"I was jus' thinkin'."

"That's an improvement."

"No, really. About me mowin' the lawn again. Maybe there's somethin' else I can do instead. After all, it's not fair to the kid ya hired. Ya know, losin' his job for four weeks when he needs the money so bad. Right?"

"Oh, that's ok," Mr. Casale said without opening his eyes. "It's nice of you to care about him, but don't worry. I'll still pay him. He just won't mow the lawn. You will. He can do the gardening and other yard work. Because you're right. It wouldn't be fair, especially when he needs the money to go to college. You know, some kids . . ."

"Ok, ok!" Eddie exclaimed, jumping up from his chair and storming towards the house. "Jus' don't start in with the lecture again. That's worse than mowin' the lawn."

After taking a cold shower, Eddie felt a little better. He lay down on his bed to rest. He thought of Ginny, and smiled. God, she was cute. A regular living doll. It would be a week before he would see her again. Damn! He couldn't wait.

Eddie looked around for something to read. He was too exhausted to dig the Playboy or Nugget out of the bottom drawer. He remembered the paperback book Bo had given him about a month ago.

"Ya gotta read this," Bo had said. It's really a great book."

"Does it have some good dirty parts like Tobacco Road*?" Eddie had asked with an eager smile.*

Bo had looked at his friend with disdain, shaking his head. "Man, don't be an asshole all yer life." Then he smiled, and punched him playfully on the arm. "Only kiddin'," Bo had said. "Read it. Ya'll love it. In fact, yer prob'ly the only other guy in the crowd who'll appreciate it."

That was all the encouragement Eddie had needed. "What's it about?" he had asked, flipping through the pages.

"I'm not gonna spoil it for ya," Bo had said with finality. And that was that.

Eddie retrieved the book from the drawer of his night table, and looked at it for the first time since that day. *On The Road* by Jack Kerouac. He turned to chapter one and read the first line: "I first met Dean not long after my wife and I split up."

Eddie was tired. He figured he would read until he nodded off to sleep. But by the end of page one he was wide awake. He read for the rest of the afternoon, and well into the night. He couldn't even remember turning his light on.

"Do you want something to eat?" Mrs. Casale

called from downstairs. Since they had already had their big dinner, Sunday evenings were always a catch-as-catch-can style of dining in the Casale household.

"No, thanks," Eddie yelled back, not taking his eyes from the book. "I'm still full from all that ziti."

A few minutes later Mrs. Casale knocked gently and entered Eddie's room. She placed a ham sandwich and a glass of milk on his night table. Then she reached over and put the back of her hand to his forehead.

"Are you feeling alright?" she asked with motherly concern. "You do feel a little warm."

"Yeah, sure, I'm fi – " Eddie stopped short, thinking fast. He let the book fall from his hands, and sighed. "Well, actually, I didn't want to say anything, but I've been havin' these, ya know, hot an' cold flashes. An' I get dizzy when I stand up. That's why I've been in bed all afternoon." He punctuated his report with a pitiful sounding moan.

Mrs. Casale leaned in, examining Eddie's eyes. "Maybe we should call the doctor," she said gravely.

"Er, I think I'll be ok in the mornin', Eddie said weakly. He paused, and sighed loudly, getting ready to deliver his big finale. "It's prob'ly jus' from mowin' that lawn in the heat. Ya know, must be a combination of sunstroke an' heat exhaustion."

He would have thrown in "heart attack" and "respiratory failure" too, but his mother certainly would have then rushed him to the emergency room of Queens General Hospital. At any rate, he prepared his audience for the punch line by moaning again, and squinting his eyes so tightly that they began to water.

"After all, it took me over three hours to cut all that grass with our little beat up old mower, while the kid with the power mower does it in less than an hour." Eddie got all the words out in one breath, then paused and waited. *Would she or wouldn't she?* There were several seconds of deadly silence. He was afraid to look at his mother.

"You're right," she said finally, nodding her head in agreement. "I'm going to speak to your father."

Eddie had to control himself to keep from jumping up and dancing around the bed. He successfully fought back a smile by biting down sharply on his tongue and causing real pain.

"Now, try and eat this sandwich," his mother continued. "I made it with nice fresh Wonder Bread. It'll make you feel better."

"I really can't, Mom. I got these stomach cramps, too."

"Well, first thing tomorrow I'll make you a nice big pot of chicken soup. If that doesn't make you feel better, then it's the doctor for sure."

"Aw, thanks, Mom. I'm sure yer chicken soup is all I need. An' some rest. I just feel so . . . " He broke off with another long sigh.

"Yes indeed. I certainly think your father went overboard this time," Mrs. Casale said with conviction as she left her son's room.

As soon as he heard his mother descend the stairs, Eddie shouted a silent "hooray" and wolfed down the sandwich and milk.

Smiling over the result of his impromptu con job, Eddie picked up the book and went back to reading about Dean Moriarty and his cool friends. I bet they'd be proud of me, he thought. He read to well past midnight, until he couldn't keep his eyes open any longer.

That night, he dreamt about him and Bo traveling the country, hitching rides and stealing cars, living on apple pie and ice cream, and rolling huge reefer cigarettes in Mexican marihuana fields, just like Dean and his friends in the book. When he awoke in the morning, he remained in bed until he devoured every last word of *On The Road.*

It was noontime when Eddie came downstairs, drawn by the good-cooking smells emanating from the kitchen.

"What's for lunch?" Eddie called out, bursting into the kitchen. "I could eat a braised horse . . . " He hesitated, watching his mother stirring a pot of soup. She turned towards him with a quizzical expression. Eddie continued, sliding smoothly into a voice which was suddenly much weaker, ". . . if I was feelin' better. But right now I could use some of yer chicken soup. It sure smells great."

Mrs. Casale studied her son through squinted eyes for several seconds. She tapped the wooden spoon slowly on the rim of the pot as she concentrated. Eddie stood there and fidgeted, and tried to look sick.

Finally, she came over and took his temperature again, touching the back of her hand to his forehead. "You don't have a fever," she said. "And, you look better than you did last night."

"Oh, I feel a little better," Eddie said. "I even managed to get the sandwich down last night, a little at a time." He looked at his mother and gave her a feeble smile. "Ya were right. I think it helped." His mother nodded with satisfaction. He was on a roll again.

"That's good," she said. "Now sit down. The soup's ready."

Eddie sat at the kitchen table, and his mother placed a big steaming bowl in front of him. He picked up his spoon and poked around the bowl of soup, but couldn't find any chicken. He glanced around and spotted a serving platter stacked with boiled chicken parts on the kitchen counter.

"Hey, Mom, ya forgot to put the chicken in," he said, getting out of his seat to retrieve the platter.

"No I didn't. I want you to eat only the soup for now, that's the most nutritious part anyway," Mrs. Casale advised. "You can have some chicken later if you're up to it."

"Right, Mom," Eddie mumbled, sitting back down. He used his spoon to push the repulsive sliced carrots and celery to the side, and spelled out "fuck you" with the alphabet macaroni floating on top.

After lunch, Eddie went down to the basement. It was always cool down there, even on hot August days. He would pass the time with his record collection, which dated back to 1952, and even included some pre-rock 'n' roll songs like Johnnie Ray singing *Cry* and Frankie Laine's *Mule Train.* He often played his records for hours, and would read the accompanying promotional material and record sleeves faithfully. He especially enjoyed checking out the other sides of the hit recordings, sometimes finding songs that were as good, or even better, than the hits. When everyone was playing *Earth Angel* by the Penguins, Eddie discovered *Hey Senorita* on the flip side, which soon became one of The Bayside Crowd's party favorites. And, he was able to pass along to his friends the fact that the group took its name from *Willie the Penguin* on the *Kools* cigarette pack.

Eddie decided to change some of the selections in the juke box, something he did every couple of weeks, and always after a party. He was proud of his collection, and always gave much thought to this project, being careful to maintain a balance between old and new, as well as slow and fast, songs. He removed three records he was tired of, and replaced them with *Little By Little* by Nappy Brown, *Ko Ko Mo* by Gene & Eunice, and *Any Way You Want Me* by Elvis Presley.

When he was finished, Eddie played the last record first, turning the volume high. He grabbed a broom from the corner, held it like a guitar, and mouthed the words as Elvis sang:

I'll be as strong as a mountain
Or weak as a willow tree.
Any way you want me
Well, that's how I will be.

". . . for you." Eddie heard his mother yelling from

the top of the stairs.

"What?" he shouted back, turning down the volume.

"I said there's a telephone call for you. Some girl."

Eddie threw the broom-guitar back in the corner and took the stairs two at a time.

"In my day a girl never called a boy," Mrs. Casale muttered, shaking her head.

"Hello?" Eddie said, hoping. A smile spread across his face when he heard Ginny's voice.

"I hope your mother doesn't mind my calling," she said softly. I just wanted to, like, thank you for the party."

"Oh, no. That's ok," Eddie said. "I'm glad ya could come."

"Well, I really had fun, and I'm especially happy to have met you," she cooed.

The telephone, mounted on the kitchen wall, was only a few feet from the stove, where Mrs. Casale was stirring a pot. Eddie looked at her.

"Hello? Are you there? Did you hear me?" Ginny was confused.

"Yes, yes. I heard ya. Er, er . . ., me, too." He kept his voice low, not wantng his mother to hear.

"What? I can't hear you. Why are you whispering?"

"I'm sorry. Must be a bad connection. Is this better?" he asked, raising his voice considerably and stretching the phone wire as far from the stove as possible.

"Now you're shouting. What's going on?"

God, I'm acting like a real asshole, Eddie thought. So, my mother's listening. Big deal. "Nothin's goin' on," Eddie said in a normal tone of voice.

Ginny relaxed. "Oh, good. Look, are you going to be down at Dick's tonight?"

Shit! Shitshitshit! "Er, no," Eddie said. "I've been pretty sick since yesterday." He was glad now that his mother was listening.

"Oh! Oh, my! You don't have that Asian Flu that's going around, do you?"

"Naw, nothin' like that," Eddie said, taking a half step closer to his mother, who was adding a shake of this and a pinch of that to the steaming pot. "It's jus' that I *mowed* the lawn in the *hot* sun, and haven't felt good since then."

"That's too bad," Ginny said, but there was a note of relief in her voice. "I hope you feel better soon. I'd like to see you again."

"Er, me too, he replied. "Look, I have yer phone number from the other night. I'll call ya as soon as I feel better. Ok?"

"Great!" Ginny said. "I hope it's soon."

"Me, too." God, Eddie thought, how many times have I said that?

"Bye-bye for now."

"Ok, bye."

Eddie retreated to the basement, elated and depressed at the same time. It was great that Ginny called. She must really dig me, he thought. But, being stuck in the house all week was a real bummer. There had to be some way to sneak out for a few hours. He smiled as he remembered one of his old records called *The Big Break* by Richard Berry. He found it, put it in the juke box, and played it for inspiration.

Sittin' in my cell lookin' through the bars
Watchin' all the cons in the prison yard
Won't be long before me an' my friend Snake
Plan to make our prison break

Well, I don't have a friend named Snake, Eddie thought, as he listened to the song, but I do have one named Bo. And, if anybody can help me come up with a plan of escape, it's him

"Yer fuckin' crazy! I ain't messin' with yer old man," Bo said flatly. "Whodaya think I am, Willy Sutton?" he added, referring to the bank robber who repeatedly broke out of jail, once by carving a gun from a bar of soap and painting it black with shoe polish.

They were down in the basement after dinner, with the TV turned up loud enough to prevent anyone from overhearing their conversation.

"Aw, come-on, man," Eddie pleaded. "I just gotta get outa here. At least for one night. Pleeease."

After twenty minutes of begging, Bo finally agreed to help his friend. The two boys brainstormed for a while, tossing out each idea as it came up.

"Well, how about this?" Bo proffered. "My mom keeps sayin' she wants to invite yer folks over for dinner . . ."

Eddie's eyes widened. "An' my mom is always sayin' it's a shame they don't see more of yer mom an' dad, livin' right across the street an' all," he said with a glimmer of hope.

"So, if we come up with a good reason, I could suggest to my mom . . ."

"My father's birthday!" Eddie exclaimed, jumping ahead and interrupting his friend. "It's my dad's birthday next week."

"Now we're cookin' with gas," Bo said, getting excited himself. "I'll tell my mom it's yer father's birthday an' it would be nice to have him an' yer mother over for dinner." He paused, contemplating. "But why this week?"

"Er, er, 'cause all next week the family members, cousins an' all, will be comin' over to wish him happy birthday?"

Bo rubbed his chin for several seconds, then nodded slowly. "Sounds reasonable to me, man. But, of course, there's no guarantee. I don't know what my folks have planned, or if yers will come even if they're invited."

"Yeah, yeah. I know, I know." Eddie was sitting on the edge of his seat. "But it's worth a try."

"Ok," Bo said, leaning back in his chair. "I'll get the ball rollin' as soon as I get home."

"Well, get goin' *now*," Eddie said anxiously.

"Be cool, fool. If I went home this early and laid this scam on them, they'd be wise something was up. Besides, the Million Dollar Movie is about to start. Put on Channel Nine."

"What's on?" Eddie asked, getting up to change the station.

"It's *Champion* with Kirk Douglas," Bo said. "I saw it once before. It's a fuckin' classic."

For the next two hours their big plan was put on hold while they watched Kirk Douglas play prizefighter Midge Kelly. And, during the commercial breaks, they did bad Douglas impersonations, repeating a line from the film, "*I can beat him, I know I can beat him,*" through clenched teeth.

The following evening at dinner Mrs. Casale asked her husband if he had any plans for the next night.

"No, not really. Why?" he responded with a suspicious glance, pausing from carving the roast pork.

"Good," she said, as if she already knew the answer. "Mrs. Brody across the street invited us to dinner . . ."

"Oh, wait, tomorrow's Wednesday, and Arthur Godfrey is . . ."

". . . and *I* already accepted."

Mr. Casale looked as if he was about to say something else, but seemed to decide against it. He went back to cutting the meat.

It worked! Eddie's heart was racing. *The goddamned plan worked.* He forked a huge piece of pork, ran it through the mashed potatoes and plopped it in his mouth, dripping mushroom gravy on his T-shirt.

"What about me?" Anna asked. She was daintily cutting a piece of meat into the size of a postage stamp. "Am I going, too?"

"No, dear. Just your father and me."

The food was halfway down his throat when Eddie heard his mother's words. Panic forced it back up. He had to spit it out on his plate.

His father gave him a disgusted look.

"Animal!" his sister sneered.

"Oh, my," his mother said. "I hope you're not still sick."

"Jus' went down the wrong way," Eddie managed to say, after he stopped coughing.

"I'll get you a clean plate." Mrs. Casale got up from the table.

"No, that's ok," Eddie said, jumping up, too. He had to get away and think. "I'm full, anyway. I'm goin' upstairs to lie down an' read."

Damn my sister, anyway, Eddie thought, as he lay on his bed and stared at the ceiling. *I didn't think of that. And, she never goes out on weeknights. Eighteen years old with a brand new car, and she stays home all week. What a square. There's no question she'd tell on me, too. Little Miss Goody Two-Shoes never does anything wrong . . .* Suddenly his eyes widened. *Well, maybe just one thing.*

Eddie jumped out of bed and tiptoed to his sister's room. He heard the water running in the kitchen. Good, she was still doing the dishes. He went over to her bureau, and methodically went through the drawers. He didn't find what he was looking for, but . . . *Mmmm, her bras and panties.* He picked up a pink bra to inspect it more closely, but was suddenly overcome with guilt. He dropped it back down and slammed the drawer shut. He turned to the dressing table, and searched the three side drawers. He found the paperback books in an old Maybellene makeup box. He took them back to his room, hid them under his bed, and laid back down, a smile of satisfaction on his face.

The next day Eddie was up early. He didn't want to miss a chance to call Ginny without being overheard by his mother. The opportunity came at twelve-thirty, just after lunch.

"I'm going to the bakery to buy a nice cake to take to dinner tonight," Mrs. Casale said. "I won't be too long."

"That's cool, Mom. Take your time. "I'm jus' gonna hang out an' play records." He tried to sound nonchalant.

Eddie waited a few minutes after his mother left before dialing Ginny's number. *Please be there,* he silently prayed, as the phone rang. Once. Twice. On the third ring he began tapping his foot. By the fourth one, he was about to hang up and re-dial when he heard that soft sensual voice.

"Helloooo."

"Hi, there, little one," Eddie said, making his voice deeper, in what he thought was a pretty fair imitation of Elvis.

"Who the heck is this?" she snapped. "If this is some kind of obscene phone call you can . . ."

"No, no. Wait! It's me, Eddie."

"Oh, it's you," she said, suddenly much calmer. "You sounded so strange at first I thought it might be some pervert or something."

"No, it's jus' me," he said disheartened. "Must be a bad connection." He winced.

"You had the same problem last time," Ginny said. "Maybe you should have the phone company check your line."

"Yeah, I will. But, anyhow, I called to see if ya want to meet me at Dick's tonight for a Coke or somethin'."

"Gee. Yeah. Swell. I'd like that a lot." She paused. "Are you sure you're feeling up to it? You know, going out and all?"

"Yeah, I'm feelin' much better. But, I guess I gotta take it easy for a while yet. No sense in overdoin' it, ya know. I'll come out for a couple of hours, anyway." He realized he was blabbering like a fool again.

"That's great. What time?"

Whattimewhattimewhattime? He seemed to remember Bo telling him once that his folks ate at seven every night. "About seven-thirty, he blurted out.

"Oh, ok. See you then. Bye for nooow," she cooed.

"Bye," he said, hanging up. God, that chick really got to him, always making him lose his cool. *Must be love, huh? I don't know, but I can't wait to see her again, that's for sure.*

That night, Eddie sat in the living room, absently flipping through the Journal-American, checking his watch every five minutes. It was after six, and his father was late coming home from work. Eddie hoped he hadn't miscalculated the time. At last, he heard his father's car pull into the driveway. Mrs. Casale greeted him sharply when he walked in.

"It's about time. Hurry up and get ready. We have to be there at seven."

Awright! Eddie thought. Right on the money.

Mr. Casale shot his son a quizzical look. "What's alright?" he demanded.

What the hell . . . ? Is he readin' my mind, Or did I actually say it? He quickly buried his head in the newspaper, scanning the columns for something of interest. He found it at the bottom of the page.

"It says that Ford is comin' out with its first luxury model car. They're gonna call it the Edsel. That's something, awright."

"Ha! I bet that's going to go over big," Mr. Casale said. "A luxury Ford. I bet Cadillac is shaking in its boots." He headed up the stairs to wash up and change clothes. He stopped halfway and leaned over the banister. What's that name, again?"

"Edsel. E-d-s-e-l," Eddie said.

"Oh, yes, that's the name of Henry Ford's son. I guess he thinks he's smarter than his old man," Mr. Casale chuckled. He continued up the stairs. "I guess all children think they can outsmart their fathers," he said before closing the bathroom door.

What did he mean by that? Shit! Eddie threw the paper aside, jumped up and began pacing. *What does he know? Naw, nothin'. Just one of his smart-*

ass remarks. But, again . . .

Mrs. Casale had made meatloaf and peas for the children's dinner, something fast and easy. It wasn't Eddie's favorite meal, but it didn't matter anyway. He was too nervous to eat. He pushed the food around the plate, and checked his watch again. "It's almost five to seven awready," he said to his sister. "They're gonna be late."

Anna looked up from her plate, and chewed a mouthful of food another ten or twelve times. *How anyone could chew meatloaf that much*? She swallowed, then dabbed the corners of her mouth with her napkin. God, he hated when she did that. *Now, the disciple of Emily Post is ready to speak.*

"They only have to go across the street, you know," Anna said. "Besides, why are you so worried, anyway?" She was about to take another mouthful of food, when she suddenly dropped her fork in her plate. *Emily Post would have been pissed off at that move*. Her eyes widened. "You're not planning to sneak out after they leave, are you?"

"Of course not," Eddie said, returning to his plate of food. He didn't want to look at his sister's accusing eyes.

Before Anna could respond, Mr. and Mrs. Casale came into the kitchen. "We'll be back in a couple of hours," Mrs. Casale said, picking up the cake box.

"Maybe sooner," Mr. Casale added, looking directly at his son.

"Well, have fun," Anna said.

"Yeah, have a ball," Eddie added, trying to sound upset that they were leaving him home.

As soon as they were out the door, Eddie jumped up and ran to the front window. He peeked through the Venetian blinds, watching his mom and dad walk across the street, ring the bell of the Brody house, and step inside. The door closed behind them.

Eddie made a wild dash for the stairs, and ran into the bathroom. He washed his hands and face, splashed some of his father's Old Spice after shave on his T-shirt, and rubbed a large amount of Brylcreem into his hair, making it gleam. He combed it in record time. When he opened the door, his sister was standing there, arms folded across her chest.

"And where do you think you're going?"

"Look," Eddie said. "I don't have time to argue. I'll be back before they get home."

"Well, I'm going to tell on you," she said with a smirk.

"Oh, yeah?" Eddie said, getting set to play his whole card. "Then *I'll* tell on you, too."

"What are you talking about?" Anna gave him a quizzical look. "I haven't done anything wrong."

"Haven't ya?" Eddie said, a big smile on his face. "Let's see." He walked into his room, reached under his bed, and pulled out the three paperback books. He returned to his sister.

"What have we here? *Peyton Place*. Hmmm. *By Love Possessed.* Not bad. An' this one by Harold Robbins. Wow!"

Anna's face turned beet-red. "Where did you get . . . ? I . . . Look, those books are literature."

"Yeah, sure," Eddie said, with snicker. "I skimmed through 'em. There's some *great* literature. I specially liked the literature about the rape of the fourteen-year-old girl. Extremely well written."

Anna's bottom lip began to quiver, and her eyes welled up with tears. Eddie eased up.

"Calm down, calm down," he said. "Jus' don't tell on me an' I won't tell on you. Simple."

"Give me those books right now," she demanded, trying to grab them.

"Not so fast," Eddie said, holding them away from her. "First, swear to God you won't tell on me."

"Ok, ok," she said, regaining her composure. "But I won't lie for you either. I'm going to go in my room, close the door and stay in there. What I don't see, I don't know. At least I can honestly say I never saw you leave the house."

"Fair enough." Eddie handed his sister the books. "But, don't worry. I'm not gonna get caught anyway. I got it all figured out."

Anna grabbed the books, turned in a huff, and stormed into her room. "You . . . you . . . beast!" she spat at her brother, before slamming the door.

Eddie gave the middle finger to the closed door and smiled. *Great! Now for the final step.* This was the tricky part, getting away from the house without being spotted by his parents. It was still light outside, and they were just across the street. One glance out the window, and it could be all over.

Eddie ran down the stairs. His heart pounded with excitement, while the chorus of the song, *The Big Break,* which he had been playing often over the past two days, kept running through his head. He . . .

Down the hall

. . .hurried through the living room and along the back hall. He opened the back door, glanced around, then stepped outside. He had to keep away from the front of the street. He would sneak along the backyards of all the houses until he came to the end of the block. Eddie grabbed one of the patio chairs and . . .

Over the wall

. . . dragged it over to the four-foot high redwood fence which separated his yard from his neighbor's. He climbed on the chair, swung over the fence, and dropped to the other side. He crouched low and . . .

Through the grass

. . . silently made his way across four other lawns, until he reached the last house on the block. He crept along the driveway of the house, made sure the street was clear, . . .

Now run, run real fast

. . . then ran like hell. He ran up one side street and down another, keeping off the main drags. He kept expecting his father to pop out from behind a tree, or to be following in his car. Finally, dripping with sweat and gasping for breath, he stopped and leaned against a telephone pole. *Christ, my old man really has me psyched out.* He was only two blocks from Dick's, and he had run all the way. He waited several minutes for his breathing to return to normal, then walked the rest of the way. However, he couldn't help checking over his shoulder every so often.

Eddie was hot, sweaty and nervous, but when he turned the corner onto Bell Boulevard, the sight of Dick's Candy Store only half a block away brought a sigh of relief. Here was his sanctuary, his safe-house. At the door, he hesitated momentarily, absorbing the sounds: the murmur of familiar voices, punctuated with occasional excited shouts, played out above the continuous musical score of the juke box, which, at the moment, was featuring *Fever* by Little Willie John.

God, I love this fuckin' place, he thought, stepping through the door. These are my friends. They always make me feel better.

"Christ, you look like shit warmed over," Joe Ross said, peering over the top of a *Tales from the Crypt* comic book he was reading by the magazine rack. "Didya have to make yer escape through the sewers?"

"Hey, douse the lights!" Shadow Silverman yelled from across the room. "The escaped con is here."

Everyone was looking at Eddie and laughing. They all knew, he thought, and they're all laughin' at me. Eddie hadn't wanted anyone to know he had been grounded like some little kid, but somehow they had all found out.

The fuckin' bastards. How'd they find out? The only one he told was Bo, of course, who had helped him with his plan. But, he'd never tell.

Eddie, standing just inside the door, scanned the laughing faces around the room. He hoped Ginny hadn't arrived yet. No such luck. She was sitting in the back booth with Judy Bender, Diane Roth and

Kate Brody. *Kate Brody!* Eddie's eyes stopped on her.

Immediately, she stopped laughing. Even her smile faded. *Bingo! Guilty.* He strode towards her, his anger rising. Kate jumped up and stood behind her brother.

"Cool down, man, cool down," Bo said, holding up his hands in mock defense, as Kate ducked behind his back. "It's really my fault. I asked my sister to help. I figured it'd sound better to my mother if the suggestion about dinner came from her."

Kate peeked over her brother's shoulder. "And, I didn't know it was a secret," she said. "After all, it's no big deal to be grounded."

Eddie winced at the word. Kate ducked back down.

"Besides," Bo added with a short laugh, "jus' take a look at yerself."

Eddie looked in the mirror behind the counter. His face was shiny with sweat. His white T-shirt was soaked through, sticking to his body. But the worst part was his hair. The front was matted to his head, like it had been pressed with an iron, while the hair in the back stood straight out, as if he had stuck his finger in a light socket. As Eddie looked at his reflection, his anger subsided. He had to admit, he was quite a sight. He chuckled softly, and glanced over at Ginny. She looked up at him with her big green eyes, a warm smile on her face.

"Not too cool, huh?" Eddie said, smiling, as he walked over to where she was sitting.

"Oh, I don't know," Ginny said softly. "I think you always look cool." Then, suddenly embarrassed, she averted her eyes.

"*You*," he said, "wait right here. I'll be right back."

He walked over to the counter, where Dick was pumping some cherry syrup into a Coke. "Can I use the bathroom a minute?" he asked. Dick looked up and actually smiled at the sight of Eddie. He nodded his head in the direction of the bathroom at the back of the store.

Eddie had to navigate around some cases of Hires root beer and Mission orange soda, and several boxes of candy and chewing gum, to get to the little washroom behind the storage area. He splashed cold water on his face and into his hair, rubbing briskly. There was a grimy towel hanging on a nail on the back of the door, which he inspected for a clean spot. There wasn't any. He rolled off several feet of toilet paper, balled it up, and wiped his face and neck.

Eddie took the Ace comb from his back pocket, and began to work on his hair. The lighting was bad, and the mirror was cracked, but, after several minutes, he was satisfied with the results. Before leaving, he smelled his armpits. *Yuck*! That Five Day deodorant pad he used hadn't lasted five hours under these conditions. He remembered one of the boxes he saw in the storeroom. He found the carton, broke it open, and pulled out a package of peppermint Lifesavers, leaving a nickel on top of the box. He emptied the entire package into his mouth, and chewed the candies into a paste. He spit the strong-smelling mixture into his hands, reached inside his shirt, and rubbed them under each arm. He sniffed again. *Better. Yeah, much better.*

The Channels were singing *The closer You Are* when a newly-refreshed Eddie, carrying two Cokes, slid into the booth next to Ginny.

"Where's ours?" Judy asked, feigning surprise, as he placed a Coke in front of Ginny. She looked at Diane and both girls giggled.

Eddie reached in his pocked and pulled out two dimes. "Here," he said, sliding the coins across the table. "Go to the counter an' get 'em yerselves. An' drink 'em there, too."

"We can take a hint," Diane said, taking the money. The two girls slid out of the booth.

As soon as they left, Hank Coleman sat down, carrying a copy of the Daily News. He was shaking his head and mumbling.

"Willya look at this ugly piece of shit?" he said, slamming the paper on the table. It was folded open to page three, which featured a three-column photograph and caption of Ford's new Edsel. "It says here," Hank continued, tapping the photo with his forefinger, "that it took three years and over two hundred million bucks in research to come up with this crap. They shoulda given me the money. I'd shown 'em how to make a *decent* car."

Eddie checked his watch. It was almost eight o'clock, and he still hadn't had any time alone with Ginny. "Hank, I don't give a shit about the fuckin' Edsel," he said. "Do ya mind takin' yer paper and botherin' someone else?"

Hank glanced at Eddie, then at Ginny, then back and forth again. A smile came to his face. "Oh, I get it. Ya two wanna be alone, right?"

"No shit, Dick Tracy," Eddie told him.

Hank grabbed his paper, got up, spotted Larry Baker alone at the counter, and headed for him. "Hey, Buffalo, didya see this monster they call a car?"

"I'm sorry I wasn't completely truthful about not being able to leave the house," Eddie said when they were alone. "But, I really didn't lie about bein' sick," he lied. "I really didn't feel too good. Really."

"That's ok," Ginny smiled up at him. "I understand." She paused. "You know, when Kate was telling everyone how you planned to get out tonight, I felt very proud. I thought, 'Wow, he's doing all that just to meet me'."

"Yeah. Well, ya know." Eddie was momentarily stuck for words.

"And, Kate was so happy that she was able to help you," Ginny continued. "You should have seen how excited she was."

"Yeah, I guess so," Eddie said, nodding his head. "She's always been a good friend. Did I ever tell ya how we met?"

Ginny shook her head. "No, but I'd love to hear."

"Well, ya know, she's the first person I met when we moved to Bayside. It was jus' after that big blizzard in '47. We were seven years old. I came outa my house that first day an' got hit in the head with a snowball. Kate had thrown it. I chased her, and washed her face in the snow. Her big brother an' his friends caught me an' packed snow under all my clothes. I ran home cryin' like hell. It took me two hours to thaw out. We've been friends ever since."

He managed to have Ginny laughing by the end of the story. Then she moved in closer, and Eddie, who had his arm across the back of the booth, dropped it down to her shoulders, and drew her tight. She snuggled against him, her head resting on the front of his shoulder. She raised her big dark lashes, and looked at him, smiling. Eddie leaned down and kissed the top of her head. They sat that way for quite some time, not talking, just listening to the music, sipping Cokes and enjoying each other's closeness.

"Oh, wow, I love this song," Ginny said.

"Yeah," Eddie agreed. "Me, too."

Eddie pulled Ginny even tighter, as they sat and listened to Ivory Joe Hunter sing:

Since I met you baby
My whole life has changed
Since I met you baby
My whole life has changed
And ev'rybody tells me
That I am not the same.

When the record ended, they looked at each other. "From now on that will be our song, ok?" Eddie said softly. Ginny smiled and nodded her agreement. With one hand under her chin, he raised her face slowly, while lowering his. Their lips, slightly parted, met, smoothly, gently. Eddie's tongue darted in and out of her mouth; Ginny's lingered a fraction longer.

They broke apart, and Ginny rested her head against his shoulder again. He raised his arm and glanced at his watch. *Shit! It was almost nine o'clock. Where the fuck had the time gone?*

"I guess I gotta get goin'," Eddie said.

Ginny lifted her head. She looked disappointed, but she managed a meager smile and nodded. "I understand." Her smile broadened. "It was really nice spending this time with you, though."

"Yeah, me – er, I enjoyed it too." Eddie was trying hard to stop himself from sounding like an asshole and saying "me, too," all the time.

"Look, would ya wanna go to the movies on Sunday? The new Elvis picture, *Lovin' You,* is playin' at the RKO in Flushing."

"I'd love to," she beamed.

"Great," Eddie said, getting up. "I'll check the times in the paper an' call ya. I'll be right back. I wanna ask Bo for a ride home."

"Alright," Ginny said, getting up, too. "I'll walk you to the door. I want to buy something, anyway."

Kate was sitting on a stool next to her brother, with Judy and Barbara standing on either side of her. When she saw Eddie walking over, she immediately started to profess her innocence.

"Look, don't start with me," she said, raising a forefinger at him. "I didn't – "

"No, wait," Eddie said, holding up his hand and stopping her. "I jus' wanna say I'm sorry for gettin' mad before. I wanna thank ya for yer help an' all."

The three girls exchanged surprised looks, obviously doubting whether he was serious.

"Oh, that's ok," Kate finally said. "I was glad to help."

"I wonder what came over *him*," Barbara said to Judy, flicking her head towards Eddie.

"She did," Judy said, glancing at Ginny, who was approaching the group. "I think it's called love." The girls laughed. Eddie shook his head. He turned to

Ginny.

As she walked up, she was putting a piece of candy in her mouth. She extended the package to him.

"Do you want one?" It was peppermint Lifesavers.

"You know, I haven't had one of these in months," she explained. "But, tonight, I don't know, I just had a strong urge for one. Strange, huh?"

"Yeah, very. But those things happen," Eddie finally managed. He quickly turned to Bo. "Hey, man, can ya give me a lift home?"

"Sure thing. Let's go." Bo slid off the stool and headed for the door.

Eddie and Ginny followed, holding hands. Someone in the store started humming *The Wedding March* very loud. Others immediately joined in. Without turning around, Eddie extended his arm backwards, with the middle finger raised. Everyone hooted and hollered. Ginny blushed.

"Vait! Vait!" They were almost by the door, when Dick came running after them. He looked strange. He was sporting a big grin.

"Yer father came in after voik an' said I should give this to ya ven you leave here tonight." He handed Eddie an envelope, then walked away, chuckling.

Eddie was stunned. He stood there for several moments staring at it. "Oh, shit!" he said.

"Oh, my!" Ginny said.

Finally, he ripped the envelope open. Inside was a Hallmark greeting card. The front had a colorful floral design and was imprinted with, "Glad To Hear You're Feeling Better." Eddie opened the card. The right side contained a standard Hallmark salutation. The left side, originally blank, was filled with Mr. Casale's familiar block printing. The message read:

Roses are red like a strawberry tart
It was a good try but you're not so smart
As long as you're out hope you had some fun
Cause now there's even more work to be done

Before I close I have one more refrain
Yes, my son, you will mow the lawn again

Eddie was crushed, embarrassed. He just stared at the card. After several seconds Ginny removed it from his hand and read it.

"Oh, wow!" She exclaimed. "This is really good. Your father is quite clever."

Eddie shot her an incredulous look.

"You really haven't figured this out, have you?" she said, surprise evident in her voice. "Lord, you should be proud of yourself."

"What the hell are ya talkin' about?"

"Look, most fathers wouldn't take the time or effort to do all this." She waved the card. "They catch their kid doing something wrong, breaking the rules, whatever, bam, that's it. Yell at him, punish him. But your father makes a game of it. Think about it. A highly educated adult matching wits with a high school kid. He must consider you to be a worthy opponent, or why bother. Just *think* about it, Eddie. I bet there are times that you get the better of him, too. Right? That's what keeps him interested. Wow, he must think you're one sharp kid. And, I *know* you are."

By the time Ginny had finished, Eddie was smiling again. "Shit, ya really know how to make me feel better, don't ya?"

"I mean it," Ginny said, seriously.

"Well, I mean *this*," Eddie said. He took her by the shoulders, pulled her close and kissed her long and hard. When they separated, he held her back, and looked into her eyes. "Ya know, I think I really, er, ya know, like you."

"Yeah, me too," Ginny said. They both laughed, realizing she was now using Eddie's line, then kissed goodbye quickly.

Heading outside, Eddie considered Ginny's words. Well, she may think my old man's pretty clever in a game of wits, he thought, but I still think he's the same sadistic bastard he's always been.

Bo was waiting on his bike. "I'll drop ya off a block away so ya can sneak back into yer house," he offered.

"Ya can drive me right into my fuckin' livin' room, an' it wouldn't matter now," Eddie said, climbing on the back.

NINE

EDDIE MY LOVE

Eddie hopped off Bo's bike in front of his house, nodded his thanks, and walked around to the back door. He stopped, took a deep breath, then stepped inside. Silence. Great, he thought, they ain't home yet. He made a dash for the stairs without his customary stop at the refrigerator for a snack.

In his room, he turned on the radio and laid on the bed, fully dressed, his hands folded behind his head. *No sense getting undressed, I'm sure I gotta face the old man when he gets home*. Meanwhile, he reminisced about the night with Ginny.

"And, this one goes out to Wally in Bay Ridge, from his gal, Pat," Alan Freed announced, as he played the record *Crazy For You* by The Heartbeats.

"'Atta boy, Wally," Eddie said to the radio. "She *must* be crazy 'bout ya to dedicate a song to ya."

An' I'm crazy about Ginny, Eddie thought. *Shit, man, I have to be. We didn't do nothin' but sit there sippin' Cokes hardly talkin'. An' I had a great time. Like, I didn't even bullshit with the guys. I just wanted to be with her. Shit, man, it's scary. Maybe I'm really in . . ."*

". . . And for Kenny in Astoria, this is from Kay, Listen now, Kenny, to *I'm In Love Again* by Fats Domino."

Eddie stared dumbfounded at the radio for several seconds. He couldn't believe it. *They took the words right outta my mouth.* Suddenly, he shouted, "me, too." He jumped off the bed, turned the volume up, opened his closet, and, facing himself in the full-length mirror that hung on the back of the door, gyrated, while singing along with the record:

Yes it's me an' I'm in love again
Had no lovin' since you know when
You know I love you yes I do
An' I'm saving all my lovin' just for you

"We're home. What's all that racket up there?" Mrs. Casale yelled from the bottom of the stairs.

As Eddie ran to turn the radio down, he heard his sister's door open. Christ, she can't wait to blab on me, he thought, promise or no promise. *I guess I can't blame her, though, after all the shit I've given her, includin' all those Indian rope burns that turned her arm black an' blue. Well, she'll be disappointed when she finds out the old man already knows.*

"I'm in my room reading," Anna called down. "And, Eddie was . . ." she paused. *Here it comes, the fink!* ". . . er, is blasting his radio like usual. It's terrible." *Well, whadaya know. She didn't rat me out, not yet anyway, but she had to take a shot.*

"Yes, dear. But *you* forgot to clear the table and do the dishes," Mrs. Casale admonished her daughter. "That's not like you." *Yea, Mom. Go get her.*

"Gee, Mom, I'm sorry. "I'll do them right now," Anna said, rushing down the stairs.

Eddie waited for his father to come up to his room to confront him. He tried hard to think of the best way to deal with the situation. Whining never worked. And, he always seemed to know when Eddie lied. Then he had to hear shit like, "honesty is the best policy." Suddenly, he sat up, his legs swinging to the floor, as an idea hit him. *Awright! Aw-fuckin'-right! He wants honesty, I'll give him honesty.* He paced his room, planning his exact words. When he felt he was ready, he practiced "sincere expressions" in front of the mirror for several minutes, before heading downstairs.

Mr. Casale was sitting in his easy chair watching *Dragnet.* Mrs. Casale was in the kitchen helping her daughter with the dishes. Eddie sat on the uncomfortable straight-back chair facing his father. Mr. Casale's eyes remained on the TV, where Officer Joe Friday was telling a witness, *only the facts, mam.* But his dad's smile seemed to be saying, "I gotchya."

"Dad, can I talk to ya for a minute?"

"That's funny," Mr. Casale said, finally looking at his son. "There's something I want to say to you, too."

"I know, I know," Eddie said dejectedly. "But, let me go first. Please?"

His dad got up, lowered the sound on the TV, and returned to his chair. "What is it, son?" he asked, a touch of concern in his voice.

"Look, Dad, I'm really sorry for what I did tonight," Eddie began, looking his father straight in the eyes. Mr. Casale's eyes widened, then seemed to go soft and gentle. Eddie paused and sighed, before continuing. "I know I was wrong an' I can't blame ya for anything that ya do. I know I don't have any right to ask, but please, just let me go to the movies on Sunday. I don't care whatever else ya do. Ya see, Dad, I met this real nice Italian girl that goes to a Catholic school, an', well, I sorta really like her a lot. An' that's the reason I snuck out tonight. Only now I feel kinda bad about the whole thing." Eddie dropped his eyes, and stared at the floor. "That's the whole story. Honest to God, Dad."

There was a long silence as Eddie studied the lint on the beige pile carpet and wondered if he overdid it with the "Italian" and "Catholic" bit.

Mr. Casale got up from his chair, and walked over to his son. "Stand up," he said. Eddie stood up. "Look at me," he ordered. Eddie lifted his eyes. Mr. Casale raised his hands. Eddie flinched, but his father only placed them affectionately on his son's shoulders and squeezed gently. "I'm really proud of you," Mr. Casale said. "Usually you either make up a ridiculous story, or come up with a stupid excuse. But, this time I believe you. I really think you're telling me the truth for the first time."

Holy shit! It's workin'. Eddie fought to keep a straight face, even managing a slight quiver in his lower lip. "I am, Dad, I am."

Well, son, if you've learned *that* lesson, then that's all I can ask. And, as a reward, the remainder of your punishment is cancelled. Everything is back to status quo."

Eddie didn't know what "status quo" meant, but he didn't care. He understood the gist of what his father said, and wanted to jump for joy. When he had come downstairs, he was hoping only to keep next Sunday free. He had ended up with the whole kit and kaboodle.

"Gee, Dad, thanks a lot." Eddie, with a subdued smile, tried to sound grateful. "Yer a great father."

"Now, don't overdo it," Mr. Casale said with a chuckle. "By the way," he added, "is this new girl of yours really an Italian from a Catholic school, or was that an exaggeration you thought you had to slip in?"

"No, really," Eddie said, happy to be able to provide proof for his story. "Her name's Ginny Marcessi an' she goes to St. Agnes."

"Marcessi, huh? That's a Sicilian name. Good." Mr. Casale settled back in his chair. "Invite her over for dinner sometime. And, turn up the TV."

"Sure thing." Eddie adjusted the volume as Joe Friday and his partner, Officer Frank Smith, were questioning another witness. He headed for the stairs.

"Oh, wait just a minute, young man," Mr. Casale called after him. "I don't think you've told me *everything."*

Eddie stopped short. *Shit!? What did I miss?*

"You didn't tell me what you thought of my little poem," Mr. Casale said, laughingly.

Eddie relaxed, the look of alarm dissolving into a smile. "A Longfellow yer not. But, your timin' was perfect." And my timin' wasn't too fuckin' bad, either, Eddie thought, taking the steps two at a time.

Anna, finished with the dishes, was upstairs waiting by her bedroom door. "I can't believe you got away with that," she whispered to her brother. "He let you off scot-free. You're so full of . . . of . . ."

She just couldn't bring herself to say the word. Eddie put his thumbs to his temples, and wiggled his spread fingers, while sticking out his tongue. ". . . full of shit," she spat out, then immediately put her hand to her mouth, as if she could force the word back in.

"Naw, naw na-naw, naw. Now-you-have-to-go-to-confession," Eddie said in a sing-song voice, as he calmly walked to his room.

Anna stood there, eyes turned upward, repeating over and over again, "He made me say it . . . he made me say it . . . he made me say it."

The next time I get her alone, I'll have to give her another Indian rope burn, Eddie thought, as he closed his door.

The radio was still playing, with Alan Freed dedicating the next record "to Connie up in Fordham Road, The Bronx, from her special guy, Charlie. Here's Gene Vincent with *Lotta Lovin."*

Eddie turned the volume down, and lay on the bed. It was almost ten o'clock, but he was too excited to go to sleep just yet. It wasn't everyday he scored a major victory against his father. Suddenly, Eddie jolted upright. The story he told his father tonight *was* the truth. Every word of it. *So, who actually won?*

Eddie, settling back down, smiled uneasily to himself. Well, I can't let that happen all the time, he thought. That would only spoil him. Anyway, I'm a free man, an' that's what counts. An', on Sunday I'll ask Ginny to go steady.

"Listen carefully, Nancy in Brooklyn Heights," Alan Freed announced. "Ralph is sending this out just for you. It's The Coasters singing *Young Blood."*

Eddie snapped his fingers and popped up in bed again. He reached over, opened the drawer of his night table, and pulled out the old Dutch Masters cigar box which contained his old jewelry and other assorted treasures, and rummaged through it. There was an old Captain Marvel decoder ring, a broken Benrus watch, an ID bracelet that turned his wrist green, some shiny beach stones collected from around the lighthouse at Montauk Point. The thin gold ankle bracelet with the intertwined hearts that Penny Randazzo returned to him was at the bottom. He checked the inscription. Hell, Eddie thought, it should be simple for a jeweler to change it. Three of the letters in the two names are already the same. An', the rest, like the date an' all, well, it'll be a snap. Jewelers know how to do that shit.

Eddie pulled a Kleenex from the box on the night table and wrapped the bracelet neatly in the tissue. Tomorrow he would bring it to the jewelry store. He lay back down on his bed as Alan Freed dedicated *My Prayer* by The Platters "to Ken at the Flying A Station in Whitestone, from Audrey."

Eddie chuckled to himself as he stripped to his Jockey shorts and climbed into bed. Yeah, he thought, the jeweler will fix it, I'll give it to her, we'll go steady, an' – . Suddenly, he stopped laughing. *What if she doesn't want to go steady*? The thought sent a wave of depression over him. *I mean, I know she likes me an' all, but, like, it's only our first real date.*

The record ended, and Alan Freed began a sales pitch for Clearasil, and how it helped heal "those nasty, ugly pimples which always seem to pop up right before our big date."

"Oh, no!" Eddie groaned, "that's all I need." He jumped out of bed and rushed to the mirror. Sure enough, there was a red blotch on his right cheek, and even a whitehead on the tip of his chin. He pictured himself on Sunday, his face a mass of zits. His depression deepened as he dragged himself back to the bed, making a mental note to stop at the drugstore tomorrow for two tubes of Clearasil. She'll never go steady with a pimply-faced jerk like me, Eddie told himself, as he sank back down on the bed.

"And this next song goes out to that special guy at Dick's Candy Store in Bayside from Ginny, who wants you to listen to the words of The Teen Queens' *Eddie My Love.*"

Eddie my love
I love you so
I'm lonely for you
You'll never know
Please Eddie
Don't let me wait too long

Eddie raised his head from the pillow slowly, and stared at the radio. He blinked several times and swallowed hard. *Holy shit! That's me! That's her! That's us, for Chrissakes. Wow!* No one ever played a song on the radio for him before. His spirits began to soar. *She really does love me, I guess. Wow!*

Eddie woke to the sound of Jim Lowe singing *The Green Door.* His first thought was that the timer on the clock-radio which automatically turns it off had failed to work, and it had been playing all night. When his head cleared, he realized the music was coming from his sister's room. He looked at his clock. It was only ten to eight. She was getting ready for work.

"Turn that thing down," Eddie yelled. "I'm tryin' to sleep, ya know." The music seemed to get louder, which, he figured, was her way of getting back at him for last night. The record ended, and the resonant voice of the disc jockey bellowed through the wall separating the two bedrooms.

"Hello, again. This is Herb Oscar Anderson . . . it's eight minutes to eight, and the temperature is already seventy-nine degrees. It's going to reach the low nineties with bright sunshine, so if you're just getting ready for work, wear something loose and light. It'll help you keep your cool. And, speaking of cool, here's Johnny Mathis with *Chances Are.*"

Eddie jumped out of bed, pulled on his robe, and stormed into the hall. He wondered why his mother or father didn't tell her to turn the radio down, like they were always telling him. The bathroom door was closed with the shower running. That would be Mr. Casale. Mrs. Casale would be on her way to church for eight o'clock Mass, as she was every morning. Anna timed her move perfectly so she wouldn't get caught. Eddie banged angrily on his sister's bedroom door.

"Yes?" Anna said innocently, as she slowly opened her door. She was wearing a loose-fitting, light blue dress. Christ, Eddie thought, she really listens to this guy on the radio.

"Turn that damn thing down," he snarled, "or . . ." Just then the shower stopped. Anna ran to the radio and turned it low.

She came back to the doorway, and said sweetly, "Was it too loud? I'm soooo sorry." She closed the door in her brother's face.

Eddie stood there for a moment, trying to think of something nasty to do to her, when the bathroom door opened and his father stepped out, wrapped in a maroon terry cloth robe. He looked at his son in surprise.

"What are you doing up so early?" Mr. Casale asked. Eddie looked at his sister's door. The music coming from her room was hardly audible now. He looked back at his father. "Jus' thought I'd get an early start on such a beautiful day."

"Wonders never cease," Mr. Casale said, shaking his head and walking into his room.

Eddie debated briefly whether or not to go back to bed, but decided against it. It *was* a beautiful day, and he had things to do. By the time he had showered and gotten dressed, his father and sister had left for work, and his mother was back from church.

"What are you doing up so early?" Mrs. Casale asked, as Eddie walked into the kitchen.

"Oh, ya know, wonders never cease, right Mom?"

"That's just what I was going to say," Mrs. Casale agreed, taking three eggs and a package of Boar's Head bacon out of the refrigerator. "How do you want your eggs this morning?"

Eddie ate his breakfast while checking the box scores of yesterday's baseball games in the sports pages of the *Daily Mirror.* He was happy to see that the Yankees were still leading the American League, and that Mickey Mantle had gone three for four, with a homer and a double, in a game against Cleveland.

"I don't know how you can get your room so messy when you spend so little time in it." Mrs. Casale, who had been upstairs making the beds and cleaning, came down carrying Eddie's full wastepaper basket. She emptied it into the large kitchen garbage pail.

"It takes talent I guess," Eddie said, folding the last slice of bacon into a piece of English muffin, and shoving it into his mouth.

Mrs. Casale picked up the full garbage pail and headed for the door.

"Wait, Mom, I'll take that out for ya," Eddie said, jumping up from the table. He might as well make as many points as possible while still on a roll from last night.

"My, my. Wonders never cease," Mrs. Casale said.

He took the pail outside and dumped it into the big metal garbage can next to the garage. He had to press it down to get the cover back on. God, how he hated to touch garbage.

"Bring the can out front," his mother yelled from the back door. "Today is pick-up day."

He dragged the can to the front of the driveway, then went back inside and washed his hands for several minutes. He checked his watch. Almost ten. The jewelry store should be open by now. He went to his room to get the ankle bracelet, but the tissue he had wrapped it in was not on the night table. He checked the dresser. Nothing. In fact, it was as neat as a pin. *My mother just cleaned my room . . . and threw out the garbage . . . I THREW OUT THE FUCKIN' GARBAGE,* he thought in rapid succession. He bolted down the stairs and burst into the kitchen.

"Mom, Mom," he shouted. "Did ya throw out a tissue that was on my night table?"

"Of course I did. Do you think . . . ?"

But Eddie was already out the door. The grinding and churning noises from the front of the house were unmistakable. A burley colored guy was lifting the Casale garbage can, about to empty it into the back of a sanitation truck.

"STOP!" Eddie shouted, running down the driveway, waving his arms. "DON'T DUMP THAT GARBAGE!"

"Why not, kid, dat's what I get paid ta do," he snorted, still holding the can in the air.

"I gotta find somethin'," Eddie yelled. He grabbed the rim of the can and yanked. The sanitation man held tight. Eddie pulled harder, and the man let go at the same moment. Eddie fell on his back, the contents of the can spilling over him. The garbage man roared with laughter.

"Sorry, kid. We only pick up garbage if it's ina can," he said between laughs. "See ya next time." He walked to the cab of the truck, anxious to tell the driver about his joke.

Eddie was covered from head to toe with coffee grinds, potato peels, sticky stuff, gooey stuff, slimy stuff. He got up, wiped himself off, and began searching for tissues. There must have been a hundred of them, and he went through them all. No bracelet. Thinking it might have fallen out, he went through every inch of the entire contents of the garbage can. No trace of it.

Great, he thought. Not only did I lose the bracelet, but now I gotta put all this shit back in the can.

It was a half hour later when he had finally finished and walked back into the house. Mrs. Casale looked at her son in shock, and wrinkled her nose. "My, you look and smell awful. What happened to you?"

"I was lookin' through the garbage for a tissue ya threw out," he said dejectedly. "I had an ankle bracelet in it."

"Oh, that," Mrs. Casale said with a wave of her hand. "I saw it and put it back in that cigar box you keep in your drawer. Why didn't you just ask in the first place?"

After showering for the second time that morning, and putting on clean clothes, Eddie headed for Bell Boulevard, the bracelet tucked safely in the pocket of his jeans. Kate Brody had just left her house too, and was halfway down the street.

"Hey, wait up," he called, and trotted after her. She was wearing a sleeveless, loose-fitting white blouse, opened daringly to the third button, and, as usual, tight Levi dungarees which drew attention to the curves of her ass and thighs.

"How come you're out? I thought you were still grounded," Kate asked, as Eddie caught up to her. "What ridiculous story did you come up with this time?"

"No story, no bullshit," Eddie said. "I jus' went to the ol' man an' told him the truth, an' he let me off the hook. Whadaya think of that?"

Kate looked at her friend. "What do I think of that? I *think* that's called growing up."

Eddie matched her sober expression only for an instant, then his smile returned. "Yeah, well. I took two aspirins an' went right to bed. An' I'm as good as new, now."

"You're hopeless," Kate said, but she, too, was smiling again. "Let's go. I have to meet Judy."

She started off down the block, and Eddie marveled at the way her ass bounced from side to side with each step. He fell in beside her and they continued towards Bell, but every so often he held back a step or two to sneak a glimpse at her backside. After a few blocks she swung around, facing him, hands on her hips.

"Do you like the view back there?"

"I was jus' wonderin'," Eddie responded, wide-eyed. "Do ya have a porch for that swing?"

"Oh, I didn't think anybody would notice."

"Are ya kiddin'? Those jeans are so tight even Ray Charles would notice." Kate laughed, and they continued walking. "By the way, I've been meanin' to ask. How do ya girls get them so tight, anyway?"

"It's not easy," Kate said, shaking her head. "You should only know what we have to go through." She went on to explain that as soon as they buy a new pair of dungarees, they take them home, put them on, and soak in a hot tub for half an hour. Then, they let the jeans dry while still wearing them, so the fabric shrinks to the body, like a second skin. "Sometimes they're so tight we have to lay flat on the bed to pull them on."

Eddie conjured up the thought of Kate lying on a bed wiggling into a pair of jeans, and immediately felt a stirring between his legs. She looked at him, squinting, as if reading his mind. He began to blush.

"Thank God it's a lot easier gettin' 'em off," he joked.

"That's awful!" Kate exclaimed, but she was still smiling. It was obvious she enjoyed the attention her derriere was receiving. "Just wait until I tell Ginny what you said."

Oh, shit! Ginny! He thought. Here I am oglin' Kate an' forgettin' about Ginny. He took out the ankle bracelet and showed it to his friend.

She took it, and held it up to the sunlight. "Isn't it the same one you gave to Penny last winter?"

"So what," Eddie said defensively. "All ankle bracelets look the same, anyway."

She turned it over. "Yeah, maybe so. But they all don't say the same thing," she said, looking at the inscription.

"Well, I was hopin' the jeweler could change it," Eddie replied. "Ya know, just the name an' date, I guess. An' maybe the word 'cents-less' to 'senseless'."

"Oh, they can change it. I know. Hank gave me one that probably saw more ankles than an old sock. And I had to have the inscription changed myself."

Eddie laughed, then told Kate about the morning's ordeal over the missing ankle bracelet and his search through the garbage can. By the time he finished, they were laughing so hard that they had to stop walking, and lean on each other for support.

"You must really love her to go through all that," Kate said, catching her breath.

Suddenly, Eddie stopped laughing. "Well, er, ya know," he hemmed and hawed. "Well, I like her . . . er, I mean, kinda, a lot."

"You guys are all the same," Kate said with a disgusted look. Why the heck don't you just say what you really feel? We girls do."

Eddie's eyes widened. "That's right! Ya girls talk all the time." He felt a rush of excitement. "Tell me, what's Ginny said about me?"

"That's for me to know and for you to find out," Kate said, raising her head adamantly, and prancing down the street.

He ran after her. "Aw, comeon, Kate," he pleaded. "Please tell me. Does she really lo – , I mean, ya know, like me a lot?"

"You guys are really something," she said with a trace of annoyance. "You can't even say the word, can you? Well, it's very easy. L-O-V-E. Love! See? Lovelovelovelove. Now you try it."

Eddie just looked at her in silence. Kate sighed, waved her hand in disgust, and continued walking.

"Wait!" he yelled, catching up to her again. "I'll do anything. Just tell me what she says about me."

Kate stopped abruptly. She turned to him slowly with a gleam in her eye. "Anything?" she asked.

"Well, yeah, I guess. But, well . . . " Eddie hesitated.

"Don't worry," Kate assured him. "I won't make you say . . . " she turned to him, leaned close to his face, and shouted, ". . . LOVE."

At that moment, two elderly ladies were passing on the sidewalk. They jumped back in shock.

"Oh gee, I'm sorry," Kate said, looking at them and blushing.

The women, regaining their composure, looked at Kate sternly.

"It's not ladylike for girls to say words like that in public," one of them said, wagging a finger in Kate's face.

"And in front of boys, too," the other woman scolded.

They walked off shaking their heads. "Kids today have no respect for themselves," said one.

"When we were girls you would never hear talk like that," said the other.

"Tsk, tsk," they said to each other.

Kate and Eddie contained themselves until the women were out of earshot, then burst out laughing.

"See," Eddie snorted, "I told ya it was a bad word."

"Ok, ok," Kate said, getting back to business. "Here's the deal. You get Hank to take me out

Saturday night, and I'll tell you what Ginny said about you."

"Oh, no, wait a minute," Eddie protested. "That's when all the guys go to the Hide Out."

"I know," she said. "And, that's when all the girls sit alone in Dick's. But, this Saturday night I'll be going out with Hank. Either that, or not only won't I tell you what Ginny said, but while you're at the Hide Out I'll be in Dick's telling her things about you she could never imagine."

Eddie's jaw dropped as he stared at Kate. She just stared back at him, hands on her hips, with a defiant expression.

"Can't we at least talk about . . ." Eddie didn't bother finishing. He knew he was defeated when Kate took an even firmer stance, arms folded across her chest, shaking her head slowly. "But, how can I – ?"

"I got it all figured out," she interrupted, moving in for the kill like a boxer with an opponent on the ropes. "Tell him you want to take Ginny to the drive-in, and you want it to be something special because it's your first date. That's why you want to go in *his* car. If you can get him to go, I bet some of the other guys will go along, too. We could have a drive-in party, you know, maybe four or five cars." Kate hesitated, then moved even closer, her chest brushing his, giving him a seductive smile. "And, the girls will be real happy with you if you can set it up, you know," she added, ruffling his hair playfully, then wiping the grease on her jeans.

"But, I'm supposed to take Ginny to the RKO on Sunday," Eddie said, taking his Ace comb from his back pocket and running it through his hair several times.

"I happen to know, among other things which I may or may not tell you, that she'd rather go to the drive-in," Kate responded, with a smug expression.

Now she really had him going. Still, Saturday was Hide Out night. He made one more attempt. "What if we make it Sunday night?"

"Saturday night, or no deal," Kate said. "I've been going with Hank for six months, and he hasn't taken me out on a Saturday yet. And, that's *supposed* to be date night. Ha! What a laugh."

Eddie knew when he was beat. "Ok, ok, I'll do my best." He had an idea. He would try to talk Bo into going first. If Bo went along, most of the other guys would want to go, too. But Bo at the drive-in . . .? Eddie thought. I don't know. Not after last time.

It was Judy Bender's birthday, and Bo had gallantly agreed to give up a Saturday night and take her to the drive-in. And Eddie had jumped at the opportunity and volunteered to occupy the back seat with Penny Randazzo.

Since Bo's only mode of transportation was the Triumph, he was forced to borrow his father's car, a black '52 four-door Chevy sedan with automatic transmission. A typical family car.

After making the usual stops for six-packs of beer and bottles of Thunderbird wine, they had pulled into the outdoor movie just as it started getting dark. Most of the parking spaces were taken. As Bo drove up one lane and down another, Eddie checked out the cars parked side by side. It was the usual Saturday night showing. There were many louvered and lowered customs, chopped and channeled hot rods, and souped-up dragsters with exposed engines. However, there were quite a few sober sedans, too, all almost identical to the one Bo was driving. Eddie pointed this out with a chuckle.

"I guess a lot of other poor slobs had to borrow their fathers' cars, too," he had joked. "So, don't feel too bad."

Bo slammed on the brakes and jerked around in the seat. "If ya don't like it, get the fuck out an' walk," he growled through clenched teeth.

"Hey, cool down, man," Eddie said, holding up his hands. "I was only kiddin'."

"Oh, shit," Bo said, relaxing with a big sigh. "It's not you, man. I can't stand drivin' this piece a shit. Whoever invented the Power Glide transmission oughta be shot. It goes zero to sixty in an hour an' a half, for Chrissakes." Drivers in the cars behind them started beeping their horns and yelling for them to get out of the way. Bo shot an arm out the window and raised a middle finger above the roof, then continued searching for a space.

They had finally parked three rows behind the refreshment shack. Bo raised the window halfway, hooked the speaker onto it, and adjusted the scratchy volume. He grabbed a can of beer, popped the top twice with a churchkey, and settled back in the seat to watch his favorite actor, Robert Mitchum, in Second Chance. *Immediately, however, Judy was all over him, nibbling and kissing. It would take at least a six-pack and a half before Bo would kiss her back.*

Eddie, working on the Thunderbird, took another long swallow, propped it against the back seat, and pulled Penny closer. She offered no resistance. In fact, when she tilted her head back, inviting a kiss, her lips were slightly parted — a sure sign that she wanted to start French kissing. Usually, it took Eddie half an hour of trying to force his tongue through clenched teeth before Penny relented and allowed the tip to penetrate her mouth.

Eddie lowered his head and pressed his lips against hers, his tongue flicking in and out. Still, there was no resistance. Holy shit, *he thought,* maybe tonight I'll get lucky and score. *Penny's tongue responded with movement of its own, and their making out rapidly reached a feverish pitch. Eddie's right hand was at her side. He moved it up slowly, over the softness of her red sweater, until he was able to cup her breast.*

Penny stiffened slightly, but didn't remove his hand. Without breaking the kiss, she pressed her body tighter against his. The movement caused increased pressure on her tit. Her breathing quickened. She moved again. This time, as if by accident, her arm brushed across Eddie's erection, which was throbbing against his Levis. He groaned. Carefully, he slipped his other hand under her sweater and caressed her smooth skin. He brought it up slowly, the tips of his fingers dancing gently over her naked flesh. He felt her body shudder. She moaned. When he reached her bra strap, his fingers searched for the clasp. He found it, fumbled for a few seconds, and was shoved clear across the back seat.

"I think we should cool down for a few minutes," Penny had said, pulling her sweater smooth. "I don't want you to get the wrong idea."

Wrong idea? Wrong fuckin' idea? Same old fuckin' cock-teaser, *Eddie had thought. He lit a crumpled Lucky Strike, took another hit of the wine, and sulked.* Yeah, well, that's it. I'm not takin' her shit no more.

"Aw, don't be mad," Penny had said demurely, reaching over and taking Eddie's hand. "You know we can't go all the way until we're married."

"All the way? Hell, I don't think we should go all the way, either," Eddie had lied. "But, at least we can do a little bit more than jus' kiss, ya know."

"Well, I like kissing just fine," she had cooed, moving in close again. "'Specially with you." She wrapped her arms around his head and pulled his face down to hers. "You're the best kisser I've ever known," she whispered throatily. Within seconds, they were making out hot and heavy again.

By intermission time, Eddie had lost count of the cooling off periods. However, he had finished half a pack of smokes and almost two bottles of wine.

"I'm gonna take a leak," he slurred. "Anybody want anything?"

Penny ordered a root beer and Judy asked for buttered popcorn. Bo said he was ok with the beer.

At the concession counter, Eddie had wolfed down a hot dog and a Baby Ruth candy bar before heading back to the car, staggering, spilling popcorn and root beer along the way. He had wandered about for a while before realizing he had forgotten where the car was parked. Weaving through the aisles, up one and down another, he finally spotted it.

"Open the damn door," Eddie called out. "My hands are full." The back door swung open and he clumsily climbed in, concentrating on trying not to drop any more popcorn or soda.

"What took you so long," Eddie had heard Penny murmur in a thickly slurred voice. "I've been so fuckin' horny back here."

Shocked, he had looked over and gasped. She was curled up in the far corner of the seat, half hidden in darkness. However, a streak of light flickered from the movie screen and revealed her nakedness from the waist up. Eddie couldn't believe his luck. With eyes locked on those glorious tits, he dropped the popcorn and root beer to the floor of the car, and lunged at her. At the same moment, he had heard a horrible scream. He pulled back, dazed, confused.

Penny was screaming at the top of her lungs, her arms crisscrossed over her naked chest. Penny was . . . Wait a minute, Penny doesn't have blonde hair. Penny's hair. . .

"Get outa here, you pig," the girl continued screaming. "You're not Steve."

"Wait, wait, I . . ." That was all Eddie could manage before the back door opened and two hands grabbed him around the neck. He was dragged out of the car, and thrown roughly to the ground.

"Ya muthafuckin' pervert, I'll teach ya to touch my girl." The guy standing over Eddie was big, his face flushed with anger. He kicked Eddie, catching him

in the pit of the stomach. Eddie groaned and rolled over. Other car doors opened and closed, and a crowd formed around Eddie.

"I didn't . . . shit, wrong car . . ." Eddie had tried to explain, but the words were barely audible. His head was spinning and he was gasping for breath. He had felt a twinge of nausea. He rolled over on the gravel, and tried to stand, but couldn't get his legs to work.

The big guy, snarling obscenities, reached down and pulled Eddie up by the shirt-front like a rag doll. He pushed his ugly, pock-mocked face up close, and cocked a ham-sized fist, ready to unload a devastating punch. "I'm gonna rip yer balls off," he had hissed, spraying beer-flavored spittle as he spoke.

At that moment, the hot dog had begun moving. Dislodged by the kick to the stomach, the frankfurter retraced its route through Eddie's gullet, and exited through the same orifice it had entered.

The big guy screamed and jumped back, a split-second too late. A hot gush of brownish-green vomit splashed into his face.

Eddie had wobbled momentarily, then fell to the ground, now throwing up in a steady stream. After the hot dog, came the wine, then his dinner, then whatever else happened to be hanging around his stomach. The crowd went wild, cursing and yelling threats. They tried to kick at him, but each time they came close enough, Eddie heaved again, sending his adversaries in gagging retreat. Soon, others lost control and began puking, too. Even the big guy was doubled over in sickness. There was vomit everywhere, on people, on the ground, and on the once-shiny finishes of several custom cars.

Eddie had looked around at all the devastation through bleary eyes. Although he was groggy, he knew once things calmed down he would get his ass kicked bad — even worse than before — for making them all sick. He had to get out of there. He tried to get up again, but was still too weak.

Suddenly, out of the corner of his eye, he spotted a familiar face in the crowd. He blinked several times before focusing on Bo, standing on the edge of the angry mob. He was holding his sides in laughter.

"Hey, Bo," Eddie had managed to cry out in a hoarse voice. "Get me the hell outa here."

"I can't right now," Bo had said, catching his breath. "I gotta piss so bad I can taste it. Just keep barfin' on everybody 'til I get back, an' ya'll be ok."

Eddie couldn't believe it, as his friend walked off laughing. He looked around. The vomiting had stopped, and people were cleaning themselves off. They glared at Eddie, snarling "pig," "animal," "pervert." The big guy had pushed himself to the front, completely soiled with Eddie's and his own puke, hatred evident in his eyes.

"Pick him up," he said to a friend standing next to him. "I'm gonna work him over real good."

He had taken another step toward Eddie, then groaned and crumpled to the ground. Bo had come up behind and landed a powerful blow to the back of his neck, rendering him semi-conscious. A friend of his turned to see what happened, and was greeted with an elbow flush in the mouth. Teeth broke, flesh ripped and blood erupted. He dropped to his knees with a cry of pain.

Suddenly, Bo had leapt in front of Eddie, facing the advancing mob. He crouched low, muscled arms swinging loosely at his sides. His hearty laughter of moments ago had turned to a menacing snicker, lips drawn tight over clenched teeth.

"Comeon, muthafuckas," he had said in his quiet, deadly tone, nodding his head towards Eddie. "Anybody wants him has to go through me first. Let's go. One at a time, or all at once. I don't give a fuck."

It was as if someone had stopped a film and switched it to reverse. Everyone started backing up at the same time.

"Hey!" someone had shouted. "The manager called the cops. Let's get outa here."

Everyone ran for their cars. Doors slammed, engines started, and tires spit up gravel. Bo pulled Eddie to his feet and half carried him to the car. He threw him in the back seat. The girls took one look, held their noses, and stuck their heads out the window.

"Yuk! Get going fast," Judy had said, "so we can get some air circulating in here."

"I'm goin', I'm goin'," Bo had said, starting the engine and slamming the transmission lever into reverse. As the Chevy backed out, there was a loud crunching sound. In his haste, he had forgotten to remove the speaker from the window.

"Oh, shit!" Bo had exclaimed, staring at the shattered remains of the window. "My old man's gonna kill me."

"Well, one good thing," Eddie had managed weakly with a wry smile. "At least it don't look the same as all those other cars anymore."

"Well, is it a deal?" Kate asked, thrusting out her hand, bringing Eddie back to the present.

"Deal," Eddie said, shaking it. "Now, tell me what Ginny says about me."

"Oh that," Kate said, with a dismissing wave of her hand. "She never mentions you." She turned and walked away.

Eddie stood stunned for several moments, then ran after her, grabbing her by the shoulders. "Why, ya little . . ." he began angrily, but stopped when she burst out laughing.

"Gotcha!" Kate said, and Eddie had to laugh along with her. As they walked to Bell, she told him Ginny actually spoke about him *all* the time, and liked him more than she ever liked any other boy. And, yes, of course, she would love to go steady with him.

When they arrived at Goldberg's Jewelry Store, a block away from Dick's, Kate stopped.

"Because you've been so agreeable, I'll do you another favor. Give me the bracelet. He'll probably do it for me for free."

"How come?" Eddie asked, handing it over.

"Because he's a dirty old man," she smiled over her shoulder, walking into the store, setting off the little bell above the door. Eddie followed.

"Hi, there, Mr. Goldberg," Kate sang out.

Meyer Goldberg, wearing a threadbare gray sweater-vest as protection against his new air-conditioner, was at his usual position—sitting on a high wooden stool with the seat-cushion hand crocheted by his late wife, Ester. He was perched over a lighted work table in the rear of the small shop. He looked up, squinting over the top of a pair of thick horn-rimmed glasses. His hard, lined sixty-six-year-old face softened into a huge smile at the sight of Kate bouncing up to the counter. He stood up slowly, using the table for support, and ran a hand through the several strands of thin gray hair on his otherwise bald pate.

"Bubula! It is you. And, you're more pretty den ever." Goldberg, only five-feet-four, had to stand on his toes to reach over the counter and pinch Kate's cheek. "Finally, you come to visit a lonely old man. Such a sight for these tired old eyes, you are." Those tired old eyes suddenly seemed to be wide awake and caressing young curves.

"Oh, Mr. Goldberg, you're such a flirt," Kate said with a giggle. "I bet you say that to all the girls who come in here."

"Girls? Vhat do I know from girls?" Goldberg lifted his arms, palms upward, and shrugged his shoulders. "Vhen I was a boy, oye vay, did I know the girls, you betcha."

Kate walked through the shop swinging her ass, checking the various displays. Every so often, she bent over to get a closer look at something. It was a great show, and Goldberg didn't miss any of it. He kept leaning further over the counter.

"Bubula, Bubula, over here, over here," he called out breathlessly. "I vant to show you some new earrings. For you, they is perfect." He pointed to the lowest shelf in the display counter.

As Kate brushed past Eddie, she nudged him with her elbow and winked. She walked over to the counter and leaned all the way over to study the bottom shelf. As she did so, the front of her blouse fell forward. The jeweler fumbled with his glasses, which were on a chain around his neck. He finally got them on, and peered down. Kate's blouse was loose enough to expose an inch of cleavage and a bit of a white lace bra, nothing more.

"They're beautiful," Kate said, standing up and throwing her shoulders back and her chest out.

"They is very beautiful," Goldberg said, slowly nodding his head, still staring at her tits.

"But, I really can't buy anything just now," Kate continued. "In fact, I have a problem." She held up the ankle bracelet, and waved it in front of the jeweler to divert his attention. "I have to get the inscription changed on this for my cousin, Ginny, and I don't know if I have enough money." She handed him the bracelet and explained what she wanted changed.

"This is a problem?" Goldberg said, examining the bracelet. "No, no. This is not a problem." He pushed a pad and pen across the top of the counter. "Here. Put vhat you vant to say exactly and come to me in one hour. It is done. For you, Bubula, I vill need no money. Just come and visit this old man sometimes. Yes?"

"Oh, you're such a nice man," Kate said, leaning forward and kissing him on the cheek. "Of course I'll come and see you." She flashed a smile, thanked him, and swung her way out the door. Eddie followed a few steps behind, his hand to his mouth, trying to make a laugh sound like a cough.

When they were several doors away, Eddie couldn't hold back any longer. He burst out laughing, slapping Kate on the back. "Awright!" he exclaimed. "Ya were magnificent. Ya oughta be in movies."

She spun around. Her cheeks were bright red, her lips were pulled tight over clenched teeth.

"You think it's funny, huh? Magnificent, huh?" she snapped in anger, pushing her face only inches from his. Suddenly, her anger seemed to melt, eyes turning watery. "Well, then, why do I feel so low and rotten?" She turned away and knuckled the tears from her eyes. "It was stupid of me to tease him like that. I'm so ashamed of myself."

"Aw, come-on," Eddie said, throwing an arm around his friend. "It was all in fun. Besides, he loved it."

Kate shrugged his arm off. "Well, that doesn't make me feel any better," she said sulkily.

He tried again. "Hey, yer always teasin' me, ain't ya, like when we dance at parties, right? That don't bother ya."

Kate looked up, a slight smile beginning to flicker. "That's different, because you always think you're so cool. Us girls love to tease you guys to bring you down a peg or two." She paused, and smiled even more. "Or, *up* a peg or two, if you know what I mean."

"Very funny, very funny," Eddie said, feigning indignation. But he was glad to see that Kate seemed to be feeling better. "Comeon, ya can drown yer sorrows over a cherry-Coke. My treat."

As they walked, all traces of the tentative smile of moment ago faded from Kate's face, and she became very quiet.

"Do you know what makes me feel even worse?" she asked, after walking in silence for half a block, looking down at the sidewalk. "It was *my* dumb idea to begin with, not yours."

"Gee, thanks, I — "

"No, really," Kate cut him off, continuing glumly, her shoulders sagging. "I didn't have to be asked to do it, or coaxed, or dared, or anything. No, not me. I'm Miss Hotsy-Totsy. I can tease a nice old man. Gee, I wonder what I should do for an encore? Steal candy from a baby?"

The tears started falling again, and Eddie realized she was talking herself into a state of deep depression. And, the more she talked, the more stoop-shouldered she became, as if the weight of the experience was getting heavier all the time.

Christ, Eddie thought, if I don't do something she'll be crawlin' into Dick's on her hands an' knees bawlin' like a baby. He stopped and grabbed her by the arms. "Look at me," he said. She kept her eyes diverted to the sidewalk. "Look at me!" This time it was a demand.

Slowly, she turned her face upward. Tears were running down her cheeks.

"Listen to me," Eddie said, his voice more gentle, but still firm. "We all like to tease an' show off. That's why I strut around an' act cool. That's why ya girls soak yer jeans skin tight. It's all part of the game we play."

Kate started to say something, but Eddie stopped her with a finger to her lips.

"No, let me finish. Do ya really think Mr. Goldberg is stupid? He knew what ya were doin', an' he enjoyed it. Ya played yer game, an' he played his. All ya did was make his borin' day a little excitin'."

Kate wiped the tears from her cheeks with the back of her hand, and blinked a bit of brightness back into her eyes. "Y-you think so?" she asked haltingly.

"Yeah, sure," Eddie said with certainty. "Jus' think about it. He sits in that tiny shop all day doin' the same old shit, an' then ya walk in, an' his eyes light up. If ya remember, he was leanin' over that table frownin' when we went in. I bet if we go back an' peek through the window he's *still* smilin'. For that ya should feel good, not down in the dumps. An' that, my ol' friend," Eddie concluded, grinning, "is the longest speech yer'll ever get outta me."

Kate stared at Eddie for several moments, then took his arm affectionately.

They resumed walking. "You know, sometimes you scare the hell out of me, you're so clever. A few minutes ago I felt like crap. After listening to you, I almost feel like I should get a medal or something."

"Ya *should* get a medal." Eddie's smile immediately turned to a lecherous grin. After all, ya got a great *chest* to pin it on."

Kate pulled her arm out from his, and stepped back, hands on her hips. "It's amazing how fast you revert back to your old perverted self," she said, trying to look annoyed. But it only lasted for a moment. Then she shook her head, smiled and took his arm again. "You *really* are something." They were both in high spirits again by the time they arrived at Dick's.

"Walk this way, please," Eddie said with fluttering eyebrows, then stooping over and taking long strides, while flicking ashes from an imaginary cigar, in a terrible Groucho impersonation. Suddenly, he stopped, and in a stage whisper, said to Kate, "Now, let's see ya tease a couple of cherry-Cokes outa Dick."

"Why, you . . ." Kate swung a wild round-house right, but she was laughing so hard she missed, and knocked over the comic-book rack.

Dick, behind the counter, looked up and frowned. He checked his watch, and began muttering in German. Meanwhile, Kate and Eddie dropped to the floor, laughing, and quickly gathered up the comics, replacing them haphazardly on the wire holders of the rotating display rack, which they propped back up.

By the time they got to the counter, they were just barely able to contain their laughter by taking deep breaths. "Sorry, Dick," Eddie said, sliding onto a stool, "but we put 'em all back the way they were."

That did it! They both broke up again. Kate hurried to the back of the store and slipped a quarter in the juke box, while Eddie tried unsuccessfully to order the Cokes. He couldn't get the words out. Every time he looked up at Dick, standing with arms folded across his chest, face red with anger, he thought of the comics and laughed harder, while Dick fumed even more. Finally, Eddie, too, rushed off to seek sanctuary by the juke box.

Grumbling, Dick shuffled to the front of the store, where he re-arranged the comic-book rack, separating the *Archies* from the *Classics*, the *Supermans* from the *Little Lulus.*

Eddie, seeing the juke box's selection light still lit, assisted Kate in pressing buttons. He was anxious for the music to start. The store was empty and quiet. At least the music would help drown out their laughter before Dick really blew his stack. The first record started playing, and Eddie realized Kate had the same idea. She played the loudest song on the machine. It was *I Put A Spell On You* by Screaming Jay Hawkins.

"You were right," Kate said with obvious satisfaction, when she returned from picking up the bracelet an hour later. "Mr. Goldberg *was* still smiling when I went back." Judy Bender and Sarah Mullins had come in, along with Joe Ross, and the atmosphere in the store was back to normal.

Eddie checked the inscription. "It looks pretty good," he said. "An', he musta cleaned it, too, the way it shines. It looks brand new."

"Yeah," Kate agreed. "And, he gave me a message for you."

"For *me*?"

"Yeah, for *you*. He said *mazel tov* to you and your new girlfriend."

"Holy shit!" Eddie exclaimed. "An' I never even spoke to him. He's even sharper than I thought. I hope ya weren't too embarrassed."

"No, I wasn't," Kate said with emphasis. "Not at all." She hesitated. "Well, maybe a little at first. Then, I guess I started to blush, and, well, he patted my shoulder and said, 'I was young once, too, you know'. Now, he says, he gets his enjoyment just being around young people. Isn't that nice?"

"Yeah, great," Eddie said. "But, I jus' wanna know one thing. Are ya sure it was really yer *shoulder* he patted?"

"Yes, I'm sure," Kate said, feigning outrage. Then, she was smiling again. "He's just a very nice old man who's a bit lonely, and you knew that from the start. So don't try to make jokes." She turned, and walked back to the booth where her friends were waiting, giving him an exaggerated swish of ass for good measure.

Eddie got a dollar's worth of change and another Coke, and headed for the phone booth to call Ginny. She was home, but couldn't leave. She was babysitting her little brother while her mother was shopping.

"How come you're out?" she asked. "I thought you couldn't leave your house until Sunday."

"That's what I'm callin' about," Eddie said. "Everything's cool now." He explained it all, and when his change ran out, she took the number and called back. Before they hung up almost an hour later, they agreed to meet at Dick's at seven.

Eddie hung out all day. By early afternoon, most of the girls and all the guys who weren't working had wandered into the store. As usual, the girls huddled in the back booth, playing the juke box and talking about clothes and boys, while the guys debated baseball and drag racing.

Cootie and Johnny Logan argued which was faster in the quarter mile, the '57 Ford or Chevy. Then Joe Ross jumped into it by claiming the Olds 88 with a J-2 engine could blow them both away.

Dan Manning and Shadow Silverman nearly came to blows over which baseball team was better, the Brooklyn Dodgers or the New York Giants. Then they consoled each other over the fact that both teams had announced they would be playing in California the next year.

Eddie mostly mooned over Ginny, going over and over in his head exactly how he would ask her to go steady. At five o'clock, he had a hamburger, French fries and a Coke, before leaving to go home to dinner.

"Don't wash the plates," Eddie told Dick loudly for all to hear. "Just pour all that grease back into the Crisco can an' use it again." Dick grunted and frowned, but Manning and Shadow came over, laughing.

"You paid for it, so why not put it in a cup and take it home," Shadow told Eddie. "You can use it on your hair if you run out of bacon fat." Chuckling, the rest of the guys wandered over, ready to join in.

They were all laughing at Eddie. He looked hard at Shadow, who got his nickname because of his heavy beard. He always seemed to have a five o'clock shadow. He was funny and quick-witted, but very sensitive about being the only Jew in the crowd. Naturally, that was exactly what Eddie decided to attack.

"At least I *have* bacon at my house," Eddie said. "Whadaya do? Rub lox in yer hair?"

"What hair are ya talkin' about?" Ross asked. "He has more on his face than on his head."

"Hey, don't make fun of his beard," Logan said, looking serious. "His old man made a bundle of money from it. When he was born his father took one look an' ran out an' bought shares in Gillette Blue Blades."

They were all laughing at Shadow, who singled out Manning for the next victim.

"What are you laughing at?" he asked. "You're so dumb, Dan, you're the only person who'll collect a pension for retiring as a high school student."

Now it was Shadow's turn to join the rest of the guys as they laughed at Manning, repeating "Dumb Dan" over and over. Manning's face pinched up, and he scratched his head.

"Yeah, well, when ya see yer motha, ask for my shoes. I left them under her bed last night."

Manning chuckled, but there was silence from the rest of the guys.

Suddenly, Shadow stepped forward and grabbed Manning by the shirt-front.

"No mothers, man," Shadow said through clenched teeth. "You know the rules. No mothers."

"Sorry, man, sorry," Manning said. "I forgot. I didn't mean nuttin' by it."

"Relax," Eddie said, getting off the stool. "I'm splitting anyway. Halfway to the door, Eddie turned and called out, "Besides, we all know that Jewish girls only fuck *before* they're married, anyways."

"Up yours, you guinea bastard," Shadow shouted above the laughter as Eddie continued towards the door. Kate was at the front of the store buying the latest issue of Photoplay Magazine.

"Wait," she said, trying to force her change into the pocket of her tight jeans. "I'll walk home with you." She looked at Eddie and shook her head. "That was terrible, what you just said."

"Yeah, I know," he agreed with a grin. "But I jus' love gettin' in the last shot."

They walked out of Dick's and, at least ten times on the way home, Kate reminded Eddie of his part of their bargain. He knew he had some serious planning to do that night.

Spinach with pork was not one of Eddie's favorite meals, but he managed to get through dinner without too much commotion. He ate most of the pork, even though it had a "spinach" taste, and only once did his mother spot him slipping the dreaded vegetable onto his sister's plate. Finally, he waited for his father to go into the living room to watch the Huntley-Brinkley report, and his mother and sister to start on the dishes. Then, he carefully palmed a stuffed paper napkin and slyly dumped the spinach into the garbage.

"No place, nothin', I won't," he told his mother as he headed for the door.

"What are you talking about?" Mrs. Casale asked.

"Just tryin' to make it easy for ya," Eddie said, smiling.

"Go on, get out of here," she said, reaching for the wooden spoon on the stove, "before I give you one of these." But, he could see she was forcing back a smile of her own.

Walking across the street to Bo's house, Eddie spotted the Triumph in the backyard. Good, he was still home.

Eddie scanned the yard, and smiled. Besides the Triumph, there were various parts of a Royal Enfield motorcycle, not quite ready for assembling; a '49 Hudson Hornet, standing on milk crates, and a '40 Ford coupe being fitted for the huge '56 Chrysler 300 engine sitting on the ground next to it. The coupe belonged to Hank, who had no room to work on it at his own house. In between the bikes, cars, and grease stains, there were several green spots where pitifully small patches of lawn were trying desperately to grow. Now, this is my kinda lawn, Eddie laughed to himself, as he climbed the stoop to the back door. *I could mow it with scissors in two minutes.*

The Brody family was at the dinner table, but the only one still eating was Bo. He looked up at Eddie, then hunched over his food and encircled his plate with his arm.

"I hope I'm not interruptin'," Eddie said.

"No, not at all," Mr. Brody replied affably, waving Eddie over to the table. "We've just finished."

"Sit down," Mrs. Brody said, indicating an empty chair. "Have something. There's still some left."

"No thanks," Eddie said, sitting. "I really can't. I just fin — " He stopped when he saw her return from the stove with a platter of rare roast beef. "Well, maybe just one little slice. It looks so good."

Mrs. Brody emptied the platter onto a plate, topped it with a ladle of creamy mushroom gravy, and placed it in front of Eddie.

He eyed the breadbasket. There were three freshly baked Pillsbury buns left. Bo quickly grabbed all three.

"Where're your manners?" Mrs. Brody asked, taking the buns from her son and putting them on Eddie's plate. "You already had five of them, anyway."

Bo glared at his friend. Kate giggled. Eddie smiled innocently, and dug into his food. "This is great," he said between mouthfuls. "I didn't think I was this hungry. I hope everyone had enough."

"Don't worry. Eat," Mrs. Brody said. "We've all had enough, we're all full." Eddie felt Bo's eyes boring into him, but refused to look up. "The way you boys eat, I swear," she continued. "Well, I guess you're still growing."

"Yeah, right" Mr. Brody added. "You're growing your fathers right out of house and home." He looked at his wife and they both laughed.

Eddie, still avoiding his friend's eyes, decided to keep the light mood going with a little joke of his own.

"Hey, Mr. Brody, ya betta be careful," he chuckled. "If ya don't get some more cars in yer backyard soon, ya may end up with a lawn."

It was several seconds before Eddie became aware of the cold silence. Slowly, he glanced around the table. Kate's face was flushed. Bo was half out of his chair, snarling. Mrs. Brody was shaking her head, suddenly depressed. Mr. Brody pulled off the napkin which was tucked into his shirt collar and angrily threw it on the table. The smile froze on Eddie's face.

"Oh, I'm so glad you brought that up," Mr. Brody said to Eddie, without really looking glad at all. He turned to his son. "I've told you a hundred times, either fix those wrecks back there or throw them away. You're turning our property into a junkyard."

He turned to his daughter. "And, you, young lady. It's bad enough my own son is making a mess of our yard, we certainly don't need any help from your boyfriend."

Mr. Brody stood up, then leaned forward, hands on the table, glaring at each of his children in turn. "I'm warning you both. If you don't do something about that junk I'm going to have it hauled away." He stormed off into the living room, shaking his head in disgust.

"Now, now, calm down, dear," Mrs. Brody said, chasing after her husband. "You know what happens when you get so angry on a full stomach."

"You jerk!" Kate spat. "We just got him calmed down about the yard, and you have to come in and say something stupid."

"Well, er . . . I didn't . . ."

"Oh, just shut up!" she ordered. "Let me try to talk to him." She hastened into the living room.

Eddie concentrated on his plate in order not to look at Bo. He cut a piece of meat, but his appetite had dissipated. When he heard the scrape of his friend's chair, he glanced up.

Bo was no longer snarling. In fact, he was smiling, which was worse. He rose slowly and walked around the table. Eddie looked back down at his plate and continued to eat without tasting.

Bo slipped his arm around Eddie's shoulder. "Let's go outside, *pal*. We can talk, have a smoke, ya know, like *real* pals." He was doing his Tommy Udo routine from *Kiss of Death,* which meant big trouble.

"Er, I'm not finished eatin' yet," Eddie said nervously, still not looking up. "But ya go on out back, an' I'll join ya when I'm through. Ok?" He figured he could sneak out the front door.

Bo put his big hand into Eddie's plate and squashed the remaining meat, gravy and buns into his fist. "Finish this outside," he said, using his other hand to yank Eddie out of the chair by the collar and drag him towards the door. "In fact, I'll even feed it to ya."

In the yard, Bo maneuvered Eddie into a headlock and held him tight, while he pushed the mushed-up food in his face, yelling: "Comeon, ya can eat it. Ya got a big fucking' mouth." Eddie gagged, but managed to grab Bo around the waist and wrestle him to the ground. They rolled around for several minutes, until Bo pinned Eddie's arms tightly to the ground, while sitting with his knees on his chest.

"Give up?" Bo asked, pressing hard.

"No," Eddie grunted. "But ya look like shit, covered with grease an' all. Why don't ya tell yer old man ya cleaned up the fuckin' yard for him?"

"Ya don't look so good yerself," Bo said, with a smile. "But, with Italians it's hard to tell. They're greasy all the time."

The tension broke, and they both started laughing. Bo rolled off Eddie and lay on his back next to him. Each time they looked at each other they laughed harder.

"Christ," Eddie said, jumping to his feet. He looked down at himself. "Shit, I gotta get cleaned up an' meet Ginny, but I can't go home like this."

"An' I ain't goin' back inside 'til my old man cools down," Bo added.

They turned on the garden hose and took turns washing their hands and faces. Bo snatched a towel from his mother's clothes line. Wetting it, they wiped off their clothes as best they could.

"I betta get rid of this before my old lady sees it," Bo said, grabbing the soiled towel. "Turn the water off."

As Eddie bent over to turn the tap, he felt a sharp sting on his ass. He yelped, jumping up just in time to see Bo poised for a second snap of the towel. This one hit him in the upper thigh.

"Ouch! That fuckin' hurt," Eddie yelled.

Bo, with an evil grin, started circling, setting up for another attack. Eddie reached for the water faucet and turned it back on, wincing as the next snap caught him on the left hip. He twisted the nozzle of the hose to full-force, catching Bo smack in the face before he could snap the towel again.

Bo tried to run and dodge away from the on-rushing water, but Eddie chased him around the yard. Suddenly, Bo stopped, threw the towel over Eddie's head, and yanked the hose from his hands. Then, Bo chased Eddie until they both fell exhausted to the wet ground, soaked from head to toe, the hose still gushing water.

"We better check our son's birth certificate."

Startled, the two boys raised themselves up on their elbows, and looked towards the sound of the voice. Mr. and Mrs. Brody were standing on the back porch, shaking their heads and frowning. "Sometimes he acts just like a ten year old," Mr. Brody continued, walking to the tap and turning it off.

"Yeah," Eddie called out. "An' he's three years *older* than me."

"Oh, my!" Mrs. Brody exclaimed, spotting the grease-stained towel. "Is that one of my new towels?" She scanned the clothes line.

"Naw," Bo said, jumping up. He grabbed the towel and tossed it through the open window of the old Ford. "Just a rag I use when workin' on the car."

Mrs. Brody looked doubtful, but Bo was already kick-starting his bike. "You can't go out in those wet clothes," she shouted over the roar as the engine caught. "You'll catch your death."

"It's ok," Bo called back. "We'll ride around for awhile an' let the wind dry us." Eddie hopped on the back and Bo fishtailed out of the driveway.

Half an hour later, they wheeled to a stop in front of Dick's. Bo was almost completely dry. Eddie, however, blocked from the wind by being in the back, was still sopping wet.

Shit, Eddie thought, looking down at himself. *I look like hell. I shoulda gone home to change. An' on a night like this, too.* He debated whether to run home now, but decided it was too late. He had more important things to take care of at the moment.

"Wait a minute," he said, grabbing Bo by the arm as they headed for the door. "There's something I wanna talk to ya about." He explained the deal he had made with Kate, and how Bo could help by coming along, too.

When Bo had finally stopped laughing, he said, "Whadaya fuckin' crazy? I'm goin' to the Hide Out. Ya an' Hank can go to the damn drive-in, not me."

"Aw, comeon," Eddie pleaded. "How the hell am I gonna talk him into it alone?"

"Easy," Bo said. "Just buy him a case of Schaefer." He opened the door and walked inside.

"Shit!" Eddie exclaimed, standing alone on the sidewalk. "Why didn't I think of that?" He walked into Dick's with a new feeling of confidence, knowing Hank would do almost anything for a case of Schaefer.

Most of the crowd was there, sitting in booths or at the counter, or hanging out by the juke box, which was blasting *Smokey Joe's Café* by The Robins. Eddie didn't see Hank, but he spotted Ginny in a back booth talking with her friends. He headed towards her, undergoing a gauntlet of wisecracks on the way.

"Hey, man," Ox called out. "Whadya do? Wipe yer greasy hair with yer tee shirt?"

"The next time ya go swimmin'," Joe Ross joined in, "ya should wear a bathin' suit."

Eddie felt his face flush. All the guys were looking and laughing. Except Cootie. He was in deep concentration propped up at the end of the counter, the movie pages of the newspaper spread out in front of him. Eddie walked over and slipped a dime on the counter. Cootie looked at the coin, then at Eddie, questioningly.

"Yeah," Eddie said, "do it. A real *big* one!"

Cootie smiled, turned to face the store, and bellowed, "Fuck ya guys!" Then he signaled Dick. "Gimme an eggcream on my good friend, Eddie, here."

Everyone was still laughing as Eddie made his way to Ginny's booth. Judy Bender and Joan Ford, who were sitting with her, excused themselves as soon as he sat down.

"You look awful," Ginny said with concern. "You didn't get into a fight, did you?"

"Naw," Eddie said. "Bo an' me were just foolin' around in his backyard an' we got messed up." Then, seriously, he added, "I'm, er, sorry. I woulda gone home to change but I was too anxious to see ya."

"Oh, Eddie, that's so nice," she said, her eyelids fluttering. "And, I didn't mean you look *awful*. You *never* do." She looked down, suddenly embarrassed. "I meant you look . . . oh, you know."

"Yeah, I know." Eddie reached down, cupped her chin in his hand, and raised her face gently. He couldn't resist. He leaned forward.

It was meant to be a short, reassuring touch of the lips. But the touch sent an electric charge through his body, igniting his passion. They were no longer in a crowded store; they were alone on a mountaintop of emotions, with darting tongues and embracing arms. The power of the kiss forced Ginny down on the bench of the booth, almost under the table, with Eddie hovering over her.

When they re-appeared several minutes later, gasping for breath, they were greeted with loud applause, hoots, hollers and whistles by a bunch of the guys who had gathered around the booth. Ginny, turning beet-red, tried to sink further in her seat. She turned to face the wall, while Eddie gave his friends the Italian salute. Still chuckling and wisecracking, the guys wandered off.

"Don't let 'em get to ya," Eddie said, patting Ginny's hand. "They're just havin' a little fun."

"They're insensitive jerks," Kate said, slipping into the seat on the opposite side of the booth. Ginny's cousin was with her, nodding in agreement. Kate looked at Eddie. "Hank should be here any minute. Don't forget what you have to do."

"How can I," Eddie said. "With ya remindin' me every time I see ya."

Ginny looked at him and Eddie realized he hadn't mentioned anything about the drive-in yet. He suddenly panicked. *Shit! What if she didn't want to go there on a first date, or, goddamnit, wasn't allowed to go?* He explained his plan, omitting his conspiracy with Kate over the ankle bracelet.

"So, would ya like to go?" he concluded. "I mean, if I can get Hank to take us."

"Oh, wow," Ginny gushed. "Yes, of course. That'll be super. We can really have fun in the back seat." She glanced quickly around the table, then dropped her eyes as she started to blush. "I mean, if a good movie's playing."

The other girls smiled. No one ever cared what film was showing at a drive-in. And, at the moment, that was the furthest thought from Eddie's mind. He was totally engrossed in imagining exactly what Ginny meant by "fun in the back seat."

His lascivious thoughts were interrupted by a sharp kick to his shin. "What the — " he snapped, looking around the table.

"Pay attention," Kate said, waving her thumb to where Hank was sliding onto a stool next to Buffalo.

"Christ!" Eddie said, rubbing his leg as he got up. "Relax, willya? I'm goin', I'm goin'."

"Hey, man, what's happenin'?" Eddie greeted Hank with a slap on the back.

"Hey, man," Hank said. "I jus' put new glass pack mufflers on the Ford today. It sounds tough."

"That's great," Eddie said, with a bit of false enthusiasm. "Lemme hear it."

As they headed for the door, Hank explained how the glass packs added a couple of horsepower to the engine, while producing a deep potent-sounding rumble. But, Eddie's mind wasn't on mufflers; he was busy thinking of the right words to convince Hank to give up a Saturday night at the Hide Out in favor of the drive-in.

They sat in the Ford while Hank raced the powerful V-8 engine to an explosive roar, then let it back down to a resonate idle, exploding and popping, like firecrackers on the fourth of July.

"Great, huh?" Hank asked.

"Yeah. Real boss," Eddie said. "Say, man, I was wonderin' if ya would take me an' Ginny, to the drive-in Saturday night. Ya see, it's — "

"Saturday night?" Hank didn't wait for Eddie to finish. "Shit man, I — "

"I know, I know," Eddie rushed on. "I know what yer gonna say. It's Hide Out night, an' all. But, it's real important to me. An' since it's our first date, it would make it extra special to go in a hot car like this. Ginny jus' loves this car. Come-on, man. Do me this favor, an' I'll buy ya case of Schaefer.

"Ya jerk!" Hank said. "Thanks for the beer an' compliments. Now, can I finish what I started to say?"

Eddie nodded.

"What I was about to say," Hank continued, "is that I was gonna go anyway. I wanna show off my new mufflers. Ya know, cruise the rows of cars, an' stuff." He opened the door. "I'll go tell Kate," he said, getting out. Then, turning back, laughing, he added, "An', thanks again for the beer."

Ginny and Kate, bubbling with exuberance, rushed to meet Eddie when he came in the door moments later. They each grabbed an arm and hugged it.

"It worked!" Kate beamed. "I can't believe it. You really pulled it off."

"I'm so happy," Ginny exclaimed, squeezing his arm tighter. "I knew if anyone could do it, you could."

"Yeah, well, ya know," Eddie said, accepting the kudos. "It's all in knowin' how to handle people."

When the rest of the girls heard that Kate and Ginny were going to the drive-in Saturday night, they sprang into action. First, they crammed into the back booth for a hastily-called meeting. After several minutes of frantic whispering and head bobbing, they checked their make-up in compact mirrors and dispersed. Within the hour, six other guys announced that they, too, had decided to take their dates to the drive-in. Even Bo had been coaxed into submission by Barbara Saunders.

"Ya bastard!" Bo hissed, grabbing Eddie's arm in a vice-like grip. "That's the last time I give ya any bright ideas."

Eddie just smiled and said, "Ya mean, ya weakened, too, huh?" With his other hand, Eddie ruffled Bo's longish hair. "An' she didn't even haveta cut off yer hair like Samson's."

Bo swatted Eddie's hand away from his head, but a smile began to flicker. "I figured that might be comin' next," he said. "An' I don't want nobody fuckin' with my hair. Besides, someone's gotta look after ya with all those bad asses at the drive-in. Don't forget what happened to ya the last time we went there.

"Yeah, I remember, but at least this time I won't have ta ride in yer old man's clunker of a Chevy." Or so Eddie thought.

TEN

BYE BYE LOVE

Eddie ran his Ace comb through his hair, pressed several stubborn strands into place with an extra dab of Brylcreem, then tilted his head at every conceivable angle while checking his reflection in the bathroom mirror. *Cool, real cool. Now for the overall inspection.*

He ducked into his sister's room and stepped in front of the full-length mirror hanging on the back of her closet door. He was wearing his new black slacks with a sixteen-inch peg, pistol pockets, a two-inch rise above the slim-jim belt, and double rows of white saddle-stitching along the outside seams. His shoes, a new pair of black Florsheim wing-tips, were even Kiwi-shined. *Yeah, man,* he smiled, *here I come, ready or not!* He headed for the stairs, then suddenly ducked back into the bathroom for a final zit-search, another dab of Bylcreem and an extra splash of Old Spice. He was now ready for his Saturday night date.

Downstairs, he stepped smack-dab into a reviewing stand manned by his Mom, Dad and sister. Their attention quickly went from *Beat The Clock* on TV to the live show in their living room. Eddie looked from face to face. His father shook his head, his mother frowned, his sister laughed. And, Eddie's high spirits of a moment ago dropped down several notches.

"You're a little too early for trick or treating." Anna was the first to speak. "Halloween is more than two months away."

"Just don't use your real name tonight, in case you run into someone that knows me," Mr. Casale said.

"You look like one of those . . . those zoot-suiters," Mrs. Casale added. "That's the last time I let you go clothes shopping by yourself."

"Aw, comeon, Mom, this is what all the guys are wearin' these days. I bet ya guys had some wild styles when ya were kids, didn't ya?" Eddie said, although he had a difficult time conjuring up his mother in anything but a regular dress.

"Well," Mrs. Casale said, avoiding the question, "have a nice time . . . and be good! Do you have enough money?"

"Er, well, hmmm." Eddie never liked to admit to having enough money to his Mom, knowing she was usually good for a little more.

"He has plenty," Mr. Casale answered for him. "I just gave him his allowance. Don't give him another cent."

"Don't be home too late, Mrs. Casale said, following her son to the door. You have Mass in the morning." She reached into her pocket. "Here, take this just in case," she said in a lowered voice. There were three one-dollar bills in her hand.

"Gee, Mom, you don't have to do that," Eddie whispered, quickly snatching the bills from her hand and stuffing them in his pocket.

As he stepped out the door, Eddie heard Mr. Casale ask his wife, "So, how much did you give him this time?"

Eddie paused in the front of Dick's, checked his reflection in the glass door, then stepped inside the crowded store to the sound of Lloyd Price singing *Lawdy Miss Clawdy.*

As usual, the girls were huddled together in and around the back booth, while the guys milled around the counter. As Eddie headed for the guys, he glanced at the girls and caught Ginny's eye. He nodded a smile. She beamed back, stopping him in his tracks. God, she's beautiful, he thought. He started to move to the back booth when someone punched his arm.

"Hey, shithead, I'm talkin' to ya."

Eddie turned sharply. It was Hank, decked out with a powder blue Hollywood sports jacket, with a one-button roll, over his usual jeans and T-shirt. That was his "dress-up" outfit.

"Whadaya want?

"I said where ya goin' in those clothes, to a fashion show at the Appolo Theatre in Harlem?"

"Hey, it's a Saturday night date," Eddie responded, annoyed. "Show a little class, willya?"

"Whadaya mean? I got a jacket on, don't I? Bein' classy don't mean lookin' like a pussy."

"The only class you knew is when you were in high school, and ya failed *that* too," Eddie said. "Me? I'm just too cool, fool."

"Well, let's see how *cool* ya look *walkin'* into the drive-in," Hank said, annoyed at the dig. He pulled a Chesterfield from a pack, lit it with his Zippo, and blew smoke into Eddie's face.

"Hey, Eddie!" Ox said in his booming voice, from across the room. "How far didya have to chase the nigga for those clothes?"

The guys all laughed, some walking over to get in on the rank-out session. They were all wearing their usual dungarees. Joe Ross, went to the juke box, punched the reject button, and turned up the volume. The next record, *Black Slacks,* roared through the store, with The Sparkletones singing:

Black slacks make you cool daddy-o
When I put 'em on I'm rarin' to go

Eddie fumed, his face turning red. Suddenly, the girls pushed their way into the group, but they weren't laughing.

"Don't go making fun of him," Diane said, poking her finger in Ox's face. "It wouldn't hurt you to get dressed up for a date once in a while."

Carol, backing Chuck into a corner, said," I went out today and bought this new dress for our date. And, you? You show up in those same old jeans. Christ, you even sleep in them." Then she glanced around, a flash of embarrassment on her face, adding: "Er, I mean, you *probably* do."

Most of the other girls berated their dates with the same complaint, but the guys backed off mumbling apologies, wisely figuring that an argument now and the only thing they'd be doing at the drive-in would be watching the movie. However, some did flash Eddie evil looks, obviously blaming him for the state of the present situation. Kate was the only one who didn't say anything. Hank may have been wearing the same old jeans, but at least he had a jacket over them.

In the wake of the guys' departure to the outer reaches of the store, Ginny appeared, looking radiant in a blue flare skirt and yellow sweater with white collar. Her long black hair, glittery in its richness, cascaded over her shoulders to the middle of her back. Her wide mouth, the pouting lips faintly touched with red, expressed a warm, understanding smile.

"You look great," she said, simply, reaching for his hand. "Thank you."

They touched, and the contact lit a fuse that burned through his body and his heart almost exploded. Eddie tried to say something, but only unintelligible sounds emerged from his lips. Then, the record on the juke box changed, and Elvis Presley helped him out, singing:

I will spend my whole life through
Loving you, just loving you

"Listen to the words of this song," Eddie finally managed.

"I do," she said softly, beginning to blush. "Over and over again."

"Well, this is how . . .er, like I mean . . . er, well . . ." He broke eye contact, looked down at the floor for several moments, took a deep breath, and looked back into Ginny's dark green eyes, ready to try again.

"That's ok," she said with a gentle smile. "I feel the same way."

"Oh, wow!" Eddie beamed.

"Yeah, *wow* is right!" Ginny responded. Her smile widened to match his.

They were silent for several seconds, listening to Elvis speak for each of them. "Oh, wait a minute," Eddie said suddenly, breaking the reverie. He reached into his pocket and came out with the little box the jeweler had provided for the re-worked ankle bracelet. He thrust it at her.

"For *me*?" she exclaimed. Eddie noted that her words were a little too animated and figured Kate had already broken the news.

"It's beautiful," Ginny gushed. She took it out of the box and held it up to the light for closer inspection, then rushed over to a booth, sat down, and put the bracelet around her left ankle. She held out her leg and inspected it again, before returning to where Eddie was still standing.

"I love it," she said, "but why'd you give it to me? I mean, it's not my birthday or anything." There was a teasing lilt to her voice.

"Well, er, ya know . . . I thought, er, like, maybe . . ."

"Are you asking me to go *steady*?" she asked, helping him out, as if the thought just came to mind.

Eddie just nodded.

"I accept!" Ginny almost shouted. She stood on her tip-toes, put her arms around his neck, and pulled his face close to hers.

The kiss was long, sweet, delicious, and sent a whirl of emotions spinning through Eddie's head. When they slowly began to settle, one thing was clear. Eddie was really in love, for the first time.

All this was going on in the time-span of a kiss, and he wanted it to go on forever. But it was over too soon, rudely interrupted by a loud chorus of whistles, cheers, and applause, as they were jolted back to the reality of standing in the middle of Dick's candy store.

"Forget about them," Ginny said softly, as they separated. "You know how they are." A slight blush caused her cheeks to redden even more. Then she smiled seductively, stood on her tip-toes again, and whispered into Eddie's ear, "We'll continue this – and more – at the drive-in."

The combination of her warm breath blowing into his ear as she spoke, plus his interpretation of the words themselves, conjured up erotic mental visions of the night to come.

"Are you sure ya don't want another one?" Hank called over his shoulder from the front seat of the car, popping a can of Schaefer.

"No thanks, I had enough," Eddie said, his mouth watering for another beer. He looked down at Ginny, cuddled in his arms, and she smiled her approval at his decision to stay sober.

"Enough? Ya only had two beers, ya candy-ass," Hank snorted. He raised the can to his lips and chug-a-lugged it.

"Leave him alone!" Kate ordered. "If he doesn't want anymore, don't force him."

"Who's forcin' him?" Hank responded. "Shit, it jus' means more for me." He popped open another can. "I jus' think it's stupid to be makin' out when there's still some beer left."

Kate glanced into the back seat, where Eddie and Ginny were embraced in a passionate kiss. She looked back at Hank, head thrown back, can to his lips. "Yeah, some people certainly are stupid," she said, shaking her head. "Here, have another one. In fact, I'll have one, too." Kate popped two cans and handed one to Hank. When he threw his head back to guzzle it, she poured hers out the window. Hank was already too far gone to notice.

"Shit, we shoulda got more beer," Hank slurred, shaking the last drops of Schaefer into his mouth, and chucking the can out the window. "Maybe I –"

"Shut up," Kate interrupted, sliding across the front seat, and wiggling onto his lap. A moment later they were making out hot and heavy.

"Kate reads him like a book," Ginny whispered, looking up at Eddie with those dark green eyes. "She really knows how to handle him."

"She should," Eddie replied. "She's been readin' that same book for years, an' it ain't exactly *heavy* readin'."

"Shush!" Ginny cautioned, raising a finger to her lips, while trying to suppress a giggle. The sound was musical. He cupped her chin with his fingers and caressed her sensuous lips with his thumb, while tilting her head up to meet his. The kiss was warm, wet, and now Eddie caressed her lips with his tongue.

She responded with her own tongue movement, while pressing her body closer, arms around his neck, maneuvering half unto his lap, her flare skirt bunching up above her thighs.

The movement caused Eddie's cock to stiffen, his hard-on jabbing into her naked left thigh. *Oh, please touch it.* His mind was clouding, and he wasn't sure if he said the words, or just thought them. She didn't exactly *touch* it, but she *did* press her body even tighter against him, while moving her left thigh slowly, back and forth.

Eddie moaned. His hands, caressing her back, slowly made their way to the bottom of her sweater. When they reached bare flesh, he began making circular motions with his right thumb, while inching her sweater higher and higher with his left hand.

Ginny's hands, which were clasped behind Eddie's head, separated. The splayed fingers of her right hand gently rubbed the back of his neck, where the short hairs met smooth skin. She used the index finger of the other hand to trace an imaginary route across his chest, heading south. Their tongues played tag, their breathing, heavy, rasping, was in unison. At the same time Eddie's thumb reached her bra snap, Ginny's index finger arrived at his belt buckle. Eddie fumbled with the clasp, wishing he had practiced with one of his sister's bras like he planned. More deftly, Ginny's fingers found the sliding tab of his zipper, and drew it down slowly, the sound of the unzipping like music to his ears.

Eddie moaned again in anticipation, expecting momentarily for her fingers to reach into his pants and caress his erection. Instead, she quickly raised her hand to his chest, and shoved hard, pushing herself off Eddie's lap, while causing him to crack his head sharply on the window frame.

"Whadya do that for?" Eddie asked, startled, rubbing the back of his head. The sudden pain had caused his erection to subside rapidly.

Ginny looked confused, too. "I . . . I'm not sure. No. Yes, I am." She took a deep breath, smoothed her skirt down to her knees, and straightened her sweater. "Look, Eddie," she continued, her flushed face turning warm with a soft smile. "I, er, like you. I mean *really* like you. But, we can't do this. We have to control ourselves."

"Aw, geez." Eddie's frustration was getting the better of him. "If ya *really, really* like me, you'd let me do it."

Ginny looked up at him, the smile fading. Her eyes turned even darker than usual.

"I can't believe you said that," she said slowly. "I was really hoping *you* wouldn't use that stupid line." Tears welled up in her eyes.

"Whadaya mean?" Eddie sounded confused, not realizing what he could have said wrong. "Aw, comeon, don't cry."

Ginny sniffed back her tears and took another deep breath. "It's ok," she said, her voice showing a trace of annoyance. "It's just that I thought we had something special, and then you have to say something like *that.* Well, comeon, give me the rest of it. You know, like 'it's ok now because we're going steady'. Isn't that how it goes?" She looked at him defiantly. "Well, isn't it?"

Shit, how'd she know I was gonna say that? "Naw, that's not what I was gonna say. What I was *gonna* say was . . . er . . . " Luckily he was interrupted by a commotion in the front seat.

"No! Hank, stop that right now. I mean it!"

"Aw, comeon, honey, at least let me *touch* 'em. It's ok, we're goin' steady, ain't we?"

Eddie and Ginny looked at each other. She just nodded, her expression saying, *There, see what I mean.* Eddie felt his face redden.

"Look, Eddie," Ginny started, reaching for his hand, and squeezing. "Like I said, I really like you. Maybe . . . er, maybe even love you. And, I want to be with you, go steady with you. But, look, no fooling around, ok, no *dirty* stuff. Promise?"

Eddie just looked at her for several moments, searching for the right words. It was difficult. He felt choked with emotion. He couldn't explain it. Ginny just told him she wouldn't put out, not even a little, yet he felt even closer to her. "Yeah, I promise," he said, huskily, taking her by the shoulders. He pulled her close and kissed her, closed mouth, because he wasn't sure what she included in the "dirty stuff" category.

"You don't have to go that far," Ginny said, pulling back, smiling seductively. "I kinda like French kissing."

Within moments, Ginny and Eddie were back to some heavy making out, with the new rules established early. In addition to French kissing, Eddie was allowed to stick his tongue in her ear and put his hands under her sweater, but only on her back. Hickies were strictly forbidden (*my father will kill me)*, no kissing below the shoulders and no touching above the thighs. In spite of the restrictions, Eddie managed to maintain a rigid erection, while breaking the "rules" three times within the first five minutes.

"That's it, let's cool off," Ginny said, removing Eddie's hand from her inner thigh, and pulling back. She was breathing quite heavy herself, while Eddie sounded like an asthma patient without an inhaler.

"Oh, God, not now," Eddie groaned, groping after her.

"Stop! Have a cigarette!" Ginny ordered, holding him off with the palm of her hand.

Reluctantly, Eddie shifted to his side of the back seat. He fished a crumpled pack of Luckies from his pocket. He had one left. "I gotta go get some more smokes," he said, not adding, *It looks like I'm gonna need 'em.*

When Eddie returned from the snack bar, Hank was leaning against the front fender, holding two cans of Rheingold, which he had just bummed from Kenny Fletcher, parked in the adjoining space.

"I hate this fuckin' beer," Hank said, opening the first can and taking a long swallow. "It tastes like piss-water," he added, before draining the rest of the can and tossing it away.

"Yeah, right," Eddie said, knowing that when Hank ran out of Schaefer he'd drink anything, even piss-water. He opened the car door, but Hank stopped him with a hand on his arm.

"Hey, buddy, howaya doin' back there?" Hank said with a lewd smirk, in what he thought was a whisper. "Gettin' lucky, or what?"

"Stop the shit," Eddie said, annoyed. He pulled his arm away. "She's a nice girl, ya know."

"Ha! Nice? They're all nice. They're even nicer when they play with this, right?" Hank said, grabbing his crotch and winking.

"Knock it off, will ya. I told ya, she's not that kinda girl."

"Sure, sure, then why's yer fly open? Jus' to get some fresh air," Hank said, snorting a laugh, as he popped the top of the other beer.

Eddie looked down, suddenly turning red. *Shit, I forgot to close my zipper.* He reached down and quickly pulled it up, while Hank laughed even louder.

"Don't worry 'bout it, ol' buddy." Hank threw an arm around Eddie's shoulders. "They're all the same. Ya jus' tell 'em put out or get out an' they come across all the time."

Eddie, really angry, shrugged Hank's arm off, and stepped back from the car. He felt like hitting him just to shut him up. He didn't have to. Behind Hank, Kate flew out of the open door, and the fire in her eyes could have melted steel. She was swinging her huge shoulder bag. Hank, still snorting with laughter, put the can to his lips and took a long swallow. On the third swing Kate's bag connected with the back of Hank's head. He almost swallowed the can.

"You . . . you disgusting pig," Kate roared. "Is that what you go around telling everybody about me? You animal." She began swinging her huge bag again.

Hank had fallen to one knee, his upper lip was bleeding. He shook his head, trying to clear it.

"Calm down, calm down," Eddie shouted, moving fast, grabbing Kate's arm before she could land another devastating blow. "Ya know how he talks bullshit when he's drunk. My God, ya *should* know by now."

"Yeah, I know. But I never heard him say *those* things." Kate's anger was subsiding, but suddenly she was on the verge of tears. "What are people going to *think* of me when they hear things like that?"

"Aw, comeon," Eddie said, comforting his friend. "First of all, he wasn't talkin' 'bout *you*. He was jus' runnin' off at the mouth. Ya know, man-to-man shit."

"Yeah," Hank said in a subdued voice, still on one knee. He wiped his lip with the bottom of his shirt. "Ya know I'd never say anything 'bout ya, yer my sweetheart." He inspected the blood on his shirt, then looked up at Kate. "Shit, baby, ya really hurt me," he whined.

"Oh, God, I'm sorry I got so carried away," Kate said, her voice suddenly filled with remorse. She walked over to Hank and helped him to his feet. "Let's go to the bathroom and I'll clean you up, honey."

"Ok," Hank said meekly. "Do ya forgive me, darlin'."

"Of course, honey. Do you forgive me, too?"

"Oh, for sure, baby."

And they walked off arm in arm.

"Do ya believe those two maniacs," Eddie said, after climbing into the back seat. "Either they're gonna kill each other or get married. Whichever happens first."

"At least there's more action outside than in this stupid movie," Ginny said with a laugh. "I've been trying to watch it while you were gone, but it isn't worth the effort."

"Then why watch it?" Eddie said, a lilt in his voice.

"Good question," Ginny responded in the same tone.

They threw their arms around each other and resumed making out. Eddie, breaking another rule, was so intent on administering an award-winning hickie on Ginny's neck, he didn't hear his friends return to the car a few minutes later. Suddenly, he heard the deep roar of the glass-packed mufflers, as the powerful V-8 Ford engine fired up.

"Hey, whereawe goin'?" Eddie's head suddenly shot up, startled. He untangled himself from Ginny's arms.

"Shit, man, I can't make out," Hank grumbled. "My lip is all swollen, an' hurts too much. I sure ain't jus' gonna sit here an' watch this fuckin' movie."

"Aw, comeon man, willya," Eddie complained.

But, Hank wasn't listening. He removed the speaker from the half-open window, shifted the Hurst transmission to reverse, and began backing out of the parking slot. He glanced up to check the rear-view mirror. What he saw was Kate pursing her lips, applying fresh lipstick. She had turned the mirror in her direction, and, in his present condition, Hank's reflexes weren't all that quick.

"Fuck! I can't see a thi – "

A loud crunching sound drowned out the rest of his words. He threw the shift into neutral, and jumped out of the car, with a very upset Kate right behind him. He had backed into a speaker stand, smashing his custom-made, bullet-shaped taillight. His face contorted with anger, as he glared at his broken light, then at Kate.

"It's yer fault, ya bitch," he yelled. "Can't ya use a fuckin' compact like yer supposed to?"

"Don't curse at me, you jerk," Kate yelled back. "If you had an ounce of sense at all you would've looked *before* you backed up."

"Jesus H. Christ, I musta told ya a hundred times not to turn the mirror."

"Well, then, you should have learned by now I don't listen to you."

"I oughta . . ." Hank snarled, stepping forward.

"You ought to, what?" Kate held her ground, raising her bag.

"Ain't love grand," Eddie said to Ginny, laughing, as they watched the scene unfold through the rear window.

"Shouldn't you do something?" Ginny asked, concerned. "It looks like he's going to hit her."

"No way," Eddie said assuredly. "He'd never raise a hand to her."

"Are you sure?"

"Sure I'm sure. He really does love her, ya know, in his own way. Besides, she has insurance."

"Insurance?"

"Yeah, the *best.* She's got Bo for a brother. An', speakin' of Bo, let's find him. "He's here someplace with an empty back seat. We just gotta be sure we find the *right* old Chevy clunker."

Eddie and Ginny were together almost every day, and the final days of summer seemed to fly by. They would meet at Dick's around noon, play the juke box, sip Cokes, snack on burgers and talk for hours. Then they would kiss goodbye, go home to dinner, and meet back at Dick's a couple of hours later. At night, the two lovers usually played out the same routine, with occasional variations. Sometimes Eddie would still go off to the Hide Out with the guys, and Ginny would sit with the girls trading stories. But, most of the time they would spend it together, discovering more and more about each other.

Ginny was an avid reader. Eddie said he loved to read, too, when he got the chance.

"Oh, I see, you're too *busy* to read a good book, I guess," Ginny said.

"Yeah, I guess," Eddie said, defensively. "Ya know, hangin' out with the guys, and, er, you, now. But I did read a great book a little while ago. It was called *On The Road* by some beatnik guy."

"Jack Kerouac. That's his name," Ginny said. "He's ok, but you should read books by some other writers, too, like John Steinbeck, and Hemingway, and maybe something by Sinclair Lewis, even

Thomas Wolfe. They're like the greatest American writers."

"Wow, you've read books by all those people?" Eddie sounded impressed, recognizing some of those names from English class.

"Yeah, sure," Ginny said proudly. "Even some Russian writers like Tolstoy and Nabokov. Yeah, you'd really *love* Nabokov's book," she added with mischievous grin. "It's called *Lolita*."

"Ya know, I . . . " Eddie hesitated, then glanced around the store. They were sitting alone in a back booth, but most of the Friday night crowd was in attendance. He looked back at Ginny and leaned closer. "Ya know, I never told anybody this before. They'd probably rib me, like. But I've always wanted to be a writer. Don't laugh."

Ginny didn't laugh. If anything, she became more serious. "Eddie, you can be anything you want. You're really a very bright guy. You can be a writer, but you have to work at it."

"Ya really think so?" he said hopefully, unable to contain the excitement in his voice. "Ya know, English has always been my best subject. I always get, like, Bs on my compositions, an' Mr. Mazer, my English teacher, says I'm a good writer. He says I'd even get As if it wasn't for my spellin'."

"That's great," Ginny said with enthusiasm. "But, don't you do book reports, too, in your school? You must have read a Hemingway book, at least."

"Naw, I don't think so. My last book report was on *Shane* by a guy named Jim Schaefer. I got a B-plus on it."

"Well, at least you read *that.*"

"Er . . . well, not exactly. But I saw the movie twice. An' read the *Classic* comic."

"*Eddie!* What are you going to do when you go to college? Do you know wha . . . ?" She hesitated, noting the sudden change in Eddie's expression. "What's the matter? You *do* know you have to go to college to be a writer, don't you?"

Eddie's glance dropped to the Formica table-top, his fingers suddenly intent on creating multi accordion folds in a plastic soda straw. "Yeah, well, we'll see, I don't know," he said very softly.

"Eddie! What do you mean you – ?"

"I said I don't know right now, ok?" Eddie interrupted, looking up, suddenly angry.

"Ok, Ginny said, annoyed. "Don't bite my head off!"

Eddie's face softened, as a smile took shape. "Hey, I'm sorry," he said gently, dropping the straw and reaching across for Ginny's hand. She hesitated momentarily, then extended her hand, too, her smile faltering at first, then matching his.

"It's . . . it's ok. I understand . . . I guess."

"Hey! I just remembered. "There's a Robert Mitchum movie at the Bayside. *Fire Down Below.* Wanna go?" Eddie asked, then his smile broadened. "See? Told ya I was a good writer. I just wrote a poem: *Fire Down Below, Wanna go.*"

"Wow! Move over Whitman, here comes Casale," Ginny said, sliding out of the booth. They walked out of Dick's hand-in-hand.

The next day they decided to go to Coney Island. "Were ya ever here before, an' have a Nathan's hot dog?" Eddie asked, on the Subway ride to Brooklyn.

"Well, my father took us all once," she explained, "but my mother packed a picnic basket. She wouldn't let us eat a frankfurter from one of those stands. She said you never know what they put in them."

First stop after leaving the train was Nathan's, where Eddie introduced Ginny to the foot-long hot dog.

"*Whatever* they put in them, it sure tastes great," Ginny said, wiping mustard from the corner of her mouth. Eddie had only enough money left for a couple of rides, plus the train fare home. They chose The Cyclone and The Whip. Against Eddie's not-too-enthusiastic objections, Ginny treated them to two more Nathan's hot dogs before hopping on the BMT back to Queens.

Over the next few days, Eddie, flush with an advancement of his next week's allowance, took Ginny to Radio City Music Hall and miniature golf at Kiddie City. Then, when he was broke again, they spent their time sitting by the pond in Crocheron Park making out. They crammed as much time together as possible those last days of August, knowing that once school started again Ginny's free time would be at a premium, limited to weekends only, perhaps even just Saturday nights.

Eddie was so wrapped up in Ginny he wasn't aware of, and really didn't care, what else was going on around him. It was for that reason he couldn't say exactly when Jim Miller started hanging out at Dick's. Of course, he heard his name, and spotted him talking to Johnny Logan and Joe Ross, but didn't pay much attention. That is, until he had overheard some of the girls talking about *what a doll* he was. And, Ginny had been one of those girls.

Jim Miller had just moved into Bay Terrace, the new development of garden apartments built on the site of old Meyer's Woods, near Fort Totten. He was seventeen, with a sinewy, but languorous body contained in a six-foot frame, which was tanned to a shade of rich, golden brown that would make any Jones Beach lifeguard envious. He wore his long, blond hair, brushed up from his forehead, pompadour style. He had blue eyes, and, when he smiled, he flashed a set of Pepsodent-perfect dazzling white teeth.

Everyone in the crowd seemed to like him. Eddie hated him. He hated him for the way he smiled at Ginny. And, he hated him even more for the way Ginny returned his smile.

"Who the hell does he think he is," Eddie said to Johnny Logan, "God's gift to women?"

Johnny laughed. "Have you taken a good look at him?" he replied. "*Any* of the girls in here would *love* to get a gift like *that*." Eddie shot him a sharp look. "Er, well, *almost* any of the girls," Logan quickly added.

Over the next few days, Eddie began sensing a change in Ginny, as well as in the rest of the crowd. The guys stopped talking about Miller in front of Eddie, and the girls avoided his eyes whenever he mentioned Ginny's name. Then, just before the Labor Day weekend, as they sat in the back booth at Dick's, sipping cherry-Cokes and listening to The Moonglows sing *We Go Together*, they had their first serious fight.

Their conversation had been stilted, with Eddie struggling to come up with topics for discussion, while Ginny offered only monotone, or one-word sentences.

"So, you wanna go to the movies?" Eddie asked. It was early afternoon, and there were only three other people in the store.

"No." Ginny replied, concentrating on placing her straw at exactly the right angle in her glass.

"Aw, comeon," Eddie urged. "They're playing *High Noon* again."

"I saw it before," Ginny said.

"Well, hell, I've seen it twice, but it's the best western ever made, an' it won all those academy awards," he said, trying to generate some enthusiasm.

"Westerns bore me," Ginny replied. "If you like it so much, you go see it. I won't mind."

Eddie hesitated momentarily, thinking about his next words. He was reluctant to broach the subject. "Er, well, maybe *I'm* startin' to bore ya, too, huh?"

She looked up from her glass. "What do you mean by that?" she said, a little too quickly.

Now that he had opened the door, he figured he would jump right in. "I'll tell ya what I mean by that," he said, his anger rising. "It seems all ya wanna do lately is hang around here an' wait for that creep Miller to come in so ya can make goo-goo eyes at each other." There it was, finally out in the open.

"I don't know what you're talking about," Ginny snapped.

"Oh, get off it! Whadaya think I am? Stupid?"

"No, not stupid. Just a jerk!" Her anger was now on par with his.

"A jerk, huh?" Eddie responded, his voice rising. "If I'm such a jerk, then yer a fuckin' idiot for sittin' here with me." The juke box had suddenly stopped playing, and his words resounded throughout the store. Joe Ross, Johnny Logan and Kate Brody were huddled together at the counter, intent on reading the Breyer's Ice Cream and Boar's Head signs on the wall.

"How *dare* you curse at me!" she shouted back, pushing herself up from the booth. "I don't have to sit here and listen to this." She stormed off towards the door.

"Good, get outa here," he called after her. "Bein' with ya lately is the same as bein' alone, anyway."

She stopped and turned, halfway to the door. Even at that distance, he could see her eyes fill with wetness. "Well, maybe you should be alone for a *long* time then," she said, her voice now void of anger, but firm, deliberate. Then, she turned and walked out.

Later, Eddie would tell himself what he *should have* done. He should have called her back. He should have said, "No, I don't wanna be alone, I wanna be with you." What he actually said was, "Ha! That'll be the day *I'll* ever haveta be alone. An', don't let the door hit ya in the ass on the way out." He affected a smug expression for the benefit of his audience, but his friends still had their backs to him, re-reading the wall posters. Maybe they didn't even hear anything, Eddie thought, however unlikely.

Then Joe Ross walked over to the juke box, dropped a nickel in the slot and pressed a button. A moment later the words of the Everly Brothers filled the room:

Bye Bye Love
Bye Bye Happiness
Hello Loneliness
I think I'm gonna cry

Eddie winced. *Shit, nuttin's sacred with these bastards.* Then he chased Ross out the door.

That night Ginny didn't show up at Dick's. Every time the door opened, Eddie looked up, but it was always someone else coming in. Most of the crowd was there, even Jim Miller. *At least they're not together.* He checked his watch. It was already after eight. *Where the hell is she?* After moping around all afternoon, he had decided to apologize. He had called her number three times already, but hung up each time when her mother answered, afraid she might be screening her daughter's calls. *Hell, that's stupid,* Eddie reasoned to himself, *I'll just ask to speak to her.* Nonchalantly, he headed for the phone booth, then quickly ducked inside. He almost froze again when Mrs. Marcessi answered. He took a deep breath, then tried to affect a most cordial tone.

"May I speak to Ginny, please?"

"Are you the one that's been calling, then hanging up?" she asked, pointedly.

"Me?" he said, trying to sound surprised. "No, no it wasn't me."

"Yes, well . . ." She didn't sound convinced. "Well, she doesn't feel good and doesn't want to be disturbed. Goodbye!" Suddenly, there was dial tone in his ear.

"Shit!" Eddie yelled into the dead receiver, before slamming it violently into its cradle. He stepped out of the booth, then stopped short. Everyone in the store was in a freeze-frame position, staring at him. Then, a moment later, as if some unseen director called "action," they all resumed moving and talking at once, as if nothing out of the ordinary had happened.

Eddie tried to look cool as he strode over to the counter, but he wasn't fooling any of his friends. They respected his mood, however, and no one made any wisecracks or comments.

Eddie squeezed in between Bo and Buffalo Baker and ordered a large Coke. Bo was holding the bulbous Coke glass with both hands, staring into it intently, as if it was a crystal ball. Buffalo, leaning the other way, was explaining to Kenny Fletcher why the Harlem Globetrotters could beat any professional basketball team they played. Dick set the Coke glass on the counter, but Eddie didn't touch it. He felt lost and dejected.

He was trying to think of what to do next, when he felt a tap on his shoulder. He spun around on the stool to face Jim Miller's toothy smile.

"Hey, man," Miller started, "I jus' want to say I had nothin' to do with – "

"Get the fuck away from me," Eddie interrupted, with a finger in Miller's face.

"Comeon, man," Miller persisted. "At least let me explain what – " he stopped short again, this time his smile was replaced with a grimace.

Bo had swung swiftly around on his stool, and grabbed Miller by the upper arm. He squeezed tightly, pulling him close. Miller's eyes became saucers, as blood drained from his face, which was now only inches from Bo's.

"What's the matter with ya?" Bo asked in an ominous monotone. "Can't ya see I'm havin' a heavy conversation with my friend? An' I don't like being interrupted, 'specially by strangers. Ya dig?"

"S-sorry," Miller managed, nodding his head.

"Good boy," Bo said, releasing his grip. "Now, I suggest ya make like a tree an' leave, an' don't come back 'til ya get yerself some *smarts.*" Bo swung back around, contemplating his Coke glass again.

Miller took a step back, quickly glancing around the store. The Crowd had ignored the incident, acting as if nothing happened. He left the store without a word to anyone.

After a few moments of silence, Eddie looked over at Bo. "Thanks, man, but I really didn't need any help. I coulda handled that piece a shit."

"Didn't say ya couldn't," Bo said, still staring at his glass. Then, he turned to his friend, and draped his huge arm around Eddie's shoulder. "Lissen, buddy. Right now ya got enough on yer mind as it is, without dealin' with that asshole. Yer'll get yer shot at him, an' when ya do, it'll be the *only* thing on yer mind. Ya dig?"

"Yeah, man, I dig," Eddie said. "I know *exactly* what ya mean. An' it makes sense, too."

"Hey, ya seem to keep forgettin'," Bo beamed a smile. "I'm always. . ."

"Yeah, yeah, I know," Eddie interrupted, returning a weak smile. ". . . three years older an' one step ahead. How can I forget when ya remind me so often?"

For the rest of the evening, Eddie wandered aimlessly around the store. His friends were compassionate; no one mentioned Ginny's name. But the juke box was merciless, continually blurting out songs like *Empty Arms* by Ivory Joe Hunter and *Long Lonely Nights* by The Hearts. Finally, he went over to the juke box, slipped in a quarter, and searched for songs that didn't depress him. There weren't any. He pushed the "coin return" button but the "make a selection" light remained lit.

"Fuck ya, gimme my quarter back," he hissed at the juke box.

"Hey, how are you feeling?"

Eddie turned to see Kate by his side. "Oh, hell, I'm okay, I guess," he said.

"Yeah, great, huh? That's why you're standing here having an argument with Wurlitzer."

"Well, lookit this shit. Who put all this crap in here? There ain't one good song, for Chrissake." Eddie stopped. He noticed the look of concern on his friend's face, and his angered subsided. "Oh, hell, Kate, what am I gonna do? Ya know about the fight we had, right?"

"I was here, remember? You said some really stupid things."

"Yeah, I know, but she's been actin' strange. Ya know, like she likes this guy Miller more'n me, but she says, like, it's all my imagination. I mean, do ya know anything, has she said anything to ya?"

"Not really," Kate said, after just a hint of a hesitation.

"Oh, shit," Eddie moaned. "*Not really!* What the hell is *that* supposed to mean?"

"Look, calm down," Kate said, putting a hand on her friend's shoulder. "She just said she thought he was handsome, and, er, well maybe she flirted a little." Seeing a look of pain cross Eddie's face, she added quickly: "But so have all the other girls – it doesn't mean anything."

"Yeah, great, 'cept I'm not goin' with *the other girls,* I'm goin' with Ginny. At least, I *was* goin' with her."

"Look," Kate said, "give her a call, say you're sorry and make plans to meet and talk. I'm sure you can work it all out."

"That's jus' it, I tried to call her but she won't come to the phone. She . . . " Eddie's eyes widened. "Hey! I got a – "

"Stop right there," Kate interrupted. "Don't get me involved, I got enough of my own problems with Hank."

"Please, pleeeease," Eddie pleaded, his hands pressed together in prayer. "Jus' get her to the phone, that's all. Then I'll take it."

Kate shook her head slowly. "I should have my head examined." She extended her hand, palm up.

Eddie reached into his pocket and quickly pressed a nickel into her hand, then followed Kate to the phone booth. After speaking to Ginny's mother, there was a short wait, then: "Hi Ginny, it's me Kate. Hold on a sec." She pushed the receiver into Eddie's hand, then squeezed out of the booth.

"Hi, Ginny," Eddie said, trying to sound a lot calmer then he felt. "Please don't hang up," he added quickly.

"What do you want? I'm busy." Her voice was cold enough to freeze the receiver in Eddie's hand.

"Look, I'm sorry for the things I said today . . . I really didn't mean it."

"Ok. So?"

"So, I'd like to see ya, talk to ya, an', well, ya know, talk this thing out."

There were several seconds of silence. To Eddie they seemed like hours. He prayed she wouldn't hang up. "Well," Ginny began, her voice a bit warmer, "I think we shouldn't see each other for a few days. You know, give us time to think things over. Besides, I'm sure you agree that we need some time to ourselves."

No, I don't agree at all, Eddie didn't say. Instead, he simply mumbled "ok."

"I'll be in Dick's on Saturday around noon," Ginny continued. "And, well, if you're there, we can talk."
Ginny's words didn't sound promising. They were too set, too formal. He felt he had to say something more.

"So, then," she continued, "I'll see you on – "
"Ginny?" Eddie interrupted.

"What?"

"Ginny, I jus' want ya to know that I care for ya very much, more'n I cared for anybody in my life. Ya know what I mean?" There was no reply, and Eddie wasn't sure if she was still on the line. "Ginny? Are ya still there?"

"Yes, Eddie, I'm here."

Eddie caught a trace of emotion in her voice that wasn't there before, and his spirits rose. "Didya hear what I said? I really mean it."

"I heard what you said, Eddie," she answered, a slight quiver in her voice. She took a deep breath. "Look, you're a great guy, and we had some wonderful times, and . . . look, I can't talk anymore. I . . . I have to think. I'll see you Saturday."

Eddie held the dead receiver for several seconds before slowly placing it in its cradle. He remained in the phone booth for some time, not wanting to face anyone. He had to think. *What were her exact words? Great guy . . .* had *some wonderful times.* I don't like the sound of that too much, Eddie thought. I'll have to really work on her on Saturday. I'll get some flowers. Yeah! Girls are suckers for flowers. I know I can make things right between us again. An', if I can't, I'll kick the shit outa that bastard Miller. Hell, I jus' might kick the shit outa him anyway.

With his confidence built up a level or two, Eddie pushed open the phone booth door, ready to face his world again.

Eddie looked around Sacred Heart Church, and noted with satisfaction that this would be the most beautiful wedding ever. There were flowers everywhere – Baby Breath on the main altar; Blue Violets on the two side altars, and Lilies of the Valley along the top of the communion railing. All the people filling the pews held a single white rose. The bride, in a floor-length, white satin gown, and the groom, in a double breasted powder blue tux, made a striking couple, as they stood together on the first step of the altar in front of Father Norman.

Bo, the best man, handed the groom the ring. He slipped it on Ginny's finger. A moment later the old priest mumbled, "I now pronounce you man and wife . . . you can kiss the bride."

The bride turned and raised her veil, and Ginny's face was more radiant than all the flowers combined.

The groom turned, and Jim Miller flashed a dazzling toothy smile.

Eddie was confused. He looked around. It suddenly dawned on him that he was standing at the rear of the church, not at the altar.

"Stop! he yelled. "That's not me!" He started running down the aisle . . . and running and running. The aisle seemed endless. All his friends in the pews were laughing at him. "This is for making Dick spit in my hamburger," Joe Ross shouted. "This is for ranking out my mother," The Shadow sneered. "Oh, Eddie, I'll still marry you," Helen Roberts, swooned, grabbing his arm. Eddie broke free and continued running. He finally reached the altar, breathless. "Stop the weddin'," he gasped to the priest. "This guy's a fuckin' impostor. He's not me!"

"It's too late," Father Norman snarled, showering the area with cigar-whiskey spittle. "They're already married. And you, young man, will suffer eternal damnation for cursing in God's house."

Eddie turned to Ginny. "Wait, we have to talk, don't ya remember?" She ignored him, walking off arm-in-arm with her new husband, tossing a bouquet of Princess Pink Carnations over her shoulder.

There were tears in Eddie's eyes. He turned to Bo. "How could you do this to me," he sobbed.

Bo smiled warmly, draping an arm over his friend's shoulder.

"I didn't do it to *ya, I did it* for *ya," Bo said. "I know ya really didn't wanna get married. Remember, I'm still three years older and one step ahead."*

"But, I do wanna get married . . . I do . . . I do . . . I . . ."

"Wake up! Wake up!" Mrs. Casale was shaking Eddie's shoulder firmly, but gently.

"Wha – huh?" Eddie popped up in bed. He was clammy with cold sweat, his eyes caked closed. He rubbed them open with a knuckle, and saw his mother standing over him. "Mom, whadaya doin' here?"

"You were crying, yelling . . . I don't know what," Mrs. Casale said with concern. "What on earth were you dreaming?"

"Er . . . I don't know," Eddie lied. "Jus' some crazy nightmare, I guess." He suddenly realized he had tossed off his sheet during the night. Mortified, he quickly checked the crotch of his Jockey shorts. He didn't have his usual morning hard-on. Nevertheless, he snatched the sheet from the floor and covered himself. "Mom? Comeon, willya? Get outa my room."

"Oh, stop it," Mrs. Casale said. "I just wanted to make sure you were alright. You sounded terrible."

"Yeah, yeah, Mom. I'm fine. Probably jus' those White Castles I had last night." Eddie knew what his mother needed to hear.

"Aha, I thought so," Mrs. Casale said, nodding her head. "You can just imagine what they put in those hamburgers when they sell them for thirteen cents. I'll fix you a good breakfast and you'll feel better."

After his mother left, Eddie remained in bed, thinking of his dream. He remembered every detail, and he was sure it was a bad omen. His depression was sinking faster then the Titanic. It was Saturday, and in a few hours he'd be meeting Ginny. *Oh God, what am I gonna do?*

After his shower, Eddie felt a bit better, but couldn't fully shake his feeling of gloom. He chose his clothes carefully, selecting the shirt he knew Ginny loved, a maroon Gaucho with blouse sleeves. Together with a pair of black chinos and black Wellington boots, his ensemble was complete. He devoted a good half hour to his hair before checking himself in the mirror. His spirits clicked a notch higher. He liked the cavalier image that his attire inspired. *If I play it as cool as I look, maybe, jus' maybe, I can pull this thing off.*

Eddie arrived at Dick's shortly after eleven, after stopping at the Bell Florists for a bunch of daisies and two long red tapered candles.

Kate Brody, who was the only one he had told about his impending meeting with Ginny, was sipping Cokes at the counter with Carol Michaels and Joe Ross.

"Hey, you look great," she said, after rushing over to greet him. "Love that shirt. And, wow, flowers and candles, really smooth."

"Ya think so? I mean, like it's not overdoing it?"

"No way! Girls *love* things like this," Kate said. "It's just too bad other guys aren't more like you."

"Thanks, Kate. I really needed to hear that. I'm really nervous, ya know."

"Hey, Eddie," Ross called out from the counter. "Ya look like a Spic who jus' robbed a church."

Eddie's face dropped, but, before he could respond, Kate spun around.

"Shut your stupid trap!" she barked. "One more wisecrack out of you and I'll dump your Coke over your head." Wisely, Ross took the threat seriously, and spun back around on his stool and sulked.

"Don't pay attention to that jerk," Kate said. "You look really cool. Just sit over there in the back booth and I'll get everything ready for you."

Kate took the flowers and candles from her friend, walked behind the counter and had a whispered conversation with Dick. He grunted, shook his head, shrugged his shoulders, then disappeared into the storeroom. A few minutes later he came out with everything Kate needed. And, a few minutes after that, Eddie was sitting at a table that could have been in the Copa rather than a candy store in Queens. Kate had covered the Formica table with a clean white cloth. The flowers, in a large tulip-shaped malted milk glass, were in the center, with the candles, stuck with melted wax in ice cream sundae dishes, on either side. Then, she put a nickel in the juke box, pressed a button and pulled out the plug.

"Looks good, Eddie, really good," Kate said, admiring her handiwork. "Now, sit down, think about what you'll say to Ginny, and don't worry about anything else. I'll take care of everything. I'll give you a high sign when I see her." She walked over and positioned herself on the first stool to keep watch on the front door.

Eddie felt foolish sitting at a "formal" table in Dick's. And, he knew he *looked* foolish, too. Every time one of the Crowd came in, he braced himself for ridicule.

However, Kate was effective in stopping them with a few whispered words. She also intercepted anyone heading for the juke box. In the next half hour she threw more body blocks than the defensive guard for the Green Bay Packers. Finally, she gave the "thumbs up" sign, and Eddie's heart began beating like a bongo drum.

Ginny walked in a few minutes after twelve. She greeted the other kids with a nod and a smile. When she spotted Eddie in the decorated booth, she hesitated only momentarily, before continuing toward the back of the store. She was wearing tight black toreador pants, a flowered cinch belt and a white peasant blouse, and Eddie took as a good omen the fact that they were both wearing Spanish-style clothes.

As soon as Ginny slipped into the booth opposite Eddie, Kate plugged in the juke box, and The Platters began singing, *I'm Sorry.* With eyes beginning to water, Ginny looked at Eddie, the juke box, the table set-up, then back at Eddie. She tried to smile, but her lips only quivered.

"I-I don't know what to say," she stammered. "You did all this for me?"

"Well, no, actually I was waiting for Cootie." That broke the ice and Ginny smiled warmly.

Kate came over with two Cokes, set them down, and left without a word.

"Of course I did it for ya," Eddie continued. "For us, actually." He lifted his glass and held it forward. "*To* us."

Ginny raised her glass, clinked his, but offered no return toast. Instead, she said, "I just love that shirt on you. You look really nice."

Eddie, receiving alarm signals from his nervous system, tried to keep it light. "You too," he offered. "*Mucho* nice." Ginny managed a joyless giggle. An uncomfortable silence followed, during which Eddie looked at Ginny, and Ginny read her straw wrapper. Then, they both started speaking at the same time.

"You first," Ginny said.

Eddie didn't argue. He looked into her eyes. "Look, Ginny, I thought of alotta things I wanted to say, but, like it all comes down to this. I . . . er . . . love ya, an' I never said that to another girl. I don't wanna lose ya, Ginny."

She looked up, locking onto Eddie's eyes for the first time. "Look, Eddie, you're the nicest guy I've ever known, and I . . . er . . . care for you an awful lot, too. . ."

She hesitated, and Eddie anticipated her next word. He closed his eyes, as if to shut it out.

". . . but, I've been doing a lot of thinking, too, and – "

Eddie opened his eyes and reached for her hand. "Ginny . . . " he implored.

She pulled her hand away and put a finger to his lips. "Wait, let me finish." She started speaking more rapidly, her words void of emotion, sounding rehearsed. "Look, next week we'll be going back to school and, well, since we're in different schools we won't be seeing much of each other anyway. Right?" But she didn't wait for an answer. "Sooo, let's see what happens over the next couple of months and, if we still feel the same, well, we can be together during Christmas break. How does that sound?"

"W-whadaya sayin'? I mean, like, say what ya mean." There was a trace of annoyance in Eddie's voice. "Yer breakin' up with me, right?"

"Well, no, not really," Ginny said without conviction. "I just want things to cool down for awhile and see what happens, you know? I mean, like, I'll continue wearing your ankle bracelet if you want. I have no intentions of dating anyone else, anyway."

Eddie sat in silence, re-playing her words. And, as he did, his annoyance was turning to anger. *Cool down? . . . see what happens? . . . no intentions of dating? Bingo! Those were the key words. She didn't say "wouldn't date." She said "no intentions of dating." Big fuckin' difference!*

"Well," Ginny asked, "aren't you going to say anything?"

Eddie hadn't planned on turning this into a confrontation, but the words were out of his mouth before he could stop them. "It's that asshole Miller, ain't it?"

"Don't be silly," Ginny replied a bit too fast. "It has nothing to do with him." She averted his eyes, and began reading the straw wrapper again.

Eddie reached out and grabbed the wrapper, ripping it several times. "Can't ya even look at me when ya say that," he challenged.

Slowly, Ginny raised her eyes to meet his. She looked at him for several seconds before speaking. When she did, her voice was soft, gentle. "Look, Eddie, it isn't any one thing, ok? It's like I said, I just need some time. Please. Can't you understand that?"

The look in her eyes, her words, the tone of her voice – they had a calming affect on Eddie, and his flash of anger subsided. He reached out and took her hand, squeezing gently. "Ok, Ginny, yer prob'ly right. We both could use some time. Besides, yer'll still be comin' to Dick's, like on Saturdays, right, so we'll see each other sometimes."

"Oh, Eddie, I just knew you'd understand. You're such a swell guy." Her face brightened. "Look, I want to go over and talk to some of the girls, ok? I'll see you later."

Eddie, depressed and alone in the booth, wondered what had just happened. It wasn't what he had planned. Somehow, Ginny had managed to get him to agree to exactly what she wanted. Then she was gone, now sitting in the front booth laughing with her friends. He just knew they were talking about him. He looked around the store, noticing for the first time that it was fairly crowded for an early Saturday. This was a bad idea, Eddie thought, suddenly self-conscious about sitting in the booth. *I gotta get Kate to take this stuff away.* He spotted her at the counter, talking to her brother.

Eddie walked over, but before he had a chance to say anything, Jim Miller, together with Johnny Logan, sauntered in, flashing his Pepsodent smile. Spotting the flickering candles and bouquet of flowers, his smile widened.

"Hey, Johnny," he nudged his friend with an elbow and hooked a thumb towards the back. Then, in a voice that carried throughout the store, "I betcha Dick serves Cokes in champagne glasses at *that* table." Miller looked around. The only one who laughed with him was Logan. In fact, a hush fell over the store.

"Hey, what's goin' on, what's the problem?" he asked, glancing around. "Somebody die, or what?"

When Eddie looked at Miller standing there with a big ass grin, all the anger and frustration of the past hour came to a head. This was the guy responsible for all his problems. He started for Miller, but was stopped when a big hand grabbed his arm. Eddie turned.

"Don't try to stop me, Bo. Not this time."

"I ain't tryin' to stop ya, my man," Bo said softly. "Ya *have* to do it, an' he needs it done. Jus' be cool, slow an' easy, an' take him outside."

Eddie nodded, and as he approached Miller he noticed the rest of the Crowd pull back, except for Logan.

Ginny jumped up from her seat, and started to say something, but Diane grabbed her arm and pulled her roughly back down.

Eddie planted his six-foot-four frame about three inches in front of the slightly smaller Miller.

"What's yer problem?" Miller asked, not backing up. He was no longer smiling.

Eddie poked a finger into Miller's chest. Hard. "Yer my problem. You've been fuckin' with my life, now I'm gonna fuck up yers." His punctuated the last word with another finger in the chest.

"Hey, Eddie," Logan said, trying to shoulder in between. "Why don't ya leave him – ?"

Eddie turned to Logan with an icy stare, shoving him back hard, confused and annoyed that Logan was taking sides against him. "I don't know where yer comin' from, but ya better go back to wherever it is, an' keep outa my face."

Logan, red faced, glared at Eddie, and looked ready to respond. Miller held up his hand, signaling Logan to stay out of it.

"I don't know what yer talkin' about," Miller said, turning back to Eddie, his voice taking on a hard edge. "An' don't poke me again."

Eddie gave him a cold hard smile. "Well, let's go outside an' I'll explain *in detail* what it's about." He poked him again, this time hard enough to move Miller a step back.

Miller's face flushed with anger. "Ok, ya wop bastard, let's go."

"No fightin' in front of my store," Dick hollered as the two boys started out. "Ya vant to kill each other, ya crazy kids, you vill go to the empty lot across the street. You hear me?"

Eddie and Miller went out, crossed the street, and walked about ten yards into the lot, stopping by an old maple tree. The entire store had emptied out behind them, and the Crowd now formed a semi-circle, about five feet back.

The two boys faced each other. Miller was not backing down. He couldn't, and still hang out at Dick's. But his confidence waned as he stood toe to toe with Eddie.

"Look, if this is about Ginny, I jus' want – "

"Fuck ya," Eddie snapped. "This is about me an' you. I don't like yer looks. Ya got too many teeth, so I'm gonna remove a few. Make sure ya never do a Pepsodent commercial."

"Ok, ok, ya wanna fight," Miller said, his anger returning to full tilt. "I'll fight ya. But let's keep it straight. No dirty fightin', just boxin', ok?"

"Yeah, no problem," Eddie said, starting to circle left as he spoke. "I'm a nice guy. I'll give ya yer beatin' anyway ya want."

"Yeah, right!" Miller said, now circling in the opposite direction. "If ya fight as stupid as ya sound, yer ass is mine."

Eddie figured Miller had had some training as a boxer. He saw it in the way he moved his feet and his shoulders, the way he held his hands.

They sparred for a while, each throwing harmless jabs, feeling each other out. Then, in less then a heartbeat, Miller ducked in, connected with two quick hard jabs, followed by a powerful right cross, catching Eddie full on his left cheekbone, breaking the skin. Blood began running down his cheek.

The Crowd moaned in sympathy – and shock. Eddie staggered back a step or two, obviously hurt. But his mind remained clear, and it registered the fact that he had to take Miller more seriously. The guy was fast, very fast. Eddie shook his head, wiped at the blood with the back of his hand, and stepped forward, a little more cautiously this time.

Miller seemed more confident now. He sensed a slowness in Eddie, a little sluggishness due to his big size. He danced around, light on his feet, constantly flicking lefts and rights to Eddie's face and body, working for another opening.

Eddie deflected most of the punches. Several slipped in, but without much steam. Then, when he was busy blocking a two-fisted assault to his head, he was suddenly hit with a left-right combination to the mid-section. The wind swooshed out of Eddie and he went down on one knee, trying to catch his breath.

Seeing Eddie down, Miller suddenly changed tactics. He went back on his word and switched to street fighting, and the creed: *once you get your opponent down, keep him down.*

Eddie was still on one knee, leaning forward, when Miller's boot caught him in the chest with a force that lifted Eddie off the ground. He landed flat on his back among the debris of the lot, his head slamming into the ground only inches from a broken brick. Eddie was still conscious, but very groggy.

A couple of the guys wanted to jump in, but Bo held them back. "One on one, let 'em finish it," he counseled, mostly for his own benefit. He wasn't happy seeing his friend getting the shit kicked out of him.

Miller, inflamed with the sense of victory, leaped on top of Eddie, pinning him to the ground with his knees. Eddie shook his head, trying desperately to clear it. *This is boxin'?* he thought. *Ok asshole, now yer in* my *ring.*

Eddie started to maneuver Miller off, but suddenly something smashed into the side of his head. A white light flashed in his eyes, then he felt the pain. His vision blurred, and he was barely able to focus on the snarling face above him – but there was no mistaking the broken brick in his right hand, poised, ready to strike again.

Eddie twisted his head to the left, while, at the same time, summoning up all the strength he could muster to shift his body. The movement was just enough to throw Miller off-balance, causing the second blow to only graze Eddie's temple.

Eddie screamed, not from pain, but to give vent to a rage so ferocious it seemed to provide a superhuman level of strength. He put all his weight to his right hip, and pushed up, while, at the same, kicking his legs. Miller was thrown off like a bad bronco rider.

Eddie, now on his feet, reached down and grabbed Miller as he tried to scamper out of reach. With one hand on Miller's shoulder, the other on his leg, Eddie lifted him over his head, like Gorgeous George administering a body slam. Eddie threw him into the maple tree, sideways, and Miller's back seemed to bend around the trunk. He slid to the ground at the base of the tree, and Eddie was on top of him in an instant. Suddenly, the broken brick was in Eddie's hand, and he was smashing it into Miller's face, over and over again, until a pair of arms grabbed him around the chest, and pulled him up.

"Get the fuck away from me," Eddie screamed, struggling to break free. He twisted around, swinging the brick wildly, but Bo easily sidestepped the move. Eddie's eyes were still full of fury as he glared at the intruder, ready to strike again. Then, recognition set in, his eyes cleared slowly and the brick dropped from his hand. "Oh, God, Bo. I . . . I'm sorry. I . . . I don't know what happened."

Bo pulled his friend close and hugged him. "It's ok, my man, it's over," he whispered, "it's all over."

A buzz of excitement filled the air as the Crowd swarmed around the fight scene.

Kate and Carol rushed up to Eddie with a wet towel, wiping blood from his face and head. They decided he didn't need stitches, but they told him to keep the towel on his head for a while. They wrapped it like a turban. "Never mind me," Eddie said. "How's Miller?" The two girls looked at each other, but neither spoke. Eddie looked over and realized a hush had come over the crowd around Miller. Logan was cradling Miller's battered head in his arms.

"Oh, God," Eddie cried, raising his head and closing his eyes. "Jesus, please, let him be ok. . . please, Jesus, let him . . . "

Just then there was a moan and everyone began talking at once. Bo went over to check on Miller and returned several moments later. "My man, ya got the power of prayer," Bo told Eddie with a smile. "If I ever get hurt, I hope ya pray for me, too. Looks like he'll be ok."

"Oh my God," Ginny screamed, just coming into the lot. Not wanting to see the fight, she had stayed in the store. She began crying. "All that blood, oh, my God."

"Hey, calm down, Ginny," Eddie said. "It looks worse than what it is. I only got a couple of – "

"Not you, you big bully." She ran over to Miller. "What did he do to you? What did he do to you?"

Bo, noticing his friend's expression, said, "Let's split. Ya don't need anymore hurt comin at ya.

"Wait!" Ginny yelled as they started to leave. She was still crying. She ripped the ankle bracelet from her leg and threw it on the ground in front of Eddie.

"I wouldn't wear that now if you paid me!" She glared at Eddie waiting for his response.

Eddie looked at Ginny, looked at the bracelet, then, with the toe of his boot, he ground the bracelet into the dirt. "That fuckin' thing's been nuttin' but bad luck for me since I got it."

Eddie and Bo hopped on the Triumph and roared off just as the first sound of sirens could be heard coming up Bell Boulevard. They rode around for a while, then pulled up in front of their houses. It was still early in the day.

"Well," Eddie said. "Might as well go in the house an' face the music. Maybe I can sneak in the back."

"Ya wanna hang in my room for a while," Bo said.

"Naw. I'm ok." Eddie still sounded depressed.

"Didya take a look at yerself?"

Eddie looked down. His Gaucho shirt was torn in the sleeve and collar, and it was covered with blood and dirt stains. His chinos were ripped at the right knee, and his Wellingtons were scuffed and gouged. "My clothes are really fucked up, huh?"

"Oh, it's not yer clothes so much," Bo said with a smile. "Yer old man's seen ya like that before. I jus' don't think he could handle his son becomin' an Arab."

"Oh, shit!" Eddie pulled the bloody towel from his head and tossed it in the garbage can as he headed for his house.

"Hey, Eddie."

He turned to face his friend.

"Look, man," Bo said. "Ya only did what ya hadda do. That's all. Nothin' wrong with that."

Eddie nodded. "Thanks, buddy. But it don't make me feel too much better."

Any hope of sneaking up to his room vanished as Eddie came around the back of his house. His mother and father were sitting out on the back patio in the late afternoon sunshine.

"Dear Lord!" Mrs. Casale exclaimed, jumping out of her chair.

"What the . . . " Mr. Casale mumbled, rising up from his chaise lounge.

"Relax, relax," Eddie said. "I'm fine, really. "Jus' got a little banged up playing choose-up football in the park."

"Football?" Mr. Casale said doubtfully. "It's still baseball season."

"Football, baseball, what difference does it make?" Mrs. Casale said. "Our son has been hurt and you're talking seasons. Come inside," she said to Eddie, "I want to look at you. And, I'll make some soup." She dashed into the house.

"I don't know what you've been up to," Mr. Casale said. "But you better hope and pray the police don't come to our door."

"What for?" Eddie asked, heading inside. "To gimme a summons for playin' football outa season?"

ELEVEN

BE BOP A LULA

"John Doe" was a wanted man.

A squad car had arrived at the scene across from Dick's only seconds after Eddie and Bo roared off in the opposite direction.

After calling for an ambulance, the cops had gone through the perfunctory questioning, receiving the expected answers.

"I saw nuttin'."

"Don't look at me."

Then, when Jim Miller told them he had been jumped from behind and couldn't identify his attackers, they considered the case closed.

Miller had been treated and released at Queens General. He took seven stitches in his scalp, four on his left cheekbone, plus he had two broken teeth and a mild concussion. He was ordered to stay in bed for a few days and check with his family doctor.

Mrs. Miller had taken one look at her son and went into hysterics. The first thing she had done, after calming down with the help of a valium, was to storm the 111 Precinct to demand action.

The old desk sergeant, remembering the incident from the patrol officers' report, had assured her that they would give it their full attention, in spite of the fact that they had neither a name nor a description. He took a blank arrest warrant, rolled it into his old Underwood typewriter, and with deliberate, one-finger proficiency, typed in the offense as "assault &

battery," listed its time and location, then punched in "John Doe" as the prepetrator.

Satisfied that justice would prevail, Mrs. Miller had thanked the sergeant and left. As soon as she was out the door, he tossed the form into the inactive file drawer, together with all the other "John Doe" warrants.

Eddie, not taking any chances, stuck close to the house. Although Kate had stopped by Tuesday afternoon to assure him that everything was cool, he couldn't help feeling there was something she wasn't saying. He figured it would be best to keep away from Dick's and Bell Boulevard, at least until school started next week. He was in a state of depression wondering if the cops may get a bug up their ass and decide to really try to find him. And, what if Miller's mother somehow forced her son to tell who it was? But, most of all, he was distressed with thoughts of Ginny.

Eddie didn't leave his house until Friday night, when Bo stopped by and coaxed his friend into going down to Kiddie City on Northern Boulevard for some hot dogs and beer and hitting on chicks.

"So, what's happening at Dick's?" Eddie asked, as soon as they sat down at an outside table.

"Nothin' much. Ya know, when *you're* not there it's kinda quiet."

"Very funny, very funny," Eddie said without smiling. "Er . . . ya know what I mean?"

"Hmmm, let's see," Bo pondered. "Ya asked, 'what's happening at Dick's,' but ya meant, 'has Ginny been in,' right?" Bo smiled. "Is *that* the $64,000 question?"

Eddie looked at his friend, and nodded.

"The answer is *no, she hasn't been in*. Now pay me my fuckin' money."

Bo kept joking around, trying to bring his friend out of his doldrums, but Eddie noticed an uneasiness in Bo which wasn't usually there. Between Kate and

Bo, he was now certain there was something his friends weren't telling him.

It wasn't until Monday morning that Eddie found out what was really happening. When he arrived at the park across from Bayside High, it was bustling with an excitement unique to the first day of school. Hundreds of students crowded the grassy area as they renewed old friendships or forged new ones, talking over each other in their eagerness to relate, with animated gestures, exploits of summer past.

As Eddie picked his way through the crowd, searching for his own friends, he was overcome with a feeling of alienation he never experienced before.

Except for an occasional nod of vague recognition, he realized he didn't really know any of these other kids. No one called his name, no one was anxious to tell him of their summer adventures. He was relieved to finally spot Joe Ross, sitting stationary on a swing, alone, in the playground area. He was looking glumly at the ground.

"Hey, little boy, whadaya waitin' for, someone to give ya a push?" Eddie quipped, attempting to shake the uneasiness he had just experienced.

"Shit! There ya are," Ross said, jumping off the swing and rushing over. "I've been waitin' for ya." There was urgency in his voice.

"Hey, man, take it easy," Eddie said. "What's goin' on? Where're the other guys?"

"That's jus' it, there ain't no other guys, it's jus' me and you." Ross was speaking rapidly.

Eddie looked confused. "I don't understand, did somethin' happen durin' the week that I missed?"

"Ya bet yer ass somethin' happened!" Ross continued. "I wanted to stop by or call ya, an' tell ya, but Bo said ya had enough on yer mind at the moment. He said if I said anything to ya he'd kick my ass, an' that I should stop bein' a chicken shit. Who the hell is he to call me a chicken shit?"

Eddie was annoyed now. "Well, Joe, why don't ya jus' go *ask* him? But for now, *tell me what the fuck is goin' on!"*

"Ok, ok," Ross took a deep breath. "Well, first of all, Johnny Logan don't hang out with us no more, he went over to the Bombers."

"Well, fuck him," Eddie said. "He's had a bug up his ass ever since we had that fight last year, an' I smacked him a couple a times."

"Yeah, man, maybe. But that's not all. Like, suddenly, he's real tight with Miller, ya know, best buddy shit. He even went in the ambulance with him, an' saw him at his house durin' the week. Then, when Miller was a little better and could go out – Thursday I think – Logan took him over to meet Jack Callahan."

Eddie just stared at his friend, shocked by this latest news. But even worse, he could see where it was leading. "An' . . . comeon, what else?" he urged.

"Well . . . " Ross hesitated, attempting to control the tremor in his voice. Eddie waited. The bomb was about to be dropped. "Callahan promised Miller that he'd help him even the score with you."

"Oh, great!" Eddie said. "An' where are ya getting' all this shit?"

"Johnny was jus' here. He split when he saw you comin'. He tol' me to keep away from ya, that they have nothin' against me. "I . . . it's jus' you they want." Joe hesitated. "Hey, but ya know me. I'm with ya all the way," he added without much conviction.

The school warning bell resounded throughout the park, to a collective moan from the students. But they were anxious to get to class, and the park emptied rapidly. Eddie and Ross held back in the playground.

"An' when is this *pay back* supposed to happen," Eddie asked, getting angry and fearful at the same time.

"He didn't say. But I got a bad feelin' about it. Like, it'll be soon, real soon."

Eddie checked the park. It was almost empty, except for a few stragglers.

"Hey, where's Manning? How come he ain't here?"

"Oh, shit, that's right. Ya ain't been around this week. He quit. He turned nineteen las' month, 'member? An' he says he wants to get outta high school while he's still a teenager." Ross forced a chuckle. "Besides, he says they don't give no draft exemptions for high school. Pretty funny, huh?"

"Great, jus' great." Eddie wasn't amused. He was busy checking the park, and the street beyond. The final bell rang and the last of the students headed through the school doors. Now, they were alone in the park, except for a pair of gray squirrels casually exploring the latest debris of candy wrappers and sandwich bags. Suddenly, the rodents' heads popped up, ears alert, noses twitching. As soon as the first of the Bombers entered the park from the far side, the squirrels scampered up the nearest tree. Eddie spotted the intruders at the same time.

As usual, Jack Callahan led the way. But this time he was flanked by the two new Bomber recruits – Jim Miller and Johnny Logan – while Don Gilmartin and Tippy O'Connor brought up the rear.

"E-Eddie . . . er, ya want me to go get some help?" Ross was unable to conceal the fear in his voice.

Eddie expected something like that, and would have suggested it himself just to get Ross out of the way. Hell, this was his fight, anyway. "Good idea, Joe. Go out the otha way and see what ya can do."

Ross took two steps then froze. A car had jumped the curb, swung into the park by the playground, and slid to a stop on the grass. The Shaw brothers – Willy and Dutch – came out from the front, while three other gang members piled out of the back.

"Oh shit," Eddie heard Ross mutter. He didn't have to turn around to see what happened. He knew how the Bombers operated, the punks. Besides, he was too busy concentrating on the advancing group. He decided to walk out of the playground area to meet them, preferring the advantage of a grass cushion to that of unyielding concrete.

"Jus' stay here an' keep it cool," Eddie said over his shoulder as he began to move. "This is my fight."

Trying desperately to keep from faltering, Eddie strode on to the grassy area, stopping several feet from the group. Callahan, hands on his hips, came a few steps closer, until his face, fixed with a cold smile, was only inches from Eddie's.

"Well, well, if it ain't the WOP bastard," Callahan said through clenched teeth. "Yer old friends, here, tell me ya like to play with bricks. Is that right?"

Eddie didn't answer. He looked at Logan, who refused to meet his stare. Then, Eddie glanced at Miller, who was trying to smile without showing his broken teeth. His face was a mass of bruises and gashes. His lips were broken and puffed, one eye was closed. But the anger glaring out of the other eye was evident. He wore white gauze bandages on his left cheek and forehead. When he brought his hands up from his sides, he was clutching a red building brick, which he started tossing slowly, tauntingly, from hand to hand, back and forth.

"My friend Miller wants ya to know what it feels like to get your face massaged with a brick," Callahan continued, in a cold, lilting tone. "But, first I'm gonna warm ya up."

Eddie heard the words, but his eyes were transfixed on the moving brick. The combination sent a chill of fright jolting through his body. Reflectively, he uttered, "But he started it." He hadn't realized what he had said, until he actually heard his own words. He wished he could pull them back. He knew he sounded like a punk, and he shuddered again, this time from embarrassment.

Callahan's laugh was cold, cruel, and it was followed immediately by a flurry of punches.

Eddie's eyes were still on the brick when Callahan's fists exploded in his face. The shock, and the force of the blows, sent Eddie down in a heap. By the time his head began to clear, he realized his nose was bleeding and he was being held flat on his back on the lumpy grass, with Gilmartin on his arms and Tippy O'Connor on his legs.

"Keep yer eyes open, punk," Miller said, leaning over Eddie. "I want ya to see this comin'." He raised the brick in his right hand.

Eddie struggled, but it was useless. "Yer a fuckin' punk," Eddie yelled up at Miller, not knowing what else to say. "An' all this time I thought ya were a stand-up guy 'cause ya didn't fink to the cops."

Miller hesitated, still holding the brick over his head. "Ha! That's rich! An' what would the fuzz do anyway? I wanted to get ya myself."

Eddie thought fast, and tried speaking even faster. "An' ya call *this* getting' me yourself? With all these assholes around? Why didn't ya bring Ginny, too? I betcha she'd be really proud to watch ya."

"Ya fuck!" Miller yelled, cocking the brick. "Ya better keep Ginny outa this or I'll . . . " But, a look of confusion crossed his battered face, and his arm slackened, as if the brick had suddenly become too heavy.

"Hey!" Callahan yelled at Miller. "Cut the bullshit an' do it, ya stupid bastard. "We've been here too long awready."

Miller straightened himself and turned to Callahan, shaking his head. "It's over," he said, a calmness coming into his voice. "This isn't what I really want." Then, he threw the brick as far as he could across the park, and turned to walk away.

Callahan spun Miller around by the shoulder with his left hand, and popped him with his right. Miller went down, the stitches on his cheek breaking open. "I'll tell ya when it's over, ya chicken shit fuck. Logan, get me that brick!"

Logan took a few quick steps towards the brick, then hesitated. He was suddenly unsure of what to do. He searched the faces of Eddie and Miller, as if *he* was the one who needed help. He looked back at Callahan.

Callahan raised a fist to Logan. "Whadaya waitin' for? I told ya to get the – " His threat was interrupted by the familiar sound of a police siren coming up 35th avenue, putting it three or four blocks from the school.

Knowing it was now over, Gilmartin and O'Connor released their restraints and stood up. Saved by the bell, again, Eddie thought, managing a smile and a sigh of relief.

"Ya think this is funny?" There was rage in Callahan's face as he looked down at Eddie, still lying on his back. "Well, have a good laugh at this!"

The kick was unexpected, violent, and caught him at the junction of his splayed legs. The pain was intense. Eddie screamed, vomited, then momentarily blacked out. When his head cleared, the Bombers were gone, but Miller was kneeling on the grass next to him, dabbing at his mouth with the end of this shirt.

"I'm sorry," Miller said softly, with watery eyes. "I'm so damned sorry. I thought this was what I wanted, and Logan kept egging me on, but . . . no, it's over, as far as I'm concerned."

Eddie took several deep breaths. He wiped his messy hand on his pants leg, and held it out.

"Ok, it's over with me, too." Without hesitation, Miller grasped it, and the two boys shook hands, before helping each other up. Joe Ross, his face pretty well banged up, compliments of the Schultz brothers, joined them. They waited, arm in arm, as the green and white squad car jumped the curb and slid to a stop just inside the park's perimeter.

"The cops are gonna have a shit-load of 'John Doe' warrants after today," Eddie said, and all three boys managed a snort of laughter.

"I swear to God it's real," Joe Ross screamed, as Cootie, the latest arrival at Dick's that night, knuckle-rapped the bandage on Ross' head.

"Bullshit!" Cootie said, unconvinced. "Does this hurt?" he questioned, pushing his big thumb into another bandage.

"Ouch!" Ross yelled. "Of course that hurts, ya stupid son-of-a-bitch."

"I dunno," Cootie said doubtfully. "It could be yer actin' is gettin' better. Ya know, yer track record for duckin' fights precedes ya."

"Willya tell 'em? Willya tell 'em?" Ross said, grabbing Eddie by the arm, and dragging him to where Cootie was propped up on his crutches.

And, for the umpteenth time that night, Eddie told about being jumped by the Bombers in the school park, and that, yes, Joe *was* right in the middle of it, *really he was.*

When Eddie told the Crowd about Miller's role in the morning's adventure, and how he had told Callahan in the end to *fuck off*, there was a satisfying murmur throughout the store, punctuated with phrases like, *I knew it!* and *I always liked 'im.*

"Yer right, he *is* a stand up guy," Eddie said, agreeing with Al Chavello's assessment. "He's got balls, awright." Then, with a quick smile, and a tender pat at his crotch, "which is more'n I can say at the moment."

A few minutes later Miller walked in, hesitantly at first, then with surer, more determined steps as a murmur of welcome filled the air. However, most of the Crowd held back, allowing Eddie to be the first to greet him. When the two boys linked arms, in a genuine display of comradeship, the others poured forth their greetings.

Although it was Monday night, Dick's was nearly full, thanks to the "grapevine," the unique communications system powered by "girls-with-phones." By eight o'clock the entire Crowd was there, with one notable exception. The excitement pulsating through the air had risen to peak power, while heated conversations were spiked with threats of revenge on the Bombers. Nothing definite, you understand, only suggestions. They were all waiting for the arrival of Bo Brody.

And, where the hell is he, Eddie wondered, his eyes darting to the front door again.

"He said he wanted to ride around a while, do some thinking, before coming down here."

Eddie spun around. Kate Brody had come up behind him, looking really hot in tight jeans and tight blue turtleneck sweater. "Wha . . . how'd ya know?

"Ah, comeon, Eddie, you're kind of obvious, you know," Kate said. "And, like who knows you better than me, huh?"

"Bo knows what happened at the school, awready?" Eddie asked. "But, how . . . ?" He stopped, realizing that it was a silly question.

"I was watching from the top of the school steps with some other kids and a couple of teachers," Kate said. "We couldn't make out everything too clear, but we saw enough. One of the teachers called the cops." She hesitated, the corners of her lip flickering into a smile. "Does it still hurt, er . . . you know, down there?"

In spite of himself, Eddie began to blush. "I guess ya *did* see enough." Then, recovering quickly, "Yeah, of course it still hurts," Eddie said, with an expression of pain. "But, the doctor said it'd be ok after a good massage. Could ya help me?"

"Oh, Eddie, I'd love to," Kate said, feigning sincerity, "but I don't know if I'd do it right. You should really go to someone with loads of experience in rubbing that thing, like, you know, do it yourself."

"Very funny, very funny. I don't do – "

"Don't lie!" Kate interrupted. "Or your *nose* will grow, too, and that won't be as much fun as your *other* thing growing when we dance at the next party."

"Don't worry," Eddie replied, smiling broadly now. "I'll be back *up* by then. Ya jus' can't keep a good man *down*."

The two friends laughed briefly. Then, Kate suddenly became serious. "You know, I was so scared, and felt so helpless, when I saw you get kicked like that," she said in a voice cracking with emotion. She leaned against him and kissed him gently on the cheek. "I'm just so glad you're alright."

"Ya keep pressin' those boobs against me, an' I'll get better real fast," Eddie joked.

"Oh, now I know you're fine for sure," Kate said. She turned to walk away, stopping to swipe a paper napkin from the dispenser on the counter. She dabbed at her eyes.

Eddie stared at her fondly as she walked away. *She really cares,* he thought. *What a great friend.*

"What a great ass!" Leo Silverman said, as he idled up to Eddie, following his gaze. "Hank is one lucky son-of-a-bitch."

Eddie looked over at Silverman, then back at the retreating figure of Kate. "He certainly is," he said, nodding reflectively. "An' in more ways than one, that's for sure."

"You're right," The Shadow readily admitted. "She's got great tits, too."

Eddie snapped out of his reverie, and looked over at Silverman. "Ya fuckin' asshole. Ya know, sometimes yer a first class jerk." Eddie shook his head and walked away.

"What the hell is wrong with you," a confused Silverman called after him. "Did that kick in your nuts cause you brain damage?"

With the buzz of conversations remaining at a high level, and the juke box blaring out *Come Go With Me* by The Del Vikings, Eddie missed the familiar sound of Bo's Triumph as he pulled in front on the store thirty minutes later. However, when the pitch of excitement suddenly jumped several notches higher, Eddie intuitively turned toward the door,

Bo, dressed in his usual Levis and tight white T-shirt, his motorcycle jacket hooked over his left shoulder, strode confidently into the store, greeting his friends with a wink or a nod.

Walking directly to where Eddie was standing by the counter, Bo put a hand on his friend's shoulder.

"Howaya feelin'," he asked, concern evident in his tone.

"Hey, I'm cool. I feel ok, really," Eddie said, nodding his head to emphasize his words.

Bo nodded slowly in return, studying Eddie's eyes, easily reading the apprehension in them. "Sure ya are, an' yer gonna stay that way," Bo said. "I promise ya that, my man," he added, patting Eddie's shoulder.

Knowing that the Crowd was awaiting his reading on the current situation, Bo walked over and pulled the plug on the juke box. Conversations wound down as fast as the music, with everyone's attention immediately turned to Bo.

"I jus' rode through Bayside West, past the bowlin' alley where the Bombers hang out," Bo said in a voice that carried throughout the store. "It's like a ghost town. Didn't see any of 'em. I guess they figured we'd come back at 'em, so they're layin' low. The chicken shits prob'bly locked themselves in their houses."

The Crowd, fired up all evening, responded with hoots and hollers. Big Ox Zarora stepped forward raising a fist.

"Let's drag the fuckers out," he shouted. There were bursts of laughter. "No, I'm serious," he continued, moving up next to Bo. "We know where some of 'em live. Let's go up an' bang on their doors and drag 'em out to the street." When the laughing and joking continued, the color drained from his face, now both fists clenched at this side. "Don't fuckin' laugh at me," Ox said threateningly, looking from face to face. "Well, whadaya say?"

The Crowd didn't know *what* to say, but the laughter stopped abruptly. That was the trouble with Ox, they never knew *when* to take him seriously. And, he didn't like to be laughed at when he *was* being serious. He certainly was capable of breaking down doors and dragging guys out and kicking the shit out of them. In fact, he was famous for it.

It was about a year ago when some guy had crashed into the back of Ox's new Chevy. It resulted in very little damage, only cracking the right taillight, but it was enough to send Ox into a rage. The guy got so scared that he jumped back in his old Plymouth and raced off. Ox followed him right to his house, kicked in his front door, dragged him outside, and beat the shit out of him on his own front lawn, while the guy's mother screamed for help from the ruined doorway.

Ox continued to look around, menacingly, as an uneasy silence fell throughout the store. Everyone knew that when Ox worked himself into this state, he was like a two hundred and thirty pound time bomb ready to go off.

"Hey, cool down, man," Bo said easily, putting a hand on his friend's shoulder. "Let's not do anything crazy."

Ox's head snapped around, a fist coming up from his side. "Who're callin' cra – ?" He stopped in mid-word, his eyes locked on Bo's.

Bo, returning his stare, didn't flinch. His smile was friendly, not challenging; his hand only touching, not restraining. It seemed to take an hour for the next few seconds to tick by.

Slowly, Ox's face eased into a smile. He unclenched his fists and gestured, palms upward, shrugging his shoulders. "Hey, man, like it was only a fuckin' suggestion." He turned to the Crowd, a big shit-eating grin on his face. "Besides, ya guys know I'd *never* do anything like that, right?" It was like throwing a switch. The store sounds were back at full volume.

Kenny Fletcher jumped up, shouting, "I got it! I got it!" When he got everyone's attention, he yelled, "Knock, Knock."

"Who's there?" several of the guys called back, immediately picking up on the joke.

"Hugo," Kenny answered.

"Hugo, who?" More of the Crowd joined in.

"Hugo outside, wego stomp, stomp."

There was only a moment's hesitation, but when Ox was the first to laugh, everyone else joined in. Bo waited for the laughter to subside a bit, then raised his arms above his head.

"I think it's best we all be cool for tonight," he said. "As for me, I'm splittin'. Knowin' the fuzz, they'll prob'bly be around breakin' balls again. Er, no pun intended, Eddie."

Within twenty minutes the store was almost empty. Some of the guys took their girls to Crocheron Park to make out. Others headed for the Bayside movie house up the block. The Shadow and Joe Ross went to shoot pool next door at Buzz & Mac's. Buffalo Baker, Mike Mancuso and Al Chavello, with Cootie trailing behind on his crutches, yelling, "Wait the fuck up, willyas?" went up the boulevard to O'Neil's for beers. Bo declined when they asked him to go along, saying he had something he had to do. He tapped Eddie on the shoulder, and nodded towards the door.

Outside, Eddie climbed on the back of Bo's bike, and the two boys headed down Bell Boulevard towards Fort Totten and the Long Island Sound. The cool night air felt good on Eddie's bruised face, but he was reminded of the lingering pain in his still-tender balls every time the bike hit a pothole. He wasn't about to complain, though. Obviously, Bo had something on his mind and wanted to talk in private.

Bo swung off the road just after the main gate of the old Army base, and rode along the sparse grass. He stopped at his favorite spot, the rock jetty which jutted out about fifty yards into the sound.

Silently, Eddie followed Bo out to the big flat rock about halfway down the jetty. It was almost as big as a king size bed, and often used as one. Eddie couldn't help thinking about the two most-often told stories about this rock. One was that there were more cherries popped out here than in a Niagara Falls motel. The other was that there were more lies told about this rock than at a fishermen's convention. Judging by the number of used rubbers washed up around it, he opted for the former and wondered again when *his* time would come. *How come everyone else is gettin' laid an' I –*

"It's over," Bo said, interrupting Eddie's thoughts.

"Comeon, Bo. We've had this same conversation before an' – "

"No, man, I mean it's *over. Really* over." Bo was standing by the rock's edge, looking out into the water.

Although it was a warm September night, Eddie suddenly felt a chill. He knew it was caused by the tone of his friend's voice. He moved to where Bo was standing. He looked at him, waiting, hoping Bo's next words weren't the words he was dreading to hear.

Bo continued looking out at the water for several seconds, then turned, staring into his friend's eyes. "I did it. I signed up for the Army today."

Eddie was unable to speak immediately. He squeezed his eyes shut, and shook his head. When he finally opened them again, his words came out as a plaintive whine. "Aw, shit, man. Why? Whadya go do that for?"

"I can't take this shit no more," Bo said, still looking into his friend's eyes. "I gotta do *somethin'*."

When Eddie tried to respond, Bo held up a hand to stop him. Then, he placed the hand on Eddie's shoulder, squeezed gently, and continued in a soft voice.

"Look, man, I'm twenty years old, almost twenty *one* for Chrissake. I'm gonna be drafted any day now, anyway. I figure if I join now, maybe, jus' maybe, I got a better chance of doin' somethin' good, ya know, learn somethin'. What am I gonna do, load fuckin' trucks for the rest of my life? Or, end up in jail for killin' some lowlife scumbag like Callahan?" Bo looked away, contemplating the water again.

Eddie didn't answer, not that one was needed. His mind was swirling as the consequences of Bo's words registered. Suddenly, a wave of depression swept through him.

"B-but, what am *I* gonna do?" Eddie finally managed his voice feeble, shaky. As soon as the words came out, he wished he could take them back, knowing how selfish they must have sounded. "I-I'm sorry, man, I didn't mean to –"

Bo turned back around, a smile playing on his lips. "That's cool. I dig. But don't worry. Ya'll do jus' fine. That's somethin' I'm *sure* of."

Eddie wished *he* could be sure of it, but he wasn't. "I dunno 'bout that," he said weakly, shaking his head. He took a deep breath, and tried to smile. "Shit, I just wish I could join up with ya."

"Hey, man, yer forgettin'," Bo said, "I'm three years older an' one step ahead of you. Yer turn will come."

"Yeah, I know, I know," Eddie responded. "How can I forget when ya keep remindin' me? But, hey, tell me, when are ya goin'? How'd yer old man take the news?"

"I have to report next month, October twenty first, but I haven't told him yet. I ain't told *anyone* yet, 'cept you. I wanted ya to hear it from me first."

For the next hour, the two boys sat on the rock, arms locked around raised knees. Bo speculated on the next three years in the Army, hopefully coming out with a good trade. Eddie mostly listened. He didn't have much to say. He didn't know what the hell he'd do now.

The news hit the Crowd at Dick's hard the following day. The store immediately became cloaked in a cloud of gloom so dense that even the loudest juke box music couldn't cut through it. Long faces, and Cokes gone flat from left untouched, prevailed throughout the room. The older guys, being rudely awakened to the fact that their own "Greetings" notices from Uncle Sam were about to be posted, were faced with making a decision they had been hoping to avoid for as long as possible. Mostly, for now, they decided to continue to avoid it.

"Fuck 'em!" Buffalo Baker said. "They want me, they have to come an' drag me away. After all," he added, extending his arms to indicate the surroundings, "who wants to leave all this good shit?"

Bo, of course, was the center of attention, even more than usual. His answers to all the questions of why he had joined were in his usual tight-lipped fashion: "Why not?" or "It seemed like a good idea at the time."

Eddie moped around, hardly talking to anyone. He felt as if in a state of limbo – still in school; not being able to make any of his own decisions. He looked up when he heard Kate Brody calling for attention. He knew she was as upset as he was, but she managed a big smile. And, she brought a smile to everyone else, too.

"Hey, let's not think of this as my brother going away," Kate announced. "Think of it as just *another* excuse for a party."

She invited everyone to a farewell blast for Bo on the Saturday before he departed for basic training at Fort Dix.

TWELVE

GET A JOB

The next morning, after a fretful, almost sleepless night, Eddie had to force himself, even more than usual, to get to school. He had already missed opening day, and he knew he'd have to take some shit from that asshole dean, St. Claire. Fuck him! Eddie thought. *I got more important things on my mind.*

Eddie was still trying to come to grips with Bo's decision to join the army. It was sometime during the pre-dawn hours, as his bedroom window gradually turned from black to early-morning grey, that the full implication of Bo's action hit home. Not only was his best friend leaving, but The Crowd – *my crowd* – was sure to break up. It only stood to reason. Bo was a leader. Everyone wanted to follow him. *Shit,* I'd *follow him, if I could.*

By the time the alarm clock radio switched on, with the resonant tones of disc jockey Dandy Dan Daniels reminding him that "today is the first day of the rest of your life," Eddie had a seed of an idea, which was so small, so embryonic; he didn't even realize it had been planted.

Eddie reached the park across from Bayside High just as the second bell had sounded, and the last of the students were crowding into the two small side doors.

He scanned the grassy area and spotted Joe Ross at the far end. As he called out, and began to walk in Ross' direction, he realized his friend was not alone, and something seemed to be different about him. There was a large, frumpy-looking woman in a dark blue dress imprinted with large yellow flowers standing next to him. It was only when he got a little closer, about twenty yards away, that he recognized Mrs. Ross, Joe's mother. She was saying something to her son, emphasizing her words by shaking a forefinger in his face, then turned and headed off towards the main entrance of the school.

"Hey, man, what's goin' on?" Eddie called out, still several feet away. "Why's yer old lady – ?" Suddenly, he realized what was different about his friend. Instead of his usual jeans and T-shirt, Joe was wearing dark green overalls with a red and white "Flying A" decal on the front. "What the fuck . . .?" Eddie mumbled as his mind struggled to interpret what his eyes were reading.

Joe paced in a small, tight circle, studying the sparse spring grass at his feet. "I – I got a job," he said without making eye contact, continuing to pace.

"Huh? Whadaya mean? After school?" Eddie said with hunched shoulders and raised hands, using his body as a question mark.

Joe stopped walking, but continued looking at the ground. Eddie stared at him, trying desperately to figure out what was going on. He snapped his head to the left, catching a final glimpse of Mrs. Ross entering the school, just before the huge double doors slide closed behind her.

"Oh, no," Eddie began, almost to himself. "No. Tell me it ain't what I think it is." Eddie grabbed a fistful of overalls with each hand and spun Ross around, bringing him face to face. "Joe! Tell me what the fuck is goin' on, willya?"

Joe raised his head, but still didn't make eye contact. Instead, he seemed to concentrate on a small brown mole on the left side of Eddie's chin, and spoke in short clipped sentences. "I got a job. My uncle's gas station. Ya know, the Tidewater in Flushing. Start this mornin'. My Mom's signin' me outa school now."

There it was – the whole story in a little over a dozen words, Eddie thought. *And my life continues to crumble.*

The two boys were silent for several seconds, neither knowing just what to say. Then, they both started speaking at the same time.

"Aw, geez, Joe, why'd – ?" Eddie began.

"Look, Eddie, it's – " When Eddie broke off his words, Ross continued. " . . . it's the best thing for me to do. Shit, I ain't learnin' nuttin' in this place, anyway. Might as well do somethin' to make some money – my mother could use the help, anyway."

Eddie just looked at his friend, a sudden feeling of depression and defeat sweeping through him.

"Hey, look, man," Ross said, trying to cheer things up. "Yer seventeen now, too. Ya can get outa this dump, ya know. If ya can talk yer old man into it."

Eddie was sorry for his next words even before he said them, but he couldn't stop himself. "Yeah, right, then what am I gonna to do, pump gas for the rest of my life, like you?"

The hurt was evident as Ross' face turned red. "Fuck ya, I'm not jus' pumping gas, ya know" he said defensively. "My uncle's gonna show me how to change oil and give lube jobs." He hesitated, then added: "An' . . . an' maybe I'll be a mechanic . . . someday."

Eddie was embarrassed, both for what he had said to Ross, and for his friend's dismal reply. They stood in silence for several seconds, avoiding each other's eyes, not knowing what else to say. The sound of Mrs. Ross' return, clacking heavily on the school's massive marble steps with her unaccustomed high heels, brought a welcomed interruption to the moment.

"Yeah, well, I guess I gotta get goin' to school," Eddie said, then winced at the sound of his words.

"Er, right," Ross said, "me, too. Er, I mean I gotta get to work." Suddenly, Ross' mood brightened, obviously pleased with how those words sounded for the first time. "See ya later at Dick's, right?" he added.

"Hey, yeah, right," Eddie said, still depressed. "We still got Dick's. See ya later."

Ross couldn't leave fast enough, darting off across the park to meet his mother on the sidewalk.

Eddie trudged towards the school's side doors. *Yeah, we still got Dick's, I guess.* But, deep in his gut, he wasn't so sure. Things were moving too fast, and in the wrong direction. He pushed through the steel door, and slowly climbed the "up" staircase.

Eddie walked the hallways of the second floor, peeking in classrooms. Since he missed the first day of the new term yesterday, he didn't know where his Home Room was – and he didn't want to ask at the office. Finally, he spotted some other seniors he recognized in room two ten, where the teacher's face was hidden behind an open book. This is it, he thought. *That has to be Greenbaum.*

Unlike other times, Eddie tried to enter the room unnoticed, hoping he wouldn't have to get a late pass. The door betrayed him, screeching loudly on worn hinges as it swung open. The teacher's face appeared above the book, and Greenbaum's eyes glanced over the top of his reading glasses, squinting into long-distance focus. Then he did something he never did before. He actually smiled upon recognizing Eddie.

"Well, well, well," Greenbaum said, as Eddie headed for a vacant desk in the back. "Better late than never, they always say." The teacher's smile broadened. "But, not true in *your* case, Mr. Casale." There were a few chuckles from some of the other kids, and Greenbaum seemed to be relishing the moment.

"Oh no, don't bother sitting down," the teacher continued, in a deliberate tone of voice. "You won't be staying long. I have an official correspondence bearing your infamous cognomen."

Eddie looked up, puzzled. Greenbaum held an envelope clasped between thumb and forefinger which he was waving above his head. "Oh, excuse me," he added, "I forget to whom I speak. *Dis* is for *ya*."

The room erupted with laughter. Eddie, scowling, looked with emphasis around the classroom as he made his way to the front. The laughing stopped. He snatched the envelope from the teacher's outstretched hand, without looking at it.

"Now, get out of my classroom," Greenbaum ordered, in a gruff manner he would never had used last term. Eddie glared at him, and Greenbaum ducked his head behind his book again, like a turtle drawing into its shell. With a final survey around the room, where most of the kids had taken a sudden renewed interest in their own books, Eddie, determined to appear cool, fixed his face with a smirk, flipped a finger in the direction of the teacher and sauntered out the door.

Even though the hallway was empty, Eddie made his way to the boy's bathroom, then locked himself in a toilet stall, before looking at the sealed envelope. *Bayside High School, Office of the Principal,* was emblazoned in the upper left hand corner. It was addressed to *Mr. Edward Casale.* With trepidation, he ripped it open, and withdrew the single-sheet of official school letterhead. His name was repeated at the top, followed by two short sentences: *You are hereby suspended from class until further notice. Have your father contact this office to arrange for a meeting as soon as possible.* It was signed, *Dr. H. Bruce Martell, Principal.*

"Shit!" Eddie yelled, kicking the metal partition of the stall. "What the fuck did I do now?"

"Hey, in there," someone called out in a manner meant to be authoritative, but was a little too high-pitched to achieve its goal. "What are you doing? Let me see your bathroom pass."

Eddie crumbled the paper and shoved it into the pocket of his jeans. He unlatched the door and flung it open with such force that one of its two hinges snapped off, flew through the air and shattered a mirror above a sink on the other side of the room.

"Pass?" he snarled through clenched teeth, stepping out of the stall. "Ya wanna see my pass?" He advanced towards a gawky-looking student with thick horn-rimmed glasses and a badge reading "Hallway Monitor" pinned to his shirt pocket. "This is my fuckin' *pass*," Eddie hissed, waving a clenched fist under the monitor's beak-shaped nose, and backing him into the tiled wall. "Are ya *sure* ya wanna see it?"

The student's eyes widened as they locked onto the circular movement of Eddie's fist. His attempt to speak resulted only in his pronounced Adam's apple bopping with an audible beat.

Finally, in a voice an octave or two higher than falsetto, he croaked, "O-oh, ok. T-that's good. B-bye." Eddie allowed the frightened boy to duck under his arm and scamper out the door.

Eddie leaned back against the cool tiles of the bathroom wall and took a deep breath. He let the air out slowly, feeling his anger dissipate with his breathing. He repeated the process several more times before he felt calm enough to plan a surreptitious exit route from the hallowed halls. He knew that if he encountered anyone else – like Dean St. Claire – he could land himself in even more serious trouble. He crept along the hallway, then ducked under the glass partition of the door to the teacher's lounge, and raced down the "up" staircase and out the side door. It wasn't until he was several blocks from the school that he was able to slacken his pace to a normal stride. However, his mind was *still* racing – steeple chasing – as it jumped from one possible scenario to another for that night's confrontation with his father, and what Martell was going to tell him when they met.

Fuck it, Eddie thought. *What's the worse that could happen, they throw me out? Hey, that's probably the best, anyway. My old man will never let me quit on my own.* His mood began to brighten. *Shit, none of my friends are left in school so isn't this what I want? Damn right it is. I can get a job, buy a car or a bike an' hangout. Or maybe join the army like Bo. That would be cool, too.*

Although he was still nervous about confronting his father, Eddie was beginning to feel a lot better, and even managed a smile while walking down the street. Several steps later he stopped short. A sudden thought had sent a chill sweeping through his body. He had no idea *where* he was headed. Not even now. Then he realized that unconsciously he had been walking towards Dick's. He continued in that direction.

"What's this all about?" Mr. Casale asked, using the palm of his hand in an attempt to press out more of the wrinkles from the crumpled sheet of paper, before reading it again.

"I dunno."

They were in the living room, Mr. Casale in his easy chair with Eddie in the wing-back facing him. His mother and sister were in the kitchen doing the supper dishes, while his father's plan to read The Journal-American and enjoy an after-dinner Dutch Masters became unfulfilled history. Eddie's eyes went from the newspaper, which had dropped to the floor, to the unlit cigar in the ashtray stand, to his father's deepening frown as he re-read the note.

"What do you mean, you don't know?" Mr. Casale asked, raising his eyes from the paper and boring them into his son. "You must have done *something."*

Eddie flinched under the impact of his father's stare. He began an in-depth study of the swirl design in the beige carpeting at his feet. "No, really," he mumbled, without looking up. "When I returned to school this mornin' I thought everything – "

"Returned?" Mr. Casale interrupted, his anger mounting. "Returned from where?"

"Well, ya know, after the sum – " This time Eddie interrupted *himself*, as his brain caught up with his mouth.

"After the summer? What, did we lose a day someplace? If I'm not mistaken, and I'm usually not, *yesterday* should have been your first day back. Right?"

"Well, er – "

"Look at me, Edward! What happened to yesterday?"

Eddie looked up, but just barely. His eyes stopped when they reached his father's knees. "Well, er, somethin' came up an' I jus' didn't make it."

"Oh, well, that explains it," Mr. Casale said. "At least you have a good excuse." He started to say something else, then paused, taking a deep breath. He pushed himself to the edge of the chair, and leaned forward, with his elbows on his thighs. The movement covered half the distance to his son. "Look, Edward," he began, his voice now void of any trace of anger, "you're a senior now. In just a few months you'll be graduating, and then you can do anything you want. It's a crucial stage of your life."

"Dad . . . " Eddie began, trying to cut short this version of "the same old story."

"No, son, just hear me out, ok?" Eddie nodded, and his father continued. "If you want to go to college, which I hope you will . . . well, great. You can pick your school . . . it doesn't matter what it costs. And, I'll get you a new car for a graduation present, just like I got for your sister."

This latest bit of information perked Eddie's interest. Now *he* moved to the edge of the chair, leaning forward with his elbows on his knees. "But, Anna *didn't* go to college."

"True," Mr. Casale continued. "But, it's much more important for boys to go."

"Yeah, but – "

"I know, I know. You're anxious to go out and start making a salary. So, look. I'll tell you what."

"What?" Eddie was becoming more and more interested in father's ideas. *A car . . . Mmmm.*

"You can look upon going to college as a job, if you want. And *I'll* pay you a weekly salary."

Eddie's eyes widened. "How much?"

Mr. Casale managed a chuckle. "Well, now, we can work that out. Mmmm, let's see. How about doing it like any other job? The better your work, the higher your salary. In this case, get good marks, and you'll make more money. Sound fair?"

Eddie leaned back in his chair. It sounds like bribery, but what the hell, he thought. He looked at his father and nodded. "Sounds fair. I mean, like, it's somethin' to consider. But, what if I decide *not* to go to college, then what?"

Mr. Casale frowned. He hesitated, then said: "Look, if you seriously don't want to go to college then I'll help you find a good job. I have many clients with their own business – we'll find something you'll like, I'm sure. Something with a future. But first you need to get that high school diploma. Without that, even I wouldn't be able to help you much. Understand?"

"What about the car?"

Mr. Casale smiled, shaking his head. "If you go to work, you buy your *own* car. But, I guess I can manage a *loan*, if need be."

Eddie hesitated, then decided now wasn't the time to bargain. "Ok, Dad. Like I said, I'll think about it. I mean, *really* think about it."

"That's all I ask," Mr. Casale said. "Now, here comes your mother, so let's not say anything right now." He lowered his voice. "We'll just have to see what Dr. Martell has to say. I'll call him first thing in the morning."

Eddie almost said, "Don't worry. You're a great lawyer an' you'll win *that* case too." But he stopped himself. He remembered the last time he said words to that effect. It was the first and only time his father ever hit him.

Filling his water gun with black India ink had seemed like a good idea to Eddie at the time. He had just begun the seventh grade at Blessed Savior School and had not been looking forward to another year of being teased and taunted by that tough crowd from P.S. 41, a public school four blocks away. There had always been trouble between the two schools, and last year the officials had met to discuss a solution to the problem – staggered release times. Now, P.S. 41 kids got to go home at two thirty, while those in Catholic School remained in class until three fifteen. Eddie had a hard time justifying that move, figuring he was doing "extra time" just because he was Catholic. Besides, it hadn't solved the problem. Some public school kids just hung around and waited for the Catholic kids, calling them sissies, and taunting them for staying in school longer "jus' to try an' hide from us, ya punks."

This year, one group of four tough-looking girls, all eighth graders, had already singled out Eddie as its main victim. They had waited at a bus stop on Bell Boulevard and had harassed him whenever he passed. He had a choice. Either fight them or avoid them by walking three blocks out of his way. Most days Eddie had chosen the latter, not because he was taught it was wrong to hit girls, but because he was scared shitless of them. They were all older and even bigger, and one, who acted as the leader, was a large colored girl who was the meanest looking school kid, boy or girl, he had ever seen. If Eddie was in a hurry, he would run a gauntlet of abuse and rush past his persecutors on shaky legs.

But, today, a sunny spring day just after the Easter break, he would do neither. It was payback time.

His plan had been to sneak out of school an hour early, position himself in the hedges behind the bus stop and wait in ambush for their arrival. He had even ridden his new Schwinn bicycle today, to provide for a swift getaway.

His tormentors had showed up, as usual, gathering at the corner, smoking and talking, occasionally glancing in the direction of the Catholic school. He had waited until they all had their backs to him at the same time, and then thrust his arm out of the hedges. The big yellow water machine gun sent repeated streams of the indelible black liquid across the sidewalk, spraying his victims in a wide arc. The sight of their clothing soaking up big ugly stains had sent the girls into a screaming frenzy.

Eddie had jumped on his bike and raced down the street. Two blocks away he had passed an empty lot, tossed "the weapon" in the weeds and continued home at breakneck speed, glancing over his shoulder several times to ensure no one was in pursuit.

The following morning at Blessed Savior all the boys of the seventh and eighth grades had been called to the gym where they were told to stand in single file and face forward. A minute later, Sister Mary Thomas, the principal, had walked in with the big colored girl in tow. She had been carrying a black-streaked pink wool spring jacket. Sister Mary Thomas had led her up one aisle of boys and down another. The girl had looked at each one, shaking her head. The moment she had eyeballed a nervous-looking Eddie, she screamed, "Thas him. Thas the white mutha – thas the boy that shot me!"

Eddie had denied it vehemently, but Sister Mary Thomas quickly spotted the evidence – traces of India ink under his fingernails. Charges of "they started it" had fallen on deaf ears, and Eddie had been sent home and told to return in the morning with his father.

When Eddie told his father what had happened, Mr. Casale looked at his son for a long time, shaking his head while Eddie fidgeted. Finally, he had said they would leave at nine o'clock in the morning and sent Eddie off to bed.

By nine-thirty the next morning, Eddie and his father were sitting in straight-back chairs in the sparse, but neat office of Sister Mary Thomas, with the portrait of Pope Pius XII above her desk. Also present had been Sister Katharine Paul, Eddie's seventh grade teacher. Meetings with Mr. Casale concerning Eddie's conduct had been something of a regular event – usually resulting in some extra schoolwork and being grounded at home. But this time those stern, hard faces, framed in stiff white medieval headpieces, had seemed even more ominous than usual.

Sister Mary Thomas had started by explaining that it wasn't just misconduct in class anymore, which Eddie was still *guilty of – a fact that Sister Katharine Paul attested to with a nod – but it involved outsiders now. "And we have our reputations, not only as a school, but as Catholics, to think of," she had explained. "We simply can not tolerate this behavior anymore, and – all the good sisters here are in agreement – we feel your son should be sent to a special boarding school for boys with behavioral problems. There's an excellent one up in New Rochelle run by the Irish Christian Brothers, who specialize in handling problem kids."*

The blood had drained from Eddie's face and tears welled up in his eyes. No, no. They can't send me away. *He had turned to his dad with a silent plea, but Mr. Casale sat stone-faced, listening to the sisters. Eddie had hung his head, knowing he was about to cry.*

"So, Mr. Casale," Sister Mary Thomas had concluded, "if you wish we can make all the necessary arrangements with the brothers for you."

There had been a long pause. Finally, Mr. Casale rose from his chair. He had said he agreed with the sisters. This conduct could not be tolerated.

"But, no matter how you look at it, it's still just a childish prank – yes, with very serious results, I agree – by an eleven-year-old boy," he had stated. "A boy that should be living at home with his family, not off in what amounts to a reformatory someplace." He had walked over to where the sisters were seated, looked at each in turn, and then presented one of the most impassioned, most emotional, recitations concerning the values of family life and the importance of a boy growing up in a home full of love. He had ended by imploring them to give Eddie one more chance, a sort of probation, "and help keep this good Catholic family together."

There had been another long pause, and Eddie chanced a hopeful glance at his adversaries. He was amazed to see that both sisters' faces had softened, even their eyes were watery. They had whispered into each other's ears for several seconds, then had agreed to "one last chance" starting tomorrow. They, too, like their Lord, needed a day of rest.

Before leaving, Mr. Casale had donated *a sum of money to cover any damages to the girls' clothing, and an even larger amount for "whatever charity the good sisters deemed worthy."*

Father and son had been silent as they walked towards the car. When Eddie had felt they were a safe distance away, he looked up at his father with a big smile.

"Great job Dad," he had said. "You had that jury *eating outa the palm of you hand."*

Mr. Casale had stopped short, looking down at his son. It was then that Eddie noticed the tears in his father's eyes, too. The right-handed slap that followed was unexpected. His father had never hit him before. His face stung, but the hurt had gone much deeper. Eddie hadn't been sure why, but he couldn't stop crying for most of the day.

Even after all these years, whenever he thought about that day Eddie got a lump in his throat and a warm, tingling sensation on his cheek. He could never understand the effect that slap had on him. He had been stomped in the balls, punched in the face. Big deal. *But that slap.* He never wanted to experience it again.

Eddie stayed up for a while watching television with his family, assuming his favorite position, lying on the thick carpet in front of the TV, with a pillow from the couch behind his head. The episode of *Wagon Train* was a good one, but when the following show, *Father Knows Best* was announced, accompanied by a loud *Ahem* stage cough from his father, Eddie retreated to his room. But, he couldn't help smiling as he climbed the stairs.

Maybe he does know best, Eddie thought, stripping down to his shorts and climbing into bed. *Amazing as that may be.* By force of habit, he turned on the radio, but wasn't really listening as Alan Freed played *Susie-Q* by Dale Hawkins. He even ignored his "girlfriends" who hung out in his bottom dresser drawer. He had other things to think about tonight.

By the time his alarm came on the following morning, Eddie had been wide awake for more than an hour, fantasizing about his future. Four scenarios played out in his head. In one, he was cruising through the palm-tree-lined roads of the Florida University campus in his red Corvette convertible, while all the beautiful suntanned blonde coeds waved and begged him for a ride. *Awright!* In another, he was at the water cooler of his Wall Street offices, dazzling a group of sexy secretaries with a witty story, as they smiled seductively and made indecent gestures by wetting their lips with the tips of their tongues. *Yeah, man!* In the third, he was sweating profusely as he loaded huge, heavy cartons into the back of a cavernous truck, while the fat, cigar-chomping foreman kept yelling to hurry up because he still had ten more trucks to load before lunch. *Shit!* And, then there was the fourth. . .

Breakfast in the dinette off the kitchen was an unusually quiet affair, with Eddie still deep in thought. The rest of the family was tuned into the chain of events. Mrs. Casale offered no advice other than "finish your eggs" when Eddie pushed his plate away only half eaten, then removed the plate without further insistence. His sister, Anna, in an uncomfortable gesture, gave him a hug and whispered "good luck" before leaving for work.

A few minutes before nine, Mr. Casale excused himself and went to the upstairs bedroom to call the school. He returned in several minutes saying "We're all set for ten o'clock."

It was during the short ride to the school in the big Buick, that Mr. Casale broached the subject. "So, Edward, have you thought about what we discussed?"

"Are ya kiddin', Dad? I've thought about nothin' else."

"And?"

"An' . . . an' yer right. What can I tell ya, ya presented a great argument. Ya know, with the offer of the car an' all for college, or findin' me a good job. Yeah, I'll finish high school, an', well, then, like, we'll see after that."

With enormous relief, Mr. Casale let out a deep breath, which he had seemed to be holding for quite some time. He expressed his satisfaction and assurance with the simple gesture of squeezing his son's knee. Eddie looked over at his father, at the proud expression on his face, and felt really good about it. Yeah, they were good reasons for stayin' in school, awright," he thought.

But Eddie couldn't tell his father about the other important reason – the fourth scene he envisioned last night. It was Bo Brody, who *did* graduate from Bayside, telling him how disappointed he was because Eddie couldn't do it, too.

A few minutes before ten, Eddie and his father were sitting on the hard wooden brown bench, which was standard Board of Education issue, outside the principal's office. Miriam Coolidge, his secretary, informed them Dr. Martell would see them shortly, then continued typing, her fluid fingers dancing over the keys of the old, drab-gray Underwood. Mr. Casale fished a recent copy of *Life* magazine from the rack next to the bench and began thumbing through it. Eddie shifted in his seat and inspected the small room. Everything seemed to bear an "official" stamp except an oval frame on the secretary's desk with a photograph of two teenage boys. He scanned the walls which contained all the familiar framed portraits: presidents George Washington, Abraham Lincoln, Dwight D. Eisenhower, Governor Averell Harriman, Dean St. Claire – Eddie did a double-take.

St. Claire was staring at him through the glass partition from the hallway. His face was set in a smile, but it wasn't a pleasant expression at all. In fact, it was quite scary. Then, in a deliberate movement, he used the forefinger of his right hand to make a slashing motion across his throat. Eddie looked around. Miss Coolidge was still typing. His father was still absorbed in *Life.* He looked back at the window, but the face was gone. The only thing remaining was the chill down Eddie's spine.

A buzzer sounded on the secretary's desk. She picked up the phone, listened for a moment, then replaced it. "You may go in now," she said, before returning to her typing.

As with his office fixtures, Dr. H. Bruce Martell could have been stamped as "official" Board of Ed issue. In his late fifties, he was on the short side of medium height and on the verge of losing the battle with advancing forces of overweight. His reddish-grey hairline began in the middle of his shiny scalp, then grew rapidly with wave upon wave piled high towards the back, giving his head a wedge-shape appearance. His navy blue Robert Hall "sale" suit, the kind that wrinkles as you take it off the hanger, was now shiny and permanently puckered.

Dr. Martell stood and removed his wire-rimmed glasses, but remained behind his desk as Eddie and his father entered the office. He didn't offer his hand, but allowed a hint of a smile to Mr. Casale and a definite frown to Eddie, before sitting back down. Then, almost as an afterthought, he said, "Oh, yes, sit . . . sit." He put his glasses back on and picked up a sheaf of papers from his desk.

Mr. Casale turned to his son and gave him a wink, a smile and a nod, as if to say, *Don't pay attention to his rudeness,* probably more for his own benefit than Eddie's.

They sat in the two, rather small, straight-back chairs, obviously positioned in front of the desk for their use, and allowing for optimum viewing of framed diplomas from City College of New York, and Fordham and Columbia Universities on the wall above Martell's head.

"I'll get right to the point, Mr. Casal*ee*," Dr. Martell said, mispronouncing the surname so that it came out *sally.* He removed his glasses again, and held up the papers. "This is a record of your son's three years here." He gave the papers a little wave, just in case they weren't noticed. "And, it is one of the worst I have ever read. Not only has your son failed several subjects like algebra and earth science, but his behavior has been that of a common hooligan, or worse, year after year. However, due to the laws of this state, we were basically forced to put up with just about anything in the past. But now that he is seventeen that is no longer the case. After discussing the situation with my staff of deans, we had decided that just one offence this year would be his last. And, *that* offence occurred yesterday when your son was absent from opening day of school without cause. As a matter of fact, he was seen in the park across the street roughhousing with that bunch of no-goods that often frequent the area. Therefore, Mr. Casal*ee*, we are expelling your son from this school, effective immediately."

Mr. Casale listened to the principal's recitation without interruption, in an apparently calm manner. Not many people besides Eddie could have detected the fact that he had become very angry. It was the little vein on his neck, just above his starched white collar, that pulsated the signal of danger like a Morse code message. The outward appearance of concerned parent remained in place; inwardly he had donned the cloak of a riled attorney.

Eddie glanced at his father, who, in turn, was staring at Dr. Martell, waiting, as if he expected the principal to continue. It was an old lawyer's trick that Eddie recognized from TV, and from personal experience – stay silent long enough and the witness would start talking again, blabbering. And get himself in trouble, as Eddie knew all too well. Yeah, ok, I usually fall for it, he thought, but no way would someone like Dr. Martell –

"It's like I said, Mr. Casal*ee* . . ." Dr. Martell picked up his glasses, started to put them on, then changed his mind and dropped them on his desk. " . . . we are well within our rights, in accordance with New York State Law, to take this action. Dean St. Claire has been especially vocal for some time now concerning your son's misdeeds, and Dean Moscovitz is now supportive of his colleague. Dean Nucatello . . . ah, well, he *is* of Italian extraction, after all, so . . . " He fidgeted with the glasses on his desk, while the vein in Mr. Casale's neck was now beating to the beat of a Gene Krupa solo. "Er, no matter, the decision is final. Miss Coolidge has all the necessary documents and she will assist you – "

"It's *Casale.* The 'e' is silent."

"Excuse me?" Dr. Martell said with a trace of annoyance. He wasn't used to being interrupted, a fact that Mr. Casale was well aware of.

"Our name. It is pronounced *Ca-sal,"* Mr. Casale repeated, his manner remaining most cordial. "You know, like in the song, *My Gal Sal*."

Oh, oh, Eddie thought, the old man's really pissed off now.

"Yes, well, I'm quite sorry," Dr. Martell said. "Foreign names are not always – "

"It's American," Mr. Casale interrupted again. "I'm American, born right here in the good old U. S. of A., as a matter of fact. Its heritage is Italian, but the name, *now*, is American."

Dr. Martell's jaw stiffened. He didn't like being interrupted, but he resented being lectured to even more. "I see – "

"No, I don't think you *do* see." Mr. Casale was relentless now, while all the time appearing respectful. "If you did, you wouldn't have made that other ethnic slur regarding your Dean Nucatello."

The principal's jaw now slackened, and fell open. He seemed confused, at a loss for words. "I – I didn't – I don't – "

"Now, now, Dr. Martell," Mr. Casale offered him a most understanding smile. "Don't worry. And the Board of Education needn't worry, either. Just think of me as a very concerned parent, not a lawyer with twenty years of litigation experience."

Now, Eddie's jaw dropped open, too. He stared at his dad with new admiration, not believing his ears.

"I'll tell you something else that concerns me," Mr. Casale continued, while Dr. Martell was still stuck for a response. "You mentioned that Edward failed some subjects, yet I have all his report cards and I don't recall any failing grades. You're not suggesting that certain members of your teaching staff authorized scholastic scores not earned by the student, are you?"

Dr. Martell's jaw reflected his reaction again. This time it clamped shut with an audible clunk. The two men stared at each other for several seconds. Then, Mr. Casale inched his chair forward and leaned in closer to the principal, elbows on the desk, and spoke in conspiratorial tone.

"Look, Dr. Martell, I didn't come here to make trouble, but I *did* come here to fight for my son. You and I both know that he's been a first-class jerk and troublemaker for some time now. But the important thing is that *he* knows it for the *first* time. No, let me finish, please doctor," Mr. Casale said when the principal tried to say something. "Edward and I had a long talk last night, and he really – I mean *really* – wants to graduate high school now and, perhaps, with a little luck, go on to college, too. He promised he would work hard this year and not cause any disruptions, or trouble of any kind in school." He paused, then added, "Please, Dr. Martell, give him this one last chance. If he screws up again, I'll sign him out of school myself, with absolutely no argument, I promise."

Dr Martell seemed to soften a bit, but still remained *The Principal*. "I feel for you, Mr. Casale, I really do. But we made a decision and in all good conscious I must support my staff."

"But, that's just it," Mr. Casale said, generating enthusiasm. Now he would throw the bone – a chance to reconsider on merit, rather than under threat. "You already agreed to give him a last chance, but he messed up even before he was officially advised of your edict. As only my son can do, I'm sure. In all fairness, I'm sure you'll agree this "last chance" should start right now."

Mr. Casale, apparently satisfied he had successfully presented his case, leaned back in his chair, and waited. There was nothing else he could say. Now it was up to Martell.

Eddie looked over at his father and was filled with a warm glow. Sometimes yer a real asshole, but other times yer the best dad in the whole fuckin' world, he thought.

After almost a minute of staring down at his desk, Dr. Martell came to a decision. He looked at Eddie. "Edward, your father has a great deal of faith in you. He believes you can change things around. As you know, there are certain people here that don't think that is possible. I will reserve my opinion for now, but I certainly *hope* you can. But none of that really matters because you, and only you, are the one who can make a difference. Are you willing to give it a try – I mean a *serious* try?"

Eddie looked at his father and nodded, then turned his attention back to the principal. "Yes Mr. . . . er, Dr. Martell. I really an' truly want to do it. I *know* I can do it."

Dr. Martell took a deep breath and let it out slowly. "Hmm, Ok," he said, as if still not totally convinced. "Consider yourself on probation. This is *absolutely* your last chance at Bayside High. Any infraction – and I mean just *one* – of our rules and regulations and you will be expelled faster than you can say Jack Robertson. And, that goes for *all* the rules, including the dress code. If you have any questions regarding those rules, I suggest you consult with your guidance counselor, er . . . " Dr. Martell put on his glasses and checked one of the papers. " . . . oh, yes, Mr. Conway, a good man indeed." He removed his glasses, and looked back at Eddie. "Are we clear on that, young man? Any questions?"

Eddie wanted to say, *Who the fuck is Jack Robertson, an' why the hell would I want to say his name?* Instead, he just nodded and said, "Yes, Dr. Martell, very clear." He thought of adding a *thank you* but changed his mind. He wasn't the one who really deserved it.

In the car, Eddie looked over at his father, who was concentrating on making a U-turn in front of the school. He could have said, *Ya did it again, Dad! Yer still a great lawyer! That bit about the "ethnic slur." Wow!* But the heartache of that long-ago slap was as fresh as this morning's milk. Instead, he said, "Thank you, Dad. Thanks for havin' faith in me, an', er ya know, standin' up for me."

Mr. Casale took his eyes off the road to allow for a quick glance at Eddie, just long enough to say, "But Edward, you're my son," as if the reason was so obvious it need not have been stated.

Going to school was now a whole new experience for Eddie. Gone were the days of T-shirt, jeans and boots. Now it was sports shirt, chinos and loafers. He attended all of his classes, and arrived on time. He even toted all of his required school books, plus notepad. He was a regular Joe-College-To-Be. Of course, all of the faculty was aware of Eddie's probation, and most were supportive, some even offering extra help.

There were others, however, who seemed anxious to take advantage of Eddie's tenuous situation with blatant attempts at goading him into doing something, anything, which would cause his expulsion. Chief among this small band of vigilantes was a certain Dean of Boys. For George St. Claire it was payback time.

St. Claire took to hovering around Eddie's classrooms, often harassing the boy during change of class.

"You there, Casale, step lively, no loitering in the hallways," St. Claire would yell if Eddie stopped for a moment for any reason, even if only to read a notice on the bulletin board.

"You're in violation of the dress code," the Dean would admonish in front of the other students, if Eddie's shirt wasn't buttoned to the prescribed second button from the top.

But, Eddie kept his cool. He would always flash a simulated smile at his tormentor, tell him through mental telegraphy to "kiss my ass," then grudgingly comply with the dean's superfluous edicts. It was difficult for Eddie at first, but he soon developed the right frame of mind – like conjuring up gleeful visions of maneuvering his red corvette through a high-speed curve with the current Playmate of the Month, flushed with excitement and anticipation, curled up next to him. Also, since all of his male friends had left high school, he pretty much kept to himself, no longer prone to pulling pranks or otherwise performing under the influence of peer pressure.

Of course, Kate Brody was still in school, as were two other girls from Dick's – Carol Michaels and Barbara Saunders – but that was different. As cool and crazy as they may be outside, when it came to school they were top academic students with a no-nonsense attitude. In fact, Kate always maintained a straight-A average. He shared a world history class with her in the morning and a study hall period with all three just after lunch in the auditorium.

Study hall was Eddie's mid-day break. Running back-to-back with the lunch period, it provided an almost two-hour respite from the classroom, and offered him a chance to relax in a less controlled environment. Actual studying was an option, not mandatory. Ben Wilson, the supervising teacher, left Eddie pretty much alone during this class, even allowing him to talk to his friends, as long as it was done in a subdued manner. The teacher was content with the fact that Eddie would no longer cause any more trouble, or otherwise disrupt the other students as in previous terms, thereby making his job much less complicated.

On Friday, Eddie's third day in his new role, he strolled into study, spotted Kate and the girls in the back row of the huge auditorium, and plopped down two seats over.

"Hi," the girls said in unison, keeping their voices low. Eddie nodded his response. "So, how are you holding up?" Kate asked, with sincere interest. She had already let him know how proud she was of him for staying in school and graduating.

"Hey, man, it's a piece a cake," Eddie said with a wave of the hand. "It's like, what, a few hours a day. Shit, I can do that much time standin' on my head if I had to."

"But, that St. Claire," Kate said with concern. "He's really on your case. Like all the time. He's really trying to get you to blow it, you know. You better be careful."

"No sweat, Kate," Eddie said with another wave of the hand. "He's a fuckin' asshole, an' I got everything under control. There's nothin', I mean *absolutely* nothin', he can do or say to me that's gonna bother me. I jus' tune him out, think of some cool things, an' smile. Nothin' to it."

Kate smiled. She reached her arm over and patted him several times on the back. "I'm very proud of you, Eddie. I know it's not easy, what you're doing, but, like, you're *really* doing it. You deserve a big reward." She leaned over and gave him a quick kiss on the cheek.

"Well, now if it's a reward yer gonna give me, why don't we jus' go find the backseat of a car somewhere an' ya can – "

"In your dreams!" Kate giggled. "You may have changed in some ways, but in others, you're as horny as ever."

"Right!" Eddie agreed. "An' I'm glad ya brought it up. Ya see, in my last dream ya were naked an' I – "

"Stop right there!" Kate said, holding up her hand like a traffic cop. She was still smiling. "*This* is the reward I was speaking about. Someone wants to meet you. For some unknown reason she thinks you're cute." With that, Kate put a finger down her throat and made a gagging sound. She turned back towards the girls and called softly, "Susie . . . oh Susie." Then, back to Eddie, she said, "Eddie, this is Susie Stein. She just moved to Bayside from The Bronx."

Eddie, his curiosity and expectations aroused, leaned forward and anxiously followed with his eyes.

From the last seat in the row, behind the other girls, a vision in drabness rose hesitantly, and awkwardly, from her seat. She was tall, at least five foot eight, and very thin, kind of gawky. "Hi Eddie, nice to meet you," she whispered shyly, extending a long slender hand, while staring at the floor.

Eddie, halfway to his feet, froze. He was unable to mask his disappointment. He looked at her for several seconds, while the girl blushed, providing her with the only hint of color. She had dull brown hair, the color of an old Hershey bar, tied up in an old maid's bun. The stark hairdo drew attention to smallish ears, the shape and size of overripe Brussels sprouts, which, together with black horn-rimmed glasses magnifying muddy brown eyes, perched on a rather long, haggish nose with a slight hook, gave her face an overall ungainly appearance. She wore a large dark brown sack dress that almost reached her ankles. It should have had "Potatoes-100 Lbs." stenciled across the front and, at that, she would have come up several pounds short.

"Glad to meetcha, too" Eddie mumbled before dropping back down in his seat, without taking her hand.

He shot Kate a dirty look, then leaned in close, his lips at her ear. "Thanks. Thanks a lot," he whispered. "Remind me to do somethin' for ya someday. Like give ya the plague."

"Just wait," Kate laughed. "Under that plain brown wrapper is a figure most girls would die for. We know. We saw her in gym class. And the next time we have Personal Care Day in our Home Ec class, she's agreed to let us fix her up. Can't wait."

"Yeah, right," Eddie said, "an' when yer finished with her ya can work on Quasimodo. Ya'll have a better chance of makin' *him* look good."

"We'll see, we'll see, smarty pants," Kate said, just as the bell rang for change of class.

Eddie, actually in a pretty good mood, grabbed his stack of books and headed out of the auditorium, slightly ahead of the girls. After all, it had been a long time since a girl, *any* girl, thought he was "cute." He allowed a quick glance back to Susie. *Maybe . . .* But the second look confirmed the first. No way, man, not in a million years, he thought.

"Well, well, did you have a good time in your study class?" George St. Claire demanded loudly, popping out from behind the auditorium doors.

Eddie, startled at first, took a deep breath before answering. "Look Mr. – " But St. Claire brushed right past him and stopped face to face with a shocked Kate.

"You're a regular little tramp, aren't you?" St. Claire shouted. "Can't keep your hands off the boys, even in class?"

Kate's jaw dropped, as she backed up and stared at the dean in wide-eyed shock. "Wha – what are you talking about Mr. St. Claire? I didn't do – "

"Don't talk back to me," the little man interrupted, standing on his toes in an attempt to appear taller than the girl. A crowd of curious students quickly gathered around.

"I *witnessed* the whole cheap, smutty episode. You had your arm around that bum over there, and *kissed* him. I saw you." He emphasized the last word with a poke to her shoulder, pushing Kate another few steps back. "And he had his *tongue* in your ear. If that's what you do in class, I can only imagine what you do in other places."

Tears welled in her eyes. "But, Mr. St. Claire, I just – "

"You think you can fool people just because you have good grades, don't you?" St. Claire continued, poking her again, and backing her into the wall. "Well, you're still trash, just like your hoodlum friend here."

Ridiculed and humiliated, Kate started crying hysterically. But St. Claire still wasn't finished. He hadn't accomplished his goal yet. He grabbed Kate by the shoulders and began shaking her.

"Stop that phony crying! You're not – "

Suddenly, a loud bang reverberated through the hallway. St. Claire froze. The startled onlookers, now including several teachers drawn to the scene by the commotion, turned toward the source. With all his strength, Eddie, his face contorted with anger, had thrown his books flat on the marble floor, causing an explosive-like blast.

All of his frustration of the past few days suddenly erupted. In two strides he was on St. Claire. He grabbed him by the lapels and jerked him off his feet with such force that the teacher's cheap suit split at the seam of the right shoulder. "Leave her alone ya little piece a shit," Eddie snarled into St. Claire's face. "It's me ya want, so come an' get *me*. Not her."

St. Claire's initial expression of shock rapidly turned to a satisfied smirk. "That's what I just *did*, Casale. In case you're too dumb to know it, you're thrown out of school, as of now. Now take your greasy hands off me!"

But Eddie was beyond the point of reason. The vision of Kate crying, and knowing she had been abused by this scumbag teacher, only as a way to get to Eddie himself, was more than he could deal with. "Then I guess I got nothin' to lose," Eddie hissed, half dragging and half carrying the little teacher across the hallway, where an oversized sash window was opened to the late summer sun. With a fistful of lapel still in each hand, Eddie pushed the now terrified teacher halfway out the window, dangling him above the pavement twelve feet below, "Now, yer gonna be *thrown* outa school, too."

The stunned crowd was mostly silent as the drama unfolded. A couple of students shouted encouragements, such as "go, man, go" and "drop the asshole."

A teacher, Mr. Wilson, tried to intervene, but stopped in his tracks when Eddie shouted, "Take another step an' I drop 'im." The fact, however, was that Eddie suddenly didn't know what to do. His rage was dissipating rapidly, only to be replaced with the stark reality of the situation.

"P-please don't do it," St. Claire, his voice cracking with fear, pleaded. Suddenly, the seam of the jacket's other sleeve ripped apart, and the teacher shrieked with horror as he dropped several inches more. At the same time, Eddie felt other stitching begin to break away, the jacket's seams stretching to its limits, threatening to shred apart and send St. Claire into a violent fall.

Oh my God, I jus' wanted to scare him. Eddie didn't know what to do. St. Claire stared up at him in wide-eyed terror. Eddie couldn't let go of the lapels. It was his only grip on the man. Yet if he tried to pull him back up the force of the action would most likely cause the entire jacket to rip away. Suddenly, there was movement by his side. Someone had slid up next to him.

"Take it easy, Eddie," Dean Nucatello said in a calm voice.

"I'm afraid to move him," Eddie managed, unable to keep the panic out of his voice. "The jacket's gonna rip."

"I know," Nucatello said softly. "Just stay calm. Everything will be alright. I'll help you." The dean reached out the window and grabbed St. Claire firmly by the belt buckle and shirt collar, and together they pulled the teacher to safety.

There were some *boos* from the crowd, but mostly cheers. It took a flustered St. Claire several seconds to get his footing, and a little longer to find his voice. He was shaking uncontrollably; his face flushed bright red with a combination of fear and anger.

"This time you *really* did it, Casale," he began through clenched teeth. "The police will be – "

"Why don't you just shut-up?" Nucatello ordered his colleague. "You're not hurt and that's the important thing. We'll discuss all this in Dr. Martell's office immediately."

St. Claire angrily looked from Casale to Nucatello, then back again. He started to say something more, then spun around and stormed off, muttering to himself.

"Are you ok?" the dean asked Eddie, putting a comforting hand on his shoulder. Eddie wasn't, but he nodded in the affirmative. He didn't think he could speak. "I don't know if I can help you anymore," Nucatello continued, "but we *will* look into exactly what happened today. You better go home for now, and I'll see what I can do."

Eddie nodded again.

He stepped around the dean, while glancing over at Kate, who was standing by the wall, her schoolbooks clutched to her chest. She was still sobbing, but by the way she looked at Eddie, he knew that her tears, her sorrow, were now for him. She started forward, about to say something, but Eddie spun around and walked quickly down the hall and out the door. He didn't want anyone to see his own tears streaking down his cheeks.

Things happened bang-bang fast after that. As soon as Mr. Casale came home from work, Eddie sat his mother and father down and blurted out a fairly accurate, somber account of the afternoon's events. Although attempting to emphasize the dean's part in "starting it," he readily took responsibility of his own actions.

"I-I don't know what came over me. Everything jus' got outa hand. I'm really sorry."

Mr. Casale appeared calm, implementing his ability to mask his true emotions. Mrs. Casale couldn't stop crying, puncturing her sobs regularly with a "God help us" and a sign of the cross.

Mr. Casale, with Eddie in tow, was in the principal's office the first thing in the morning. However, even he couldn't smooth things over this time, not even with the support of Dean Nucatello who testified to St. Claire's "unprofessional" behavior. Eddie was out. Period. End of story.

Yes, it seemed Mr. St. Claire may have miss-handled the situation, perhaps being a bit overzealous with his reprimanding of Miss Brody, and for that he would certainly be appropriately censured. But Eddie's response was totally uncalled for, in fact, criminal. However, Mr. St. Claire's desire to instigate assault charges had been abated, and no further action would be contemplated at this time, as long as Eddie was withdrawn from school and agreed to never set foot on school property again.

There was an awkward silence, with neither father nor son looking at each other, during the short ride home. Mr. Casale pulled up in front of the house, and stared straight ahead, remaining stone-faced, while waiting for Eddie to get out of the car.

Eddie reached for the door lever, hesitated, then turned to his father for the first time.

"Dad . . . I – "

"No, Edward," he said harshly. "Not *now*." Eddie sighed, nodded, and was halfway out the door when his father spoke again, this time with empathy.

"Look, son, what happened this morning is something that's going to affect your entire future. And, *your* future is the most important thing in my life right now, as it is yours. Let's both think long and hard today, and we'll speak when I come home from work. Agreed?"

"Yeah, Dad, ok. We'll talk later," Eddie said, his words fraught with depression. He started out of the door, but hesitated again. "What about Mom? What should I tell her?"

Mr. Casale thought a moment, then said: "Just tell her I'll call her when I get in the office. I'd rather not give her this news face to face. Maybe she'll be all cried out by the time I get home."

Great, Eddie thought as he climbed out of the big Buick, sinking to even greater depths of gloom. He headed for the back door of the house. *Think about my future. Yeah, right.* Eddie had thought about this day – when he would quit or leave school –

often. But he never *really* thought about the day *after*. Sure, he'd work, get a good job and make lots of money, and . . . *And, what? What am I gonna do? Pump gas? Load trucks? What do I wanna do?* A line from a comic book he had read years ago suddenly popped into his head. *Veronica* had asked *Archie* what he wanted to be when he grew up, and *Archie* said: *a retired businessman. Wouldn't that be nice?* By the time he walked in the back door, Eddie's mind was reeling with confusion. The *only* thing he saw clearly was his red Corvette tooling through the Florida campus with someone else at the wheel.

"So, what happened," Mrs. Casale asked as soon as he walked into the kitchen. She was at the sink drying the breakfast dishes, a dish towel in one hand and her rosary beads in the other. Her cheeks were tear-stained.

"Er . . . Dad said he'd call ya in a little while when he gets to the office." As soon as he said the words, he knew his father had set him up, the coward. There was only one conclusion his mother could get.

"Oh my God," Mrs. Casale wailed, bursting into a renewed fit of crying. She dropped the towel and began fingering the rosary beads with both hands. Eddie retreated to his bedroom and shut the door. But his mother's sobbing, interspaced with *Hail Marys, Our Fathers,* and several *Acts of Contrition,* was still clearly audible.

Dinner that night was a solemn, yet elaborate affair. Mrs. Casale had been in and out of crying spells and cooking frenzies all day. In the end she relied on the old Sicilian belief that any crisis can be dealt with better on a full stomach. When the kitchen smoke cleared, there was a pot of thick, aromatic minestrone soup, hand-shaped gnocchi with Bolognese sauce, a platter of roast veal with potatoes rosemary, broccoli with butter and garlic and warm pizza bread stuffed with sausage and peppers. However, tension around the table was thicker than the potato dumplings on the plates, and the meal was picked at in silence, except for an occasional sob from Mrs. Casale and her urging of "finish your food, I'll only have to throw it away." Eddie's sister, Anna, was the only one who complied.

After dinner, Eddie and his father retreated to the back patio. The night air held a hint of the fall to come, but was still summer-mild. Eddie plopped on a heavily padded metal chair, while Mr. Casale, who had donned a brown sweater-vest, paced slowly, looking out over the expanse of lawn, hands folded behind his back.

"So, have you thought about what you want to do?"

"Well, Dad, I guess – " He stopped suddenly when he noticed Anna hovering at the open kitchen window in an obvious attempt to eavesdrop.

But before he could complain, he spotted his mother's arm reach out and pull his sister away. "I guess," he continued, "I'll, ya know, find a job or somethin', someplace."

Mr. Casale stopped pacing. He pulled a matching padded lawn chair in front of Eddie's, and sat facing his son. "Look Edward, there's another option we can consider."

"What option? Like what?"

Mr. Casale leaned in closer, and smiled hopefully. "I called around today and found a private school in Manhattan that will take you. You can finish your senior year there, and graduate next spring, on time."

Even before his father finished speaking Eddie was slowly shaking his head. "No, Dad, I don't – "

"Now don't say no without at least thinking about it, son."

Eddie looked directly into his father's eyes. "Dad, that's all I've done all day, was think about it. I mean seriously. And I can't go back to school. I mean it's not Bayside High, or this private school, whatever it's called, it's *school* in general. Ya know, bein' treated like a child all the time. I can't take the teachers on my case no more. Ya understan'?"

Now it was Mr. Casale's' turn to shake his head. "No, I'll be honest, I don't understand," he said, keeping eye contact. His disappointment was obvious in his tone and expression. "You *must* have a high school diploma, at the very *least.*"

"Dad, I know how important it is, I really do. An' someday I will get it, I promise. Maybe even go to college, like night school, or somethin'. Who knows? But not now. I *won't* go back now, Dad. I *can't.* Please don't try to make me."

A long silence followed, during which Father and son maintained eye contact. Finally, Eddie leaned back in his chair and studied his hands. "Er . . . there is another option, Dad. Maybe I can – "

"No! I will *not* be a party to that!"

"Whadaya mean?" Eddie looked up in surprise. "A party to what?" *How'd he know?*

"The army."

"No, the Navy." *At least he didn't know everything.*

"Whatever. I will not help you join *any* armed forces," Mr. Casale said adamantly. "It's just too dangerous."

Too dangerous? Eddie thought, almost laughing to himself. *Try walkin' into a park filled with Bayside West Bombers.* "It's not dangerous, we're at peace, ya know. The Korean War is over an' there's no otha war goin' on."

Mr. Casale looked at his son and shook his head sadly. "Edward, Edward . . . this so-called peace could explode into another full-fledged war at any moment. What, between Lebanon, Cuba, Russia, China, Southeast Asia, and God knows where else. Oh, never mind, just forget about it." Then he gave his son a questioning look. "Besides, I don't understand your thinking. You think high school is strict? Do you have any *idea* what the military is really like?"

"Yeah, but, it's not the same, Dad. Ya know, at least they treat ya like a man."

Mr. Casale snickered. "And that's based on your *vast experience – "* He stopped abruptly, took a deep breath, and allowed a warm smile to return. He leaned forward and put a hand on his Eddie's shoulder.

"You'll be going into the service soon enough, on your own or with the draft, and you'll find out just *how* they treat you. But I won't sign you in. Forget about that. I'll help you in any other way, though. Like I'll help you find a good job."

Mr. Casale started to get up out of his chair, and Eddie knew, with a sigh of relief, that the conversation was over. *It didn't go* too *bad.* In fact, he was quite satisfied. His father had many contacts, clients with corporations, big businesses. Now he just had to sit back and wait for his father to line up a good cushy job for him.

"So, do ya have anybody in mind yet? Like who ya gonna call?"

Halfway up the back stoop, Mr. Casale turned and faced his son with a quizzical expression. "What are you talking about?"

"Ya know, ya said ya were gonna help me find a job."

Mr. Casale hesitated before answering. There was a hint of a smile, but only for the briefest moment. "Oh, of course I will," he said with exaggerated certainty. "The first thing in the morning I'll give you a dime for a copy of The New York Times and you can check the 'help wanted' columns like all the other unemployed *men* out there."

THIRTEEN

SUSIE Q

"Hey, here's one! Let's see: 'Boy wanted for home newspaper delivery. Must be honest, dependable and own a bicycle. Good pay'."

"Very funny, asshole," Eddie said over Cootie's snort of laughter. "Don't fuck aroun', this is serious."

"What's a matter, ya can do it. Ya still got yer old Schwinn in the garage, dontcha?" Cootie said.

Eddie shook his head and continued scanning the "Help Wanted" columns of the *Daily News*. Cootie was checking the *Long Island Press.* It was just after eleven on Saturday morning and they were sitting at the counter in Dick's, chocolate eggcreams and newspapers in front of them.

Things had been strained around the Casale household that morning, the first day of Eddie's post-high school life. He had been out of bed early in hopes of displaying eagerness in searching for a job. His mother had been uncommunicative, preparing and serving breakfast with watery eyes and a solemn expression. His sister had appeared uncertain of how to react to the current situation, whether to criticize or console. Instead, she did neither. His father had not fared well, either. The master of masking his emotions, Mr. Casale had "slipped" several times at the breakfast table – a word here, an expression there – exposing a crack in his armor which allowed Eddie a glimpse of just how disturbed he was with his son. Even more depressed than the night before. And this morning he hadn't even broached the subject of helping

Eddie find a job. Eddie had left the house right after breakfast, walking fast, anxious to reach the sanctuary of Dick's and the patronage of his friends.

"Find anything yet?" Cootie asked, still skimming newspaper columns, the tip of his tongue protruding from the right corner of his mouth.

"Yeah, sure," Eddie said, "if I wanna be a dental hygienist or stenographer." He shoved the paper aside. "There's nothin'."

"No, wait" Cootie said. "Holy cow, this one's perfect for ya. Lissen." His eyes followed his finger to the page. "Young man wanted as trainee junior 'cecutive for major corporation . . ." Eddie's head snapped around, his eyes lit up. ". . . good salary an', let's see, oh yeah . . . must be *seventeen* years old with *no* high school diploma."

"Ya asshole," Eddie yelled. He grabbed his newspaper, rolled it into a club, and swatted his friend over the head. Cootie, still laughing, flung his arms up to protect himself, knocking the chocolate eggcream off the counter. It splashed onto the front of his white shirt.

"*Shit*!" Cootie exclaimed, looking down as the brown liquid absorbed into the cotton fibers.

"No, not *shit*," Eddie said. "Actually, it looks more like *diarrhea*," He gave Cootie a final swipe with the newspaper.

The two boys looked at each other, then broke up laughing.

"Ya got me goin' on that one, though." Eddie gasped. "*Junior executive.* Yeah, right."

"I think we're even," Cootie said, inspecting his shirt.

"Hey, what the fuck's goin' on with ya two jerks?"

Eddie and Cootie tuned to see Bo walking up. They were laughing so hard they hadn't heard him come in. "Oh, hi Bo," Eddie said. "We were just, ya know, goin' through the papers lookin' for jobs."

"Shouldn't be a problem," Bo said with a straight face. "From what I've just seen, ya two can replace Martin and Lewis now that they've split."

Cootie snorted a laugh but Eddie didn't even smile.

"Er, whadaya doin' here so early, anyway?" he said, unable to contain the nervousness in his voice. He had been apprehensive about seeing Bo since the situation with school. He didn't know how his friend would react, whether he'd approve or not. He had hoped he wouldn't have to face him until later that night; that he could stall for more time. But he knew his friend had come down early just to speak to him.

The two boys looked at each other for a moment, Eddie shifting from foot to foot. Then Bo smiled, draped an arm across Eddie's shoulders and directed him to the rear of the store, next to the unusually-quiet juke box.

"Ya got into some shit, huh?" Bo said, looking into Eddie's eyes.

"Yeah. Well, ya know." Eddie's shifted his eyes, and seemed to be studying the selection panel on the Wurlitzer. Bo waited. Several seconds of silence passed before Eddie raised his eyes to meet Bo's. "OK, I know, I overreacted. But I was only tryin' to help yer sister, ya know, an' ya should – "

"Bullshit," Bo said softly.

"Whadaya mean, bullshit? She was cryin' an' – "

"Come-on man, don't go puttin' it on her. She's upset enough over what happened, an' she'll talk to ya later 'bout it, herself. But, ya know Kate can handle herself pretty good, 'specially with an asshole like St. Claire. Oh yeah, maybe she'll cry, ya know, like try an' make 'im feel guilty. An' if that didn't work, she woulda gotten aggressive, too. For sure."

Eddie broke eye contact, turning his attention back to the juke box. He fidgeted with his hands, stuffing them into the pockets of his jeans, then removing them.

"Come-on," Bo continued, prodding gently, "admit it. Ya wanted outa school an' ya used this to bring everything to a head, right? I mean subconsciously, anyway. Think about it."

"Fuck no! I – " Eddie broke off. Several moments passed before he looked back at his friend. He smiled, a sudden calmness easing into him. "Ya know, I never thought of it that way, but . . . I . . . I dunno . . . I think maybe ya could be right." More silence followed as Eddie's mind went into overdrive. "Yeah, right, makes sense. My old man was tellin' me I gotta finish school an' everything, but I just couldn't. All this crap I was feedin' myself 'bout maybe goin' to college, an' gettin' a new car an' all, was just *that* – crap. But, like I didn't want ya to be pissed at me. I, er, guess I wanted ya to say it was OK, an' that's why – "

Bo interrupted by putting a hand on Eddie's shoulder, and squeezing gently. "Whoa. Hey, ya don't need *my* approval, man. You're my friend. Ya do what ya haveta do an' I'll always be behind ya. That's what it's all about. Besides, I *know* ya. Yer'll work for a while, an' get yer shit together, then, if ya want, at some point ya can go for that thing the city gives. Ya know, the equivalency diploma."

Eddie nodded and smiled. He had never even considered *that* route before. Then the smile faded and he shook his head. "That's just it, Bo. Work. I've been checkin' the paper. There ain't any decent jobs around, 'specially without that fuckin' piece a paper. It's a real downer, man."

Bo didn't reply at first, but when he did he was nodding his head as if just coming to a decision. "Look, I'm givin' my notice at work on Monday. I think maybe I can get ya in, ya know, recommend ya to replace me before I leave in a couple a weeks. I'm pretty tight with the foreman an' maybe he'll go for it."

Eddie's face lit up for a moment, then faded. *Shit! Loadin' fuckin' trucks!*

Bo seemed to read his friend's expression. "It's just loadin' trucks, I know, but it's a good job for now, an' the pay is right. Benefits, regular hours, holidays an' all that good shit. OK, when ya work, ya work. But, hey, ya can handle it. If I didn't think so I wouldn't recommend ya, right?"

"Yeah, I guess." Eddie seemed unsure. *Loadin' trucks?* Then, slowly, he nodded his head. "Yeah, loadin' trucks. No fuckin' problem!"

"That's right," Bo said. "An' besides, yer prob'bly only gonna do it for a couple a years till ya get drafted, anyway, or join up. Like me."

Eddie smiled. *Like* me. *Like* Bo. *Yeah, I can dig that.*

As they started back to the counter Bo stopped Eddie with a hand to his arm. "Well, not *exactly* like me, ya understand." Eddie looked over at his friend. "Ya see, when I said I was *behind ya* before," Bo continued, "well, it was only like a figure of speech. Ya know I'll *always* be three years older an' – "

"Yeah, yeah," Eddie interrupted. "I know . . . an' one step *ahead.* But look over yer shoulder. I'm gainin' on ya fast. Even takin' yer job."

Eddie was in much better spirits than just a few minutes before. His confrontation with Bo had gone well, much better than anticipated. He even had a prospect of a job. Thank God for friends, Eddie thought, glancing over at Bo. *Like he said, that's what it's all about.*

As usual for a Saturday, the Crowd started arriving early, and soon the juke box was blasting and the place was buzzing. To all outward appearances, it would have seemed like another normal weekend day. But the level of intensity was down several notches, conversations slightly stilted, stories related with less animation. Change was coming on faster than a souped-up Ford at the Bridgehampton Drag Strip, its specter haunting Dick's like a white-sheeted apparition on Halloween.

It wasn't until after one o'clock that Kate made her entrance, flanked by Barbara Saunders and Carol Michaels. They were dressed in their usual attire of tight blue jeans and oversize blouses, but their somber expressions made them appear out of uniform. As if prearranged, Carol and Barbara split off to join other friends, while Kate remained just inside the door. Her eyes settled on Eddie, who was already up and making his way towards her. Without exchanging a word, they accompanied each other outside, settling under the store's rolled-down awning.

"Look Eddie," Kate began, her expression still solemn. "I really want to thank you – "

"Hold on a minute," Eddie interrupted. "Let me talk first, OK?" Kate nodded. "First of all, there's no need to thank me," Eddie continued, smiling, "'cause I didn't do anything for ya, understand?" Kate gave him a questioning look. "Yeah, true," he said. "I had my *own* reasons for dumping on that creep, as you know."

"Yes, I know, but – "

"There's no "buts," Eddie cut in again. He was determined not to let her say her piece. "This was buildin' for a long time, an' the opportunity popped up an' I grabbed it. Or, grabbed *him*, as the case may be," he added with a laugh. He was trying to make this conversation as light as possible. "Hell, I know ya can handle that weasel any day of the week, an' twice on Sunday."

"Well, yes, I can, but – "

"Didn't I say no 'buts'?" Eddie persisted.

"Besides, it turned out great, anyway. I'm outa that shit-hole for only one day an' already got a job."

Kate almost smiled for the first time. "A job? Where? Doing what?"

Eddie managed to keep his smile in place, as he told her about Bo's plan.

"Oh," she said, then hesitated. "That's good . . . I guess. You know it was never going to be a long-term thing for my brother, don't you?"

"Of course. Me neither. I got plans, ya know."

Kate looked at her friend and nodded. "OK, you did it. I feel a little better now. Let's go inside and I'll buy you a Coke to say thanks anyway." She turned and headed for the door.

"Well, wait a minute," Eddie said. "If yer still so determined to *thank* me I could think of something a whole lot better than a Coke that you can do to – "

"Kate swung around and punched him playfully on the arm. "You *never* stop dreaming, do you?"

"Ouch!" Eddie exclaimed. "Christ, ya shoulda hit St. Claire like that."

"I was about to before you stuck your two cents in," Kate responded, smiling now. She paused, shaking her head. "You're really something else," she said.

"I know, I know," Eddie said, putting an arm around her and walking her into the store. "But I just don't know *what* yet."

Things continued happening fast over the weekend. Some of the guys announced the decisions they were hoping to avoid. Paul "Ox" Zarora would sign up for a four-year hitch in the Navy, while Al Chavello decided to enlist in the Air Force. Chuck Hoffman and Kenny Fletcher chose to follow Bo into the Army, with Kenny hoping to sign up under its "buddy plan," which would allow Bo and him to serve at the same duty stations throughout their enlistments.

Leo "The Shadow" Silverman was exempt from the draft due to his status as a college student, and, of course, Cootie was classified 4-F because of his accident. Handsome Hank Coleman wasn't planning on going anyplace either. It was always assumed that he and Kate would some day get married, and on Sunday afternoon they made it official. He gave her a ring he borrowed from his mother, and an approximate date was set for as soon as possible after Kate's graduation from high school next spring. And, with luck, before he received his draft notice. It was like racing the clock with Uncle Sam.

Joe Ross and most of the other guys said they weren't volunteering for anything. They would go only when they received their "greetings" letter, and then it would only be for a minimum of two years.

Amid this state of flux at the candy store, several constants remained. The Cokes and eggcreams flowed, the juke box played on and Eddie fell in love - again.

On Monday afternoon Eddie was sitting alone in a booth sipping what would have been his "after school" Coke, reading a *Joe Palooka* comic and listening to The Cleftones sing *Little Girl Of Mine.* He was passing time until Bo came home from work, hopefully with good news about the job.

He glanced up when the front door swung open, threw Kate, Barbara and Carol a smile and a wave, then returned to his comic book. A second later he did a double take. Bringing up the rear of the group was a girl he had never seen before – and always wished he had. She was tall and slender in stature, but almost voluptuous in the crucial places – including breasts that would have caught the attention of Hugh Hefner. Her reddish-blonde hairdo was cropped stylishly short, just over the ears. It framed an angular, but attractive face that could have been pretty with some slight readjustments – like a softer jaw line and a less-pointy nose. He could only imagine the color of her eyes – *emerald green?* – since they were hidden behind large oval sunglasses. She was wearing skin-tight black toreador pants, a red plastic cinch belt drawn tight around her narrow waist and a snug, *very* snug black knit off-the-shoulder sweater which allowed a generous hint of cleavage. Her long thin neck would have been too harsh, especially with the bare shoulders, if it weren't for the red silk scarf, tied cowboy-style. She strode into Dick's like a fashion model on a runway, taking purposeful steps on black patent leather pumps. Everything about her oozed confidence except her expression. She appeared nervous, with freshly painted lips drawn tight over her almost-straight teeth.

"Hi there," Kate said when the little group reached the booth where Eddie sat staring up the new girl, eyes darting between face and chest. "You remember Susie Stein, don't you?"

"No, I never met her," Eddie said, still trying to keep his gaze above her shoulders.

"Yes you have," Kate insisted. She looked over at Barbara and Carol, and all three girls giggled as they slid into the booth opposite Eddie. The new girl remained standing, biting her lower lip.

"Come on, sit down," Kate said to Susie, indicating, with a wave of the hand, the only space available – next to Eddie. Then to Eddie she said, "In school last week. I introduced you, remember? Right before you went berserk."

Eddie looked confused. Then it began to dawn on him. He glanced at the three smiling girls across from him. He looked back up at Susie, who was still standing, gnawing at her lip with even more gusto.

"Does this help?" she said, taking off her sunglasses. "They're prescription."

He noted her eyes were dark brown, not green . . . *Brown?* Slowly it dawned on him. He envisioned ugly horn-rimmed glasses in place of the fashionable sunshades, and made the connection. *But she was a dog, wasn't she?* He tried to remember what she looked like then, but, other than the glasses, he couldn't get a clear picture. However, Kate's words of introduction were indelible: *Someone wants to meet you . . . she thinks you're cute.*

Eddie, putting on what he considered his most seductive smile, shifted further over in the booth, making more room on the seat. "Yeah, come-on, sit down. I won't bite."

Hesitantly, Susie slid into the booth, her cleavage increasing as she leaned forward. Eddie's eyes widened. The other girls giggled, and Susie's face reddened a shade deeper than the touch of rouge on her cheeks.

"I told you so," Kate said.

"What do you think?" Barbara asked.

"You like?" Carol chipped in.

"Aw come on, knock it off, you guys," Susie managed, her face going from red to crimson.

"I don't understand," Eddie said. "I mean, last week you looked so . . . er, different, ya know. I mean, how come?"

The other girls, anxious to provide an explanation, answered for her.

"Well, Susie comes from a very strict Jewish family that just moved here from The Bronx," Kate started.

"The *South* Bronx," Susie clarified.

"Whatever," Kate continued. "It was becoming a very bad neighborhood, you know, with a lot of colored and Puerto Rican people moving in, and her father never let her go out much – except for school, of course."

"And then she had to take a school bus," Carol interjected. "With a bunch of wild kids."

"So her father made her dress like that, you know, like real plain, so she wouldn't be bothered too much," Barbara supplied. "Or, like, even worse, you know?"

"Yeah, even *much* worse," Kate emphasized, leaving little doubt as to what she was referring to by '*much'* worse."

"But," Kate went on," he always promised that once they moved to a good safe neighborhood . . . "

"Like Bayside," Carol added.

". . . she could start dressing and acting like a normal teenager. So we gave her a complete makeover in Home Ec class today. Then went shopping after school."

"This is normal?" Eddie said. He was looking sideways at Susie, his height providing an excellent vantage point for staring down the front of her sweater. He was getting that familiar stirring in his crotch.

"Put your eyes back in your head, jerk," Barbara admonished. Susie looked at Eddie and immediately tugged the top of her sweater up an inch.

Embarrassed at being caught staring, Eddie forced himself to look away. "Has her old man seen her yet?" he asked Kate.

"No, of course not," Kate explained. "We told you we just finished. But we're all going to walk her home, you know, to be there when he comes in from work."

"Yeah, moral support," Barbara said.

"And, she's going to change her top before she gets home," Carol said. "There's a nice big shirt like ours in her bag."

"Yeah," Kate joined in. "We wouldn't want him to have a heart attack so soon after moving into his dream house."

This time all the girls laughed, including Susie, who was starting to shed her nervous demeanor.

Suddenly, the front door swung open and Joe Ross rushed in. He was wearing his coveralls with the red and white "Flying A" decal. "Hi everybody," he called out. "Gotta get to work. Just stopped in for a quick Coke." When he reached the booth he stopped short. "Holy shit!" he exclaimed, staring at Susie. "Where have ya been all my life, sexy?"

"Hidin' from ya, ya asshole," Eddie shot back.

"One thing we can always count on with Joe," Kate said with a frown to the rest of the table, "is his total absence of any class."

Immune to the cutting remarks, Joe squeezed his way onto the seat next to Susie, almost dropping into her lap. She reacted by pushing herself over on the seat, and up against Eddie. The body contact generated instant heat, even through two layers of clothing. Eddie's dick, which had momentarily stood down, was rising to attention again.

"Hey, who invited *you* to sit with us," Kate said.

"Yeah, thought you were late for work or something," Carol chimed in.

"Aw, comeon, ya guys," Eddie said with a euphoric smile brought on by the leg-on-leg caress of the girl next to him – which he wanted to prolong for as long as possible. "Don't be like that. He can sit with us if he wants to."

The girls across the table groaned.

"Suddenly he's 'Mr. Hospitality'," Carol said. "Wonder why."

Eddie ignored the sarcasm, and dropped his arm, which had been draped over the top of the booth, to Susie's naked shoulder. She snuggled closer.

"Hey, there's nothin' I have that ya can catch, ya know," Joe said.

"And there's nothing you have that she *wants*!" Kate said.

Joe glanced over at the new "couple" and shook his head. "Well, it's her loss anyway," he said with a smile. "I'm the guy with the good job makin' lots of money, an' I coulda shown her the *highfalutin* life."

Everyone at the table laughed, then Kate introduced them, explaining that Susie just moved to Bayside.

"Well, nice meetin' ya, anyway," Joe said, getting up to leave. "So, ya gonna hang out down here, or what?"

They all glanced at Susie. She was looking up into Eddie's eyes, and he sang along softly to the juke box. Her friends answered for her, in unison: "Ab-soo-lutey!"

"An' another one bites the dust," Joe said, waving his arm in disgust as he walked out.

Eddie couldn't believe his luck. Here he was cuddling with this great girl he'd only known for a few minutes. He couldn't remember if he made the first move or . . . *screw it, who cares.* Susie, still snug in his arm, lifted one hand and began playing with a paper napkin from the table, sliding it around in continuing larger circles on the smooth Formica top.

"Ooops!" she said, as the napkin slid off the edge of the table and fluttered to Eddie's lap. She reached down under the table and grabbed the napkin – along with a fistful of Eddie's already hard dick. She didn't just brush against it; she took hold and squeezed. Or so it seemed. Eddie froze. He didn't know what to do. He couldn't look down, it would be too obvious. No one else at the table seemed aware of what was going on. In fact, Susie was sipping her Coke with her free hand, and carrying on a conversation with the girls.

Oh my God, Eddie thought. *She was still feeling . . . for the napkin?* Eddie bit his lip to keep from moaning.

Then, with a final squeeze, she said: "Aw, here it is. I've been looking for this darn thing." She picked up the napkin and dabbed at the corners of her mouth.

Eddie's mind was whirling. *This is too much. Wow! I just met this chick.* He started thinking about the first time he would be alone with Susie. *WOW! OH WOW! Down at the park . . . in a back seat* –

"Hey, jerk, I'm *talking* to you."

Eddie's thoughts were jolted back to the present. He focused on Kate. "Huh?"

"Aw, never mind," Kate said with a wave of her hand. "That answers my question."

"What question?" Eddie asked, confused. Does she know what just happened? he thought.

"I *asked* what you thought of the *new* Susie," Kate said. "But singing in her ear after only five minutes is a new record, even for you."

"And speaking of *records*," Carol added, "there's a new record out called *Susie Q* by Dale Hawkins. You better rush down to McElroy's and buy it."

"On your way there you'll pass Goldberg's," Barbara joined in. "Might as well stop off and pick up another ankle bracelet."

The girls across the booth roared with laughter, elbowing each other and pointing at a frowning Eddie. They knew him so well. Susie laughed along, although she seemed unsure of the joke.

"Very funny, very funny," Eddie muttered, not appreciating being the butt of the joke. He did, however, make a mental note to do just those two things. If what just occurred under the table was any indication, he figured he'd been going steady in a week.

For the next hour the girls explained to Susie what hanging out in Bayside was all about. They even provided a thumbnail sketch of every member of the Crowd that Susie hadn't met yet. Eddie offered a comment here and there, but mostly just listened, with an occasional wistful glance at Susie. But she didn't drop her napkin again, nor anything else for that matter, and he began to wonder if he had imagined the entire incident.

"Well," Kate said, checking the petite Lady Benrus on her wrist, "it's almost five. We'd better get going. We have to get ready for our *routine*."

"Yeah," Susie said. "My father gets home at five thirty. On the dot! He's a creature of habit."

"That's good," Kate said, "because then I got to go home, too. The 'Great One' is picking me up at the house tonight for a change. What it really means is he'll beep the horn in front of my house and I'll go running out. But, hey, it's a step in the right direction . . . I guess."

"Hey . . . where're you two goin'?" Eddie asked, trying to make it casual. His mind was already in the back seat of Hank's Ford, Susie snuggled up by his side.

"Where else?" Kate said. "Probably back here, then, I guess, to the pond in Crocheron Park . . . to watch the submarine races." She flipped her eyebrows Groucho Marx style.

Eddie swallowed hard. When everyone turned to look he realized his "gulp" had been audible. He blushed, then asked: "Want some company?"

"What, just the *three* of us?" Kate shot back to a chorus of laughs.

Eddie gave Kate a dirty look, before turning to Susie. "Wanna go?"

"Me?" Susie said, wide-eyed, pointing her finger at herself in an exaggerated gesture. "To submarine races? Sounds so exciting. I've never seen them before."

Eddie studied her for a moment. He was about to explain that there weren't *really* any submarine races, when she winked at him. *Winked! She actually winked.*

They made plans to meet at Dick's at seven, then the girls left for their confrontation with Mr. Stein.

Eddie sat alone in the booth and played back the afternoon's events. What *really* happened? They come in, introductions, sit down, Cokes, blah, blah, blah, drop the napkin. *Drop the napkin?* He thought about their first meeting in study hall last week. She seemed awkward, shy. She didn't even look at him when they met. But Kate said she *wanted* to meet me. *Strange.* Kate said too that Susie thought he was *cute*. *Well, yeah, but . . .* By the time he was finished, Eddie was convinced the intimate incident was just an innocent mistake. *Well, maybe she . . . Nah, she was nervous about sitting next to me, that's all. Dropping the napkin was just being clumsy. Most likely she never even* realized *she touched my thing. Hey, still felt great just the same.* Just thinking about it caused his dick to nod its head. He reached down and gave it a satisfying tug.

"Hey, man," Bo called out, coming up to the booth. He removed his aviator glasses and hung them over the top of his T-shirt. "Whadaya doin'?"

"Huh? Oh, hi Bo," a startled Eddie replied, his hand shooting up from under the table, freezing for a moment in mid-air, then settling awkwardly on the table top. "Uh, nothing', why?"

Bo gave his friend a quizzical look. "Well, yer sittin' here all alone with a stupid shit-eatin' grin on yer face, that's why."

Eddie thought fast. "Just thinkin' about the job. So, what's the good news?" Actually, he had forgotten about it, but he didn't want his friend to think he wasn't serious about working. He would tell him about Susie later.

Bo slid into the opposite side of the booth and signaled Dick for a large Coke by holding his hands vertically about twelve inches apart. He turned to his friend. "Well, ya got an interview for Friday mornin' at ten."

"Great!"

"Yeah, well, Andy – that's my foreman – ain't too happy that yer, er, ya know, so young – "

"Young? Aw, man," Eddie whined.

"Cool it, cool it. Stop actin' like a kid an' let me finish," Bo said. "It's because yer not eighteen yet. But, I told him ya were a big guy an' looked a lot older an' can handle it. So, he checked with management an' they're gonna see ya on Friday. Then we'll see. Look, one step at a time, ok?" Eddie nodded, trying to pay attention. "Look," Bo continued, leaning forward with his elbows on the table. "Let me explain the entire job, so ya'll know – " He broke off as Dick placed a Coke in front of him. Before resuming, Bo took a straw from the table dispenser, tapped it out of its paper wrapper and dropped it into his soda. "So ya'll know just what ya haveta do on Friday. First thing to remember is . . . "

Bo went into a detailed job description, plus some insights into the foreman and some of the co-workers. Eddie, nodding occasionally, had a hard time concentrating. His mind kept wandering back to Susie – *the paper napkin!* – and his upcoming date – *in the back seat!* Sure, he wanted this job, but he wanted to get laid, too. *The only thing is,* he thought, *which is more important right now?* He realized the answer as he mentally tuned Bo out and started planning his wardrobe for the date.

I like the way you walk
I like the way you talk
Oh Susie Q

On his way home from the candy store, Eddie did stop off to buy the new Dale Hawkins record as predicted by his friends, but decided to wait a while for the ankle bracelet - *to see what happens.*

He played the song repeatedly while getting dressed. Now, decked out in black chino pants, a powder blue short-sleeve shirt, with a dark blue turned-up collar, and his black Wellington boots freshly glossed with a coat of Kiwi Kwick Shine, Eddie was back at Dick's by six thirty - murmuring his own off-key rendition of the repetitive lyrics.

You say that you'll be mine
Baby, all the time, Susie Q

As the store was empty, he decided to double check himself in the mirror behind the soda fountain. His shirt sleeves, at almost elbow length, were deemed too long to be cool. He rolled them up, in neat folds, to about two inches below the shoulder. He fished his Ace comb from a back pocket and ran it through his already-sculptured Brylcreem-sheened hair, reaffirming the spit curl that fell to the middle of his forehead. He angled his head left, then right, then stepped back several steps to take in the entire picture. *Hmmm.* He tugged at his turned-up collar and, taking the tips between thumb and forefinger, gently rolled them back in a wing-like fashion. *Awright!*

Satisfied with his primping, Eddie eased onto a stool, spun around in a complete circle, and came to a stop with his arms spread in a grand-finale finish, with a cry of, *Da daa!*

Eddie's only audience was a dour-faced Dick, who had been standing several feet away, watching the routine, shaking his head.

"Dick, my good man," Eddie said with a flourish of his arm, "how about giving a prize of a free Coke to the coolest-looking guy in Bayside."

"Ven I see him I vill give it. But for you, you pay me a dime." Dick poured out a large Coke and placed it in front of Eddie.

"Dick, even *you* can't depress me tonight," he said, placing a coin on the counter. "*Tonight* is *my* night, ya dig?" he called over his shoulder as he headed for the juke box.

"Dig? Vhat is dis dig?" Dick mumbled, punching the ten-cent key on the cash register.

Eddie scanned the song titles, not really expecting to find *Susie Q* listed. He wasn't disappointed. He made a mental note to jot it down and leave it in the song suggestion box that was kept for the juke box vendor. Finally, Eddie pressed B-11 and was Lindy-hopping back to the counter to Laverne Baker's *Jim Dandy* as Cootie and Chuck Hoffman pushed through the door.

"Hey Dick," Cootie bellowed as he crutched his way to the back, "if I'd known ya had a floor show I woulda come earlier."

Eddie did a double twirl, ending in a knee-dip, with his right arm held high above his head and left arm thrown forward, the middle finger extended an inch in front of Cootie's face.

"Fuck ya, too," Cootie said, hopping over to a stool and propping his crutches against the counter.

"Where'd ya learn that move, from the *Dance of the Sugarplum Fairies*?" Hoffman quipped.

"Jeal-ou-sy, night an' day ya tor-ture me," Eddie sang out in a very bad Frankie Laine impersonation.

"God, yer as happy as pig in shit," Cootie said. "What's goin' on?"

"That's for me to know an' for ya to find out," Eddie replied.

A few minutes later the Crowd started arriving in force. Each time the door opened Eddie glanced at the entrance. He checked his watch. *Shit, it's after seven!* Then he looked over at the old Hamilton clock on the wall above the juke box. *OK, cool. It's only six fifty one in real time.* His mother must have set his watch ten minutes ahead again, like the rest of the clocks in the house, in her continuing campaign to get him to school on time. Well, she doesn't have to worry about that anymore, he thought.

Eddie was about to re-set his watch when Barbara and Carol walked in, together with Big Judy Bender. The volume of intensity climbed several notches as they table-hopped with the news of the day, headlined "Eddie's New Girl."

The interest in the mysterious Susie Stein intensified when Big Judy observed with obvious admiration, "Yeah, I saw her, and she's hot stuff." No one had ever heard Big Judy, who considered *herself* to be "hot stuff," attach that label to another girl.

Eddie picked up on the comments with swelling pride, and attempted to field the questions and remarks that came his way with an ease and confidence that belied his present state of anxiousness. His mind was in turmoil, jumping from one scenario to another. First, he was in a back seat making out with Susie, then he was the laughing stock of the Crowd, the butt end of another practical joke perpetrated by the girls. His eyes darted from clock to watch to the door. It was six fifty five and seven oh five, respectively. *Shit!* Calm down, she'll be here, he told himself again.

Suddenly, he had another thought. He pulled his wallet from his back pocket and, under the pretense of checking his money, ran a thumb over the lower left hand corner. The familiar circular impression in the smooth kid-skin leather was still there. He let his breath out slowly. He had been carrying that Trojan for over two years – since he was fifteen. Maybe tonight he'll get to use it. *Whadaya mean, maybe? She –*

"She isn't showing," Leo Silverman said, walking over with Chuck Hoffman, as Eddie jammed the wallet back into his pocket. His two friends were sporting mischievous grins.

"That's right," Hoffman agreed. "If she's as great lookin' as we heard she was, she probably went to Atlantic City for the Miss America contest."

"Or ran off to Hollywood," Shadow Silverman chimed in. "I mean, we got *MM* and *BB.* Now there'll be *SS,* the new sex symbol."

"Are you crazy?" Hoffman snickered, now directing his gibing towards Silverman. "Who ever heard of a *kike* sex symbol?"

"Why you kraut bastard," Silverman exploded. "I told you never to use that word. Where the hell is your armband, you Nazi prick? Besides, Jewish women are just as sexy as other women, jerk."

"To Jewish men, maybe," Hoffman shot back. "But then Jewish men think an old sock is sexy."

"I'll give you an old *sock,*" The Shadow snarled, waving a fist in Hoffman's face, "right in your mouth."

Eddie shook his head and walked off, leaving the two to their rank-out session. He wasn't in the mood for that shit tonight. He wandered over to the juke box. Cootie was propped in front of it, but leaning the other way, bumming a cigarette from Kenny Fletcher. The "select one" light was flashing, so Eddie reached in and pressed C-16 for *Girl of my Dreams* by The Cliques, and stepped away. Cootie turned back to the juke box, hit a button, then called the machine "a fuckin' thief" when nothing happened.

Eddie was too preoccupied to fully enjoy that little maneuver, but he did allow a slight smile. It didn't last long. He did another quick wrist-to-wall time check, and it was now official by both his Mother's Time and Eastern Standard Time – Susie was late. Thoughts of "the practical joke" took hold again and Eddie's spirits went spiraling down to the store's gritty linoleum floor. *They did it!* he thought. *They set me up big time. I can't believe I fell –* In mid-thought the door burst open and Kate rushed in . . . alone. *Oh shit, here it comes.* Eddie braced himself for the "we gotcha" to ring out throughout the store, followed by a wave of ridiculing laughter.

"Sorry we're late, but Hank . . ." Kate hesitated, looking at Eddie with concern. "Are you alright? You don't look good. My God, you're sweating." She studied Eddie with squinted eyes. "Hey, wait a minute. You didn't think we weren't coming, did you?"

"What? Who, me? Are you crazy? I didn't even know ya were late." Eddie did an animated check of his watch. "Is it seven awready?" He knew he was babbling, but couldn't help himself.

"Yeah, right," Kate said, not sounding convinced. "Anyway, Hank was late, as usual, then, of course, he had to stop for a six-pack. Can't go anywhere without that, you know. *And*, I had to go into Susie's house and talk to her father before he'd let her go out. You know, tell him where we're going, what we're going to do." Kate laughed. "If he only *knew.* Well, we're here, at last. And Susie's waiting outside . . ."

Suddenly, a dozen guys tripped over themselves in a stampede to the front of the store. They pushed aside displays of Whitman Samplers and back-to-school supplies to gawk through the plate glass window.

Kate hooked a thumb over her shoulder. "See? I knew that would happen. 'Specially the way she looks tonight. That's why I told her to wait in the car with Hank while I got you."

Eddie looked at Kate in astonishment. "Ya, *what?* Ya left her *alone* with Hank – an' a six-pack?"

Kate's eyes widened. "Oh my God!" she exclaimed. "You don't think . . .?" But Eddie was already heading for the door, dragging her along by the hand.

When Eddie flung open the door to the custom black Ford, Hank was kneeling on his seat, leaning over the back, holding a can of Schaefer to Susie's face. Hank's eyes, however, were locked on her breasts. Her awkward body movement of twisting her head back and away from the outstretched can, caused her chest to thrust forward, straining the buttons of her tight red blouse.

"Here we go, baby, take a slug an' – " The sound of the opening door freeze-framed Hank's performance.

Eddie hesitated. His breath caught at the sight of Susie's erotically twisted body in the back seat. Then he dove in next to her and, in a continuous motion, snatched the can from Hank's still outstretched hand. He threw his head back, and took a long swig of beer.

"Thanks, I needed that," Eddie said, handing back the empty can.

Before Hank could respond, Kate was on his case. "I can't leave you alone for two minutes, can I?" she said, climbing into the front passenger seat.

"Whadaya talkin' about?" Hank complained, feigning innocence. "I was just socializin'."

"Well keep your socializing in the *front* seat," she ordered. "Now drive."

Muttering, Hank shoved the Hurst gearshift into first, and peeled away from the curb with a roar from the glass-pack mufflers. Eddie turned to Susie, who was smoothing her ruffled blouse. "Sorry 'bout that.

Hank's a good guy. He just gets carried away sometimes. Don't be upset."

"Oh, no problem," Susie said with an easy smile. "I can handle guys like him. Besides, he's cute."

Eddie looked at her for some time as she continued to arrange her clothes and pat her hair. She didn't appear to be the least bit upset.

Since it was still early enough, Eddie suggested heading out to Port Washington, grab some Cherrystones at Lou's Clam Bar, and park by the town's harbor to catch the sunset over Long Island Sound. It was more impressive than the local reedy pond at Crocheron Park, and Eddie wanted this night to be special.

"That's a great idea," Kate seconded.

"Come-on, I'll even spring for the clams," Eddie added when Hank complained about the twenty-minute drive to Nassau County.

"Throw in a dollar for gas an' ya got yerself a deal," Hank bargained.

They headed east on Northern boulevard, making a couple of fast stops along the way. The first was for a dollar's worth of high test at the Sunoco station; the second was the compulsory six-pack stop at Vitali's deli, just over the Queens-Nassau border, where the sales tax was two percent less.

"I've saved hundreds of dollars just buyin' my beer out here," Hank said, pulling to the curb in front of the market.

"Yeah, 'specially when someone else pays for the gas." Eddie's caustic comment drew chuckles from the girls, but only a, "yeah, even better," from Hank.

Once inside the store, while waiting for old man Vitali to finish making a salami and provolone hero for the man ahead of them, Hank nudged Eddie in the ribs. "That babe out there is hot to trot," he said with a lecherous grin. "Ya know, it wasn't my fault before in the car. She was all over me, leanin' over the front seat with her boobs in my face, askin' me for a sip a beer."

"Hank, come-on, willya," Eddie said, giving him an exasperating look. "Knock it off."

"I'm *tellin'* ya," Hank said, turning serious. "I ain't bullshittin'. I mean, I took the blame an' all, not wantin' to say anything in front of Kate. Ya know, them being friends – "

"Hank!" Eddie snapped, raising his voice. "Yer fuckin' crazy."

"Boys!" Mr. Vitali called out, wagging a finger. "Shush! I be right wid ya." He wrapped the sandwich in white wax paper, took a dollar from the customer and shuffled to the cash register.

"Hank," Eddie continued in a subdued tone. "Ya were hangin' over the seat all over *her* for Chrissakes. I ain't blind."

"Yeah, well, like she sat back all of a sudden. Maybe she heard ya comin', I dunno. But – "

"Hank, ya got some imagination," Eddie interrupted, shaking his head and smiling. "That's the reason we all love ya. But just forget about it an' let's go, ok?"

"Yeah, OK, maybe so," Hank agreed. "But now I know why ya were so anxious to have clams tonight," he said, holding out a stiff forearm and making a pumping motion. He turned to the shopkeeper. "Gimme two six-packs of Schaefer . . . aw, hell, make it three."

They stood at the crowded raw-clam counter at Lou's, a sea food shack next to the harbor, and watched with fascination as the man in a chef's hat opened Cherrystone clams like a magician. A clam in one hand, a two-inch blade in the other, a flick of the wrist and – presto! – the still-pulsating mollusk is on the platter.

Eddie selected another one, tapped on a couple of drops of Tabasco sauce, and sucked it from the shell. He had loved clams ever since he was a kid and used to go on vacation with his family out to Amagansett. A local guy had shown Eddie how to dredge for them with a clam rake in the Great South

Bay. Then, sitting on the coarse sand, the guy would produce a well-worn penknife and a jar of horseradish, and they would devour clam after clam as the *old salt* recalled his adventures while working the lobster boats of Montauk.

Eddie looked over at his date, his eyes slowly sweeping over her sensual figure, and he marveled for the second time tonight at his good fortune. The first was when he helped her out of the back seat of the low-slung two-door Ford a few minutes ago. The image of Susie crouching forward, her blouse dropping just enough to reveal a rather skimpy, almost sheer pink lace bra, and her tight navy blue skirt bunching to mid-thigh as she extended a shapely naked leg to the sidewalk, was still fresh in his mind.

"You're going to have to show me how to do it."

"Huh?" He looked over at Susie. She was smiling, a clam on the half shell in the palm of her hand.

"How to eat it," she said. "I never did it before."

"Oh, yeah. Sure." Eddie took a Cherrystone from the platter. "First ya put some lemon or hot sauce on if ya want, then hold it with two fingers, like this." He demonstrated, holding the clam between thumb and forefinger and carefully bringing it to his lips. "Then ya just – er, ya – " He hesitated. He couldn't bring himself to say the word, so he continued demonstrating.

"Oh, you mean I should *suck* it," Susie said, after watching Eddie eat his clam. Her tone was quite innocent, but her smile seemed teasing, taunting. "Like this?" She slowly wrapped her lips around the shell and slurped loudly.

Eddie felt a rush of heat to his face. He glanced over at his friends. Hank had spilled beer over his shirt; Kate was staring wide-eyed and open-mouthed.

"I swallowed it," Susie proclaimed proudly. "Was I supposed to?"

"Wha . . .?" was all Eddie could manage.

"Swallow it? Is that how you do it? I mean, you don't chew it, do you?"

By now, other people were watching with looks of wondered amusement. Even the counterman stopped shucking clams for a brief moment and gaped. Susie, who had first drawn a few admiring glances just by walking from the car to the counter, seemed unaware that she had become the center of attention.

Eddie studied her expression. *Is she putting me on?* Susie blinked back a questioning look, like a student anxious for her teacher's reply. *Naw. No way. She's so damned innocent she has no idea what's she saying. But still . . .*

"Well?" she asked, looking up at Eddie with a tilt of her head.

"Are ya sure ya never had clams before?" Eddie asked.

"Now, where do you suppose I'd find clams in the South Bronx, silly?" Susie said. "Plenty of Guoya beans these days, but no clams."

"Well, it's just that ya . . . oh, never mind. Yeah . . . I mean *no . . . yer right, ya* don't chew them – er, the clams – "Eddie stopped when he realized he was unable to put together a coherent sentence. He didn't know what to say next. Luckily, Kate came to his rescue.

"Hey, it's getting late," Kate said. "Let's finish up and go. I don't want to miss the sunset after coming all the way out here."

As they headed to the car, Eddie glanced back at the clam bar. Most of the men were watching them. One even caught Eddie's eye, then nodded his head with an animated wink and a smile. *A fuckin' wink*! Eddie thought of running back and punching the guy's eye closed, but a sharp elbow to the ribs stopped him.

"Yer a cool bastard," Hank whispered with a salacious smile as the two girls walked ahead. "*Oh, let's stop for some clams on the half shell,*" he mimicked. "Shit, that scene was better than the last stag movie I watched."

Eddie shot him a look, but didn't say anything. Yeah, real cool, he thought. That's why I can't put three words together. He was confused. On one hand he was certain what just happened was totally innocent. Just like what happened this *afternoon when they were sitting in Dick's. But, what if it wasn't? he couldn't help thinking. What if she* did *have experience in those things?* Of course he had hoped to get lucky tonight, but this would be more like a miracle – like breaking the bank at Monte Carlo. But he kept thinking of the first time they met – the *plain* Susie. The shy girl whose father never let her out of the house. He smiled to himself and shook his head. *I ain't fallin' for it. I'm not gonna build this up in my mind an' then be disappointed again.* By the time they reached the car, Eddie was convinced that there was no way a girl with such a sheltered life could have *that* kind of experience.

Hank maneuvered the low-sitting Ford slowly along the gravel road that hugged the harbor, and groaned every time a loose stone kicked up and pinged the underside of the car. They were headed for a spot they knew on the far side of the rambling parking lot that served the boat yard and docking area.

"I should make ya all get out an' walk," Hank muttered at one point.

"Yeah, right!" Kate replied with a snicker. "Just hurry up and stop worrying about your precious car."

A few minutes later they were settled on a small rise overlooking Port Washington bay – just in time to catch the final rays of sunset, with the huge red-orange ball sinking behind the New York skyline across the sound.

"It's just beautiful," Kate said.

"It sure is," Susie agreed. "It even makes the South Bronx look good from here."

"Look! Ya can actually almost see the sun movin' when it gets like this," Eddie offered.

"Not fast enough," Hank mumbled, popping the top of a Schaefer.

Suddenly, the sun was gone, dropping from sight, and leaving in its wake a halo-like glow around the high-rise buildings of the city.

"Wow. It just, like, disappeared, but the sky's still pretty, huh?" Eddie said with a trace of too much enthusiasm, continuing to stare out the window. "I love the way it – " He cut himself off, knowing he was talking too much again. *Why am I so nervous?* He realized he was trying to prolong the sunset in order to postpone the start of making out. *But why?*

"Well, the submarine races should be startin' soon, but I can't see 'em yet, heh, heh." Eddie was unable to control his inane prattle. When there was no response, he glanced around the car. Hank was swigging beer with one hand, while his other arm was around Kate, who had snuggled close, her head on his shoulder. Eddie turned to Susie, who was leaning against the far side of the car, hands folded in her lap, while a half-smile expression seemed to say, *Well?* And still Eddie hesitated, unable to come to grips with the fact that he was intimidated, perhaps for the first time in his life. He knew she was waiting for him to make the first move, but he couldn't will his arm to action.

"Well, maybe we can see them better down by the water," Susie said. "Let's take a walk."

"Yeah. Great idea. OK." Eddie was grateful to have Susie take the initiative. "Hey Kate, we're getting' out. Open the door."

"Just when I get comfortable," Kate groaned, but she was already moving, pulling the front seat forward.

"We'll try not to be too lonely, havin' the car to ourselves for a change," Hank said. "Come back in about an hour. An' *knock* before ya come in. We may be in the middle of something *private.* Ya know?"

"In your dreams," Kate said, as Eddie helped Susie out of the back seat, catching another intimate view.

"Don't do anything we wouldn't do," Kate called after them.

"An' if ya do, name it after me," Hank added.

Eddie took Susie's hand. They had to maneuver through the boat yard to reach the water. Due to the lateness of the season, there were many dry-docked yachts of all shapes and sizes. The residents of Port Washington, an affluent community in Nassau County, took their boating seriously. Vessels made by Chris Craft, Contessa, Owen and Bell Boy – schooners, sloops, catamarans, cabin cruisers, speedboats, with not a single Boston Whaler among them – occupied most of the immense dry-dock area. There was a watchman in a shack off to the far end, but, because the light was fading fast, there was only an occasional boat owner or workman in the yard.

"Wow! Look at this one," Susie said, stopping in front of a huge craft. She stared up in awe at a 42-foot Chris Craft Bullnose Cruiser, looming even larger due to its perch high up on the keel and bilge blocks.

"Yeah," Eddie agreed, "it's a regular ocean liner. But, come-on, let's go." He was anxious to find a quiet spot down by the small sandy beach.

"No, wait," Susie said, yanking her hand free of his. "Look! A ladder. Maybe we could – "

"Don't even think about it," Eddie said, in a hushed tone, glancing around. "They have a watchman here, and it could get us in big trouble. Now, come-on, it's gettin' late." He reached for her hand, but she drew it back with a mischievous grin.

"Aw, come on, let's just take a look," she whispered, starting up the ladder which was leaning against the side of the yacht. "Don't be chicken."

"I'm not chick — " He looked up, and froze. Susie had hitched her skirt up over her thighs for the climb and he caught a full view of her naked legs clear up to a patch of pink panties. *Ohmygod, are those hairs sticking out?* Beads of sweat broke out on his forehead. He did a quick check of the immediate area. There was no one in sight. He grabbed the ladder and, like a donkey after a carrot, followed her, his eyes glued to his goal.

"Hurry up," Susie called softly, glancing down over her shoulder to check his progress. But Eddie, his cock turning rigid in anticipation, was already just one rung below, in wide-eyed pursuit. "And don't go trying to look up my dress either, you pervert," she said, smiling to herself while swinging her right leg extra wide for the final step.

"Wow, lookit the size of this," Susie said when they were standing side-by-side on the spacious deck. "It's huge!"

Feeling his face flush with guilt, Eddie's first reaction was to try to hide his erection by folding his hands in front of the bulging crotch of his pants. An instant later, realizing she was referring to the boat, he blushed even more.

"Wait, stay down," he finally managed, hunching over. He peered over the deck railing and did a 360 degree scan of the boatyard from his high vantage point.

The watchman, his wooden chair perched back on two legs against the front wall of the shack, was reading a newspaper. A naked light bulb above the door glared in the deepening dusk. The few people scattered around the yard seemed too immersed in their own activities to have noticed the teenage intruders.

"OK, nobody saw us but we still gotta – hey, whadaya doing? Don't do that!"

Susie was trying the door to the main cabin. "Wouldn't it be great to see inside, I mean just to look how rich people live? I bet they have great big bedrooms, with huge soft beds." The door was locked. She pushed harder, but it still didn't budge. "Damnit, come here and help me with this."

Eddie hesitated, momentarily pondering Susie's description of the beds. Then, reluctantly, he caught himself. It's bad enough if we get caught on this boat, without causin' any damage, he thought. "Naw, comeon over here instead," Eddie said, taking another look around. "There's a really nice view from up here." He was torn between his nervousness about being alone with Susie, and his concern over being caught by the cops or the watchman – and having his hoped-for intimate evening interrupted. Suddenly, he spied the thick seat cushions, which doubled as floatation devices, on benches built into either side of the deck. "An' here, we can put these on the floor," he said, pulling several down and spreading them out side by side.

Susie walked over, smiling now. "It's the deck, silly, not the floor. Don't you know anything about boats?" She helped him with the cushions and they soon had a make-shift mattress the size of a double bed.

"This is comfortable," Eddie said, dropping to his knees on the cushions.

"And what do you suppose we do down there?" Susie asked in an animated tone.

"Watch the submarine races, of course," was Eddie's matter-of-fact reply.

"I don't think we can see them from all the way down *there*," she said, continuing the game.

"Sure ya can. Look, they're startin' right now." Eddie pointed over the railing towards the water. "Hurry up or yer'll miss 'em."

"OK, but I hope you're not just trying to take advantage of me," Susie said, unable to control a giggle. She dropped to her knees beside Eddie. "Where are they?" she asked softly, leaning closer, as if for a better look.

Eddie was still nervous, but gaining more confidence with each passing moment. He thought he was handling the situation well. But he had loads of experience just making out. It was the next hurdle – the moment of truth – he was concerned about. Just concentrate an' do it by the numbers, he thought, but his mind was racing. *But take it slow. I can't let my dick take control. Start by simple kissin', then some French kissin', then a little feelin' on the outside, then go under the blouse and head for the clasp on the bra, an' then . . .*

Eddie turned to her. He cupped her face in his hands, and leaned in. He started with a gentle kiss, his slightly-parted lips barely touching hers. It was a tender moment, and Susie's response was encouraging. His hard-on, which had been in a constant state since first climbing the ladder, was now showing signs of further aggression. *No!* he mentally shouted to it. *Not this time!*

Carefully, he moved into step two. He slipped his hands from her face and slid them around her back, pulling her tighter, wisely keeping his hips pulled back, denying his boner the slightest contact with her body. At the same time he parted his lips a little more and began to maneuver his tongue. *Easy, now, easy.*

He wasn't sure exactly how it happened – like who made the first aggressive move – but suddenly their bodies were in a tight embrace, prone on the padding, their tongues deep in each other's mouth. The kiss held for almost a minute, while Susie maneuvered on top of Eddie, her hips grinding into his, his erection pressed into her thigh. When she began moving her leg in a slow, circular motion, Eddie moaned and broke the kiss.

"No, stop," he gasped, a moment from shooting his load in his pants. "I haveta stop for a second."

Susie pulled back, supporting herself on her arms in a push-up position. She looked down at him with a wry smile. "My God, is this your first time?" she managed through her own heavy breath.

Dumbfounded, Eddie stared up into Susie's face. *Jesus, what's happening here? I'm supposed to ask* that *question.* It took him several seconds to form a response. "Er, of course not. It's just that, er, ya know yer so hot an' sexy an' . . . well, ya know."

Susie's smile widened. "Oh yeah, I know," she said. She pushed herself off Eddie and rolled onto her back next to him. Eddie continued to gape as she hitched her skirt up to her hips and pulled off her pink satin panties, tossing them off to the side. "You do at least have something, don't you?"

"Wha – " Eddie was transfixed by the sight of those flimsy panties rolling down her naked thighs and the patch of dark pubic hair only half hidden by the top of her hiked-up hem.

"A rubber. Don't you have a rubber?"

Eddie blinked several times and broke his trace-like state. "Yeah. Sure. Of course. Whadaya think?" He sat up, pulled out his wallet, found the Trojan in the secret compartment and held up the plastic package as evidence of his considerable experience. "Always make sure I have a new one of these with me."

"Good," Susie said, snatching the packet with one hand, and reaching for his zipper with the other. "I'll help you. I'm really horny now."

"No!" Eddie almost shouted, grabbing the rubber back. "I'll do it." He was afraid that the moment her fingers touched his cock it would explode. He didn't even trust his own hand at this moment, and knew he had to be very careful.

"OK, but hurry up," Susie said in a husky voice. "I'm so horny I'm already soaking wet.

Eddie was getting more nervous by the minute. He never heard a girl speak like this. He unzipped his fly and reached in through his Jockey shorts.

"What are you doing?" Susie asked, her impatience growing stronger. "Aren't you at least going to take your pants down?"

Eddie stopped. "Yeah, of course I am." He changed direction and unbuckled his belt with unsteady hands. He raised his hips and pulled his pants and shorts down to his knees, while his dick, only faintly visible in the darkening shadows, sprang up and waved in the air. He tore open the packet and placed the rolled-up Trojan on the head of his cock, then carefully rolled it down to the base of its shaft. He rose to his knees and positioned himself between Susie's spread legs. With eyes closed, he hesitated briefly to reflect on what was about to happen. *Here it is.* His mind was racing. *Finally.* Then he began to lower himself into Susie.

Suddenly, the palm of Susie's hand pushed against his chest. "No, stop!" she cried, pushing him back. "Look at your *thing*." When he had raised himself off the cushions, Susie had caught a glimpse of something in the fading light.

"Shit," Eddie muttered, rolling onto his back. He propped himself up on his elbows and looked down. The rim of the condom was like a rubber band at the base of his shaft – the rest of his penis was naked. The old Trojan, hidden in the depths of the wallet for years, had dried up and all but disintegrated upon use. "Shit!" he repeated.

"Shit," Susie confirmed. She was sitting up, staring at his shaft in disbelief. "How long have you had that rubber?"

"Whadaya mean?" Eddie said. "I just bought it. I'm gonna get my money back."

Her excitement subsiding, Susie shook her head in disbelief. "Do you have another one?"

"No!" a frustrated Eddie almost barked. "Whadaya think, I'm a walkin' drugstore?"

"Don't bite my head, it's not my fault, you know. I'm disappointed, too."

"Yeah, but I'm the one who's gonna end up with a case of blue-balls."

A sly smile crept across Susie's face. "Well, maybe there's something I can do about *that."* She licked her lips and slowly lowered her head towards his crotch.

Eddie's eyes widened as he watched Susie's head fade down into the shadows. *She's gonna give me a blowjob! Oh boy, oh boy.* Eddie took a deep breath and tried to conjure up a replay of the Reese to Robinson to Hodges double play that sparked the Dodgers to beat the Yankees in the '55 World Series.

"Ooooh," Eddie groaned, as a pair of warm sensuous lips touched the head of his cock for the first time in his life.

"Huh?" a startled Eddie grunted a moment later, as those lips withdrew from their intended task.

"Ugh," Susie grimaced, quickly sitting up. *"Ptoo, ptoo,"* she turned her head and spat several times.

"Whadaya doin' that for?" Eddie cried, sitting up.

He was immediately fearful that his penis tasted like shit and no lips would ever dare touch it again.

"There are tiny little bits of, I don't know, that stuff from the rubber, all over your *thing."* She made a face. "It tastes awful."

"Oh shit," Eddie whined, trying to think. "Wait, lemme try to wash it off or something."

"No, don't worry," Susie said, pushing him back down. She already had a white silk handkerchief in her hand and was moistening it with her tongue. "Just relax. I'll take care of it," she said, leaning down for a closer inspection as she set about her task.

Eddie panicked. "No, don't do tha – ahhhhhh." It was too late. By the second stroke of the damp smooth cloth on his shaft, Eddie lost control and erupted into a massive orgasm.

"*Goddamn!*" Susie exclaimed, jumping back a moment too late. She glared at Eddie. Gobs of semen dripped from her face. "You asshole," she screamed. "I can't *believe* this happened." She wiped the semen from her face, then began working on her shirt. "You ruined my brand new blouse, too."

Eddie waited several seconds to catch his breath. Then, not bothering to remove the latex ring from the top of the rubber which still engulfed his now limp penis, he pulled up his pants and stood. He was torn with emotions – sad, angry and, of course, quite satisfied.

"I'm sorry," he offered, "but I tried to tell ya not to do that."

"Oh, excuse me," she said sarcastically, "it's just that I'm not used to guys who shoot their loads in three seconds." She shook her head. "I can't believe I thought you were so cool, like you've been around a little. Boy, was I wrong."

"Used to guys?" Eddie repeated, looking confused. She seemed like such a different person than the one he first met. "Whadaya mean? I thought ya used to, like dress plain, ya know, so guys wouldn't bother ya an' things."

Susie dabbed at her blouse one more time, then stuffed the hankie into the waist band of her skirt. She looked at Eddie. "Are you serious? You really believed that stuff? Look Eddie, for your information all that crap was only for my father's benefit. I used to keep my things at a friend's house, my *normal* clothes, all my make up and everything. I mean, I used to hang with the guys from the Fordham Road Baldies, for Chrissakes. The *coolest* guys in town."

Eddie remained silent. He wasn't angry anymore, just sad. He couldn't believe he never picked up on any of this. Suddenly, it started to fall into place. The scene in Dick's when she touched his cock. *Some accident.* Then the way she carried on at the clam bar. *Do you suck them? Yeah, right.*

"Come on, we may as well get out of here," Susie said, climbing onto the ladder.

Eddie took a last look around at the seat *cushions on the deck. Shit, I was so close to actually doin' it this time, he thought. Yeah, close but no cigar. The story of my life.* He spotted the crumpled pink panties between two cushions. He picked them up, stuffed them in his pocket, and started after Susie.

He caught up to her before they reached the car, and put a hand on her shoulder. He decided to give it one more try. "Susie?" She stopped and turned to him. "I'm sorry about . . . er, about what happened. Do ya think we could, ya know, get together again?"

"I'm sorry, too," Susie said, without looking very sorry. "You know, I really wanted it, too, back there. But I just don't think sex is ever going to happen between us – we're too different. You'd be better off to find yourself a high school freshman to, ah . . . you know, practice with." She swung around and continued walking back to the car.

Eddie's face flushed with anger as he watched her swing her ass away from him. *Nasty fuckin' bitch!* He stuffed his hands in his pockets. His hand touched the panties. Fingering the soft material had a soothing effect on him.

A smile came to his face as he started walking. Oh yeah, bitch? he thought. *Well here's a news flash. I already* had *sex with ya. An' I got a pair of panties in my pocket an' a ring around my dick to prove it.*

FOURTEEN

SOLDIER BOY

The ride back to Bayside was cordial enough. Kate, twisted around and leaning over the front seat, carried on most of the conversation with Susie, who acted as if nothing happened. Of course, according to her, nothing *did* happen. Eddie, when forced to make a comment or reply, grunted something unintelligible or made one-word responses, a smile as fake as a circus clown's pasted to his face. Kate kept throwing him inquisitive glances. She knew something went wrong between the two. Eddie's stupid smile, and the fact that they were sitting far enough apart so that a tractor-trailer could have passed between them, made it quite obvious. Kate was dying to know what had happened in the boatyard, and had to bite her tongue to keep from asking the direct question. She'd find out soon enough, she figured, knowing they would drop Susie off first.

"Do ya want me to walk ya to the door?" Eddie asked without much enthusiasm as they pulled up in front of Susie's house in Bay Terrace.

"Oh, no, that's ok," Susie said. "My father's probably looking out the window, and he's not used to me dating boys yet."

No, just fuckin' 'em, Eddie thought, watching his latest hope for a love life climb out of the back seat and wiggle away from him.

"Ok, ok, let's go," Kate snapped at Hank, giving him a sharp elbow to the ribs. He had been gaping at Susie's ass, her tight skirt pulling even tauter as she climbed the steps to her front door.

"Put your eyes back in your head, and your foot on the gas," Kate said, then immediately turned to Eddie in the back seat.

"So? Tell me, tell me. What happened?" she asked, as Hank grumbled that he wasn't doing anything, and pulled away from the curb with a peel of rubber.

Eddie hesitated, momentarily considering telling Kate the truth. Then he glanced at Hank, driving with his head tilted towards the back in an obvious effort to hear every word. He had to say something, knowing Kate would eventually get it out of him. He decided to give them a slightly edited version. He told them about the boat, Susie's aggressive moves, and how she'd been fooling her father back in the Bronx. However, when it came to the ending, *the climax,* he let them fill in their own imagined details, by conjuring up a lascivious smile, and closing with, "Hey, ya know, a gentleman don't kiss an' tell . . . *everything*."

"Oh my God," a subdued Kate said, turning back in the front seat. Suddenly, she was caught up in her own thoughts. *Her* friends just didn't do these things.

"I *told* ya so," Hank affirmed. "Didn't I tell ya? "I still know my women," he snickered, as Kate sent another elbow crashing into his ribs.

The story of Eddie and Susie on the deck of the boat became the stuff legends were made of at Dick's candy store. The very next day, Hank had told all the guys and Kate had filled in the girls. The guys hungered to hear all the juicy details. The girls had heard quite enough. They immediately labeled Susie a slut, and decided to cold-shoulder her at school.

Eddie was locked into the story with mixed emotions. His sense of right and wrong told him he shouldn't lie about a girl when it came to something like this. But, basking in all this sudden carnal glory certainly made him feel good. An', I'm not lyin', he reasoned with himself. *If they want to jump to their own conclusions, I can't help it.* Of course, Eddie provided enough material to make the "jump" more like a very short skip. An', he reasoned further, it's not like it wouldn't have happened if that damn rubber wasn't broken.

"So, comeon, ya really got laid on yer first date with her?" Cootie asked again, as a group of guys crowded around Eddie in a back booth.

"Look, I told ya it ain't right for me to talk about it," Eddie repeated, with that same lascivious smile which he had now mastered to perfection. "All I can tell ya is I didn't go home with another case of blue-balls *this* time."

"How was she?" Joe Ross persisted. "As good as she looks?"

"Whadaya think?" Eddie responded.

"I don't know," a doubtful Kenny Fletcher said. "Yer not the smoothest guy around when it comes to girls."

"Oh yeah?" Eddie said, slipping the pink satin panties from his pocket and waving them up in front of his friends. "An' just how *smooth* is this little item?"

The guys oohed and ahhed, and Eddie reveled in his new-found role as a "stud."

Susie never did return to Dick's, and Kate reported the word from school was that Susie was hanging out in Bayside West, with the Bombers. That news gave birth to a new spate of gibes, such as, *One night with Eddie and she defects to the enemy*, and Eddie was relegated back to being the butt of the joke in a matter of days. However, the story persisted, and even intensified in "detail", and it soon became dogma that Eddie *fucked the shit outta her* that night in the boatyard. In fact, in some strange way, time distorted the facts in Eddie's own mind, and, he could imagine himself many years later, whenever he would be asked about his "first time," he would always be able to relate in exquisite detail *that night with the Jewish girl on the deck of a boat.*

By the end of the week, life returned to normal at the candy store, or as close to the norm as it could be with so much happening at once. The conversations in the booths and along the counter, which, until recently, mainly concerned rock 'n' roll and making out, were now permeated with talk of military duty, high school graduation, and the specter of finding employment. However, these new topics co-existed with the old ones, and they all played out to the ever-constant rhythm of the juke box. In that way, at least, there was a pretext of permanence, a feeling of continuity, and the new agenda could be relegated to the ranks of other teenage adventures, like a Saturday night party or a gang fight with the Bayside Bombers. The subliminal subjects, the ones dealing with the pending break-up of *The Bayside Crowd* and the imminent concerns over the responsibility of "growing up," remained *just below the threshold of conscious perception.*

Friday morning, dressed in a new pair of Dickies twill work pants and denim shirt purchased the previous day at the Army and Navy store, Eddie stood across the street from Blue Star Automotive Parts on Northern Boulevard in Long Island City. He checked his watch. It was a few minutes before his ten o'clock appointment. Five minutes had passed since his last time check.

For the past half hour, Eddie had been rooted to the same spot, watching the busy loading area adjacent to the company's business offices. Two trucks were backed up to the platform, and another was waiting its turn. About a dozen powerful looking men, both white and colored, had been working non-stop. The boxes they were lifting, the crates they were maneuvering *looked* heavy, and, of course, they were. After all, engine parts weren't made of plastic. Although they worked with an easy fluid motion, seemingly belying the extremely laborious nature of their task, Eddie could see the exertion etched in their faces, the occasional grimace when a crate was perhaps even heavier than anticipated. And, most of them were sweating, evidenced by the dark stains around the collars and under the arms of their shirts – even though it was a typically cool, mid-October morning. What the fuck is it gonna be like in July? Eddie thought, knowing how much he hated to sweat.

Eddie had arrived early for his interview, anxious and confident, with the intention of making a good impression by showing his eagerness for the job. Then, he had decided that walking in a full half hour ahead of schedule may be overdoing the *enthusiasm* bit. He would wait a while, and go in only about 10 minutes before the appointed time.

Partially hidden behind a telephone pole, Eddie had thought he would put the waiting time to good use, and check out just what this job would entail. He had a good angle of vision, allowing him an unobstructed view of most of the loading platform. He had been watching for more than a minute before he became aware that one of the men up there was his friend, Bo. The fact that he hadn't spotted him immediately startled Eddie. Somehow it didn't seem to be the same guy who would stride coolly into Dick's with that easy smile, acknowledging greetings from the crowd with a slight nod or a short flip of the hand. The guy on the platform – *this Bo* – was one of a group of brawny, hard-working "men" – practically indistinguishable from his peers.

This had sent a shiver down Eddie's spine. He had tried to imagine himself working side by side with these men, lifting and heaving enormous weights eight hours a day. A feeling of apprehension had begun edging its way into Eddie's psyche, elbowing his confidence to one side. He just couldn't visualize himself on that platform. Within minutes, the apprehension had spawned the siblings of doubt and confusion, and any remaining traces of the aplomb that had fueled Eddie's earlier intentions had dissipated like morning dew on a sunny day.

Getting out of there and going home suddenly seemed like a good idea. However, the thought of facing Bo, and what he would say to his friend, was too intimidating.

When Eddie checked his watch again it was exactly 10 o'clock. Shit, it's now or never, he thought. He took a deep breath, and tried to conjure up whatever resolve he had left.

As Eddie stepped off the curb to cross busy Northern Boulevard, he took another look at the loading platform. The sound of a blaring horn and screeching brakes was like a blast of artic air, freezing Eddie in mid-step. The only body parts which continued to function were his eyes, which widened in fright at the Cadillac that skidded to a stop, its garish chrome bumper practically brushing against the twill of Eddie's pant leg.

Immediately, more horn blowing mingled with angry shouts as traffic quickly backed up on the westbound lanes of the congested thoroughfare. It was only seconds before Eddie regained mobility, and jumped back to the sidewalk, but, with the incident being played out in slow motion, it seemed more like several minutes. With another shout of "asshole!" the Cadillac driver rolled up his power window and drove off, and traffic was soon moving along at its normal mid-morning pace.

Eddie's composure was coming back much slower than his mobility. He braced himself by leaning against the telephone pole with one hand and took several deep breaths. Finally, the last nervous tremor dissipated and he was able to stand without support. He looked again at the loading platform. Work seemingly continued without interruption, as if nothing happened. But, something *did* happen. That was a sign, Eddie thought. *Someone's trying to tell me something.* Eddie wasn't sure who that *someone* might be, but what that *someone* was saying was crystal clear. Without another look back, he turned and headed off in the direction of the IRT subway stop a block away.

If Eddie would have looked back, he would have seen that there was, after all, a slight interruption on the Blue Star loading docks. One worker, a muscular young man with reddish-brown hair, had stopped loading boxes. He stood on the edge of the platform, hands on his hips and shaking his head slowly, watching Eddie walk away.

"Don't worry 'bout it," Bo said. "I dig."

"Yeah, well, I dunno," Eddie faltered, avoiding his friend's eyes. "It's jus' that, er, I dunno."

"Yeah, I know, you've made yer reasons *extremely* clear," Bo said with his easy smile. "Ya don't haveta to keep repeating it." He reached over and placed a hand on Eddie's shoulder and squeezed gently. "Seriously, it's cool. I mean it. No need to explain."

The two friends were sitting in a back booth in Dick's. It was the moment Eddie was dreading since that morning. He thought about it all day, but couldn't come up with anything to say that didn't sound *faggy*.

"Yeah, but . . . well . . . ah, Christ. I jus' wish I could go into the army, like you," Eddie said, still looking down at the table. "But my old man still won't sign for me, an' they won't take me without his ok."

"Look at me," Bo said. When Eddie continued looking down, he squeezed his shoulder much harder. "Look at me!" he repeated, no longer as a request. "I've got something to tell ya that I've never said before."

Eddie eased his gaze up and nervously stared into the face of a very stern-looking Bo. He didn't know what to expect.

"I know ya wanna go into the army like me," Bo began, his words etched in a resonance of understanding. "But there's two very important reasons why ya can't, an' I hope ya understand what I'm about to say."

Bo paused, his expression becoming even more serious. Eddie waited, leaning forward and eagerly awaiting his friend's next words.

"First of all . . ." Bo began somberly, and then paused again. Suddenly his face broke out into a big grin. ". . . I'll always be three years older, and, secondly, always one step ahead. Asshole."

It took Eddie several moments for the words to sink in. But, when they did, all the apprehension and nervousness that he had been harboring throughout the day, ebbed from his body. There was nothing else to say. Bo understood. "Fuck ya!" was all Eddie had to say, and the two friends indulged in each other's smiles.

The following week Eddie settled into a daily routine. He would get up fairly early, and, after a leisurely bacon-sausage-eggs-toast breakfast, go down to Dick's, buy the *Daily News* and *Long Island Star-Journal*, and quickly scan the classifieds. It didn't take him long to dismiss job after job. The one for "Messenger" required riding a bicycle, something he hadn't done since he was fourteen. In "Stock Boy Wanted" he objected to being called a "boy." And the one for "Window Washer" – well, enough said.

With job hunting out of the way, Eddie would spend the rest of the morning reading the two newspapers, comic sections first, while waiting for some of his friends to show up. After catching up with *Blondie, Alley Oop* and *Dick Tracy*, he learned that local Mafia don Tommy Lucchese, also known as "Three-Fingers Brown," was taking over the Queens garbage racket; that, sadly, the Milwaukee Braves beat the mighty New York Yankees in the world series, and that President Eisenhower celebrated his sixty-seventh birthday.

He didn't know what he'd do with this information, since he would probably be the only one of the crowd so informed, but, if he was still in school, his social science teacher, Mr. Albright, would be proud.

By Friday, Eddie was convinced that, in the entire world of American business, there was not one single job suitable for his particular interests. He was just about to toss aside the latest copy of the *Daily News* when, on the bottom of page seven, the headline, *Rockaways' Playland To Close For Season,* caught his eye.

The story, just three paragraphs in length, announced that this would be the last weekend for New York's second largest amusement park, after Coney Island, before shutting down for the winter and re-opening next Memorial Day.

Great! Eddie thought, reading the story again. *Just what we need to pick our spirits up . . . things have been too down aroun' here . . . some laughs, some good rides . . . yeah.* Sure, Kate's party for her brother was coming up the following Saturday night, but it lacked the usual enthusiasm associated with other parties. Too much was going on, too many of the guys were leaving. It was already being referred to as *The Last Party,* which was a totally depressing notion.

Eddie hung around Dick's for the rest of the day, downing a couple of greasy burgers for lunch, and, as the crowd drifted in at irregular intervals, he touted his idea for taking a ride out to Rockaway. He beamed, really proud of himself for coming up with the idea, as most of his friends responded with remarks like "sounds cool," "good idea," and "great, count me in." A few said "we'll see" or "anything else happening?" but Eddie knew what they really meant.

When Bo arrived and nodded his approval, the "undecided" immediately committed. Those that couldn't make it for various reasons, reluctantly expressed their regrets in a tone etched in disappointment. Despite the spontaneity of the excursion, or, perhaps because of it, everyone seemed to realize this would be a special night.

By seven o'clock, the crowd was ready to go. Minutes later, a caravan of four cars, packed with 10 guys and seven girls, with Eddie riding "shotgun" in Al Chavello's Chevy, turned onto the Cross Island Parkway on its way to the fun and games of Rockaway's Playland.

The crowd rolled slowly along Rockaway Beach Boulevard and hit the amusement park at Beach 97th Street, where the first of the rides was spotted.

"Hey, the bumper cars!" Eddie shouted. As if on cue, the four cars dispersed in different directions and, within the length of the block, were able to park three of the cars – one legally, one in a driveway and another at a fire hydrant. Only Larry was left in the middle of the street cursing his friends for beating him to the spaces, leaving him stranded as in a game of musical chairs.

"Hey, wait," cried Ox. "Here's a bumper car that must have gotten away from the ride," he said, walking up to a yellow and white Nash Metropolitan convertible sitting at the curb. With its top down, the tiny car was less than four feet high. "Let's return it, and you can park here."

Six of the guys descended on the car, grabbing bumpers, fenders and door handles, and, with only a slight effort, carried it half a block, depositing it on the metal floor of the bumper car ride. The Nash was barely indistinguishable from the 20 or so gaily-painted electric cars racing around the oval track.

"Whadaya crazy?" the ride's operator yelled, hitting the "off" button and bringing all the electric cars to a stop. "You punk kids," he snarled, charging from his booth, fists clenched at his sides. "I've got a good mind to . . ." He stopped suddenly, faced with the formidable wall of Ox, Bo and Eddie standing shoulder to shoulder, arms folded across their chests. ". . . t-to call the cops," he finished lamely, rushing back to the safety of his booth.

That little prank seemed to set the mood for the evening, and the crowd maneuvered through the Playland looking for new adventures. They filled several cars of the Cyclone Roller Coaster and then played "cowboys and Indians," shooting thumb-and-forefinger guns while riding the horses of the merry-go-round.

Being mid-October, the sun had set early and darkness was settling in, bringing with it the coolness of the night. Most of the visitors had departed and, one by one, the attractions were shutting down. When the crowd approached The Whip, it was already locked for the night.

"Shit!" Eddie said. "I really wanted to ride The Whip."

"Well, be my guest," Ox replied. He had found a large rock, and, with a powerful blow, smashed the cheap padlock on the control box. The lock snapped, the door of the box opened, and, as Ox pressed the "green" button, the ride rumbled to life.

Eddie and his friends jumped into the cars, and, within seconds, they were twirling around at full speed. By the time Ox hit the "red" button, bringing the ride to a stop as the crowd jumped out, there were six other people waiting in line for the next ride.

"Special tonight, only twenty five cents for an extra long ride," Ox announced, holding out his hand. When he collected a buck fifty, and the newcomers were seated in the cars, he hit the "go" button and ran off with the rest of his friends, leaving his "customers" screaming in delight.

After a 20-minute escapade in the Fun House, the crowd drifted across the boulevard to Boggiano's Clam Bar for some Little Necks and cold beer.

The outside serving counter was already crowded but Eddie and Bo edged their way to the front, where a colored counterman with long fingers and sinewy forearms was rapidly shucking clams with a small flat knife.

"Lookit him move that blade," Bo said. "He's a real artist, ain't he?"

"Yeah, well, a knife to a nigga is like a paint brush to Rembrandt, right?" Eddie said, with a laugh.

Eddie thought his remark was really clever, and was disappointed it didn't solicit the response he expected. In fact, the expression on Bo's face didn't change at all, only his eyes narrowed as they focused on a spot over Eddie's right shoulder.

"What da fuck ya say?" The voice was high-pitched and came from behind Eddie.

Tipped off to a possibility of trouble by the look in Bo's eyes, Eddie turned quickly and took a backward step, which put him side-by-side with Bo . . . and-face-to-face with a mean-looking colored guy wearing black jeans and a grey satin baseball jacket emblazoned with the name *Black Barons* and a red high hat and walking stick embossed emblem. He was almost as tall as Eddie, but at least 30 pounds lighter. Crowding around him were at least five other colored guys all wearing similar jackets.

"I say, muthafucker, what da *fuck* ya say, man?" the colored guy said, taking a step closer, crowding Eddie. "I'll show ya what a *real* artist is like, *honky*."

There is nothing quite like the sound of a switchblade snapping open, and Eddie recognized it immediately. Then, everything happened very fast. Eddie felt a pressure on his chest, which caused him to stumble backwards into the counter. He first thought he was stabbed, and that it didn't really hurt. Actually, it was Bo's left elbow slamming into his friend, forcing him out of the way, as Bo jumped forward, lunging at the black guy, his big right hand swinging up from the waist.

The switchblade caught Bo in his right side at the same moment his fist landed on the bottom of the black guy's jaw, snapping it up, breaking bone and teeth. Suddenly, there was screaming, with people running everywhere. Bo was down, clutching his side, blood oozing between his fingers. It took Eddie's friends only several seconds to react and they did so with almost precision movements. With fists flying, they waded into the Black Barons with a fury seldom seen before. They all did . . . except Eddie. He was kneeling down next to friend, tears rolling down his cheeks.

"Bo, Bo, are ya awright?"

"How the fuck can I be awright, asshole, I've been fuckin' stabbed!" Then the familiar smile returned to his face as Bo added, "See what I mean? I keep tryin' to tell you . . . I'll always be three years older and *one* step ahead."

As quickly as it started, the brawl ended less than a minute later, due to the quick arrival of two police cars from the 100 precinct, located just two blocks away. Ambulances quickly followed from Rockaway Beach Hospital, also located nearby on Beach Channel Drive, which had its relatively quiet evening shattered with the arrival of Bo, in one ambulance, and two members of the Black Barons in another, one with a shattered jaw, the other with several broken ribs and fractured arm.

The police separated the two warring groups but made no arrests, since the switchblade had mysteriously disappeared. The cops warned the Bayside Boys that if there was any more trouble they would all be hauled in. Then they rounded up the rest of the Black Barons and escorted them to the subway station, telling them to get their black asses back to Bedford-Stuyvesant, slapping their nightsticks into their palms for emphasis.

"If we ever see those punk-ass jackets in our precinct again, you'll wish you never left your shacks in the Georgia swamp," a big, red-faced Irish sergeant called out just before the group disappeared into the subway car.

One police car headed back to the precinct, while the two officers from the other remained at the scene.

A distraught Eddie tried to ride in the ambulance, but was told it was not allowed, so, together with the rest of his friends, they ran to the hospital, arriving only minutes after the ambulances.

Unable to go into the treatment room with their friend, the group paced the waiting area of the emergency room, under the watchful eye of a uniformed security guard. But the wait was amazingly short. Less than an hour later, a still-smiling but somewhat pale Bo emerged through the swinging doors into the reception area, explaining that the knife wound was a slash, not a stab. They closed it with fourteen stitches, gave him a tetanus shot and sent him on his way.

"Let's keep this quiet," Bo said. "My old man will shit if he hears about me gettin' cut."

But the news of the "knife fight," and Bo's heroics, was too big of a story to keep under wraps, and immediately became the number one topic of conversation around Dick's Candy Store . . . and beyond.

When it finally made its way to the Brody household through "unknown" sources," Mr. Brody comforted his wife with the rationale: "at least he'll be off the streets soon and in the army. With no war going on he'll be a lot safer there."

Mr. Brody repeated those same words to Mr. Casale when they met the next morning as they were leaving their houses for work.

"What are you talking about? Mr. Casale said.

"Oh, you haven't heard," Mr. Brody said. "Our sons were involved in an altercation with some colored guys. Robert got cut with a knife that was apparently meant for Edward."

Mr. Casale turned white. Visibly shaken, he abandoned any thoughts of going to the office, and returned to the house. The specter of Eddie lying on the street someplace bleeding to death was unbearable. He thought he would not tell his wife what he just heard and make up some excuse why he didn't go to work.

"Oh, my God, what happened?" she nearly cried after taking one look at her husband.

Getting her seated in the living room, Mr. Casale, as calmly as he could, told his wife what he just heard. She became hysterical. He put his arm around her shoulders and she sobbed into his chest.

"What are we going to do?" she managed after several minutes. "He won't go to school . . . he can't get a job . . . he's always hanging around the streets . . ."

As he sat there consoling his wife, he replayed the words of Mr. Brody: *At least he'll be off the streets soon and in the army . . . with no war going on he'll be a lot safer there.*

For the next thirty minutes, Mr. Casale and his wife sat in their living room discussing the future of their only son, and how best to protect him from the evils that were becoming more and more prevalent to the streets of New York, which, obviously, are rapidly expanding into the suburbs. Mr. Casale suggested, and his wife, finally, reluctantly, agreed that he would sign his permission for Eddie to join the army.

Soldier boy why feel blue
Don't you believe that she will be true

The song by The Four Fellows, recorded a couple of years earlier, spent more time spinning on Kate's new hi-fi than any of her new records, including *Wake Up Little Susie,* the current number one hit. The party was in full swing, but it lacked the usual spark of parties past. In fact, the consumption of alcohol was probably at an all-time low. It was nearing midnight, and Barbara Saunders, as she had been doing all night, was telling her friends how much she would miss Bo. She was grouped together with all the other girls with "steadies" who were soon to be in the service, consoling each other over their impending loss, explaining how they would *write everyday.*

The guys, too, at least those that would soon be in uniform, had their own group, but the main topic of discussion, for a change, was not about girls or fighting. Actually, the talk concerned the future, a subject which had not been too common in the past. Each had their own idea of what the next couple of years would be like, and each in turn expressed their thoughts of the paths they would follow. Eddie was proud to be a member of this particular group, of finally being "grown up" and going on his own. But, somehow he couldn't shake a feeling of depression that had been bothering him all night. A feeling of loss. He thought about all that had happened in the past year, and how it was abruptly about to change. So, in the middle of soon-to-be sailor Ox Zarora's dissertation about how "the Navy got the gravy and the Army got the beans," Eddie interrupted with:

"Hey, ya guys, remember when we . . . "

EPILOGUE

In the case of The Crowd from Dick's Candy Store in Bayside, the military service worked its magic, giving credence to all those soothsayers who predicted *the army will straighten them out.* After serving their minimum enlistments, the guys returned to their home neighborhood carrying a new-found feeling of responsibility along with their discharge papers. But one thing remained the same. The special bond that brought them together while coming of age in the 1950s held tight as they stepped back into Bayside in the early 60s to begin the rest of their lives.

Hardly a year or two went by without them all getting together for a reunion party, mostly through the efforts of Kate Coleman, nee Kate Brody, who made it her life's vocation to keep The Crowd together.

Yes, Hank's plan to stay out of the army came to fruition. He and Kate married shortly after she graduated high school, the only two from within The Crowd to tie the knot, and had four children in rapid succession, distancing himself even further from the draft board.

One by one, over the following five or six years, most of the other members of The Crowd were married, with each wedding reception serving as a reunion as well. In fact, most of the guys served as best man or usher for each other.

A stranger glancing at the various wedding albums might well assume it was a professional wedding party, with the groom, best man and ushers occasionally switching places.

Also, everyone seemed to find the right niche in the labor market. Bo, with his powerful personality and easy-going style, made him a natural for selling, and soon became the national sales manager for a major corporation.

Eddie was just 20 when he was discharged, having received his equivalency high school diploma in the service. At first, he followed his friend's lead and tried sales. He went door-to-door with a display case of cutlery, and failed miserably. After a few months of selling knives almost exclusively to his family, he maneuvered a job as copy boy for the New York Journal-American and enrolled at New York University to study journalism at night. Between his studies and on-the-job training, he was promoted to full reporter in a fairly short tim

Bo's job had him on the road for two or three weeks at a time. When was back in town, he and Eddie, and sometimes one or two of the other guys, would regularly get together for a couple of beers at O'Neil's, since Dick had retired and the candy store became a laundry, and talk about what was happening in their lives . . . and, of course, about old times.

Bo married first, and had two children, and Eddie was godfather to the first born, a boy. Eddie married a few years later. He asked Bo to be godfather to his daughter.

Throughout the years – the 60s, 70s and early 80s, whatever Bo and Eddie encountered in life, their special friendship remained set in stone.

In 1985, Eddie decided to accompany his new wife, Maria Papas, to Greece to meet her family and settle there in early retirement. The *goodbyes* were not too difficult, since Eddie planned on coming back at least once a year to see his family and friends.

Then, only two years later, the motorcycle accident and the devastating news. BO IS DEAD.

For the next three weeks in the hospital, Eddie remembered and wrote about their friendship in every detail. And, he was right. It did help him deal with the news that brutally awaited him after the operation. But, the one thing he wasn't able to put on paper was that strange feeling that seemed to be haunting him from the moment he regained consciousness. And, it continued to elude him until he called Kate as soon as he returned home. She told him Bo had the heart attack at around 10:30 a.m. and died a little more than an hour later at the hospital, at 11:47. Eddie's accident, rendering him unconscious for several minutes, was at 6:45 p.m. There's a seven hour time difference between New York and Crete. Eddie and Bo were unconscious at the same time. A chill raked up Eddie's spine, then, almost as suddenly, he experienced a satisfying calmness. And, for the first time in weeks he was truly happy.

"Don't worry about not being here for his wake," Kate said. "He would understand."

"Yes, he *did* understand," Eddie replied.

And, it was then that Eddie was sure Bo stayed around just long enough to tell him, with that easy smile, one last time: *I'll always be three years older and one step ahead.*

ACKNOWLEDGEMENTS

There is only one place to start, and one person to start with, and that's Patricia Coulaz, my friend for over 50 years, who inspired me more than anyone in the writing of this book. Without her indefatigable support, I would have probably abandoned the project years ago.

My thanks, also, to Keith Eardley, Martin Coates, Ken Bloomfield, John McLaren and, of course, to my wife, Sofia. Their readings of the manuscript, their useful suggestions and their proofreading talents were invaluable to me, and allowed me to finally write "The End" to the story I've trying to finish for over 20 years.

ABOUT THE AUTHOR

When Lou Duro was nine years old, his parents gave him a toy printing press for Christmas, and he immediately wrote and published his own four-page newspaper which he distributed to neighborhood families. He's been writing and published ever since. Along the way, he became an award-winning newspaper reporter, a contributor to numerous national and international magazines, and editor/publisher of newspapers in both the United States and Greece. His book of poetry, *the sadness of happy times,* originally published in 1970, has been a perennial seller ever since, most recently being re-issued in a bilingual English-Greek edition. Lou lives on the island of Crete with his wife, Sofia, but commutes to New York regularly to visit his daughter and her family who reside in (where else?) Bayside, Queens.

The author in 1957

Made in the USA
Columbia, SC
11 March 2020